## Let everybody know what you thought of this book!

| It was great! | It was okay. | It was awful. |
| --- | --- | --- |
| | | |

Go to http://waynebookdis~~~~~~~~~~ ~~~~ tell us
more about this book, or a~~~~~~~~~~~~~~~~~~~~~ng!

# Stalking Death

Thea Kozak mysteries by Kate Flora:

*Chosen for Death* (1994)
*Death in a Funhouse Mirror* (1995)
*Death at the Wheel* (1996)
*An Educated Death* (1997)
*Death in Paradise* (1998)
*Liberty or Death* (2003)

Also by Kate Flora

*Playing God* (2006)
*Finding Amy* (2006, with Joseph K. Loughlin)

By Kate Flora, writing as Katharine Clark:

*Steal Away* (1998)

# Stalking Death

Kate Flora

CRUM CREEK PRESS
The Mystery Company
*Carmel, Indiana*

STALKING DEATH

Copyright © 2008 by Kate Clark Flora

ISBN: 1-932325-06-9

Cover art by Robin Agnew (Aunt Agatha's, Ann Arbor, MI)
Cover design by Pat Prather

First published by The Mystery Company, an imprint of Crum Creek Press

First edition: June 2008

Crum Creek Press / The Mystery Company
484 East Carmel Drive #378
Carmel, IN 46032

www.crumcreekpress.com

*To the next generation*

*Jake and Max Cohen,*
*Sara and Lisa Clark,*
*Kate and Robbie Lloyd*

*May you be strong, brave, wise, and kind*

# Acknowledgments

This story would not have been possible without the generous assistance and support of many people.

For help with managing crises in the private school world, Thea's mentor is always Margaret Milne Moulton.

For help understanding stalking and stalkers, special thanks go to Victim Witness Advocate Heather Putnam and attorney and stalking victim, Laurelyn Douglas, as well as to the Concord area Domestic Violence Victim Assistance Program.

For help with police procedure, Deputy Chief Joseph K. Loughlin of the Portland, Maine police department, my Citizens Police Academy at the Waltham, MA police department, Concord, MA police chief Len Wetherbee, and my never-met but always generous New Hampshire source, Mike Sweeney.

The story was critiqued by my writing group, Hallie Ephron, Linda Barnes and Sarah Smith. My readers included Diane Woods Englund, Nancy McJennett, Jack Nevison, Brad Lovette, and my late mother, A. Carman Clark.

Special thanks go, always, to my husband, Ken Cohen, who has always believed in my writing. Thanks also go to my personal hero, and publisher, Jim Huang, whose steadfast support of the Thea Kozak series both lightens my heart and moves me to tears.

I have been well, and generously, advised. The errors and the liberties I have taken with fact, process, and law are entirely my own.

# CHAPTER ONE

I raised the heavy gun, trying not to flinch in anticipation of what was coming, the loud explosion and flash of fire, the ejected shell flying at me, the bone-jolting kick. I steadied it in two hands and tried to line up the site and the target. Andre had called it a bottle target. It didn't look like a bottle. It looked a bowling pin or one of Al Capp's shmoos.

Andre hovered behind me, a big, reassuring bulk. Not quite touching me, but close enough to keep me from running away. If he hadn't been there, I would have set the square, ugly weapon he'd loaded down on the counter, very carefully, and run like a gazelle out of this basement room, darkened with the lead and powder of thousands of explosions, out of the chilly air heavy with the brimstone scent of exploded gunpowder, and into the glorious brightness of a September day.

Andre was right. I had to push myself through this. This was part of my recovery. Last summer, I'd pointed a gun at a fellow human being and pulled the trigger. I hadn't touched a gun since.

He said it was like remounting after falling off a horse, but I'd fallen off horses before. Falling off a horse isn't premeditated. It happens so fast you're on the ground before you know what's hit you and you have to get right back on or you walk home. I've never heard of anyone with recurring nightmares from falling off a horse. Shooting someone, even when it's necessary, is different. You have to bring the gun. Load the gun. Release the safety. Point, aim, squeeze, and watch the other guy fall. When you put the gun down, you never want to see it again.

But I was Thea Kozak, recovering nice girl. Someone who genuinely believed that when the going got tough, the tough got going and that if I backed down, the girls and women coming

9

behind me also lost ground.

*Enough, Kozak. Time to get down to it.*

I had ear protection. Safety glasses. I had Andre only inches away. His voice was soft. "Relax, Thea. Breathe in. Breathe out. And squeeze." He straightened my body, turning me slightly. *Okay*, I thought. *I can do this. I have to do this.* Sensing my determination with that uncanny ability to read body language that some cops have, Andre stepped back.

I breathed in, breathed out, sited down the barrel, and then I wasn't looking at a shmoo. I was watching two men struggling to carry a third across a dark field while a fourth man they couldn't see raised his gun and aimed at them.

"No way," I muttered. "No way."

Always aim for center mass. I steadied my gun. I breathed in, breathed out, slowly increased the pressure on the trigger, and shot the shmoo, eight times, right in its generous little chest. Then I put the gun on the counter and walked out.

Driving home, Andre said, "I know that was hard for you. You were great." He slid one hand off the wheel onto my thigh. "I was thinking of a cheeseburger, but how about a hat trick?"

A hat trick was one of those sports concepts I'd never grasped. All I knew was it was fun. Dash in the front door, shed our clothes, and make love on the soft living room rug. Move to the bedroom for round two. Then once more in the shower. This was my reward for being brave at the shooting range. We'd finished round two and were lying together, his strong thigh against mine, watching the patterns of light on the ceiling, when the phone rang.

"Don't answer it," Andre said. "You're busy."

But it was fall, the most intense part of my working year. I'm a partner in an educational consulting firm, EDGE Consulting, and when the independent schools which are our bread and butter geared up for the fall term, so did we. Weekends were a big time for problems, and problems were my specialty. I grabbed the receiver.

"Sorry. I was in the office when the phone rang. St. Matthews has a problem." My partner, Suzanne. Her voice was light, but I read overtones of seriousness. Like me, and despite a husband and small child, Suzanne was a workaholic. "How'd it go today?" she asked. "Shoot off any toes?"

"Still got nine. That should be enough."

"Seriously. You got through it okay?"

"Tough as a bowl of Jell-o."

"That's what I was afraid of. Sometimes that guy pushes you too hard."

Andre pushed himself up on the pillows. "Suzanne?" I nodded. "Tell her you're busy."

"Andre says to tell you I'm busy."

"Oh." Her voice dropped a register. "Am I getting you at a bad time?"

She knew our penchant for midday quickies too well. "A good time, actually. We're between rounds. What's up?"

I couldn't tell whether her sigh was prompted by St. Matthews or me. Lately, she'd been sighing a lot. "St. Matthews has a problem student. Or student problem, depending on how the facts turn out. The kind of thing that could blow up in their faces if it's not handled right. What's your Monday look like?"

It was application season. Not the time for a headline-grabbing scandal if St. Matthews was to attract the applicants they wanted. "Hold on." I crossed to my briefcase and fished out my Blackberry. Blackberrys and cell phones. Two disagreeable accessories that had become necessities. My latest "get rich quick" fantasy was a line of colorful cowgirl belts like little girls wore in the '50s, with dual holsters for PDAs and cell phones. Instead of rows of little wooden bullets, the belts could have batteries. I'd make 'em in purple leather and faux cowhide and glittering plastic, become a hot product millionairess and retire.

I checked my schedule. "I'm chained to my desk, writing proposals."

"Not any more, you aren't." Her firm voice reminded me I was too busy for get rich quick. Still caught up in get rich slow. "You're going on a road trip."

I looked over at Andre. I've always been a slave of duty and a glutton for work. Six months ago, if a school had called, I would have been out the door in a flash, pleased that I'd become well-enough established as a trouble shooter in the private school world to be the one they called. Now I hesitated. If St. Matthews' problem was big, it could mean an overnight. I hadn't spent a night away from Andre since the wedding. Having come so close to losing him, I didn't like Andre more than an arm's length away, and I hated being alone with my dreams.

"They give you a rundown?"

She made an affirmative noise. "It's bad, Thea. Classic case where they should have called us sooner. You know the headmaster, Todd Chambers. He's neither an incompetent nor a nincompoop. In this case, it sounds like he's being a bit of both. In danger of really putting his foot in it."

Chambers was young for a headmaster, only early forties, but his preppie veneer and stuffy manner were from an earlier generation. He was so clearly born to the private school world I could picture him as an infant in diaper and tweed sports jacket, pacifier and horn-rimmed glasses, drooling onto his bow tie as he waved a Princeton pennant from his perambulator. In fact, he *was* born to the private school world. His father had been a legendary headmaster who, over a twenty-five year stewardship, had taken a second-rate school and made it one of the best in the country.

Chambers had been the trustees' pick to replace a headmaster who'd been way too liberal, his mission to put a very traditional New England boarding school that had been slipping towards progressive back on a more conservative track. Reportedly he was doing a good job, but the student body, having grown accustomed to laxity about dress code and other regulations, was testy and resentful. Some of the younger faculty had also resisted returning to a more authoritarian regime. Jackets and ties and all they signified were harder to phase in than out.

I pulled out a small reporter's notebook and a pen. Andre, giving up, folded his hands under his head and closed his eyes. He knew all about the call of duty. Just let the Maine State Police call for his services and he'd be gone before I could say SOP, his parting words some version of "Don't know when I'll be back. I'll call you." It might be one hour, or ten, or twenty-four, before I heard from him again. He wasn't plain old Andre Lemieux, the man of my dreams. He was Detective Andre Lemieux, a Maine State Police detective, the man in the white hat. Although, of course, his hat wasn't white. Too good a target, white hats.

I shuddered and tried to concentrate on Suzanne. "You got his number?"

"I'm afraid so. Problem number 207. Man about to have foot stuck in mouth."

"Could you be more specific?"

"It's all waiting on your desk, partner. My succinct notes on the nature of his problem. Minority scholarship student, athlete, loner, claims she's being stalked and has the whole community in a twitter. He says she's making it up. Doing it for attention. Or revenge."

She gave me a New Hampshire phone number. "He has a letter explaining the situation he wants to send to the parents. As a last minute thing, he wanted to run it by us. By me, actually, but I told him you were our crisis person. I didn't tell him I had to do a faculty tea."

She paused. "My psychic bones sense something fishy. Maybe a worried trustee in the background or more than he's telling. He's waiting for your call."

I pictured Chambers, done up in tweed, sitting in a prim wing chair beside a shiny black phone, the dignity of his posture marred by the twisted leg, the toe of a polished wing-tip stuck between his lips. "If we've got the draft letter, then shouldn't a phone call do it?" I was already pushing away thoughts of leaving.

"I think this needs the personal touch."

13

"You mean hand-holding? Is he nervous about this?"

"I was thinking more along of the lines of your having to sit on him," Suzanne said. "When you see the letter, you'll understand." There was a howl in the background, and a man's soothing voice. Her husband Paul comforting their son. "Call him, Thea. He's waiting."

"It's Sunday. Doesn't he have a life?"

"You're a fine one to talk. You've worked plenty of weekends. This is boarding school, which is a seven-day-a-week operation, as you well know. Besides, he's young and ambitious, not like anyone we know, right? The school *is* his life."

"Phooey," I muttered. "All right. I'll call him. But I hope he's not really sitting by the phone, 'cuz it's going to be a while." I looked at Andre and lowered one eye-lid in a lurid wink. "I've got some things I have to do first."

"Spare me the details," she said dryly, "I've got things to do, too. Like mucking out the downstairs, removing one ton of baby detritus, and making things genteel and serene for an afternoon tea. New faculty today."

"I may only have nine toes now, but I am not green with envy."

"I didn't expect you would be."

She didn't sound mellow. Lately she rarely did. "This being a wife business is awfully demanding sometimes. You'll see."

Suzanne was very happily married but Paul's new job as headmaster had added the social obligations of being headmaster's wife to her already hectic life. We'd moved our business to Maine to accommodate her, but she was finding there were a lot of other accommodations she had to make as well. Like fitting tea parties into her schedule. It was a good thing the female brain was adept at multitasking. A legacy of keeping the baby from falling in the fire while sweeping the cave while watching out for the saber-toothed tiger.

"Becoming Mrs. Detective Lemieux was the achievement of a lifelong dream," I said. "Luckily, policemen don't have tea parties. They have balls." Suzanne made an exasperated sound.

Andre grinned at me, tossed off the sheet, and headed for the bathroom. "I've gotta go. Mr. Detective is getting restless."

"That's what you get for choosing a man with appetites."

"Is there another kind?" I spoke to an empty line. Suzanne had gone to police the parlor.

I pushed the buttons that would connect me with Todd Chambers. He answered so quickly it looked like he *had* been sitting by the phone. "Todd? It's Thea Kozak, from EDGE. Suzanne Merritt says you have a problem?"

"Thanks for returning my call." He expelled his breath with a sigh. "I'm afraid we do. I was hoping we could get together this evening. Don't want to let any more time slip by on this one."

There was a faint rustle as he raised a sleeve and checked his watch. I'm such a fine detective I can sort rustles into categories. Sniffs and snorts, too. "I figure what, two and a quarter, two and a half hours you could be here. Five-thirtyish?"

It was precisely that peremptory confidence that had made him the trustees' choice, but I didn't have to jump when he said jump. I would jump when I was ready. "I could meet with you at 7:30." He didn't need to know what else was on my agenda. If I wanted to get up close and personal with Andre and off-load some of the emotional baggage I'd acquired during my session at the range, that was my business.

"Seven-thirty?" He was on the cusp of protest, but held back. "That would be fine. I've faxed some background documents," he said. "We've got a student who claims she's been harassed. Stalked by someone leaving obscene pictures in her room. Our internal investigation says she's doing it herself. Maybe for attention, maybe revenge. She hasn't been happy here. Now she's got other students stirred up, and that concern has spread to the parents. I need to put their minds at rest. I've faxed a letter I want you to review."

"Yes. Suzanne said it was at the office. I'll go by and take a look at it. Maybe we can do this by phone."

"I'd rather do this face-to-face, put you in the picture, maybe even have you speak with this girl, see if you can straighten her out. She needs to understand ..." He stopped without finishing.

Straighten her out? I didn't want to talk myself out of a job, but this wasn't up my alley. The letter and related communication strategies, yes. Counseling a troubled student, no. "Isn't that something one of your counselors should do? Or her advisor?"

"Well, you know adolescents. She's blown this way out of proportion, says she doesn't trust anyone here. I thought you might... that she might relate to you. I'm afraid we've... well, I'm afraid she feels alienated. We're having trouble reaching her. We thought someone from the outside might help."

As if my job were psychology and not PR. Troubleshooting. Admissions advice. Image counseling. I guess it all did involve psychology. Whatever the story was, it sounded like I could be walking into a nasty mess. A school community is like a small town. News travels fast and rumors get exploded like an enormous game of gossip. The parent community can be even deadlier. Once word of trouble gets out to them, it can spread coast-to-coast in a matter of hours. We live in an instant messaging world.

So probably he was right. I'd have to see the documents and get put in the picture. And we'd have to do this face-to-face. I needed to see his reactions to my suggestions, to get a read on him and the situation. When I got there, we could identify the best person to deal with an irate student. One thing seemed sure—if she'd gotten to the point where she'd inflamed the campus, then they hadn't handled this girl well, nor, by extension, the rest of their students, especially the female half.

I was about to hang up when it occurred to me that a stalking complaint could have legal implications. "Have you run this by your lawyers?"

"Yes. They didn't see a problem."

That was good news. Many times, schools put their heads in the sand and refused to take the obvious steps. "Seven-thirty, then," I said, and wrote down his directions.

Andre was already in the shower, singing a ridiculous song to which he didn't know the words, bellowing snatches of song interspersed with bits of humming. I opened the door and stepped in. "I've got to go to New Hampshire tonight."

He twirled an imaginary mustache. "Not before I can work my way wiz you."

I twirled my own mustache right back. "I thought I'd work my way with you."

"Sounds like a plan." He dropped a hand on my thigh, worked its way up until it nestled against my body, and made a deep sound in his chest, somewhere between hunger and contentment.

Even as I soaped his broad chest, smiling with anticipation, another part of my mind was already racing ahead, working on the problem at St. Matthews.

## CHAPTER TWO

Andre lay on the bed like a male odalisque, artfully draped with a bit of sheet, watching me get ready to leave. He was reluctant to let me go. He didn't say anything, he wouldn't, it was just that by now we knew each other like the punchlines of old jokes. A word, a phrase, even a look could be shorthand for whole speeches. Sometimes, keying in to his moods was as simple as listening to him breathe.

"Don't try to drive back tonight if you're tired," he said. "Find a motel." This from the man who would drive all night to be by my side if I needed him.

"I'll try to make it quick. You know I will."

"You're driving to New Hampshire to give this man a quickie?"

"Andre …"

"Yes, dear?" he said innocently.

I threw his clothes at him. "Get dressed, will you. I can't stand the temptation."

"I've married a woman who can't handle temptation?"

"Where you're concerned, you're damned right you have. It would be easier if you were fat or ugly. Or dressed." I grabbed a fistful of underwear and shoved it in the suitcase. My hands hurt. I wondered if there was a job-related injury called trigger-blister, if you could get carpal tunnel from steadying a firearm. I'm a big, strong woman but Macho Man had chosen a cannon for today's exercise instead of some sweet, ladylike Barbie-pink Smith & Wesson.

"Black lace underwear to sort out a confused headmaster?" he said.

"Honey, darling, sweetie-pie," I said, sticking out my chest, "a bra this big in hot pink looks like a pair of beach umbrellas.

And white is boring."

He leaned back against the pillow, hands behind his head, showing off his arm muscles, his chest muscles, his rock-hard abs. "I like big girls out of their underwear."

"Not out on the public street you don't. Not behind the wheel."

"Good point," he agreed, reaching for his tee-shirt. "At least, not when they're you. Other girls?" He shrugged. "When I was a highway trooper, you wouldn't believe the things I'd see. Walk up to a car to check some girl's license and registration and she'd have her skirt up to here and her blouse unbuttoned down to there." He demonstrated with suggestive motions of the sheet. "I'd just lower my eyes and look away."

"Oh, right."

The phone rang. "It's your mother," he said, checking his watch.

She was calling to complain that we still hadn't sent her wedding pictures, and I wasn't in the mood for it. I had to get on the road. "Tell her I'm not here."

He picked up the phone. "Hi, mom."

I could tell he was getting an earful. Didn't I understand that decent people didn't work on Sunday. They played golf or visited their mothers. Dusted the dracena or taught manners to their almost perfect children. But I was not letting her upset me.

Andre murmured some soothing sounds and put down the phone. "Brace yourself," he said. "She wants to know if we have any good news for her."

She, with her own history of miscarriages, shouldn't be hinting about pregnancy. I was getting a headache. She sends them, telepathically, to punish me for being such a rotten daughter. Even now, she was marching into my father's office in high dudgeon to tell my father, for the zillionth time, what an impossible girl I was. At thirty-one, I'm old enough to stop letting her give me headaches. Some of us are slow learners.

I grabbed my toiletries bag, shoved it in and started zipping my suitcase. "Don't forget to pack a sweater," Andre said.

19

"Warm socks. And your umbrella."

I made my hand into a gun, and pointed it at his heart. "Don't start."

"Can't help myself," he said. "You're too much fun to tease. And admit it. You do sometimes need looking after."

"And you're just the man to do it."

"You bet your ass." He stood there, grinning, letting his eyes travel over me in an imitation of rude cop attitude. When other cops do it, it makes my blood boil.

"I'm late." I jerked the suitcase off the bed.

"Aren't you going to wear a suit?"

"Why? It's just a meeting."

"For when you meet the press."

"Not meeting the press, honey."

"Better take a suit. With your track record, you'll get there and all hell will break loose."

"That's reassuring. If my clients thought like you, I'd never get any business." I narrowed my eyes. "What's this stuff about a suit, anyway? You don't like me in suits."

"Exactly," he said. "Suits make you look grown-up and dumpy." He was grinning again. Bastard. He had the most backhanded way of giving compliments.

"So no one will notice me, right?"

"Right," he agreed. "It's so easy to miss a beautiful woman when she's 5' 11" and stacked."

"Stacked?" I crossed my arms defensively over my chest and glared at him. "What has gotten into you today?"

He turned toward the window. "Guess I'm having trouble letting you go."

Our history read more like an adventure novel than a romance. We had good reason to fear separation. Still, duty called and I had answered.

I was wearing black pants and a green sweater. I walked to the closet, got my black jacket, and put it on. "You see," I said, pirouetting slowly. "Suit."

"Damn," he said. "Hot damn. You don't look the least bit

dumpy." I could have dragged him to bed once more, but we were out of time. And, like Scarlett O'Hara's mammy, my mother had tried to teach me to exhibit ladylike appetites.

I stopped by the office and picked up the papers Todd Chambers had faxed, reading through them on my way to the car. Someday I'm going to fall and break my neck trying to do two things at once, one of which involves forward momentum.

Even a cursory reading told me I had to stop him from sending the letter. While it might calm some worried parents, if he already had an upset student on his hands, sending a letter suggesting she'd made it all up would be like throwing gasoline on a fire. It stopped just short of calling her a crazy liar. There had to be a better way. My job was to figure that out between here and his office, then present it to him diplomatically.

The roadsides were banked with a thick tangle of flowers— goldenrod, chicory, Queen Anne's lace, and masses of pink and purple asters. In the fields, the drying cornstalks were turning gold and pumpkins growing orange. The mountains of Western Maine were a mixture of late summer's fading greens sprinkled with bits of yellow-green and deeper gold and the occasional early maple in brilliant reds and oranges. The wide lakes reflected the blue of the sky, quiet after a summer being churned by propellers. Wedges of birds were gathering for the journey south.

I wanted to savor this before October's chill and November's bleakness. But the day was already softening into darkness, the shadows deepening and lengthening as I pressed westward. Todd Chambers' problem had begun to permeate my mind. I felt uneasy about what was waiting for me.

I switched on the radio to distract me, but the word "news" is just shorthand for "bad news." After a domestic murder, a 12-year-old girl who'd been snatched off the street and assaulted, and two fiery crashes on New Hampshire highways, I turned it off, but I couldn't quite forget that girl. After years working on girl's education issues, I'm proud of young women's growing independence, but the danger also seems to be growing. Too

21

often, when I pass a barely dressed female jogger who's tuned out the world with headphones, my admiration for her athleticism wars with my desire to stop and ask if she's lost her mind.

I went back to the beauty outside my car and the job inside my head. Schools hired me because I was the competent outsider who could help them handle thorny problems. I didn't doubt my ability to do that. When I got to Chambers' office, I'd help him figure out what to tell his parents. We'd craft language reassuring them that their children weren't living in a place where students were stalked and terrorized. Tell them a careful investigation had found no evidence anything scary had taken place except in the overwrought imagination of a student. Our challenge was to make the school look good without making the student look bad.

I hoped he had conducted the investigation properly and been sensitive and kind in handling his troubled student. I didn't want to get into this too deeply or have to spend a lot of time on campus establishing the facts. I was already too busy. Sometimes it happened. I'd arrive thinking there was one job to be done and find myself up to my ears in another.

I left the winding Maine roads and set off across New Hampshire. St. Matthews was located in the heart of the state, in one of those picture-perfect New England towns with a green sporting the requisite Civil War memorial and a pristine white bandstand, surrounded, at this season, with vibrant orange mums. Facing the green were a few blocks of big white houses with rolling lawns and wide porches with wicker furniture and porch swings, punctuated by the rare and even more imposing brick house.

I never entered such a town without a brief longing to live there. Small towns had a down side, though. Unless you worked like the dickens to keep your secrets, everyone knew your business. Private schools were like that, too, little inbred communities where people lived in each other's pockets and secrets were hoarded like gold, their keeping traded like favors.

I flipped on my blinker and steered down something called

Academy Lane, which, according to my directions, would bring me to Bishop Hall and the headmaster's office. Bishop Hall was one of those imposing white houses I'd been admiring. A discreet black and white sign identified the visitor parking, empty now in the darkness of a Sunday evening. I pulled into the space closest to the door and shut off the engine. Closest to the door out of habit. Despite the eye-glazing sound of it—consultant to independent schools—my work life has been anything but uneventful.

But the night was pleasant and benign, the area well-lit, and I'd only come to talk about a letter. The only danger I could foresee was that Todd Chambers wouldn't like what I was about to tell him and that despite his good breeding, he might express that displeasure in a loud voice. Guys who like to yell are tiresome, but that's all.

I got out and walked briskly to the door, looking neither left nor right to see if there were bad guys in the bushes, firmly repressing the skin-prickling sensation that someone was watching.

A woman waiting just inside the door popped out of her chair when I came in. "Ms. Kozak?" Her voice was throaty and slightly accented. I nodded. "If you would follow me?" She turned and glided down the dimly lit hall, assuming I would follow.

She wore a flowing dress in a deep shade of purple, and was draped in a vast scarf in intricate swirls of purple, lilac and turquoise blue, caught at the shoulder with a rhinestone brooch. Her black hair was confined in an impeccable chignon. She was slight, no more than five feet tall, and elegant in the striking, bony way of some Frenchwomen. Next to her, I felt like a giant. She didn't look much like a secretary, even if Chambers had a secretary who would work on Sundays. She didn't introduce herself and I wondered who she was.

She led me to an imposing door, nearly 8 feet high and painted a dramatic, shining black, stenciled, in gold letters, Headmaster's Office. She knocked and opened the door to a lovely room, long, high-ceilinged and well proportioned. The books on the shelves were old, with gold-embossed leather bindings. The four fine paintings had elaborate gold frames and small signs identifying the painters, like old paintings in museums. A dark cabinet held a magnificent set of Cantonware. It conveyed St. Matthews' tradition of austere Yankee gentility perfectly.

Todd Chambers, blond, trim and slightly supercilious, was behind his desk, playing with a letter opener. When we entered, he stood but didn't come forward to greet me. His failure to come out from behind the desk told me that he expected me to work for him, not with him. Also, that the trustees might have hired him for his manner, but not for his manners. It didn't bode well for the discussion we were about to have.

Seeing him, I remembered that the other time I'd met Todd Chambers, he'd reminded me of those arrogant and unlikable fraternity boys in Animal House who'd made me root for the losers.

Normally, when I met with a school on a sensitive matter like this, the headmaster would have his deans with him, and often one or more trustees. Except for the silent woman, Todd Chambers was alone. I sat in one of the chairs facing his desk— chairs comfortable enough to be welcoming to visitors, yet sufficiently formal to convey the dignity of the office to students who were being "called on the carpet," and waited.

He didn't waste time on polite preliminaries, but dropped into a big leather chair that gasped slightly at the impact of his body. He scooped up some papers from his desk. "You've read my letter?" I nodded. "What did you think?"

The woman in purple had taken a chair to the side and slightly behind me, the indoor equivalent of being in my blind spot. Her silent presence spooked me. There's something eerie about a person deliberately sitting where you can't see them. Like the cop in the back taking notes during an interrogation, except the cop has an identified function.

"I think it's a good start," I said. "You've got an extremely

24

sensitive situation here. It calls for some rather delicate draft-ing."

"You didn't like it?" he interrupted. "We thought it was pretty good. You have no idea what things have been like around here since that girl started stirring things up. No idea. My phone's been ringing off the hook."

"I have a pretty good idea, Todd. That's why you called me."

He waved the papers back and forth, like someone fanning a fire. "Of course. Of course. Just a figure of speech. Naturally. So, with your experience, knowing how fast rumor travels, you can certainly understand why I'm… why we're all… so anx-ious to get this letter out as quickly as possible. Did you want to suggest some changes?" His eyes flitted briefly to the woman behind me.

Of course he was eager to get the letter out, if he was being deluged with calls from parents, but that made the content more important, not less. If he'd wanted someone to rubber-stamp the awful thing, Suzanne could have done that over the phone. But he'd insisted on having me here. Now that I'd driven this far, I was going to do my job.

"Before we start working on the letter, you need to put me in the picture more fully. You didn't go into much detail about what's been happening."

There was a rustle behind me, but when I looked, the woman was silent as a stone. Chambers shook his head dismissively, then quickly scanned the papers. "I had hoped, with all your expertise, that reviewing the letter would be sufficient. That's our real focus here, after all."

"I thought your real focus was managing a tense situation on your campus involving a student who claims she's been …" I raised my eyebrows quizzically, "… is being stalked, and the resulting rumors and concerns among the rest of the student body, which have gotten back to the parents."

He looked past me at the silent woman. "Is that really necessary?" There was another rustle.

"Todd, I can't help you draft a tactful and reassuring letter to parents about events I don't understand myself. In such a volatile situation, it's essential to ensure that what goes into your letter is accurate. If this girl is bent on causing trouble, you don't want to make statements or take positions you can't defend and you want to be sure you've done everything possible to look out for her well-being. You don't want to do something which will blow up in your face."

"Blow up? How?"

"She could go to the press with her story. It's the sort of thing newspapers love. To the police, since stalking is a crime. Or hire a lawyer and sue the school or her alleged stalker."

He blinked in surprise, as though his only concern was discharging his responsibility to the bill paying segment of his community by sending out an appropriate letter, not the state of things on his campus. Maybe I was misjudging him, but he seemed surprisingly unconcerned with the delicate matter of managing the student whose claims to being a stalking victim he wanted to label lies and paranoia. Or with the potential effect that declaration could have on the rest of his female students and his applicant pool, 50% of whom were presumably female, and most of whom had mothers. Parents take safety seriously and stalking sounds threatening and unsafe.

Maybe he hadn't listened to the news, but it seemed likely to me that if the abduction of a young girl in this part of New Hampshire made the national news, it would add new dimensions to parents' concerns about a potential stalker.

"I'd like to deal with this letter first." He snapped the paper loudly. "Then if you have other questions, we can discuss them. It's all here anyway. We conducted an investigation and determined she was making it up. There is no stalking problem on this campus."

This wasn't a chicken and egg problem. I couldn't evaluate the letter without knowing who the girl was, what she'd claimed, how they'd handled their investigation, and why, if there was no evidence of stalking, the students were upset and talking about it to their parents. Nor could I predict the risks of any steps, such as this letter, St. Matthews might choose to take.

I looked at his stubborn face, tinged pink with frustration, and somewhere above my slow but still competent head, a lightbulb began to glow. Chambers didn't want advice about a letter or his campus crisis. He only wanted the imprimatur of EDGE Consulting on this mess so he could show his trustees and the independent school world he'd done his best. He'd wanted one of us physically here so he could say he'd brought in the experts to be sure he was doing it right. Was the silent woman sitting behind me there as a witness?

*Keep the incredulity off your face, Kozak*, I told myself sternly. *This isn't the first time you've been used. You ain't no babe in the woods.* Well, this babe wasn't leaving without making a sincere effort to get the facts and give my reluctant client the services he needed, even if they weren't the services he wanted.

Calmly, I pulled paper and a pen out of my briefcase and gave him my best professional smile. Once you've been executed by the right wing militia, an evasive, slightly truculent headmaster isn't so daunting.

"I can't help with the letter until I have all the facts. Let's start at the beginning, shall we?"

"The facts are that the girl is crazy," he said, giving his papers a frustrated shake. "Dangerous and crazy."

I waited.

"She's impossible."

I still didn't say anything.

"Don't you understand," he said, exasperated. "I have to stop this right now. Discredit her and reassure my parents. I can't let her go on. She's trying to destroy everything I've planned for this school."

# CHAPTER THREE

For a full five minutes after he'd declared his student crazy, he sat silently, looking anywhere but at me, twiddling his pencil, shuffling his papers and occasionally tugging on his ear. I'd never seen a grown-up professional man tug on his ear before. It fascinated me. I'd seen little kids do it. I'd seen women touch their earlobes quickly, checking for earrings, but this was serious tugging, as vigorous as pulls on those old-fashion bell ropes the rich used to have in their drawing rooms.

What was he summoning. Ideas? A coherent version of the story? Another way to con me into approving his letter? It was possible he didn't understand the seriousness of the situation. I'd seen it before. Sometimes headmasters got so caught up in the day-to-day running of their schools that they lost sight of the context, of the position of the school in the wider world of parents, alumni, and potential applicants. That was where trustees, with their broader vision, were useful, to remind Chambers that the economic security and prestige of his school depended on its reputation, and a Dean of Students to be mindful of the *in loco parentis* role.

All the while, the woman behind me stayed so silent I finally looked around to see if she was alive. My CPR was rusty — I'd only used it once in fifteen years — but I would have given it my best shot if she was lying there unconscious. She wasn't. She was sitting, still as a statue, watching him and waiting. If I lived a thousand years, I'd never develop that kind of patience.

"It started the first week of school," he said finally.

"So, about a month ago?"

"Yes."

"The student who says she's being stalked, who is she? Tell me about her." What he chose to tell would reveal as much

28

about him and his reading of the situation as it would about the girl.

"She's African-American," he said. "An athlete. Here on a full scholarship. Decent student. Not stellar, she came to us with a lot of educational deficits, but adequate. Something of a gift for poetry, I believe."

I waited for the details that would explain her more fully. What her personality was like, whether she played well with others, got along with her roommate, was quiet or loud, introverted or extroverted. Whether she observed curfews and followed the rules or was rebellious, a risk-taker or a discipline problem. If she'd come with a history of mental or emotional instability. And what her sport was.

"Actually, she's only half black. But she's got a lot of attitude. She can be …" He searched for the right word, settled on, "prickly. She followed her older brother, Jamison. He's a brilliant athlete. A campus leader. Charming. Personable. He's a senior this year. We'll be sorry to lose him."

*But not his sister.* His sister who, thus far, remained unnamed. "And her name is?"

"Shondra." At this rate we'd be lucky to get through this by midnight. Since it was clear I wasn't going to be through anytime soon, I needed to think about a place to stay tonight. But first, the girl's whole name.

"Shondra what?"

He looked puzzled, as if, she being in the wrong and all, her name didn't matter. "Jones."

I was willing to bet, just from the little he'd said, that her name mattered very much to her. I looked pointedly at my watch. "It doesn't look like I'm going to be driving back tonight, especially if you want me to meet this girl. Is there a motel or a bed and breakfast you'd recommend?"

My query was about as welcome as a skunk at a wedding. It even stirred the silent woman behind me. Now that I was asking questions instead of following his script, he wanted me gone. But it was he who'd insisted we meet face-to-face, he who wanted me to talk to this girl. Maybe that had been part of the rubber stamp—first approve the letter, then get the dirty job of explaining it to her. Had he seriously expected either thing to happen? I reminded myself that however dense or difficult he was being, he was my client, even if he was playing hard to help.

Despite the way I was foiling his plans right and left, he eased the sulky expression off his face and found some manners. "Many of our parents like The Swan. It's our local B&B. It's very nice. Our parents can be particular." He paused. "But of course you know that. You're very familiar with our little world."

He picked up the phone and made me a reservation. Of course, keeping his parents happy was a big part of his job. I didn't mind if he momentarily confused me with them. I didn't even wrinkle my nose at his use of the phrase 'our little world.' Practically speaking, he was right. The private school world did serve a small population.

But 'our little world' was an interesting and challenging one. He and the other administrators on the front lines, and Suzanne and I and the rest of the EDGE staff backing and assisting them, were in both the education business and the service business. Boarding schools not only provide the classes that are their primary purpose, they provide housing and food service, sports training and culture and recreation, medical services and guidance and structure, as well as caring adults and a safe environment to the students entrusted to their care.

How campus crises or potential crises, large and small, were handled could have a major impact on a school's ability to attract and hold the type of student it wanted. Increasingly, in a world that scrutinized and rated schools, information about the quality of the student body and their success in getting into "good colleges" was what parents considered. That and the physical plant. Parents considering letting their children live away from home were also concerned about safety.

While he proposed to slap a Band-Aid on the situation in the form of his awful letter to parents, Todd Chambers, like it or not, had a lot more to deal with than nervous parents. He had a potentially explosive situation on his hands. It didn't take a Pollyanna to recognize that a crisis was also an opportunity. Handled well, his response would reflect positively on the ability of the school to provide a safe and caring environment to all the resident students. Handled negatively, it would outrage at least one member of the student body—one with the ability to have a significant PR impact—and not necessarily reassure the rest of the female students that they were respected, supported and safe.

I was surprised he hadn't thought this through more carefully. Maybe he had and just wasn't sharing those thoughts with me. He'd have to be more forthcoming if we were going to work together.

"Thanks for taking care of that," I said. "Now, tell me a little more about Shondra. What sport or sports does she play?"

"Basketball." As though tall, athletic young black women didn't engage in other sports. He seemed so surprised I hadn't grasped that on my own that I didn't remind him black women were winning at Wimbledon, that Jackie Joyner Kersee and FloJo hadn't been basketball players, or that China had a wonderful women's basketball team. We're supposed to be learning not to make assumptions about people based on sex and race and national origin. His mandate might have been to tread on the conservative side, but I doubted that he'd been hired to take St. Matthews back to the dark ages.

"She's 6' 3"," he said, as though that explained everything, and another bulb lit up. Since I was another tall woman, he'd hoped I'd have special insights and an instant connection with his problem student. As though being tall made me a mind-reader.

"Tell me about this stalking complaint. What does she say happened?" This time, the rustle behind me was more pronounced. When I turned, she was shaking her head.

"Mostly phone calls. Phone calls of a sexual nature. Recurrent phone calls, frequent enough to disrupt her studies and interfere with her sleep."

"Weekly? Daily? Hourly?" He shook his head. "Does she have a roommate?"

"Not this year."

"So there's no one to corroborate her story." I felt a flash of sympathy for this unknown girl. Whatever was driving her behavior, she was all alone with it.

"That's right."

"Anything else, other than calls?"

He looked back at the woman behind me and I could sense her giving him permission to answer. Surely, if she were a Trustee, he would have introduced her. So who the hell was she and why was he looking to her for authorization?

"Twice since the fall term started she has come to us with rather pornographic pictures she claims to have found in her room. She says there was another one, back in the spring, that she threw away. She says her things have been rearranged. Disturbed. That messages and bits of paper have been placed in her pockets and in her... uh... undergarments."

*Bizarre. Why would someone make up such a story, what did she stand to gain?* "To whom did she go with these items?"

"In one instance, to the head resident in her dorm. The second time, to the resident on duty. Both times, we conducted a careful investigation and concluded there was no way anyone other than the student herself could have placed the items there."

I needed to know the details of his investigation. "You told her this?"

"Yes. And she went crazy on us. Hysterical. Furious that we didn't believe her. That's when she started spreading all over campus that she was being stalked and harassed, that a male student had invaded her room, and we wouldn't help her. Naturally that got other girls upset. They called their parents and you can imagine the rest."

"You didn't involve the police?"

The "of course not" from behind me almost drowned out his

32

reply.

"We preferred to handle the matter in house, as I'm sure you can understand. And we have a most adequate security force."

Maybe they did. Some campus security forces were superb, others little better than glorified groundskeepers. "Did your security force conduct the investigation?"

"No, we did."

"You, personally?"

"Of course not. Our Dean of Students and the Head of Residential Life."

"And their names are?"

For a second, I thought he wouldn't answer. Headmasters are frequently defensive when they have to call in outsiders, but usually it doesn't take long for them to realize we're all on the same side. Sometimes lower level administrators are more difficult. They often feel their jobs are threatened. But Chambers ought to be able to see that his job was more threatened by not handling things well than by doing the right thing. I was only asking the same questions he could expect parents or reporters to ask.

"Craig Dunham is Dean of Students. Cullin Margolin is Head of Residential Life."

"Do you still have the items she claims were placed in her room?"

He looked past me at the woman. "Miriam? Could you? I think they're still in Wendy's desk."

"It doesn't matter, Todd. They're irrelevant," the woman said.

"Well, she's asked. And I suppose it makes sense for her to see them."

"It's just a waste of time," she said, but she rose from her chair and glided out the door, the only sound the subtle susurration of her dress.

"Your secretary?" I asked.

"My wife." Again that slight surprise, as though I should have known.

33

Todd Chambers was reasonably polite, had a reputation for competence, and had had the good sense to call us when he had a campus problem. So why did I find him so irritating? Because he expected to have his mind read, and I'm no mind reader. Because he was being ridiculously stubborn about providing essential information. I couldn't tell whether he was being deliberately disingenuous, whether Miriam was here because she was the brains in this outfit, or whether together they had a plan to get our approval without actually dealing with their problem.

I was also irritated because of what was coming—the moment when he'd drop all pretense of cooperation, try to force me to approve his letter, and I'd say no. Then, either I'd have to persuade him to let me help or I'd have to leave. If it was leave, it would be only with the clear understanding he couldn't represent that I, or our company, had had any part in his decision to send the letter or anything else he chose to disseminate. That would be unpleasant.

Chambers' wife returned holding an envelope gingerly between two fingertips. She placed it on the desk in front of him with a husky, "Darling, it's getting late," and began her flowing retreat.

I held out my hand, stopping her. "Mrs. Chambers?"

Her expressionless eyes met mine as she gave my hand a cursory squeeze. It was like being handed a bag of bones that had been in the refrigerator. She dropped my hand without a word and glided back to her chair.

I watched him shake the contents of the envelope onto his desk. Two pieces of paper in protective plastic sleeves. I've spent too much time around cops, I guess. They reminded me of evidence envelopes. I reached toward the top one. "May I?"

"Of course," he said. "You asked to see them, didn't you?"

I picked it up and moved it into the light. A strong-looking naked black woman bound to two posts, a leather hood over her head, being approached by a masked white man wearing an enormous dildo. Scrawled between her legs were the words,

"You know you want it, baby." The message was menacing, pornographic, and stomach-turning.

Hastily, I set it down and picked up the other. Different woman, different position, different message, but equally ugly and disturbing. I tried to imagine myself at sixteen, finding such a thing in my bed, and my stomach knotted. No young woman, unless she was deeply disturbed, would associate herself with something like this. Most would have no idea where to find such pictures. The new freedom and ease about their sexuality which many young women espoused was about exactly that—freedom. Freedom was not what these pictures were about.

Seeing the pictures enforced my growing sense that I needed to meet Shondra Jones. If she was crazy enough to do this herself, handling her would be well beyond my abilities, probably beyond the abilities of the St. Matthews counseling staff. Whatever I learned from a meeting with Shondra Jones, now that I'd seen these pictures, I knew this situation would not be put to rest by any letter.

"These are very disturbing," I said, putting them back in the envelope. "Have other girls seen them?"

"A few," he said, "before we took them and locked them up." His head bobbed. "The pictures, I mean, not the students."

"So it's understandable why they're upset." He nodded. "But no other students have gotten them?"

"No."

"Getting back to the phone calls. How many? With what frequency? Duration?"

This time he answered. "She says all the time. Often enough so she can't study or sleep."

I made a note. "That also began this fall?"

"Not exactly. She claims they began last spring and continued all summer to her home. She says she reported it to her housemother. The woman Shondra claims she reported it to is no longer on our staff. And there is no record of the complaint."

"There would normally be such a record?"

"Of course."

"Did you contact this woman?" He didn't answer. "What about her last year's roommate? She doesn't corroborate Shondra's story?"

"She didn't return this year. She really wasn't St. Matthews material."

Meaning either no one had tracked her down as part of their 'thorough investigation' or she'd refused to talk to them after being tossed out on her ear. "What about friends who might have been in her room when the phone calls occurred?"

"She's pretty much a loner."

He seemed almost pleased that no one could corroborate the story, while I imagined a troubled girl increasingly isolated by the departure of anyone she was close to. Either isolated and crazy enough to crave attention, even negative attention, or scared to death with no one to share it. "Are the dorm residents also the student's advisors?" He nodded. "What is her relationship with her current house mother?"

Behind me, Miriam Chambers sniffed. His eyes shot to her, then back to me. "I told you. She's difficult."

"Has Shondra accused anyone of being her stalker? Identified anyone?"

Chambers stared steadily past me at his wife. "How could she? There is no stalker."

It wasn't an answer to my question. "Is this her third year here?"

"Second."

"So she's a sophomore?"

"Junior."

"Does she get along all right with her dorm mates?"

Chambers shrugged. "Like I said, she's kind of a loner."

"What about with her teammates?"

"I've heard no complaints. She's a hell of an athlete." He sounded annoyed.

Did that mean he hadn't bothered to find out during his thorough investigation? Anyone trying to get a handle on the matter would need information about the student, her personality, her social and academic situation both to investigate the complaint and decide what steps to take to help her. Even if he planned to con me, at some point someone, trustee, reporter, or even Shondra's lawyer, was going to ask these questions.

"What about her brother? Is he a four-year senior?"

Chambers nodded. "Getting Shondra here was his idea. He was worried about what might happen to her back home. They're being raised by a grandmother and I guess that Shondra was quite a handful. Jamison just kept at us until we agreed to take her." He smiled. "He's quite a diplomat, but he never gives up. He's very protective of his little sister, very much the responsible older brother, even though they're not much more than a year apart."

"You sound fond of him."

"I am."

"But not so fond of his sister. Why is that? Has she given you trouble before?"

He shrugged, sighed, and looked at his wife. "We might as well tell her, I suppose."

"I thought," her voice was steady and cold, a hard knot of sound in the dim, quiet room, "she was only brought here to advise us about the letter. So people would see we'd done everything we could."

"But Miriam... you've been listening. She'll understand when she knows what this is really about."

"It was just the wording, Todd. That's all we were concerned about. That's all *she* should be concerned about. The wording and the fact that we did the proper thing. Sent the letter so our parents would be reassured. That's all we hired her for. Shondra doesn't matter. We can't allow a thief and a trouble-maker to spoil what you've worked so hard for."

She confirmed my suspicion that EDGE had been called in as window dressing, not to give real advice. I hate it when people discuss me like I'm not in the room. It's rude and demeans both me and them. I turned to her. "You must realize that the proposed letter is neither produced nor sent in a void,

Mrs. Chambers. Neither the content nor the impact can be adequately assessed without the facts."

"The facts are that the girl's crazy. She's out to get us. She'll make trouble no matter what we do."

"Shondra has a history of mental illness?"

"Not that I know of." She shook her head impatiently. "I told Todd to just expel her. That would have been the simplest thing. He said we had to go through some steps. We need to discredit her and calm everyone down, then get that girl out of here before she destroys everything."

"What is she trying to destroy?"

I was watching her face, not really expecting an answer, but though she uttered no words, her eyes moved to a picture on an easel in the corner—a large colored architect's rendering of an impressive brick building.

I got up to examine it. In the lower right corner, in that incredibly neat square printing architects have, it said: MacGregor Center for Music and the Arts. I hadn't seen the rest of the St. Matthews' campus, so I didn't know how this fit in, but it had a bigness and impressive centerpiece quality which suggested it was a major project for the school.

"It's lovely," I said.

"Thank you," Chambers said. "We've got donor commitments for over nine million and we're about to begin the public phase of the campaign. The largest ever for St. Matthews. This is a particularly sensitive time, which is why we're so concerned about Shondra coming forward with her accusations now."

His wife's sudden sharp gasp stopped him before he finished the sentence. But though people, sometimes including my own clients, have occasionally wished I were deaf, dumb and blind, I am none of those things. "What is it that you and your wife are trying so hard not to tell me?" I asked.

Todd Chambers had an ability to delay without embarrassment that bordered on the extraordinary. He'd done it to me before and now he did it again. He simply sat behind his desk in the pool of yellow light while his wife and I waited, watching in different kinds of breathless anticipation as he carefully straightened and aligned three piles of papers. Finally, when he'd gotten the arrangement just the way he wanted it, he raised his head and cleared his throat.

"Actually, I misspoke earlier. Shondra did accuse someone of being her stalker. Her accusation is, of course, completely ridiculous. His name is Alasdair MacGregor and he's the grandson of the major donor of our arts center."

## CHAPTER FOUR

I did not yell out, "Aha! The plot thickens." But I wasn't as surprised as I would have been if he hadn't spent so long playing silly games with this information. Way in the back of my mind, I wondered if I was performing some strange form of marriage counseling alongside my consulting. One thing was certain. Mrs. Chambers was pissed as hell at her husband for telling me this. She'd abandoned her stillness in favor of an angry rustling. I knew if I looked back at her, I'd see those cold, dark eyes beaming icy rays in his direction. Chambers had gone back to playing with his papers.

Pissed as hell was not a nice expression. I'd been trying for months to excise it from my speech. But it was surprisingly easy to fall into bad habits, and hard to fall out of them. Even in the middle of this professional consultation, my mother's voice was in my head, chiding me about my language. Lately her voice has been there way too much. Mostly asking about pregnancy, or my lack of it. My loss. Something my mother should understand. Suddenly I was very tired.

I wondered if they had children. She didn't act like a nurturing person, but there are all kinds of parents in the world. There were no children's pictures anywhere in the room, which was the usual practice in the business. But then, most of what I'd experienced at this school didn't follow the usual practice. For everything about this matter, I had to maintain that difficult pairing—an open mind and a watchful eye.

Meanwhile, it was getting late and the only other people in the room were silently at war. It was time for me to take charge. I flipped to a fresh sheet of paper. "Okay, here's your situation. You have a minority student who claims to be the victim of a stalker. The stalker's behavior has involved, according to her, phone calls to her at all hours of the day and night, and, most recently, pornographic pictures and messages which have been left in her room. Right so far?"

I put on my best "we are going to get along and get to work" expression. Chambers grunted. Mrs. Chambers sniffed loudly and, when I turned, she looked pointedly out the window. It was dark and there was nothing to see. I was losing patience. It was inconsiderate to the point of being antisocial to sit behind someone in a meeting involving only three parties. Good thing I wasn't here to teach manners.

"To complicate matters, the student has identified her stalker as the grandson of a prominent alumnus and important donor, correct?" He nodded. "And your internal investigation has indicated that what she says is untrue?" Another nod.

"Dean Dunham conducted the investigation and you didn't involve the local police department? Dean Dunham didn't consult them or ask for advice?"

"He already told you," Mrs. Chambers snapped. "We wanted to handle the matter quietly. Todd, she's supposed to be working for us, isn't she? So why is this girl being so uncooperative?"

Ignoring her, I asked, "So no one ever checked the documents or her room for fingerprints or anything like that?"

"We don't have that capacity," Chambers said. "I doubt that any school's security services do."

"What about phone records? Is there anyway verify her claims about harassing phone calls, at least as to frequency or source?"

"If they had come from him, they would have been part of the internal system. There wouldn't be any records. But the calls were never made, so it's a moot point," Chambers said.

"Your investigation consisted of?"

I waited while he played with paperclips. Finally, he said, "Interviewing her and interviewing people in her dorm."

"And there's a written report?"

"Craig just reported his findings to me."

"Surely you anticipated ..." I stifled the words, anxious, given what I was hearing, to try and save this man from himself. "Did she tell you how she identified her stalker?"

"She said she recognized his voice."

"What about the boy? Her alleged stalker. Did you interview him?"

Miriam Chambers' voice was an icy blast from behind me. "Aren't you listening? You think we gave any credence to her crazy claims?"

"I would have assumed," I said quietly, "that you would have listened to both sides before dismissing such a serious claim. Doesn't the school have a harassment policy? A written procedure for handling such matters?"

"Of course we do," Chambers said, "all schools do. But in this case we felt ..."

"That she wasn't entitled to be accorded the same procedural safeguards as any other student? That he shouldn't be subjected to a hearing on the matter?"

"I think we were entitled," he began, "when the accusations were so outlandish...to deal with it before it got to the formal accusation stage."

His wife cut him off. "We're trying to keep this quiet, Ms. Kozak. Whose side are you on here, anyway?"

"Well, it hasn't been kept quiet, has it?" I countered. "You have one very unhappy student who is determined to make it as public and noisy as possible and your failure to follow your own procedures hasn't helped. You've said she was already difficult, perhaps known to be a trouble-maker. Didn't you anticipate that she might react this way?"

"We expected her to cooperate. That she'd be grateful," Mrs. Chambers said. "Frankly, I don't see why all these questions are necessary, why any of this is. We only asked you here because we wanted your advice about the letter. Because we wanted things done right."

I'd already explained why I was asking questions. If she didn't want to hear it, fine, but the words had been spoken.

42

Something I've learned from my years in headmaster's offices and trustee's boardrooms—you can talk until you're blue in the face but you can't make people listen.

"Are your trustees informed about the situation?"

Chambers opened his desk drawer, selected a large paperclip, and carefully fastened some papers together. "Our chairman, Charles Argenti, has been kept abreast of the developments. The rest of the board, well …" He shrugged. "Charles and I hoped it wouldn't be necessary."

"And you consulted your legal counsel?"

"They sent one of their associates out last week. Nice girl. She seemed to think there wasn't any problem."

His statement ruffled my feminist feathers. All the people in positions of authority he'd mentioned were men, and he'd referred to them by title. Come to the one woman involved, he calls her a girl and omits her name. He'd done the same with Shondra Jones. Maybe I was being too sensitive. I'm a hell of a sexism barometer.

"You told her about Shondra Jones' accusation, whom Shondra had named, and why that was significant? Did you share your concerns that Shondra might have a strong reaction to your dismissal of her complaint? Did you show her the pictures? Brief her on your written procedures for handling sexual harassment complaints?"

My father's a lawyer, and lawyers always say you shouldn't ask a question if you don't already know the answer. So far, I hadn't asked anything I didn't believe I knew the answer to. Todd Chambers wasn't the first naïve headmaster I'd ever met, and he certainly wasn't the first person to make a situation worse by trying to sweep it under the rug. I just needed to know how bad things had gotten.

I also needed a softer tone. This guy was my client, not Shondra Jones. However irritating his naïveté might be, however badly he'd bungled, I had to take these situations as I found them.

"We gave her the facts."

He was getting sullen as I dismantled the house of cards he'd constructed, spoiling his fantasy that things were under control, his problem solved, and that all he had to do to tidy up was send that letter. How he avoided thinking about strategies for dealing with a 6' 3" minority woman who claimed she was being stalked and was mad as hell escaped me. But whatever he was trying to do in his own head, that didn't absolve his lawyer of her responsibility to ask the important questions.

"I'm surprised she let you off so easily," I said. "It's hard to believe any lawyer, hearing that a female student who claims to have been the victim of a stalker who leaves images suggesting sexual violence in her room has had those claims dismissed, and hearing that the claimant has essentially been called a liar and a fraud, would say you didn't have anything to worry about. Especially when it all took place without the benefit of the school's written procedures."

I hesitated, but there were things I had to tell him. He was being frighteningly complacent in the face of a potential disaster. "Todd, I'm sorry to be saying this, but I think you have a lot to worry about. Just for starters, you have a ton of negative publicity to worry about. You have a frightened female student population to worry about. You have a potential lawsuit for slander to worry about. Stalking is a crime in most states, so you have a failure to report an alleged crime to worry about."

I forced myself to stop. I was dumping it all on him too fast. Better take it slowly, give him a head's up about potential issues I saw, and lay out a strategy after I'd gathered the facts.

Miriam Chambers rose with an angry rustle. "How many times do we have to tell you." Her voice was unsteady. "There was no stalking. There is no stalker. The girl is a mental case. She needs help. That's our only problem."

I hadn't yet asked what kind of support and services they'd offered Shondra. Somehow, I didn't think they'd be responsive to that question right now.

I looked down at my notes. "Tomorrow, I hope I'll be able to talk with the people involved. And we needed to begin

44

devising a management strategy. Your biggest challenge will be communication—reassuring your student body and their parents that there is no stalking problem on your campus and that the students are perfectly safe, without doing so in a way that will embarrass or enrage Shondra Jones."

"That's impossible," Miriam Chambers said flatly. "She's already enraged."

My neck was getting sore from swiveling around. "It's unfortunate that it's gone that far. We'll have to find a way to calm her down. Show her that St. Matthews cares about her and wants only the best. Do you disagree, Mrs. Chambers?"

She glided down the room to join her husband, setting a possessive hand on his shoulder. Her previously expressionless face had congealed into an icy, dismissive glare. It was a practiced look, and probably normally quite effective. But if looks could kill, I'd have been dead a thousand times. So far, knock on wood, not even the real killers had succeeded. If she meant to intimidate me, she'd have to work pretty damned hard.

"I think you should get the school's attorneys back here," I said. "Get their feedback on the details of your investigation. On your failure to follow your own procedures. Get them to clarify the issue of slander. Get their sign off on not involving the local police."

Todd Chambers put a cautionary hand over his wife's and manufactured a yawn. "Excuse me," he said. "Long day. I'm afraid I'm losing my concentration. What if we get together again in the morning?"

He was the client. "What time?"

"Eight-thirty?" he suggested. "Come to the house. We'll give you breakfast."

Miriam Chambers looked like that was the last thing on earth she wanted to do, but she nodded.

"Fine," I agreed. "Could you arrange for me to meet with Dean Dunham afterward? And the faculty residents from her dorm? And, of course, Shondra herself?"

He nodded.

A thought struck me. "What about her brother? You said he was very protective toward his sister. How is he reacting to all this?"

"Oh, Jamison is a very sensible boy. I think he'll stay out of this."

"Well, you might check in with his advisor and his coach, see what's going on." This was so basic. Chambers was supposed to have his fingers on the pulse of his school, and he hadn't considered this? Maybe there hadn't been time, if they'd just delivered the bad news to Shondra. But he'd said she had inflamed the whole community, and that took time. "When did you tell Shondra you couldn't substantiate her claims?"

"Tuesday evening."

And it was Sunday. She'd had plenty of time to get steamed up. "And what form did that communication take?"

"You know," Chambers said, "you make me feel like I'm on the hot seat here. You sound more like a cop than a consultant."

"Todd, my specialty is damage control. I can't help if I don't know the situation."

But his remark had gotten me thinking. Not long ago, someone had mistaken me for a cop. At the time, I'd thought it was ridiculous. But hanging around with them so much, was some of it was rubbing off? A natural curiosity. A deep skepticism about everyone's story. A sensible instinct to test the offered version of the facts. I'd have to watch myself. The last thing I needed was to start scaring away clients.

Suzanne was the charmer and the diplomat, I was the heavy, brought in for the hard cases to help clients in trouble. It was part of my job to make people face the facts. It was also my job to handle the process with sensitivity and to make it as easy for them as possible. It didn't sound like my client was experiencing that just now.

"Sorry. I didn't mean to sound like the Grand Inquisitor. I'm used to getting called in on emergencies where I'm coming in from outside, having to quickly gather the facts and work out strategies for handling things. I guess sometimes I do tend to sound like a drill sergeant." I waved an apologetic hand. "It's your show. If my approach is not what you want, just tell me."

Just as suddenly as he had flared up, he was effusively apologetic, as though he feared I was about to flee. "No, no. I didn't mean it like that. We do need your help. I was just thinking we might all function better in the morning."

"Morning is fine," I agreed, shoving my notes into my briefcase. "If you could just tell me how to find The Swan?"

For a second, he looked puzzled, as though he didn't understand where swans came into this. Then he smiled. "It's very easy. You go back down the drive the way you came, turn right onto the main road, and it's half a mile down on the right."

"And your house?" He looked blank. "For breakfast tomorrow?"

He pulled a campus map out of his desk, circled the building we were in, then followed a curving drive with his pen and circled another building. "We're right here."

"Eight-thirty," I said. Then remembered something. "The boy she's accusing. Has there ever been a relationship between them?"

Their "no" was quick and unanimous.

"What's he like?"

"Resolute and determined," he said. "Clever."

"Handsome and inventive," she said.

"Popular?" I asked.

He let it go a beat too long. "Alasdair's kind of particular about his friends."

"He ever been in trouble?"

Their eyes met, and like two computers networked, information flowed quickly back and forth, encrypted so I couldn't read it. "No," he said. "Nothing significant."

I wondered how the school, or Chambers, differentiated between significant and insignificant. "Your student handbook sets out the rules for conduct, academic and social?" He nodded. "So by not significant you mean he's never broken a major rule?"

I watched the exchange of data again. His face was bland but there were tell-tale signs. He was deciding to lie. "No. Nothing major," he agreed.

I lifted my bag to my shoulder and checked my pocket for keys. "I'd like a copy of the handbook." I waited while he reluctantly went to the shelf and found a copy.

"Thanks." I gave him a smile I hoped was reassuring. "See you in the morning."

He said a polite goodnight. She stared through me like I wasn't there. I thought of Suzanne, my partner, now a headmaster's wife herself. She would never intrude into Paul's business like this, however much they might have discussed it in private. Nor, should she ever be drawn in, would she forget her manners because her nose was out of joint. Fierce, formidable and icy though she was, Miriam Chambers had many of the qualities of an ill-mannered child. And both of them, polite and impolite, were showing the strain of holding things back.

I stood in the dark parking lot, watching them through the window, huddling together at his desk, wishing I *could* read minds. Unconsciously, I formed my hand into a gun, aimed, and fired. She staggered backward, her hand at her chest. But it was something he'd said, not what I'd done. I turned away and clicked the unlock button.

My instinct for impending disaster told me to drive straight home. Back to security and normalcy and Andre. Especially back to Andre. It warred with the businesswoman in me, which told me to stay and soldier through or people would stop calling me for cases like this. It also warred with the part that, like a bloodhound, was on the scent of something and wanted to follow it. The self that relished the challenge of a difficult case.

Overarching it all was an ironic detachment, born of having lived too long on the cusp of danger, which saw the whole thing cinematically. Like in one of those volcano movies, on the surface, everything was placid and normal, with an everyday set of problems to be dealt with. I walked on grass and asphalt on a peaceful New England boarding school campus, breathing air scented with wood smoke. Underneath, masked by this benign surface, violence and danger roiled like molten lava, waiting to explode.

*"Oh, get over yourself, Kozak,"* I mumbled as I started the engine. *"It's just a job."*

# CHAPTER FIVE

Craig Dunham was a Todd Chambers clone, though I doubted either man knew it. A big, preppy, confident man with Chambers' slightly supercilious air and enough starch in his bright pink, orange and blue striped shirt to hold him up should his own body ever fail. He had the annoying habit of looking past me, as though he was still waiting for the 'real' consultant to arrive. I didn't know what my failing was. It could have been gender, or age, or the fact that I'm inappropriately sized for a woman. Men are sometimes disconcerted to find that we see eye-to-eye. At least, in the literal sense.

I'd come to my meeting with him straight from a sterile and cold—in the interpersonal sense—breakfast with the Chambers. It was clear he hadn't married her for her cooking. People in New England joke about the Brattle Street and Beacon Hill fathers sneaking out in the evening for a burger after one of their wives' meager feeds, and we've all heard those stories about the Yankee millionaires trying to feed six people on a pound of meat. Miriam Chambers, though clearly not old Yankee herself, had embraced that style with a vengeance.

She'd presented me with one sad and lonely egg, quivering on the wide expanse of empty plate next to a decrusted piece of pallid white toast and a single strip of limp bacon. Hungry as I was, it had seemed downright cruel to molest those lonely bits of food. I wondered how he kept his big, robust body running on such a slender allotment. Probably made it his duty to check out the dining halls on a regular basis. There had been American coffee, too, the kind you can read through. Six quick cups might cause a slight buzz, but then you're committed to spending the rest of the morning in the bathroom.

I didn't know why they'd asked me to breakfast, since the

talk was as spare as the meal. I could have lingered at The Swan, feasted on quiche, homemade muffins, fresh fruit and heaps of bacon and sausage, and been a happier person. I'd looked longingly about as Chambers conducted me to Dunham's office, but we passed no easy source of food. Unfortunate, since I'd skipped dinner. I skip a lot of meals. One of the downsides of being a workaholic. It means that when I do get to eat, I need to EAT.

The one thing I had learned was why Miriam Chambers had been at last night's meeting. Todd might have a reputation as a tough conservative and a brilliant fund-raiser, but she obviously played a major role in creating that image. He could hardly chew without looking to her for approval.

Now I was sitting on a sturdy wooden chair listening to Dean Dunham deliver a description of his investigation into Shondra's accusations as meager as the meal I'd just left. Brevity might be the soul of wit, but I wasn't here for wit, I'd come for information. I waited, pencil poised, from beginning to end, and found nothing to write down.

As soon as he finished, I pounced. "Tell me about the hierarchy," I said. "The reporting system from dorm residents to you."

He looked puzzled. "Todd said ..."

"Do the residents report directly to you?" I interrupted.

"We're a pretty small school," he said.

"Do they ..."

"Yes."

"And you keep student records here, in your offices?" He nodded. "So if Shondra had reported a harassment problem last year, it would be here in her records?"

"If she had reported it...but there was no report."

"That's what Todd said. So let's back up. When a student comes to a dorm resident, or an advisor," I paused. "Are they the same? Their advisors are the dorm residents?"

"Yes." A silence while he appeared to be counting windows. "Well, usually."

51

"What's the procedure for noting a student's concerns? What kind of record-keeping takes place?"

He explained it to me. A form filled out, copies in their file at the dorm and in his. "But of course, not everything gets written down."

"Of course not. But serious things? On-going things?"

"I would hope so."

You would *hope* so? Mister, you're supposed to be in charge. Was this the Walt Disney school of management? Wishing will make it so? "When Shondra's complaints first came to light this fall, did they begin with her expressing concern about telephone calls or did you first hear about it because of the pictures?"

"The pictures," he said. "But you know she ..."

"So she never spoke to any of the residents about being bothered by phone calls?"

"Why do you ask?"

"I'm trying to get the big picture. What you knew when and how you, by which I mean St. Matthews, responded, so we can present a favorable picture of St. Matthews that's grounded in fact."

"I'm sure Todd told you. She complained about the first picture. We investigated. Concluded that she'd done it herself. Then there was the second picture. We looked into that and reached the same conclusion. That's when she really started making trouble. When she said Alasdair had done it."

"Tell me about your investigation."

"I thought I just did," he said. "Anyway, I don't see why it matters. Todd said you were here to help us communicate with our parents. To reassure them that there is nothing untoward happening on this campus."

Untoward was a pleasing locution. Too bad we weren't here to discuss language. Today I'd vowed to stay pleasant, so I flashed him an apologetic smile. "I know it seems strange, but sometimes I have to go backward before I can go forward. I need to know what I'm dealing with. The last thing St. Matts needs is to send out a letter that will expose it to claims for libel or slander. So if you could run me through it?"

Dunham looked like I was speaking in a foreign tongue. "I thought that truth ..."

I raised a hand to stop him. Truth was a defense, assuming you could establish truth, but we were trying to avoid a situation where we had to defend ourselves. I often think I should give up consulting and go to law school. At the very least, I am always a lawyer's daughter. Truth, established by a trial, or even a battle of lawyers, was something St. Matthews didn't need. In the world of pop celebrity, any press is good press; in this world, public recognition for anything other than academic, arts or sports achievement, or major donations was to be avoided. Mom and Dad didn't ante up 30K a year to send junior to a tony school whose campus scandals made the nightly news.

"Believe me, a fight about what the truth is is something you want to avoid. And I bet it wouldn't be hard for Shondra Jones to find a lawyer who's dying for the publicity a fight with St. Matthews would generate." I steered him back to my question. "So...your investigation?"

Dunham's unguarded face veered between puzzled and annoyed. He looked longingly at a stack of waiting papers. "But I don't see ..."

"Please." I gave him an encouraging smile.

If I lived a thousand years, I'd never understand why schools hired me to do jobs and then stalled, second guessed, or disagreed at every step. But people had a habit of keeping the difficult questions and bad news from themselves and therefore, also, from me. Self-deception was a common thing. At the management level, it took the form of policy. The US military weren't the first to practice forms of don't ask, don't tell.

I practiced Andre's skill of maintaining an opaque cop's face while I waited for his detailed explanation. When I left this room, he should still be thinking of me as a pleasant woman who was helping him solve a problem, not a cynical witch who was beginning to sympathize with Shondra Jones.

He ran me through it. It was as slipshod, cursory and

conclusory as I'd feared. Their "thorough inquiry," to quote the language from their letter, had consisted of interviewing the resident advisors and a few of the girls on her hall, plus two girls who lived downstairs near the entrance, as well as Shondra herself. On the basis of this, they had concluded that it was impossible for anyone to have come into the dorm unobserved, never mind making it to the third floor and Shondra's room. The prior year's resident advisor, to whom Shondra had reported the harassment, hadn't been contacted, nor had the former room-mate who'd allegedly lived through it with her.

When I asked if anyone had spoken with Alasdair MacGregor, his "of course not," was as sharp and dismissive as though Alasdair was a taboo subject.

"Are there written reports?"

"We didn't think that was necessary."

I thought of matters I'd dealt with at other schools, of the comings and goings that actually took place, and wondered whether they were being impossibly naïve, simply lazy, or deliberately dishonest in the interest of protecting a major donor's family.

I pulled out my campus map and laid it on his desk, standing beside him so I could see it from his point of view. "Can you show me where Shondra's dorm is?"

He pointed. "She's in Cabot Hall." I circled it in red.

"And where her room is?" He looked puzzled, but complied, and I marked the place where her window would be.

I pulled out a blue marker. "Now, can you show me where Alasdair MacGregor's dorm is?" He circled another building, Pearsall Hall, directly across from hers. "And where his room is?"

Dunham balked. "I'm afraid I have no idea," he said.

And I was born yesterday. I let it go. I'd find out eventually. "Now," I began, and realized that I was beginning too many sentences with the word 'now.' I took a deep breath and forced the inquisitive tone out of my voice. "I don't envy you, having to deal with so many adolescents. It must be a challenge." He smiled and nodded. "Do you have Shondra's file available?"

He patted a thick folder sitting on his desk. "Got it right here."

"Let's double-check the dates she reported finding those pictures in her room. All I've seen is Todd's letter, and they weren't in there."

I peered eagerly over his shoulder as he rifled through, finding the papers he wanted and running his blunt finger down the pages, searching for dates. He read them to me and I jotted them down, wishing there were a way to get him out of the room so I could see what else was in there. For now, unless fate intervened, I'd have to rely on him. Hugging my notes to my chest, I walked around the desk and sat facing him again.

Was I being overly suspicious? Weren't my clients entitled to a presumption of goodwill? Increasingly, though, I was being called in when there was already trouble. Maybe that's why I was becoming more like an investigator than a consultant. But I heard Suzanne's voice in my head. "Kid gloves, Thea. Despite the cutting edge population they serve, this is a very genteel business. At least, it thinks it is."

"Todd says that Shondra has a reputation for being difficult." He nodded. "Can you give me some examples of ways in which that has manifested itself?"

I watched him prepare to disagree and didn't let him get there. "I know we both realize one of the most important aspects of handling this, from a PR standpoint, is to emphasize the school's deep concern for Shondra's welfare, not to identify her as a problem student, but as a student with a problem, and to delineate the steps taken to provide her with the best in support and counseling."

I sounded like such a weasel, like we were all conspiring to play a dirty trick on the girl that would derail her credibility and make us look good. But wasn't that why they'd called me? I was glad there wasn't a mirror in sight. I didn't want to see my sharp nose, pointy teeth or bright, beady eyes.

"That's a good way of putting it," he agreed. "We aren't

heartless, whatever the girl may think. She's certainly not the first student with problems." He bent over the file, occasionally removing a sheet and marking the place with a yellow sticky. Then he evened up the edges so it was a neat little stack and passed it across the desk. "This ought to give you some idea," he said.

I took my time going through the papers. This was the first glimpse I'd had of how they kept their records and performed student evaluations. It was all very orderly and professional. Every term, along with her grade, each teacher had written evaluations. So had her coaches. Everyone except her basketball coach felt she had problems with authority. Resisted taking direction. Didn't like to ask for help. They all felt she could do better, that she wasn't working up to her ability.

Words like 'quick-tempered,' 'moody,' 'inattentive,' and 'solitary' also appeared, as well as the wish she would cooperate and participate more. The word 'attitude' didn't appear, but it was always there in the subtext. So she didn't exactly play well with others, off the court at least.

Even her basketball coach, who seemed to like her a lot, noted that she was wary and quick to perceive slights. Had it begun with her feeling that she hadn't gotten into St. Matthews on her own merit? If everyone felt she could do better, what had they done to help her along?

Increasingly, despite the unfavorable picture of the girl I was being given, I found myself curious about her side. Whatever the underlying cause of her behavior was, it was important not to lose sight of the fact that she was the child, the student, the one for whom, presumably, this institution existed. Nothing I'd seen made it clear why everyone believed she had done this herself, but I could see why, faced with so many negative messages, she might engage in a defiantly "in your face" attention getting gesture. I could also see why, if she was a victim and the school refused to believe her, she wouldn't take it lying down.

At least she hadn't folded her tent and fled. That was the

other way to go—believe the message and become a failure. In the next hour, I would be meeting her. I wondered what it would be like.

"Alasdair MacGregor," I said. "When did she tell you that he was the one who was stalking her? When she went to her advisor with the first picture?"

"No." He gave a vigorous shake of his head and set a broad hand on the closed file, as though reading something through the cover. Or was he holding something in? "No. Then she said she didn't know. It was later. After the second picture. When we were interviewing her, I asked if she had any idea who might be doing it. She looked me right in the eye and said oh yes, she knew exactly who was doing it. I asked her who and she said Alasdair MacGregor."

"Did she say how she knew?"

"She said she'd recognized his voice. But if he was calling all the time, why did it take so long?"

This next question was tricky, but I had to ask it. "So you didn't believe her. Was her delay in identifying him the only reason?"

He just shrugged. Perhaps he'd also remembered he was supposed to be charming, that he wanted me on his side, because he followed the shrug with a warm smile. "Ms. Kozak...Thea...May I call you Thea?" I nodded. "Picking him? It just wasn't credible. Alasdair doesn't need to chase girls. He's got them lined up for blocks."

In four short sentences, he undid any good a truckload of smiles and charm might have done. This wasn't about chasing girls, about attraction. This was an allegation of stalking. It was about controlling and harassing girls and shaking their sense of self and safety. About playing on their vulnerabilities and terrorizing them. Stalking was also about refusing to take "no" for an answer. As dean of a population of students that was half female, he should know that.

"Any idea why she would have picked him?"

"Not really. But if she was angry and frustrated and really

wanted to get back at St. Matthews, he'd be a good choice. Everyone on campus knows about the capital campaign and his grandfather's contribution…and he's, well…it's a hard term to use for one so young. They're just trying things on at this stage—sexual identity, personal style, political beliefs…but Alasdair has positioned himself as a bit right-wing. Conservative. A bit of a bigot, even, and he's pretty outspoken about it. I expect …"

Dunham's eyes circled the room as he debated the propriety of sharing this with me. "Well, to be frank, he'd be about the last male on this campus to be interested in a minority female."

I appreciated his honesty, but there it was again. He was equating stalking with normal attraction. I forced my hands to unclench and swallowed the lecture rising in my throat, shelving my soapbox with an effort. I needed to wrap my hands around something before they headed toward him in an un-gentle way. "Any chance there's a cup of coffee around here?"

I expected him to pick up his phone or push a button. Instead, he shoved back his chair, smiling with what I recognized as relief. On this point, at least, we were simpatico. "I'll get you one," he said. "How do you like it?"

"Cream and sugar?" I didn't add lots of cream and sugar. He didn't need to know that some days I lived on the cream and sugar in my coffee because it was the closest to food I got.

"Mind if I look at her file?"

"Help yourself." He pushed it across the desk.

I opened it and started thumbing through, looking for dates around the end of the previous year, something other than teacher's reports. What I found was a memo from the previous May, from an advisor named Deborah Zucker, reporting that Shondra had approached her about a series of anonymous phone calls she'd received. The phone calls came at all hours, from an unknown male, and the content was sexual and disturbing.

I looked through the adjoining papers but couldn't find any further references to the problem, nor any information about how it had been handled. I made some notes about the date and contents, and when he returned with my coffee, I handed it to him. "I can't find anything in the file, but perhaps you might remember. How was this handled?"

He read through it, put it back in the folder, and closed it. Instead of answering my question, he said, "So I guess this craziness of hers has been going on longer than I thought." Unembarrassed about his earlier statement that there was no prior report, indifferent to the implications.

I was beginning to share Shondra's frustration. "What if there really is a stalker?" I asked. "What if the poor girl is honestly terrified?"

"Wait 'til you meet her," he said. "She's even bigger than you are. Great big girl like that can take care of herself. What's she got to be scared of? It's not like someone's actually touched her or anything. Even if she weren't doing it herself, what's the harm in a few phone calls or pictures? It's no big deal."

"Have you seen those pictures?" He nodded.

He'd seen the pictures and could still say this? At that moment, it clicked for me. He didn't get it at all. Not about stalking nor about how serious the school's situation was. If she'd created those pictures herself, she was a deeply disturbed person engaged in a battle against St. Matts and they had let things go on far too long without appropriate intervention. If she *was* being stalked—and for the first time, I was entertaining that possibility—they had failed her miserably. It would be hard to repair the damage now.

Either way, the problem went well beyond Shondra Jones. Everything Dunham had said made it obvious he didn't have a clue about stalking and he was the Dean of Students. Whatever I was able to do for them in the present situation, St. Matthews had another serious problem they didn't seem to know they had—a cultural problem of blindness, insensitivity, and care-lessness, particularly toward female students.

"This Deborah Zucker, who was her advisor. She's left the campus?

"She found St. Matthews too isolated, I'm afraid. She was a city girl. Missed the bustle and excitement."

"But you could tell me how to reach her?"

"I suppose she must have left a forwarding address." He didn't offer to find it.

"Who is her advisor this year?"

He opened the file again. "I really don't know." How could he not remember? Both he and Todd Chambers had told me he'd spoken with her advisor several times in the course of investigating her complaint, yet it hadn't mattered enough to stick in his brain. I knew if I asked what steps they'd taken to give Shondra counseling or support, I'd get another blank stare.

"It must be in your notes—the ones you made when you investigated her complaint," I said sweetly. "I'll have to check with you later for that information. It's time to go meet Shondra. And given her current state of mind, it's probably a bad idea to keep her waiting." As a casual afterthought, I added, "Maybe by then you could also find me contact information for Deborah Zucker?"

I slung my briefcase strap over my shoulder and picked up my coffee. "Where am I meeting Shondra?" Dunham blinked a few times, like he had something in his eye.

"I have no idea," he said, "I'll check." He reached for the phone, then hesitated. "I hope you realize what you're getting yourself into, meeting Shondra."

"What do you mean?"

He rolled his eyes. "You'll see," he said ominously, and made his call.

# CHAPTER SIX

I saw immediately how she could get someone's back up. There was nothing warm and fuzzy about Shondra Jones. She wore "fuck you" attitude from her braided-head and jutting jaw to the tips of her big, sneakered feet. She stalked into the room with a ball handler's feline grace, dropped her backpack on the floor, dumped herself into a chair, and proceeded to stare out the window with an air of exaggerated boredom. The arms that dangled from her tee-shirt were taut with muscle.

Physically, she probably intimidated most people, but as a big girl myself, I was delighted to encounter a strong, fit young woman who was taller and meaner and didn't walk around with stooped shoulders and a hanging head. Adolescent attitude can be a pain in the ass, but in girls I'll take it over passivity or airheadedness any day. And I know it's intolerant, but group giggling stimulates my gag reflex. I doubted if Shondra did much giggling.

"Thank you for agreeing to talk with me," I said. She continued to stare out the window. "My name is Thea Kozak and I'm an educational consultant. The St. Matthews administration has brought me in to help them deal with this stalking situation."

Her eyes shifted from the window to me, narrowed with disbelief. "Situation?" she sneered. "The Administration says they is no stalking situation, except in my head." Making the word "administration" about three blocks long. "All in my head." She tapped her temple for emphasis. "How you gonna deal with that?"

"What about you? What do you say?" I kept my voice neutral and my face blank, trying to give her nothing to jump on.

She swept me with a disdainful look, and went back to

staring out the window. She had exotic eyes. Large, brilliant, slightly tilted. They hadn't told me she was beautiful. "Buncha honky ass-kissers so busy snuggling up to the folks with money they got no time or interest in what's really going on. People like me, brought in to provide diversity, they don't give a damn about us." She gave the word "diversity" four long exaggerated syllables and a nice long pause to let it sink in. "'Cept it bothers them when we don't know our place. We supposed to kiss ass and be grateful."

Her eyes swept back again, giving me a glimpse of how angry she was. Angry and something else. Something I wasn't supposed to notice. Uncertain or frightened. I didn't think she meant me to see that. Underlying her youth and strength, there was an air of jaded weariness that made her seem much older than sixteen.

I didn't think authority frightened her, nor having to interact with adults or fear of discipline, but something had shaken her profoundly. The revelation had been accidental. But I've been badly scared, with good reason, often enough to recognize it.

I thought of Craig Dunham, asking what did a big strong girl like her have to be afraid of? No one had touched her, had they? I wondered if he'd ever had his peace of mind deeply disturbed. If anyone had ever shaken his arrogant self-confidence enough to give him profound self-doubts? How well he would cope if his privacy and concentration were constantly and relentlessly interfered with? And he was an adult. She was sixteen, far from home and living alone among strangers.

"I did all the right things, according to their rules," she said. "It hasn't changed a damned thing. I bet they never even talked to him 'fore they decided I was crazy and makin' it all up. While that boy ..."

Her voice caught on the words and hovered there, temporarily paralyzed. "That boy...with all the harm he's done, and I ain't...I'm not just talkin' 'bout what he done to me, he can do any damned thing he wants, and ain't nobody going to say boo for fear his rich grandaddy will take the money and run."

Suddenly, the bravado and fear fell away, and she was just an angry teenager. "I've given them their chance. I tried to do it their way. I've got my rights, too, though they won't admit it." She spread her arms wide in a dismissive gesture, shaking her elaborate concoction of braids. "Well, you can tell them not to worry. I'm done waitin' for them to do their job. I'm taking care of it myself."

She rose and turned toward the door, her back arrow straight, her shoulders wide and square, speaking to me over her shoulder. "You tell them that, okay. Tell 'em take their effing dorm residents and their expensive consultants and their asshole letter to parents and shove the whole damned mess."

What did she mean, taking care of it herself? In a second, she'd be gone and I'd miss my chance to ask. "Hold on," I said. "Maybe you've got real reasons to be angry, but not at me. I'm just trying to figure out what's going on."

"What's goin' on?" She turned back, her shoulders slumping like she was too exhausted to maintain the posture of outrage any longer. "What's goin' on is a whitewash." A smile flickered, so brief I almost missed it. "Hey. That's fine, isn't it? A whitewash."

She stretched her arm up the wall and rested her head against it wearily, gathering her attitude back around her. Then she pushed away again. "You tell them to relax, okay. They can go ahead and do whatever they want. Send their lying letter. Pretend nothin's going on with Alasdair and them…all the things they done. No skin offa my ass. They had their chance. Best they could do was call me a crazy liar. So you tell them I'm handlin' it. Tell them, just wait and see what this crazy nigger bitch does next."

She snatched up the pack and slung it over her shoulder. "I be goin'."

"Shondra." I made my voice deliberately loud and commanding. She was tired of people who either patronized her or treated her with suspicion. "Sure you don't want to tell your side to someone who doesn't give a damn about the MacGregor money?"

MacGregor money might be paying my salary, but I had to come into these things with an open mind. If EDGE started walking in and approving whatever schools wanted to do, our reputation would suffer. They didn't come to us because they wanted "yes" women. They came because we brought an experienced and unbiased outside opinion and were willing to call it the way we saw it. When the chips were down, we could be tough for them and tough to them.

She half-turned toward me, giving me the benefit of her elegant profile. "I guess that would be you?"

"That's right."

"I'm supposta believe you might be on my side even though theys paying you?"

"They're paying you, too," I pointed out, "and you're not on their side."

She folded her arms and leaned back against the door frame. "You got a point there," she said. That was all she said, but she didn't leave.

I walked down the room and leaned against the wall, facing her, imitating her posture. "When did the stalker first start bothering you?"

"Didn't you hear?" she said. "They is no stalker."

I repeated the question. She was silent so long I thought she wasn't going to answer. "Last spring."

"April? May?"

"April, I think."

"What did he do?"

"Phone calls."

"Obscene phone calls?"

"I guess."

"You guess?"

"They weren't obscene at first, just anonymous, like he'd go, 'do you know who this is?' and stuff like that. I didn't know who he was. He called a lot. I was trying to work and the work's hard for me, so I asked him to stop botherin' me. He kept it up, so I

64

got nasty. That's when it got ugly."

"Ugly how?"

"Ugly sex talk. Sayin' disgusting things he'd like to do to me." She looked down at her shoes. "Now mostly he doesn't say anything. He just calls, knowing that's enough. Knowing I'll worry and won't sleep."

"You had a roommate last year, right?"

"Yeah."

"She know about these calls?"

"Sure. She was the one insisted I report them. I wasn't gonna. I wanted to tough it out." She clasped her arms more tightly against herself. Muscle definition I would have killed for, that I couldn't have if I spent my life in the gym. "I thought they'd stop."

"She got some of these phone calls, too?"

Shondra shook her head. "He'd always hang up if she answered. He was smart. Creepy smart. After a while, it got so he only called when I was alone in the room."

"So your roommate never heard his voice?"

"No. But she saw me getting enough so she could see how they bothered me."

"Any idea how he knew you were alone?"

"No. That's why it was so creepy. It was like he was watching. She'd leave the room and bingo, the phone would ring."

"What was your roommate's name?"

"Allie. Allison Schwartz. Why?"

"I thought I might talk to her."

"Check up on me?"

"More like confirm."

She gave me a 'yeah, right' look. "Tough luck. Allie's gone. Dropped out. They told her she was a loser so many times she started believin' it."

"You stay in touch?"

"No way. Allie's trying to forget this place, what it done…did…to her head. She don't want to hear from me. Not from you, either."

Reading between the lines, she missed Allie. I wondered if the girl had been a friend. The picture they'd given me, and the way she presented herself, suggested loner. Social isolation was a common problem among minority students at places like this. Maybe she had friends on the team.

"You spoke with Deborah Zucker about the phone calls?"

"That a question?"

"I guess not. How did she respond?"

"You mean, what did she do besides actin' like I got two heads?"

"Yes."

Shondra's shrug was a big gesture. "She got me an answering machine so I could screen calls. It worked. I guess he didn't want his voice on tape or something, because for a while, the calls stopped."

"Doesn't the school have voice mail?"

"Yeah." Her jaw jutted sullenly. "But I had a boyfriend back home, and he didn't wanna leave no voice mail. He could only call certain times. So with the machine, I could listen for his calls…pick up when it was him."

"You said 'for a while.' Then what happened?"

"Someone stole it. The school wasn't about to spring for another."

Her face dared me to ask why she didn't buy another one. "Did you report that?"

She gave me one of those 'do you think I'm stupid' looks. "Of course I did."

"And?"

"And nothing. They didn't have a clue what had happened, so they did what they always done. Figured I'd stolen it myself. Sold it so I could take a trip to the mall." She gave me a sideways look, watching for my reaction. "I mean, how much did they think I could get for some piece of crap answering machine, even if I could find something at the mall that might fit me?" She stretched out in a way that showcased her long limbs and large feet.

I understood the problem of dressing a tall body. "Why would they assume that?"

"Lady, you're closer to 'em than I am. Why don't you ask them? Anyway, it's not like they come right out and say this stuff. I just know that's what they thinking."

"Do you take things?" I asked.

"Once or twice I did. In the beginning. They all had so much and I …" She didn't finish. "Jamison got on my case. Told me I was shamin' the family and asked how would Grandmamma feel if I got my sorry ass kicked out for being a thief after all he'd done to get me in here. Jameson's got some temper on him. Said he'd beat my ass. So I stopped. I never done…did it again. But to them, that's who I am."

She gripped her bag. "I gotta go. We just wastin' time and I've got class. Look, I know it's my own fault, but other folks get second chances."

I needed the rest of her story. "Did anyone else overhear any of the calls? Ever had anyone in your room when he called?"

"Not that I remember. Maybe Jen or Lindsay, once?"

"Who are Jen and Lindsay?"

"Girls on the team. Look, I gotta go."

"When can I talk with you again?"

She stared into my face. Her eyes were hard and cold, and this time, all I could see was anger. "We done talkin'."

I took out a card and offered it to her. "In case you change your mind."

She looked at doubtfully, then shoved it in her pocket. "Doesn't matter what I say to you or anyone else. It'll always come down to the same thing. Stuff happens. I report it. They decide it isn't really happening. Talkin' to you won't change that. Nobody 'round here's gonna stand up to Alasdair. I got no time to waste on things that don't matter. I got school, I got basketball, I got work."

She gripped the strap of her bag with a white knuckled hand. "I'm too mad at those motherfuckers to be polite anymore. You guess they ever think 'bout how it will be when my Grandmamma reads that letter? So if you'll excuse me."

"Deborah Zucker believed you, didn't she?"

"Yeah. And they couldn't wait to get rid of her sorry self. Did they really think we believed that stuff about her wanting to go back to the city? No way. She was like me. She didn't fit in. Allie believed me, too. And they're both gone. If you start believing me, you be gone, too. Wait and see. So if you value your job ..."

She leaned in close, this strong, furious, wounded young woman I had to look up to, and whispered, "...better get your white ass back over there to the Administration Building and tell 'em what a crazy, mixed up nigger I am. Tell 'em, whatever I said, you could see with your experienced professional eye that I was just a lyin' ho. Not that it matters what you say. They already got their minds made up." She turned and left, her long strides carrying her quickly away.

I watched her go, those broad shoulders so straight it must have hurt. Shondra Jones had come to St. Matthews with a chip on her shoulder. In a little more than a year, the school had turned it into a boulder.

# CHAPTER SEVEN

I followed my campus map to Cabot Hall, where I was meeting Maria Santoro, the resident advisor Shondra had gone to with the second picture. As I climbed the wide, slightly shabby staircase to the third floor, I thought about other times, other dorms, and how much sameness there was from one campus to another. Some were cleaner, homier, some more modern or more elegant, but they all possessed the same mingled scents of cleaning products, grooming products, pizza and popcorn. Except at times like this, when everyone was in class, there was always the background hum of music, the rush of showers, the rising and falling cadence of voices.

So far, I'd spotted two staircases, two fire escapes, and a convenient tree, all of which afforded access to the building, as well as all the ground floor windows, and the dorm hadn't been locked. I'd walked in unobserved and climbed two flights of stairs without meeting anyone. On the third floor, searching for Ms. Santoro's room, I'd passed two students and a janitor. No one had challenged me or shown any curiosity about my presence. True, I wasn't male, like Shondra's alleged stalker, but I was a stranger and I looked too young to be someone's parent, even if the last six months had aged me ten years.

At Ms. Santoro's door, I read the very picky sign about when she could and couldn't be disturbed. Neither welcoming nor supportive of a poor, homesick freshman, never mind the rattled victim of a sadist playing mind games. Dorm residents had to set limits, I knew, but tone made a big difference. Brief as it was, the tone of this note was whiny and petulant. I wondered if the writer was aware of that.

I raised my hand to knock, imaging Shondra standing here in my place. I could see her anger and her fear—I'd witnessed both of those today—but I didn't have the story yet, so I couldn't imagine what she'd said or how she'd proceeded. I knocked and waited. When nothing happened, I knocked again, harder and louder. I'd asked Craig Dunham to call ahead. She was supposed to be expecting me.

Finally, a stocky young woman with a peevish face and spiky punk hair snatched the door open and glared up at me. "What's your problem?" she snapped. "Can't you read? I'm not on duty right now. I'm trying to work."

With those few sentences, she'd put me in Shondra's shoes. I looked down at her with my best predatory smile—the one I learned from the heron about to stab a fish—and said, "Maria Santoro?"

She hadn't bothered to look at me before, assuming I was one of her young charges. Now she reddened and gave me a slightly apologetic "Yes."

I stuck out my hand. "Thea Kozak, from EDGE consulting. Todd Chambers has brought us in to assist with the Shondra Jones matter."

The flush darkened as she opened the door wider and jerked her chin toward the room. "Oh, right. Craig's secretary called with some garbled message about them sending someone over. Come on in."

I stepped past her into a pig sty. Papers and books littered the floor, warring for space with empty pizza boxes, take-out Chinese cartons and soda cans. Obviously, she didn't believe she was supposed to be a role model, but I was surprised she hadn't made some effort to pick up, knowing the administration was sending someone to see her. She shifted a litter of books and papers off a chair and invited me to sit. I wondered if she even bothered to do that when her visitor was a student or if she left them standing. What I really wondered was why she hadn't been fired long before this, whether the dorm head was paying any attention.

With a wince for the fate of my good pants, I brushed crumbs and other detritus off the chair, and sat. "Tell me about the night

Shondra found the second picture," I said.

"Ha!" A sharp little fox-like bark. "That girl is a menace to society."

"About that night?"

"It was almost lights out time. Nearly eleven. I was grading papers when she came banging on my door." She rolled her eyes.

"She came to you because you were the resident on call?" I wanted to back up and take her through the normal evening routine but the room was hot and the smell of old food mixed with the cloying sweetness of incense was sickening. I wondered if she burned incense to cover up more incriminating smells.

"Yes."

As I waited for elaboration, she flipped idly through the pages of a book. I took the book out of her hands, closed it, and set it on her desk. "Maybe you could concentrate on my questions?"

Santoro shrugged. "She said she was sure that someone had been in her room and she wanted me to be with her while she looked around. I went back to her room with her."

"How did she seem? Was she calm? Upset? Angry?"

"Upset. And angry. Shondra's always angry. So, we went back to her room. Opened the door. The light was on." She hesitated. "It looked okay to me, but she said things had been disturbed."

"Did she say how she could tell? Was the room neat? Messy?"

"That girl should have been a nun. The only thing not perfectly orderly or neatly aligned was the laundry bag on the floor."

"That's how she knew her things had been disturbed?"

"That's how she said she knew," Santoro corrected. She picked up a pencil from the desk and began doing a mini-baton twirling act. A ray of sun through the window illuminated her face and I could see several empty holes in her ears and a small

71

one in her nose. I wondered if she also had a pierced tongue. Not quite the image Todd Chambers' trustees were looking for.

"Then what happened."

She halted the pencil and looked at me quizzically. "Are you a cop or something?" she asked. "You don't sound like any consultant I've ever met."

"You meet a lot of consultants?"

She shrugged. "I've met some cops."

Why was I not surprised? "I do a lot of this," I said. "Trying to figure out what went on so I can advise the school about the best way to handle the situation. They're paying for my time, and time is money."

The pencil twirled. "They should expel her and be done with it."

"Why?"

"Because she's a born troublemaker, that's why. Because now that she's got this thing set up, she's gonna milk it for all it's worth. Drag St. Matthews over the coals if she doesn't get her way. Probably sue for defamation, walk away with a bundle of cash."

"What is it she wants that she's not getting?"

"You don't know?" I shook my head. "She wants a formal hearing before the disciplinary board. She wants Alasdair MacGregor to admit he's been stalking her. And she wants him kicked out of school." The pencil flipped onto her desk.

"She told you this?"

"No. But we all know that's what she wants."

"Do you know Alasdair MacGregor?"

"I've had him as a student." She tried to hide it, but the thought of Alasdair MacGregor lit her up.

"What do you teach?"

"Spanish."

"Getting back to Shondra," I said, "when you got to her room, what did she want you to do?"

"She said she was sure there was something in her bed and she didn't want to find it. She said someone else had to find it

72

because the last time we hadn't believed her."

"The last time meaning the first picture?"

"Yes."

"She found it in her bed?"

"That's what she says."

"No one was with her that time?"

"No."

"At that point, before you found the picture, how did she seem?"

"Seem?" She blinked her exophthalmic eyes and checked her watch.

"Yes. Her affect. Her demeanor. Her mood." I didn't give examples. I wanted her words.

"She was quiet. Tense."

"What did you do?"

"I pulled down the covers and found a picture. I picked it up and held it out to her. She refused to touch it."

"Why?"

"Because she didn't want her fingerprints on it is what she said."

"How did you react to the picture?"

"Naked lady. Big deal." She shrugged. "Not worth getting upset about."

"Not even if you're a frightened sixteen year old?" She shook her head, as if the idea of Shondra Jones as a scared adolescent was incomprehensible. "And then?"

"I held out the picture so she could see it. She looked at it, then ran down the hall to the bathroom and was sick."

I waited for a 'poor thing' or a comment on the shock of such a finding to a young girl, but there was none. "Was anyone else around besides the two of you?"

"I think maybe Alice Demers walked by. She's such a mousy little thing. I'm not sure. And Cassie MacLeod. She's across the hall." She checked her watch again.

"Then what happened?"

"Shondra came back from the bathroom, looking like death

warmed over, and insisted we had to take the picture to Mrs. Leverett, the house mother, right away. So that's what we did."

"And?"

"And what? You know. I'm sure Chambers has gone over this with you. We promised her a careful investigation and she said 'yeah, right, just like last time. Ask a few dumbass questions and walk away from it.' She said she couldn't take this anymore and asked, 'When are you going to talk to him?' I said, 'Who?' And Shondra said we already knew who."

"Did you know who she meant?"

"Of course." Santoro picked up the pencil and started twirling it again, a dumpy, incompetent, indifferent little drum majorette. I couldn't wait to rain on her parade.

"You know how Shondra has that flat, infuriating way of talking. That's when Mrs. Leverett lost her temper. They started yelling at each other. Then her husband came in and said the noise was going to wake the children. Shondra yelled an obscenity and walked out."

"What were they yelling about?"

Santoro laughed. "Her rights."

"And then?" I knew they hadn't called the local police, but I wondered what they had done. Called the campus police, perhaps? Certainly called Todd Chambers. Held an emergency meeting about what to do?

"Camilla…Mrs. Leverett, said it would be best to wait until morning, when everyone was calmer. She put the picture in an envelope, put it in a drawer of her desk, and we all went to bed."

I like to think I've left my impulsive, temper-losing self behind, but sometimes things still make me flare up like a Fourth of July rocket. How could any group of responsible adults end an evening like that by simply going to bed? Even if they believed she'd created that picture herself, even before their 'thorough investigation,' a student that disturbed should have triggered a call to the headmaster and to counseling services.

And if she hadn't done it, which was what they were

supposed to have believed at that point? I pictured Shondra climbing back up the stairs, going into her room and shutting herself in with the vision of someone else in the room, touching her things, putting that revolting picture in her bed.

I knew what I needed to know, but I wanted to hear her say it. "No one checked on Shondra to see if she was okay?"

"Of course not," she said. "She'd just told us to go…uh…well, fuck ourselves, so why would we?"

Because you're the grown-ups and that's your job? "She'd just found a picture that could be construed as a rape threat directed at her, in her bed. You didn't think that warranted some extra attention? You didn't call security?"

Maria Santoro dropped her pencil. "Of course not. She put the picture there herself."

"That was determined through a subsequent investigation, wasn't it?" She didn't deign to answer. "You didn't know that at the time."

"Everyone knew she was a troublemaker."

"Is she one of your advisees?"

She shook her head, a vigorous "no," as though even when she was the resident on duty, she had no real responsibility for the students. "She belongs to Mrs. Leverett."

I'd have to speak with Mrs. Leverett, then. "Tell me about Alasdair MacGregor."

"What about him?"

"You had him as a student. What's he like?"

"Bright enough. Quick. Manipulative. Actually, he's very smart. He's just a little lazy."

"Doesn't get good grades?"

"I didn't mean …" She shrugged. "He does okay. He could do better if he wanted to."

Just like Shondra. I wondered what his evaluations said. "Is he popular?"

"Yes," she said. "No. I mean, I guess it's kind of mixed."

"Why?"

"His repu…uh…his politics." She stared longingly down at

the pencil, at a loss without a prop.

"Could you elaborate?"

"Why? Why are you asking about him? He's the real victim here, if anyone is. It's obvious Shondra picked him because his political views offend her."

"What is your basis for that conclusion?"

"My what?" Her eyes narrowed suspiciously. "You said you weren't a cop, right? So how come the interrogation, anyway?" She explored her ear, checking each of the empty holes, then quickly dropped her hand when she saw me watching. I manufactured a look of surprise. "Interrogation? I'm just trying to get the big picture. It's not like I'm asking whether you smoke dope in your room or were ever arrested or are sleeping with a student."

I'd just thrown out some random problems other schools had, but one of those was a bingo. I could tell by the way her eyes widened and her shoulders hunched. Before she could regroup, I said, "So, about Alasdair MacGregor? Is there a history between him and Shondra?"

Her eyes flashed to her watch and she popped out of her chair. "I'm sorry but I have to go. A class."

"It says on your door that you're available for the next hour."

"That's an old sign."

"It says Fall schedule. You're less than a month into the semester." The mean part of me wanted to see her squirm.

She flopped sulkily back into her chair. "He's like a lot of the kids we see. Macho exterior, insecure interior. He's really haunted by the pressure from his family. St. Matthews is the family school. MacGregors always go here. They're always campus leaders. Alasdair is trying to find his own niche. Looking for a place he can excel. Sometimes he…sometimes they…make bad choices. All the kids, I mean."

But she didn't. She meant Alasdair, who was deemed worthy of some slack, while Sondra wasn't. "What kind of bad choices? Has he been in trouble?" She didn't answer. "What about his relationship with Shondra?"

76

"I don't believe there is one." She said it too quickly, then scooped up the pencil and went back to being a mini-majorette.

I shifted my eyes away from her, circumnavigated the room, looking for clues about her personality. The messy room, with the Indian bedspread thrown over the sofa and the Papasan chair, looked more like a student's room than an adult's. So did the heap of kicked-off shoes and sandals under her desk. Of course, I have a heap like that in my place, too, or did until I started sharing quarters with Andre. He's so neat I'm lucky he doesn't make me spit shine them and lay them out in rows. Not that I would. Something I shared with Shondra Jones—a lot of attitude.

"To your knowledge there's been no fight, argument, insult, feud or rivalry which might have made her want to get back at him? No ugly words, no racial slurs? No sexual advances?"

She dropped her eyes. "No."

"What about a romantic relationship?"

"You're kidding, right?"

"Why would I be kidding? Shondra's a very pretty girl."

It came out before she could stop herself. "Because she's black. Alasdair has these...I told you...conservative views. He would never be interested in someone black."

"Are you basing this on things he's said or things you've inferred?" She just blinked at me with a slightly stupid look I wanted to slap off her face, and didn't answer. "Were you in the dorm last year?"

"I was in a different dorm."

I'd had enough. Often, I learned as much from what people didn't say. And she hadn't told me plenty. I snapped my notebook shut and stood up. Held out my hand. "Thanks for your time," I said.

She returned the handshake as minimally as was humanly possible. A quick stab in the air in the vicinity of my hand. Handshakes are another thing that can tell you about people. As she hurried to open the door, I swept the matchbox on her desk neatly into my pocket. She closed the door behind me so quickly she almost took my ass off.

I went down the hall, into the bathroom, and shut myself in a stall, a bit breathless at my own behavior. Holding the little matchbox neatly between my fingertips, I slid it open and stared at the definitive evidence that she smoked dope in her room.

I wondered if Shondra knew about this. If people weren't just intimidated by her size, but because she knew their secrets. Secrets could be a form of currency. Had secrets like this contributed to their reluctance to call in the police? Had her ability to trade in their own currency been part of their eagerness to see her gone?

## CHAPTER EIGHT

I hadn't arranged to speak with Mrs. Leverett. From Maria Santoro's description, it would probably be more of the same, but I was here anyway so I stopped on the first floor and knocked. The noise level had increased with girls returning from class. A student passing behind me said, "She teaches a math class this block."

"Maybe I could catch her afterward. Do you know where the class is?"

"All math classes are in Eaton." The look she gave me was wary now that I'd revealed myself to be a stranger. She backed away even as she asked, "Do you know where that is?"

She was a 'pastel blonde,' with baby-fine hair and skin like porcelain. She wore pastel colors, too, a long tan skirt with a pale aqua twin set. Her toes, peeking from open shoes, were painted to match her top. She had hopelessly innocent blue eyes, a slightly snub nose, and a small mouth gelled a shiny soft pink. She twisted a strand of hair around her finger and waited for my answer.

"I have a map," I said.

"Are you a reporter?" she asked.

"Nothing so glamorous, I'm afraid. I'm an educational consultant." It had the usual effect. As she turned away, I asked, "Have there been reporters around?"

"One," she said. "But he was black and a guy. So he didn't come into the dorm."

"Did you talk to him?"

The blue eyes widened. "Oh, no. Not me, I'd never. But he tried to talk to Alice. I heard her telling the other girls about it."

Trying not to make her nervous, I asked, "What's your name?"

She glanced quickly around, as though looking for permission to tell her name to a stranger. "Cassie McLeod," she said quickly. "I'd better go."

"I was hoping you could show me the way to Eaton."

But Cassie was spooked. "It's not hard if you've got the map."

"I guess you're right. And I'm sure you've got important things to do." I turned toward the door, elaborately casual.

"Is this about Shondra?" she blurted out, flushing a becoming pink. "Excuse me. I've got to go." She turned and hurried up the stairs.

Todd Chambers hadn't mentioned a reporter. Had that omission stemmed from ignorance or because he didn't want me to know? With whom had that reporter spoken? What had he learned? And what potential fallout could we anticipate?

This was a can of worms indeed. Right now I was wishing I'd just rubber-stamped that letter and gone home to Andre, leaving St. Matts to handle its own problems. If only I were a lazy slacker like Maria Santoro. But Andre was working and so was I. I checked my watch—still an hour until I met with Todd Chambers—and headed off to Eaton.

I followed the map and was almost at Eaton when a deep voice from behind said, "Excuse me?" I turned, found myself about level with his shirt pocket, and kept on looking up until I found a handsome face that was much too young to be so troubled.

"Are you the consultant lookin' into my sister's problem?" He had a preacher's voice, which, in this soundbite age, would probably end up doing sports commentary or voiceovers. Selling products instead of values or responsibility.

"If you're Jamison Jones." I held out my hand. "Thea Kozak. EDGE Consulting."

He wrapped his hand around mine with the studied gentleness of the very large and strong. "Have you got a minute?"

We sat on the stone wall in front of Eaton Hall, looking out over a rolling green campus punctuated by vibrant trees. The beauty of the day seemed to have no effect on his spirits. After a few sighs and some shifts of his restless body, he began. "I'm real worried about my sister. About what she'll do," he said. "She's been pressurin' me to help her out. And I don't know."

He sighed again, shrugging his big shoulders. "I'm tryin' to stay out of it, but hey, the way Mr. Chambers and them are actin', I just may have to."

"What does she want you to do?"

He gave me a calm and careful examination, taking in my color, my suit and my briefcase, then countered with a question. "What does Mr. Chambers want *you* to do?"

Sign off on a bad letter, I thought. Aloud, I said, "Help him draft a reassuring letter to parents so they won't worry about a campus stalker."

"But you talked to my sister," he said, "and people in her dorm. Why'd you do all that if you're only supposed to write a letter?"

I wasn't the only one who sounded like a cop, was I? I was glad to see they were teaching them to think and question here at St. Matts, and not just learn by rote. And to learn how fast information traveled on this campus.

"What's that letter supposed to say, anyway?" Before I could respond, he answered his own question. "That everything here at St. Matts is just fine and my sister's a crazy, paranoid minority who's makin' it all up because she don't...doesn't...like someone's politics, right?"

Got it in one. Despite Jamison's poise and maturity, I was a little surprised Chambers liked him so much. Administrators of Chambers' stripe weren't usually kindly disposed to this level of student insight and questioning. At all schools, there was a strong, and necessary, element of 'because I said so.' Maybe he pulled his punches with Todd Chambers, but didn't think he had to with me. Or maybe it was enough that he was putting the St. Matthews' basketball team on the map.

"I'm really not at liberty to discuss it." Which, much as I wanted to tell him the truth, I wasn't.

"Not at liberty? Thought this was a free country?"

"I've been retained by the Administration to ..." Too stuffy. "I mean, I ..."

Before I could finish, he pushed himself up off the wall, his geniality gone. "No. I don't suppose you are. Not if they're payin' the bill. You think what they tell you."

He jerked his chin in the direction of the Administration Building. "What's wrong with their heads over there, do you suppose, that they think sending some lyin' letter's gonna make this thing go away? I tried to tell Mr. Chambers that, after Shondra asked me for my help, but he's got that witch wife whisperin' in his ear. He used to be a half-decent guy, when he first come...came here, but he doesn't listen anymore. All he thinks about is that building and what he's got to do to get it paid for. He don't care about us no more."

Did Chambers know this was his community's perception? "What does your sister want, Jamison?"

"I guess," he said, "according to what I've learned in my constitutional law class, that she wants due process." His eyes, fixed on my face, dared me to be surprised.

"A hearing, you mean, on the harassment charge, with Alasdair forced to be involved? I should think, if she's telling the truth, that what she'd want is to have the whole thing stop."

He studied me carefully, like I was something he was going to have to write a paper on, then nodded with surprise and approval. "Sounds like maybe you believe it's really happening."

"I'm keeping an open mind," I said.

"What did Shondra tell you?"

"When it started and how it escalated. Then she decided she didn't want to talk to me and told me we didn't have to worry, she was going to handle it herself. I take it that means getting you involved?"

His shoulders slumped. "That's part of it."

What was the rest? A lawyer? The press? Some national black students association? "What does she want you to do?"

"Talk to Alasdair."

I wondered if either of them had actually used the word 'talk'? "You going to?"

"Probably. Won't do any good, though."

"Why not?"

His full lips lifted in a cynical smile. "Because Alasdair is a devious, vicious, arrogant son-of-a-bitch who knows he can do whatever he wants and nothing will happen." His spread his hands wide. "Look what he's already gotten away with."

"So you're sure he's doing it?" He looked so surprised I wondered if he'd been referring to something else Alasdair had done. That something everyone hinted at and no one would talk about. Then his face hardened and a wary look came into his eyes. "You think my sister's makin' this up?" He looked away, considering, then back at me with those studying eyes. "You see those pictures she got?"

I nodded. "Have you?"

"Where the f ..." He caught himself before the word came out. "Where your brains at, lady? She sure ain't making them herself." There was a strangled quality to his voice. Anger, grief, or a combination of both. I thought about those ugly pictures. About the things we do for our little sisters.

He misinterpreted my silence. "You think she did that herself? There ain't no way that my sister...She did that, she'd have to be crazy. Shondra's got her problems...she got kind of a bad attitude, and other stuff...like maybe lovin' basketball too much, and kinda holdin' herself off from other people, but she ain't crazy. She's decent. Those pictures weren't decent."

He started away, then turned back. "You gotta wonder," he said, shaking his head, "how so many smart people can act so dumb. It's all gonna come out sooner or later. You can't hide shit like this. I wish you all weren't forcin' me to do your jobs for you. I'd rather stay out of it. But if you all gonna act like assholes, then me and Shondra...we gotta stick together. Comes down to it, family is everything. You know?"

I knew.

He turned on his size sixteen feet and lumbered away, leaving me with a sinking feeling in my stomach and a bunch of questions I'd never gotten to ask. I worried about what he was going to do, how Alasdair was going to react, and what the fallout would be. It didn't bode well for Chambers' plan of sending the letter and then sweeping this under the rug. Trying to sweep Jamison and Shondra Jones under a rug would be like covering a couple elephants with a tarp and claiming they were rocks.

Luckily, worrying about Jamison Jones wasn't my problem. I'd only been asked to look at a letter and talk to Shondra Jones. Sure, I'd needed to understand the situation, and sure, there were things I'd learned that ought to be addressed, things I'd suggest when I met with Chambers if he could get his head out of the sand, or shake off those visions of sugar plums and dandy new arts centers long enough to focus. But I wasn't volunteering to try and straighten out Shondra Jones, and I certainly wasn't getting between Jamison Jones and Alasdair MacGregor. That was a job for Todd Chambers, his deans and his security staff. Or Godzilla.

I'd forgotten Mrs. Leverett. I hurried inside and checked the classroom. Empty. In the math department office, they told me she'd returned to the dorm. By the time I'd hiked the ten minutes back there, I'd only have fifteen minutes left for an interview. Not enough time to do a decent job. Sighing, I picked up my briefcase and headed for Chambers' office. It had been a totally unsatisfactory morning. I was longing for some satisfaction and didn't expect I'd find it at my next destination.

On the way, I passed a building that smelled like lunch and thought hungrily of thick sandwiches on decent bread. Eye-opening coffee. Anything that looked like serious food. As I frequently tell Andre, I'm a big girl, and big girls need to eat big meals. Usually I'm telling him this while he's trying to steal the food off my plate. He reminds me that big boys need big meals too, distracts me somehow, and steals the food. It's how I stay slim and he stays happy.

I didn't follow my nose into the building that smelled like food, I detoured into one that, despite its modern brick façade, smelled a little of moldy old books—the library. I asked for a copy of last year's yearbook, then sat at a table and thumbed through it, looking for pictures of Alasdair MacGregor. Because of the name, I'd been expecting fair hair and sturdy features. What I found surprised me and explained Maria Santoro's dreamy look when his name was mentioned. MacGregor had the sculptured-cheekbones and slightly bruised and vulnerable look of a young Gregory Peck.

He was in a lot of pictures, and in every one, a single twisted dark curl graced his forehead as though the stylist had just arranged it and ducked out of the frame. Then, for no reason other than I had some time left, I checked for pictures of Shondra, of which there were a few, and of Jamison. Like MacGregor, he had many, towering above his classmates, generally smiling, looking like a big man on campus.

I checked my notes and then looked for the two women who were gone, leaving no one to corroborate Shondra's story. Her last year's roommate, Allison Schwartz, had the hunch-shouldered droop of the chronically depressed and a sullen look that marred her pretty features. There was only one picture of Deborah Zucker, looking fit and athletic, wielding a field hockey stick. It gave no clues to why she hadn't fit in.

Unenlightened, I returned the book to the shelf and went back out into the fall sunshine, ignoring the rumblings of my stomach as I traversed the busy pathways back to Chambers' office. My watch said I was on time—I am a compulsive slave of the clock—but he wasn't at his desk. I went back down the hall to find his secretary, a bright, cheerful woman whose nameplate identified her as Wendy Grimm. She smiled at me over her half-glasses. "Todd? Oh, I think he's at the gym. He usually plays squash with Dean Dunham on Mondays at eleven."

"I'm Thea Kozak, from EDGE Consulting? He asked me to meet him here at eleven." I managed to get just the right degree of confused disappointment into my voice. "Do you suppose he forgot?"

"Oh, dear." A plump, freckled hand went to her lips. "I really don't know. He's been so distracted lately...getting ready to launch the new campaign. I suppose it might have slipped his mind. He's usually so prompt."

"Well," I said, "I'm sure he'll be along any minute. Something else you could for me? I need a couple of addresses. A staff member and student who are no longer here. Could you look them up for me?"

She smiled, relieved I wasn't angry and glad to do something for me. She grabbed a pen. I gave her Allison Schwartz and Deborah Zucker's names. "No problem. I'll have them when you ..." She trailed off, staring over my shoulder. The smile stayed in place, but her brightness vanished. "Mrs. Chambers...this is Ms. Kozak, the consultant...she was supposed to meet with Mr. Chambers."

"I know who she is and why she's here. You can get back to whatever you were doing. I'll take care of it." Wendy Grimm returned her attention to the documents on her desk, but not before I glimpsed the intense distaste on her face.

"If you'll follow me." Miriam Chambers turned and glided out of the room. At breakfast she'd been wearing a green caftan. Now she wore black slacks and a blue blouse that revealed a fashionably gaunt body. The clothes were expensive and well-cut, and with the elaborate makeup she wore and her black hair piled up, she looked quite elegant. Without the rustle of fabric, her silent way of moving was unnerving.

She led me into her husband's office and nodded toward a chair, floating back behind his desk and settling into his big leather chair. She tented her hands together in what I hoped was an unconscious imitation of her husband. "I'm afraid we got off on rather an awkward footing last night," she said, as though we hadn't had an equally awkward and chilly breakfast just a few hours ago. "I'm afraid Todd is...we're both... rather preoccupied with the new arts center project. It's the biggest thing St. Matthews has ever undertaken. So very important for the school's image…for the future."

She gave me time to absorb her words. Unnecessary. The importance of the project was obvious, as was its relevance to the matter that had brought me here. It didn't negate any of the concerns I'd expressed last night, though I knew she hoped it would.

"Obviously, nothing can be allowed to get in the way," she continued. "That's why we have to manage this situation with the Jones girl before it gets out of hand."

Too late for that. It was already out of hand. I wasn't sure any of us knew how far, but I wasn't discussing that until her husband appeared. He was my employer, not her. Some instinct for self-preservation made me switch on the tape recorder I always keep in my briefcase. Probably highly illegal, I didn't know New Hampshire law and 'Live Free or Die' might not cover everything, but what I did know was that after what she'd just said, I wanted EDGE protected in case they didn't take our advice and later claimed we'd supported their actions.

"It looks like a very exciting project," I said.

"Oh, it is." She walked to the easel and began flipping plans, pointing to various parts of the building, describing the ways they'd be used, the architect's clever ideas for creating multi-purpose space, the focus groups they'd had with faculty and students to identify needs and create the design. For the first time, she was animated, her pale cheeks coloring as she talked. "And this is just the beginning. It is going to be Todd's legacy, bringing the campus into the twenty-first century."

Wasn't it a little soon to be thinking about a legacy? Chambers had only been headmaster for two years, and it usually took the first year to settle in. "What do your fundraisers say about the timeline for raising the money?"

"The MacGregor family foundation is putting up most of it, and we have firm commitments from several other prominent alumni. We only have to raise about five million. The materials for the general solicitation are at the printer right now."

I tried not to goggle at her use of "only" and "five million" in the same sentence. That seemed like a lot of money. But these old New England boarding schools had connections. I once heard a headmistress describe a West Coast fundraising event in which she got pledges for ten million in a single evening. I thought about my friend Jonetta's school for poor black girls in New York City. She busted her butt to raise every precious dollar. But as my mother often said, only the naïve expect life to be fair.

Shondra's timing couldn't be worse, from a PR standpoint. I wondered if she was more calculating and devious than she seemed. The genteel and ornate face of the tall clock said Chambers was now twenty minutes late. "Do you think Mr. Chambers will be much longer?"

"I really don't know," she said. "But we don't need to wait for him. Todd and I redrafted the letter after breakfast this morning, taking your concerns into account. I think you'll find it substantially improved." Reluctantly, she returned to the desk, opened a file, and passed me a single sheet of paper.

Without looking at it, I said, "As I've tried to make clear, the contents of this letter are only a small part of the problem. No matter how tactfully your draft your communication to the parents, it will not put an end to your difficulties with Shondra Jones. The matter has gone too far, and gone on too long, without a satisfactory resolution from her point of view."

"Shondra doesn't matter," she said. "One crazy trouble-maker cannot be allowed ..."

"I think we should wait for Mr. Chambers," I said. "Ultimately, how to proceed is his call, but I have some concerns to discuss with him before any decisions are made. My conversations this morning with Dean Dunham, with Shondra Jones and her brother Jamison, and with Maria Santoro, have raised a number of issues I hadn't anticipated."

"Just read the letter," she insisted. "Todd has delegated everything to me."

One thing about being a consultant, at least in our business— just when you think you know how to deal with what comes along, something completely unexpected rises up, like the shark in Jaws, and shows you its pearly whites in what isn't a smile. I didn't know whether she really had the power to act for him or only wished she did. It didn't matter. My concerns properly went to the Headmaster and his deans and trustees, not to the Headmaster's wife. I was just being practical. Headmaster's wives usually don't have the authority to sign contracts or pay bills.

To test my assumptions, I said, "You have the authority to sign contracts that are binding on the school?" I got out our standard contract and started filling in the blanks.

"You want me to sign a contract?" As shocked as if I'd asked her to shuck her designer grab and dance naked.

"Standard procedure," I assured her. "Business relationships work better when the expectations of the parties and their mutual understanding about the work to be performed are discussed and put in writing at the beginning." Especially in cases where the client wanted to use our name without taking our advice. I should have done this last night.

Miriam Chambers raised her chin until the tendons stood out in her neck. She flapped a hand at the letter, trying to regain control of the situation. "Just read that over for me, would you please?"

"Happy to," I said, passing her the contract. "And you can take a look at this."

She almost snatched it out of my hand. Not that there was much to see. A clause setting out our rate for the initial consultation and our rates for work thereafter was already in the boiler plate. The details still needed to be agreed on and written in. All I'd done was fill in names, places and dates and begun a paragraph describing our involvement thus far—reviewing the draft letter and the school's handling of a student complaint, including our proposed process for thoroughly reviewing the complaint and the school's adherence to its own rules.

While she frowned over our rates, I read the new version of the letter. It was better. It still referred to a thorough investigation, which I now knew was baloney. It reassured parents that no stalking had taken place, which I suspected was also baloney, and it now characterized the situation as a misunderstanding between students, which was a more tactful view of Shondra, though I doubted that she'd see it that way.

"It reflects a fairer view of Shondra," I agreed, "but it still makes some statements which could be considered misleading."

"It just describes what happened. What we know."

"I'm afraid it doesn't. It says that you conducted a thorough investigation. You didn't talk to her last year's advisor, or last year's roommate. You didn't talk with Alasdair MacGregor, or his friends. Or ask the local police for advice."

"That was unnecessary."

"You've ignored the evidence of your own records. You have a report from last year, from Deborah Zucker, concerning harassing phone calls to Shondra Jones."

"Oh. Well. Deborah. She was such a bleeding heart she'd believe anything."

"The school bought Shondra an answering machine to help deter the calls. The school's own records and behavior suggest a belief that she was being stalked. How are you going to deny that, if challenged?"

She shrugged. "Those records can disappear."

"Shondra's not going to disappear."

"She could. Given her record, we've ample justification for asking her to leave. Whose side are you on, anyway?" she demanded, shaking the draft contract. "You want us to pay you these big bucks to side with that impossible girl?"

"No. I want St. Matthews to pay reasonable bucks to discover the truth, defuse a potentially volatile situation, calm Shondra Jones and the parents, and to keep something like this from happening again." The help they'd asked for. Sometimes I got so tired of people who thought they were entitled to make a reasonable living while Suzanne and I were supposed to work for peanuts. Clients who wanted us to drop everything and come running when they called, but who refused to try and work

90

as a team.

"It was a big mistake, calling you," she said. "You just don't understand the issues here. Your partner, Suzanne, wouldn't have given us all this trouble. She'd have approved the letter, and gone back home to help out her own husband, just like I'm trying to help mine. She would have understood our situation."

She looked over at the plans. "Like his father before him, Todd is a born headmaster. This is his legacy that we're building, every bit as good as his father built at Riverdale—a school with strong ties to its history and strong alumni support. Why, the naming opportunities alone." She swiveled the chair to face me. "Nothing is going to get in the way." She tore the contract into pieces and dropped them in the wastebasket. "I think you might as well leave. Obviously, we're going to have to handle this ourselves."

Todd Chambers, pink and sweaty and vastly more cheerful than when I'd last seen him, appeared in the doorway, still in his gym shorts. He dropped a gym bag by the door, and smiled. "Sorry I'm late," he said. "Hope I didn't miss anything."

# CHAPTER NINE

"I've fired her, Todd." Miriam Chambers, in just four words, summed up the situation. "She wouldn't approve the letter without speaking with you. She produced an outrageous contract." She searched for it briefly before remembering that she'd just torn it up. "... and she seems to be taking that awful girl's side against us."

Chambers, hovering beside the desk, looked meaningfully at his chair. His wife, with an audible snort, got up and came around the desk, dropping neatly into a chair beside me and crossing her legs at the ankles. Movements very different from her eerie glide but just as theatrical. Chambers settled himself into his chair, his sweaty skin squeaking slightly as it met the leather. "Miriam," he said, as though I were invisible, "do you think this is wise?"

Normally I would have waded in at this point and stated my case—but the couple's interaction was giving me too much insight into St. Matthews' current situation, so I just watched.

"I do," she declared. "I think we're better off without her. She wants to turn this into a federal case, well beyond the scope of what we need. It was Suzanne Merritt we wanted anyway. She wouldn't have given us all this trouble."

Their assumptions about my partner rankled. They weren't talking about the Suzanne I knew. She wasn't trying to run any school, just being a good, supportive wife while running her own business. They must have mistaken Suzanne's reputation for tact and diplomacy for something more saccharine and obliging. I considered correcting their assumptions, but it would have served no purpose, so I bit down again on a tongue that was getting ragged.

Chambers smiled wearily at his stony wife. "Well, she's here and her partner's not and we've got to do something." He shifted his gaze to me. "You read the redrafted letter?" I nodded. "And?"

"As I told your wife, it's much better." His smile widened. "But, while it may allay some of your parents' concerns, it doesn't address the bigger problem. And it isn't factually correct."

"What's not correct?"

"You see," she said, "we did just what she wanted, and now she wants more. It's just a way to pad her fee, Todd. That's all. Gets her nose in under the tent and suddenly she wants to run the whole show."

Run it? I much preferred the idea of watching the curtain coming down on this show and seeing St. Matts in my rearview mirror, but I wasn't leaving until I'd shared what I'd learned and tried to help him face reality. "The bigger problem is that you've got an explosive situation here, as well as gross misconceptions on the part of your staff about what stalking is…but, assuming we're going to concentrate solely on the letter, it is factually inaccurate in the following ways."

I outlined what I'd told Mrs. Chambers in greater detail, adding some of the stuff that I'd known was baloney. "You can send that letter, but if Shondra Jones, on her own or acting through a legal representative, questions your assertions and brings out the facts, your efforts to calm the situation will backfire and make the school look far worse."

Chambers' pleasant smile was gone, replaced by an angry frown. I was sorry. We all want to be loved, even if we don't need to be. But I'd come here to help, so I soldiered on, offering them an abbreviated version of my solution.

"Why not send a letter saying you don't feel there is a stalking situation on the campus, but rather a misunderstanding between students. Affirm that this is a very safe campus with a concerned and accessible security service. Say that to be absolutely sure everything is done to ensure student safety, you intend to conduct a detailed investigation of the student's

93

complaint according to the school's procedures, and will make a full report when the investigation is concluded."

I felt like a weasel, but it was a sensible suggestion. It gave them an out and, hopefully, committed them to doing the proper thing, both from a procedural standpoint and because it might appease Shondra Jones. I didn't mention the second part of my agenda—workshops on stalking and sexual harassment. I'd be lucky if I could get them to accept this.

Their faces were disappointingly stony. I waited, practicing the kind of patience and self-control that builds character. If character building is anything like muscle building, I'm becoming a moral colossus. I built my character in a silence that went beyond awkward. She sat beside me, rigid as a student at a military academy, while he studied his fingers like he was learning to draw the prints from memory.

A lesser woman would have let the silence force her into blurting something out, but I've got a determined nature. They'd called me and I'd given up part of a precious Sunday with Andre to come here. If they wanted to dismiss my advice and ask me to leave, they'd have to take the initiative. And I'd still send them a bill.

Finally, Chambers forced a little, self-deprecating smile. "I guess we don't exactly have a meeting of the minds here, do we?" He picked up the redrafted letter and reread it, nodding, then looked at me. "I think this is a pretty fair letter."

I'd already given him my opinion and advice, so instead of repeating myself, I said, "And what about Shondra Jones? How will you handle her reactions?"

"That ought to be easy," Miriam Chambers said. "Everyone knows the girl is a thief and a liar."

"Does that 'everyone' include her brother?"

Chambers shook his head. "Jamison is applying to colleges this fall. There's no way he's going to jeopardize his standing with the faculty and administration."

I almost asked, 'and how would standing up for his sister's honor do that?' but Chambers' meaning was obvious. He believed Jamison Jones could be blackmailed into silence even if his difficult sister could not. I wasn't sure I agreed. The young man I'd just met had evinced a strong sense of family honor and solidarity, as well as a lot of self-confidence. If push came to shove, I thought he'd step up for his sister.

I thought something else, too—that I was wasting my time here. I didn't believe the trustees could have known what they were getting, hiring Chambers to put this school back on track. There was a big difference between conservative and corrupt. In my presence, the headmaster's wife had spoken glibly about destroying student records, now he was telling me that he had no compunction about blackmailing Jamison Jones into silence. It was ugly and dishonest. Put that together with a Dean of Students who was clueless about sexual harassment and stalking, and I was looking at a bad situation. No wonder they hadn't wanted any trustees sitting in on our meetings.

I wanted to be gone. Back to my desk, already groaning with work, to our still understaffed office, back to my searches for a secretary and a house. Back to my own piles of dirty laundry, which I knew how to handle. Most of all, back to Andre. Suddenly the distance between us seemed vast.

Chambers looked at his wife, then at me, and down at the letter in his hands. Something like a smile played around his mouth. It didn't take a mind reader to know what he was thinking. "I guess there's nothing more to say," he said. "Thank you for coming."

Bad as their situation was, his decision meant it wasn't my problem. All that remained was to cover my ass, and EDGE's reputation, so this wouldn't come back to haunt us when it blew up in Chambers' face. I pulled the small tape recorder which had just memorialized our conversation out of my briefcase. "Just for the record," I said, "so there can be no misunderstanding about what has happened here."

Chambers looked like he wanted to vault the desk and snatch it. In his agitation, he crumpled up the letter into a ball as I summarized the events which had transpired, up to and including their refusal to sign a contract or take my advice about the letter. "So, since it appears that you do not want any on-going relationship or follow-up from EDGE Consulting, we'll bill you for our time to date and send a report of my interviews and preliminary advice."

I smiled at them. A genuine smile. I was leaving. "I know this seems very formal, but we don't want any misunderstandings about our role in this or about the advice given and not taken. I have my professional reputation, and the reputation of our firm, to protect."

I switched off the tape recorder, tucked it back in my briefcase and swung the strap onto my shoulder. "Good luck," I said, and headed for the door.

The small blonde girl rushing in almost knocked me off my feet. "You've got to come quick, Mr. Chambers," she panted, planting her hands on her thighs as she bent to catch her breath. "Out behind the gym. Alasdair MacGregor and Jamison Jones. They're fighting, Mr. Chambers, and I'm afraid someone's going to really get hurt!"

It was the girl from Shondra's dorm who'd told me where to find Mrs. Leverett. Her porcelain skin had lost its pink underglow and she looked like she was in shock. Still, I wasn't surprised when they went rushing out without any concern for her welfare. Alasdair MacGregor was their prize student.

I located the gym on my map, then took her by the arm and led her out to Wendy Grimm's desk. "She's just seen a fight and she's upset. Look after her. And in case no one else has, call security and tell them two students are fighting behind the gym."

"I'll take care of it," she said. She held out a piece of paper. "That information you wanted."

"Thanks." I shoved it in my pocket and headed over to the gym.

It was a typical student fight, wary combatants circling each other, sweaty and gasping with bloody faces and fists, oblivious to anything but what was between them. The jostling crowd watched like violence was great good fun, mumbling commentary and observations with no intention of interfering. Jamison was bigger and angrier, and clearly getting the better of his slighter opponent, but Alasdair was the one who seemed to be enjoying it. Each time Jamison dropped his fists and backed away, Alasdair smirked and taunted him until he was drawn back into the fight.

Chambers stood at the side, alternately commanding them to break it up and urging the watching students to help him. Both efforts were equally ineffectual. Except for pushing him away with bloody hands when he tried to get between them, the fighters ignored him completely. A group of students in shirts and ties and fierce grins clustered together, calling encouragement to Alasdair and heckling Jamison. On the other side of the crowd, another group, marked by their height, were giving similar encouragement to Jamison. A little beyond them I saw Shondra, standing a little apart from a bunch of tall women, hands clenched, her face creased with worry.

Eventually, a carload of campus cops rolled up, sirens screaming, and skidded to a stop, barely missing the watching crowd. Four of them poured out, grabbed Jamison, and manhandled him across the field and into the back of the car. It took all four. He was a huge guy and way past mad. All the time they were dragging him away, he was shouting at Alasdair, a steady stream of threats, profanity, warnings to stay away from Shondra, and that this was far from over.

A second car arrived and two cops led Alasdair, much more gently, over to that. As he was getting into the car, Alasdair looked over at the car Jamison was in and smiled a blood-streaked smile through battered lips. He looked back at his cohort, gave them a victory sign, then ducked his head and disappeared from view.

Two cops stayed in the car with Jamison while the other two approached the crowd of excited students and one of the cops ordered them to disperse. His actual words. "You are hereby ordered to disperse."

97

I wondered where their chief was, what kind of relationship he had with the students, and why Chambers was standing there like a wooden soldier while all this was going on. The cop's instructions fell on deaf ears anyway. The crowd grew as students milled and stared, filling in newcomers on what had taken place and asking the cops questions about what was going to happen next.

Through it all, Chambers and his wife stood together, Chambers staring bleakly at the car holding Alasdair. I was too far away to hear what was being said, but her mouth never stopped moving and he never acknowledged that she was speaking.

Much as I hated leaving unfinished business, I'd been fired, so I didn't run over and grab Chambers' arm and yell, "Do you have any idea what's going to happen now?" Instead, I turned with a grateful sigh and walked back to my car.

There was a note under my wiper. "Why don't you ask what Alasdair and them do to girls?"

I had a pretty good idea who'd written it. If I were staying, I might have done just that, but while I was disturbed by the situation I was leaving behind, and frustrated that I hadn't been able to reason with Chambers, St. Matthews' problems were no longer my business.

Maybe, on the way home, I'd pick up a bag of apples so I could make a pie.

# CHAPTER TEN

Andre, the man who loves to eat, was delighted with his apple pie. Suzanne accepted my explanation of the events at St. Matthews with a shrug and a sigh, agreeing we couldn't win them all. I spent the rest of the week working on a report for a school that *did* want my services, and interviewing the hopeless cases who wanted to be my secretary.

My last secretary, Sarah, left behind when we moved the business from Massachusetts to Maine, had spoiled me. She'd griped about the workload, the copy machine, and her impossible husband, but she'd been a jewel. I'd gotten used to having my needs anticipated and to finding neatly typed stacks of work on my desk every morning. Sarah had also fielded my mother's cranky calls. Now I was willing to settle for someone who could type and spell, and even that seemed like too much to ask.

Friday night, Andre cooked steaks on the grill. We shared a bottle of red wine and ate deadly chocolate cake while watching Barbara Stanwyck in *The Lady Eve* and *Ball of Fire*. Her costumes were so cute I asked Andre how he'd like it if I ran around in harem pants and a little bolero that stopped just below my chest.

"I wouldn't let you out of the house," he said.

"Let?" I tried to inject a dangerous note into my voice but I was too mellowed by wine to sound very menacing.

"No way," he said. "You ran around in public in something like that, you'd cause traffic jams, serious accidents, lust attacks, and be a general public nuisance. So no, I wouldn't let you out of the house. I wouldn't leave the house, either. Just stay home and run my fingers across your bare tummy until you begged for mercy."

"Go ahead," I said, tying my shirt in a stomach-baring knot.

"Make me beg."

When the phone rang in the middle of the night, my heart stopped, even though Andre was snuggled so close I could feel his breath against the back of my neck. Phones ringing in the night were an occupational hazard of living with a homicide detective. They were never good news. With a grunt, he pushed himself across the bed and snatched up the receiver, already awake and alert as he said, "Hello?"

There was a silence after his hello which I assumed was a brief description of where the crime scene was and what he'd find there, until he said, "Hold on. She's right here," and handed me the phone. "Some guy named Dunham," he said, "with a private school emergency." With a satisfied sigh at getting to hand it off, he snuggled back into the covers and pulled his pillow over his head.

I paused before I said hello, racking my brain for who might be calling, but the only Dunham I could think of was Craig Dunham at St. Matthews, and they'd sent me packing. It would take more nerve than I could imagine most people having, or an incredible emergency, for him to be calling me at 2:00 a.m..

I stared out the window, where a shaft of moonlight painted the lawn silver. Outside that streak of light, it was a still, black velvet night. I wanted to go back to sleep and let these people handle their own problems. I slid my leg across the bed until I was touching Andre, then lifted the phone to my ear. "Thea Kozak."

"It's Craig Dunham, at St. Matthews. I apologize for calling at this hour, but we've got a major crisis on our hands and we need your help."

"You fired me, remember?"

"We made a huge mistake," he said, "and believe me, we're regretting it. If you want, when you get here, I'll go down on my knees and apologize. Just please listen to what's happened and say you'll come." The panic in his voice crackled across the miles.

"Hold on." I slipped out of bed, crossed the cold floor to my

100

office, and switched on the light. "Okay," I said, grabbing a pen. "What's the emergency?"

He grabbed a breath. "Around 11:30 last night, a body tentatively identified as Alasdair MacGregor was found smoldering in a pile of leaves."

"A body?" My voice dropped to a whisper. "A dead body?" As though there were any other type of body that prompted calls at this hour, except from horny jocks.

I fought my desire to put the phone down. This should have been a call for Andre, not me. I was a consultant. Give me admissions glitches, faculty members downloading pornography or seducing students, financial peccadilloes, mass food poisoning, student pregnancy, chemical spills or a bus accident, but please, no more dead bodies. I'd had enough of death and violence. I was treating my PTSD and trying to live a normal life.

I wanted to crawl back into my warm bed and forget this call. If I closed my eyes, I could picture it. Shadowy figures circling, the smoky blaze against the darkness, the pungent smell of leaf smoke with a nauseating undercurrent of burned flesh. Flashing lights and cop radios and the controlled chaos of a crime scene. Alasdair MacGregor's gorgeous face, which I'd last seen streaked with blood and smiling, now blackened and blistered. My imagination, always going for the telling touch, carefully arranged that curl on his sooty forehead.

"Did he die in the fire?" I asked.

"We don't know yet. We don't know much, really. Only that he's dead. You know how police are." He sounded infinitely sad and weary, a place I'd been too often and understood too well. "I'm sorry," he said. "But this is familiar territory to you and we're way over our heads." As though other schools had their plans in place and were cool with campus death. Or as though because I'd dealt with it before, I was a pro and unfazed by it. Nobody was cool with death.

I'd deal with campus death before, but that was with a strong headmistress with whom I'd had a good working relationship.

I had no relationship with Chambers or Dunham, never mind the other deans or campus security and little reason to believe I could work with them. But this was an emergency. Against my will, because the creeping horror of other times and other bodies was coming over me, I clicked into gear.

"Got a pen?" I waited through the rustling while he found one, wondering who makes an emergency phone call without a writing implement. *Cut him some slack*, I reminded myself. *He's in shock.*

"Ready?" He made an affirmative sound. "Better get some of the other deans in to help you, you've got a lot of work to do. As soon as we hang up, call all your resident advisors and let them know what's happened. If you can disturb me, you can certainly disturb them. Tell them that until further notice, everyone is on duty at all times. Also alert your counseling staff. You need them to make themselves available as many hours as possible. Even if they're just sitting in their offices, knowing they're there will be comforting to your students."

I gave him time to write that down. "Now, your students. I assume some of them know, that there's been gossip, but no formal announcement?"

"Right. I don't think many of them know. It was in a pretty isolated place."

"So that's the first thing you have to do. An early morning assembly to deal with it right up front, acknowledge their concerns, and to be sure they know that their counselors and advisors are available."

I waited for the sound of pen scratches to stop. "Food. Food is critical. Not just in the dining halls, but in their dorms. Lounges. In the student center. Any place they're likely to congregate and talk. Sodas, sandwiches, chips and cookies. Bowls of fruit. It will cost you, but in the long run, it pays."

What else needed to be done immediately? "This one is critical, Craig. You have to control the flow of information. Get your PR people on this immediately. Only one person speaks to the press and you agree in advance on what is said—a written script so no one deviates. Do not allow reporters to speak with your students. That means controlling access to the campus and especially to campus buildings. You've got to get your directors of security and grounds and buildings on board right away. You can't wait. The press will have been following the police scanners. Now, parents ..."

"Wow," he said. "I had no idea." He cleared his throat. "Something else you need to know ..." It sounded like more bad news, as though what he'd already said wasn't bad enough. "Jamison Jones was found standing over the body. He's been arrested."

I supposed the one followed from the other and wondered if the whole business could have been prevented if Chambers had been willing to take advice. So much for Chambers' confident assertion that Jones could be controlled. Too late now. What was done was done.

"About your parents," I began again, not quite ready for the Joneses, but I had a question about whether it even made sense for me to be doing this much. "Why are *you* calling me?"

He knew what I meant. I read the knowledge in his silence. I studied the mottled purple and white patterns on my cold feet, doodling on the pad in front of me.

"You mean why not Todd, and am I authorized to speak for the school?"

"That's right."

"He's...I don't know...fallen apart? This new building meant so much to him. Too much, I suppose. When he left the scene, he went back to his house. He refuses to answer the door or the phone so I authorized myself to call you. That is, first I called Charles Argenti. Chairman of the Trustees? He said go ahead and call you. I'm expecting him any minute. He's driving up from Boston."

"He likes his coffee black," I said, "and be sure you have a supply of legal pads and sharp pencils ready for him. And you'd better reserve us both rooms at The Swan. What's your relationship with the local police chief?"

"Pretty good," he said, sounding puzzled.

"Because we'll need his cooperation. And what about Shondra? How's she doing?"

"Shondra?" he asked, as though he didn't see where she fit into this.

*Come on mister, start thinking, anticipating what may happen. Protect your students and put out fires before they blow up in your face. You had enough sense to call me. Now keep on using it.* "Yes, Shondra. Jamison's sister. Is there someone on the staff who has a good relationship with her?"

"Mrs. Leverett's her housemother."

I supposed it was progress. Last time I asked, he hadn't known. But it was still the wrong answer. "I said *good* relationship, Craig, someone sympathetic. What about her coach?"

"Jenna?" he said. "Oh, she's good. I'll give her a call."

"Do that right away, too. Please. If she doesn't already know, I don't want her getting the news about Alasdair and her brother from anyone but a caring adult. Okay, you've got your list. Start making calls. I'll be there as soon as I can."

I hesitated, but I had to say it. "Craig? You've got to get Todd Chambers out of his room, suited up, and acting like a headmaster. I don't know how you'll do it, but you have to do it. Maybe Argenti can help with that. Now, what about the boy's family? Have they been called?"

His sigh almost blew me across the room, and I was a hundred miles away. "Out of the country. We can't reach them."

"The grandfather, too?"

"This is really not my job." Dunham sighed again.

Whether he liked it or not, for now, it was. I hadn't cared for him. He'd been too complacent and slipshod. Still, I didn't envy the position he was in and I appreciated the way he was stepping up to the plate. It was Chambers' behavior which was deplorable. "You've got to make that call, you know, and you can't put it off. You don't want the family learning it from a reporter or a news source."

"But I don't know what to …"

Make something up, dammit. "Dead in a campus accident, regrettable circumstances, still under investigation," I suggested. "Can he come at once and does he know how to reach the parents?"

"Accident?" he murmured.

"As far as you know, pending police investigation. It could turn out that MacGregor was stinking drunk and fell in the fire and Jones was trying to rescue him. Despite having been arrested, Jamison Jones is innocent until proven guilty. If you're uncomfortable with accident, say fire."

I didn't care. My feet were cold. I wanted to be in a warm bed, not giving advice and packing for a drive. I did not want to think about Shondra and Jamison Jones. About the way death found its way to my doorstep the way stray cats found their way to others.

"Get me a room at the Swan and write down my cell phone number," I said. "And stay calm."

Ridiculous advice but he needed to hear it. "Thanks," he said. "When will you be here?"

"As soon as I can. Around seven, seven-thirty."

I disconnected and called Suzanne. She sounded sleepy and cranky and her mood didn't improve when she heard my news. We agreed I'd stop at her place on my way out of town. Paul, Junior was an early riser anyway.

Then I did the math. It was now three a.m. I needed an hour to prepare and pack. Had to be at Suzanne's by five. That left me an hour to sleep. Not adequate to make me bright eyed and bushy tailed. Not enough time to reconcile myself to leaving Andre again so soon.

I set my watch for four and slipped back into bed, planting my icy feet against Andre's strong thighs. He shuddered, then turned and flung an arm around me, pulling me against him. "What's up?" he whispered.

"Dead student, another one arrested," I said. "I have to go help them out."

"They fired you, didn't they?"

"A victim's family treats you badly, do you walk away from a murder?"

He ran a line of kisses down my neck. My feet were getting warmer and St. Matthews was retreating. "I don't want you to go," he said.

"Me neither. Don't want you to go when you get calls, but sweetie, that's the way it is. If I locked you in a tower, you'd knot your sheets together and climb down."

"And *vice versa*. You'll be careful?" he whispered.

"Very, very careful."

"Make that very, very, very."

So it was going to be okay. We clung to each for our remaining hour, remembering how it had felt to be apart. Remembering the wedding that didn't happen. When my alarm went off, I rose, cursing, to pack. He fixed me breakfast, then carried out my suitcase and put it in the trunk. I couldn't seem to get in the car.

"What's wrong?"

"The life we lead. Always leaving. Always chasing death. It's not normal. And I can't help remembering …"

He pulled me up against him. "We picked these lives, Thea, because there's a lot about them we do like. You need to go there because you're the best person for the job. You know what you're doing and you know what they need. Same for me. What would you rather do?"

"Stay in bed with you."

"Forever?"

I considered. "For a big chunk of forever."

"You want me to come with you? It's the weekend."

"What would you do? Lounge at the B&B, eat brunch and read novels? I've got an 18-hour day ahead."

"Lounging? Eating? Reading? I could do that. As long as you stopped in occasionally for a little recreation." He twirled his imaginary mustache, a gesture so goofy it was endearing. I thought, for the millionth time, how lucky I was to have found

106

this man. I was about to say, 'why not?' when his beeper went off. He pulled it off his belt, checked the number, and grinned. "Looks like blood and gore is calling both of us."

"That's not funny."

"Cop humor," he said. "I'll call you as soon as I know what's up."

"Promise you'll be careful."

"I promise." He stood, his hands on his hips, watching me leave. For richer, for poorer, in sickness and in health, so long as we both shall live. It took all my willpower not to turn back.

# CHAPTER ELEVEN

"Oh, I don't know," Suzanne said, balancing Paul, Jr. on her hip as she tried to fix his cereal. "It's just damned ..." Her eyes rested on the soft blond head nestled against her shoulder. "...darned inconvenient. Next weekend is Parent's Weekend and we've so much arranging to do. I mean yes, I know I ought to be there...I'll have to be there, but honestly, Thea, after the way they've treated us, I can't muster much enthusiasm for dropping everything and rushing over there to help."

"A student is dead," I reminded her. "They've got an A-list crisis on their hands. This is when they need us."

"And I've got all these parent who expect to be catered to."

She was on both sides of this and I sympathized. But the clock was running and she was the one who'd modeled compulsive behavior and made me a partner in this firm. "Then don't come. Send Bobby or Lisa to help. It won't be you, but we've got to face reality. You've got a lot going on in your life."

"Yes, dammit, I do!"

She set the baby in his high chair, put down his cereal and a spoon, then dropped into a chair and buried her head in her hands. "I never meant for things to get like this. You know how much EDGE Consulting means to me."

I looked at the small blond boy, eagerly spooning up his cereal. "As do the men in your life."

"Just you wait," she said. She flushed. "Oh dear. Oh, Thea. I am so sorry. I didn't mean ..."

My life has been disturbingly public. Things other people get to do in private, I tend to do with an audience. I'd had my miscarriage in the company of several tough Maine State Troopers. Andre was eager for a baby and so was I, but I couldn't stand the way everyone cast clandestine looks at my waistline and asked hopeful questions. I was ready to get some t-shirts that said, 'Bug Off, I'll let you know when I'm pregnant.'

"I know what you meant."

But Suzanne had popped out of her chair and was fretting around the kitchen, feeling guilty about what she'd just said, and guilty about work, and guilty about leaving her husband and son, even though her husband had a staff and her son had a good nanny. And none of it was getting me any closer to the door.

"They're waiting," I said. "Come if you can. If not, send Bobby or Lisa. Call me, either way, so I'll know who's coming. These people are clueless. I can't do this alone."

I slung my briefcase over my shoulder. The baby gave me a delighted smile, said, "Teea," just like my little sister Carrie used to do, and flung a big spoonful of gummy cereal. It hit me square in the chest, rolled in two gray tracks down my front, bounced off my knees and landed on my toes. Not bad for a kid who wasn't even two.

Suzanne squawked, dove at me with a sponge and a bottle of club soda, and did a valet number that would have qualified for Guinness. I was sick of hearing her mutter "sorry," so I told her to shut up. "Babies do that," I said. "It is no big deal. I'm not known for my sartorial splendor anyway."

Suzanne, who used to buy my clothes before she got too busy, rolled her eyes. "You don't have to be splendid," she said, "I just don't want you squalid. Give me a full report as soon as you know what's going on, okay?"

I draggled out into the gray morning, fired up my sleek red Saab, and headed for New Hampshire. This time, there was no sunlight gracing the fields, but the cold night had laid silver frosting over everything and the valleys and hollows were filled with a wispy mist that gave a ghostly cast to the roadsides. It hovered about the lakes and rose up from fields like the ground was smoking.

Driving through that haunted landscape, it was hard to fight off memories of other times when I'd set out to handle a crisis and found much more than I'd bargained for. This time I would stay strictly professional, give my advice, and get out of there.

My resolution lasted until I arrived at St. Matthews. Craig Dunham had not told them to expect me. I had to talk my way past the security at the gate, a chore that wasted several minutes. I took off down the drive much too fast, only to find Shondra Jones, a full 6' 3" of abject misery, standing by the roadside.

It had started raining. When she stepped into my path in her dark raincoat and held up a hand, I thought she was more security until she threw back her hood. Suddenly revealed like that, her glistening, set face looked fierce and tribal and a dozen years older than sixteen.

At my nod, she got in and slammed the door, her wet braids tossing like snakes. She sat silent, staring out through the windshield. She was jittery, shivering from the cold and it was obvious she hadn't slept. If they'd sent her coach to help, it hadn't worked, but Shondra at the best of times was probably hard to help.

Abruptly, she burst into sobs that shook her strong shoulders and sent sympathetic reverberations through me as well. "Can you pull over, please?" I stopped the car.

"This is all my fault," she said. "For tryin' to stop this. For thinkin' me and Jamison could handle it ourselves. I should have just let him go on doing like he was doing and not got Jamison involved. Alasdair said I'd be sorry and he was right. I am so goddamned sorry. Ain't nobody can stop what he do."

I had no idea what she was talking about, but before I could ask, she said, "You gotta help Jamison, Miz Kozak, you just gotta. Someone's gotta figure out what's goin' on here. He's only in this 'cuz of me. My brother'd never do anything like this, and he's got no one on his side."

"The first thing your brother needs is a good lawyer, Shondra."

"Oh, yeah. Right. What we gonna pay him with? Jamison didn't do this, you know. And that's the truth."

"That's what his lawyer is for, Shondra. To protect his rights and help him prove that."

"And how's he gonna find a good one up here in fuckin' Cow Hampshire?"

"There are good lawyers everywhere," I said quietly. "And that attitude of yours isn't helping anyone."

"So now you gonna get on me 'bout my attitude, too?"

"Hey," I said, "you came looking for me, remember? You've got a pretty damned funny way of asking for help."

"Yeah, well, they say I got funny ways." She was flexing the fingers of her big hands. Flexing. Flexing. Flexing. Then tapping in a jittery beat on her knees. All the while staring at me with her exotic, tragic eyes.

I tried to be patient. This girl was in the middle of a crisis, after all. She obviously wanted something, but I was no mind reader and the clock was ticking. "Shondra, I know this is a bad time for you, but I've got a lot to do. So spit it out, because I'm already late. Believe it or not, you aren't all alone on this planet."

"Might as well be," she said. "Way everybody acts."

"That's really good," I said. "Put yourself way off in a corner, then complain because everyone acts like you're way off in a corner. Does that really make sense?"

"Nothing about this goddamned place makes sense. This place, or this thing that's happened, the way everyone acts. It's like something from bad TV, only it's real."

This was going to be like pulling teeth. Even though her situation was terrible and someone ought to pay attention to her, I just didn't have the time. "Look, I'd like to help you, Shondra. I want to. But right now, I've got to figure out what kind of help the school needs. That's my job. Once I've got that under control, we can talk." I started driving.

"I don't know why I bothered. You're no different from the rest of them. Later, Shondra. Catch you later. You gotta be patient. You gotta calm down. We're takin' care of it. Just wait. Wait. Wait. We'll get back to you. Yeah, like I've never heard that before. And them numbskulls just go on doin' what they're doin'."

Even though the car was moving, she unsnapped her seatbelt and grabbed the handle. "I don't know how, but somehow, Alasdair set this up, him or those friends of his."

"Shondra, for heaven's sake. Alasdair's dead."

"I sure hope so. He deserved it. But Jamison didn't do it. I did. I'm the one who told him there were pictures."

"Shondra, what are you talking about? What kind of pictures?"

But she was gone, jumping out of the car and going down hard on one knee, then bouncing back up and taking off at a run. She disappeared into the trees along the road, swallowed up in their darkness.

I found Craig Dunham in Chambers' office, along with a man I recognized as Argenti, two others who were unfamiliar, and a woman I hadn't met. There was no sign of Chambers. Dunham looked shaken and exhausted, Argenti calm and in charge. It was Argenti who came to greet me, giving me one of those alpha male handshakes that cripple little old ladies and leave the rest of us with frozen smiles and tears in our eyes.

A table by the wall held a coffee urn and cups, and a tray of pastries. Wendy Grimm hurried toward it, looking back at me over her shoulder. "Did you want coffee, Ms. Kozak?"

"Please. Cream and sugar. Thanks."

Argenti was already speaking. By the time I tuned in, he was saying "…your advice about what to tell our parents."

"Pastry?" Wendy Grimm asked.

"No thanks."

"You certainly took your time getting here," Argenti said, dropping into a chair and waving to the one beside him. "We want to get right on this. Now …"

I opened my briefcase, pulled out a pad of paper, and signaled for Craig to join us. "Can you bring me up to speed, please? What are we dealing with?"

"Cold blooded murder," Argenti said.

"Is that what the police told you?"

"They arrested the boy, didn't they?"

I shrugged. This was not the moment to suggest that cops didn't always get it right. Except my own personal cop, of course. "If you could describe what happened."

Craig Dunham sighed, shifted his broad shoulders, and sighed again. Today he'd traded his cheery stripes for a somber white shirt and dark suit. He didn't sit down. "The police haven't told us anything, so we still don't know much more than I told you on the phone. Last night around 11:30, one of our security guards spotted what he thought might be a fire back in the woods. It happens sometimes. A group of students will slip away and build a fire. Usually to sit around and talk. Sometimes to drink. Normally harmless, of course, but it's against the rules, so he went to check."

He fiddled with his shirt cuffs and then with his collar, like a kid uncomfortable in Sunday clothes. "When he got closer, he could see it was a fire, but it appeared to be unattended. Then he realized that someone was kneeling beside the fire, pulling on what looked like a human leg."

His own legs suddenly seemed to give way. He dropped into the chair beside me, taking a few seconds to regain his composure. "Sorry. I'm not...God...I don't know how to say this."

"Go on," Argenti barked, running manicured fingers through his thick silver hair. "We haven't got all day."

He was right. We *were* in a hurry. But first we had to get a handle on what we were dealing with. Then we could start managing it. "Mr. Argenti, are the other trustees aware of the situation?"

"Called 'em all myself, soon as I heard."

I nodded. "Craig, please continue. Have you eaten anything?"

"I can't remember."

We needed some real food, not hollow carbs. I called Wendy Grimm over. "I know it's early, but can you get dining services to send us some sandwiches?"

"Oh. Of course. I should have thought of that." She hurried

out, grateful for a chance to escape the frenetic atmosphere of the room.

"The security guard called out something like, 'hey, what's going on,' and the kneeling figure jumped up and ran."

"So, how are they so sure it was Jamison Jones?"

"Oh, for heaven's sake," Argenti said. "How many 6' 7" black students do you suppose there are at St. Matthews? Pity, though. Boy's a fabulous athlete. Guess you can take the boy out of the city but you can't take the city out of the boy." He raised his heavy eyebrows. "You know the two of them were fighting earlier this week?"

"I saw it."

"Oh…uh…right." The eyebrows dropped.

I wondered what version of the story Chambers had given him.

"The guard had called for back-up as soon as he saw the fire," Dunham continued. "But when Jamison ran off, he was still alone, and he'd gotten close enough to the fire to see that someone was lying in or near it. He grabbed the leg Jamison had dropped and hauled the person out. But it was too late. The boy was already dead."

"Alasdair MacGregor?" He nodded. "Was there any trouble identifying him?"

"Well, they haven't done that yet. Officially, I mean. But they were MacGregor's clothes. MacGregor's wallet was in the pocket. The face was badly burned, though, so they may have to use dental records."

I looked down at my hands, squeezed white-knuckle tight. The others had clustered around us, listening. I wondered if he hadn't told the story before, or if they needed to hear it repeatedly to accept it? This wasn't just some story on the news, it was their new reality, and sudden, violent death is a hard thing to process, especially when it involves someone you know.

Suddenly Dunham looked at his watch, jumped up, and started pacing the room. "We've called an assembly for 9:15," he said, rubbing at his forehead. "I've got to think about what

I'm going to say."

"Where's Todd?"

Argenti answered for him. "Headmaster Chambers," he said sourly, "appeared briefly, looking distraught, asked if anyone had seen his wife, and then dashed off without another word, apparently to look for her." He stared around the room, seeking confirmation. "If we had known, when we interviewed him, about her history of mental illness, he never would have been chosen. A headmaster's wife is a vital asset."

I wondered how Suzanne would have responded to being called, 'a vital asset?' "Can we get your security chief in and get his version of the story? Also, has there been any contact with the police?"

"They're coming at 10:30," Dunham said. "The cops, I mean. New Hampshire state cops. A Lt. Bushnell. Wants us to help him coordinate his interviews." He walked over to the window and stared out, his shoulders drooping.

Argenti gave him a disapproving look, then shifted his sharp gaze to me. "Well, what do we need to do?"

Find some backbone, I thought. I began ticking off my list. "Prepare for the assembly. Notify all the parents. Control the information flow. Do what we can to help the police."

He held up a hand. "One thing at a time. How do we deal with the parents?"

"We need to write a script and then you need to call all the parents and reassure them that things are under control here and that their children are safe."

"I need to call all the parents? Me, personally?"

"Of course not. But it's best if the calls come from Trustees or senior administrative staff whose names will be familiar to the parents."

"Are their children safe?"

It was his school, his call. But Argenti wouldn't want to hear that. And in Chambers' absence, he was the client. "Assuming Jamison Jones is the perpetrator and Alasdair MacGregor is the victim, this was personal. And they are safe."

115

Big assumptions, since we didn't yet have an identified victim and no one had talked with Jamison Jones, but Argenti was satisfied. "How do we do it?"

"Grab your deans, administrative staff, and a bunch of faculty, give them their script and a list of names, and start making calls."

"Right." He rose decisively from his chair and turned to the woman I still hadn't met. "Cristabel, Craig's got a lot on his plate. Can you take charge of this?"

She nodded, turning to me with a weary smile and holding out her hand. "Christabel Ivers, Dean of the Faculty. And these," she indicated her colleagues, "are Cullin Margolin, head of residential life, Aidan Lamont, Director of Counseling Services, and Jordan Perry, Associate Dean of Students."

We all shook hands. Dean Ivers was a small woman with an elaborate coil of shiny dark hair. She was at least part Asian, and used a cane. She was the only woman I'd met so far with a title, and a mean part of me noted that on the diversity scale, she was a three-fer: woman, ethnic, and handicapped.

"This is just such a tragedy," she said. "And the timing couldn't be worse." As though there was ever a convenient time for violent death.

I supposed, from St. Matt's standpoint, there was. After the school had secured pledges for the new arts center and collected the checks. During the summer, when most of the students were gone. Or even during Christmas break. But it's a fact of life that death is always inconvenient.

I was about to sit down with Deans Dunham and Ivers to plan for the assembly when the front door banged open. There was a commotion in the hall outside. A fist thundered on the room's tall, black door and a furious voice, theatrically loud, preceded the man who flung it open and entered without waiting for an invitation. "...someone who can tell me just what the hell is going on here. Where is my grandson?"

116

# CHAPTER TWELVE

Grandfather MacGregor had the coloring I'd imagined for his grandson, along with the full voice, larger-than-life presence, and grandiose delivery of a Shakespearean actor. He catapulted into the room, a broad-chested, bulky man, nodded at Argenti, and barked, "Where the hell's Chambers? Man's got some explaining to do, leaving that ridiculous message." Once he'd entered, though it was a large room, he took up all the space and air.

"Actually, Mr. MacGregor ..." Craig Dunham stepped forward cautiously. "I was the one who left that message. I...we...there's been ..."

Argenti was wringing his rolled-up papers like a man killing a chicken. I didn't have to be a mind reader to get his thoughts. How had it come to this, that he found himself surrounded by stumbling incompetents?

I could have told him: hiring Chambers, who valued fundraising, enhancing facilities, and his own prestige over educating students and then not keeping a close enough eye on things. No doubt Chambers had had good credentials, despite the crazy wife and a bad case of blind ambition, but any new employee, however much he may exude confidence and competence, bears watching.

Ignoring Dunham, MacGregor fixed his angry eyes on Argenti and beetled his heavy golden-white eyebrows. "Charlie, where the hell's Chambers? I need some goddamned answers." He peppered the rest of us with machine-gun glares. "Don't you people have work to do? I need to speak with Charlie."

We retreated to Dunham's office to prep him and Dean Ivers for the student assembly. As I walked them through the basics, I was sadly aware of the hollowness of their responses. Instead of drawing on some genuine concern or compassion for their students, they simply took down whatever I said. Even Lamont, who, as Director of Counseling ought to have had helpful suggestions, waited for me to tell him what to do. True, they were in shock, but looking after a community of teenagers was their job.

I laid much of this at Chambers' doorstep. Culture comes from the top and what was coming down was a careless indifference to what ought to have been their primary mission. I'd had my quarrels with the way Dorrie Chapin had handled a death at the Bucksport School, but while there had been systemic problems, she hadn't forgotten the basics of her job as Headmistress or lost sight of her fundamental responsibilities to the students in her care. Here it felt as though the word "care" would be out of place.

We were woefully short of time, and I passed out directions like a cruise ship social director during the mandatory lifeboat drill. Maintain an atmosphere of peace and calm. Act like you're in command to reinforce their sense of security. Emphasize and support their sense of community. Reassure them that there are grown ups available to listen. Express an understanding for their conflicting emotions in a situation where both the alleged perpetrator and the victim are their fellow students. I wished our emergency kit included a few spare spines I could give these people.

Beyond the walls, MacGregor's voice rose and fell like a foghorn. Outside, sheets of rain poured from a sky the color of dust.

One of our biggest challenges was that the students were going to be looking for information and we had very little. I summed up what we knew. "A body believed to be Alasdair MacGregor was found in the woods last night, an apparent homicide. Jamison Jones has been arrested. The details are sketchy because the police are still investigating. Tell them you'll update them as details become known. For now, call your security chief. He's the campus cop, works with the local

118

police. He's got to know something. Or call your local police chief." Dunham sighed and lifted the phone.

Margolin and Perry would work with Wendy Grimm and Dunham's secretary to divide the parent list into manageable chunks while I wrote a brief script for callers to use. I'd been at the school a little over two hours. It felt like ten. It was clear I needed my own staff, but Suzanne hadn't called, so I didn't know when I'd have one.

Eventually, they went off with the secretaries, giving me a moment to catch my breath and think about what else needed to be done. When I stared down at my notes, I saw Shondra's frozen face and heard her certain voice. Jamison didn't do it. Wouldn't do it. Yet wasn't that the obvious conclusion? Something had finally pushed him too far.

I thought of him sitting in a cold gray cell, surrounded by people who thought he was a murderer. Did he have anyone to call, and if so, would they be able to give him competent help? Who was going to take care of finding him a lawyer? Would the school take on that responsibility?

There were so many people affected. An event like this, in a close community, was like throwing a stone into a still pond. The ripples spread until they rocked the whole pond. I thought about the students we needed to pay special attention to. Jamison's teammates and friends, MacGregor's teammates and friends, Shondra's. And Shondra herself. So far, although she was at the center of this, no one had mentioned her.

Dunham came back from the assembly beaded with sweat, his face white. Dean Ivers looked better, but only because she'd applied her color to the surface of her skin, where it couldn't drain away. They both dropped silently into chairs and sat staring at opposite walls. The detectives were due in fifteen minutes, but I didn't remind them. They needed the down time.

I left them and went to the other room, where MacGregor and Argenti were still going at it. MacGregor might represent a major donor as well as chief mourner, but Argenti, in Chambers' absence and until we found Dunham more backbone, represented the other 598 students at St. Matthews. I opened the door, knocked perfunctorily on the wood, and spoke before they could dismiss me.

"The police will be here in a few minutes. Do you want to meet with them here or in the Trustees Room, and whom do you want at the meeting?"

"The Trustees Room," he said. "It's more formal." Where he could sit at the head of the imposing table and try to control the seating. "I guess we'd better have Dean Dunham and Dean Ivers. And Woodson, from Security."

MacGregor announced loudly that he was going to the toilet. I took advantage of his absence to raise something I should have thought of earlier. "What about the school's attorneys?" I asked. "Have they been called?"

"Good catch," Argenti said. "I'll ask Wendy. It's a Saturday. I don't know whether we can reach anyone." He went off to do that and I went to find a toilet myself, to "freshen up" as the euphemism goes. I didn't announce my attentions loudly.

Fifteen minutes later, we were sitting around the big table like members of a dysfunctional family, watching Gregor MacGregor going head-to-head with the cops. It was not a pretty sight. MacGregor's interrogation style was early battering ram, and his personal volume control was busted. He was up against a pro, though, and his first volley of barked queries bounced off the lead cop like bullets off Superman.

Lt. Bushnell, the state police detective, was tallish, lean and graying, with the cropped hair that revealed those too naked cop's ears. Behind utilitarian glasses, he had smart eyes. I knew he'd been up all night, and it showed. Even his jacket looked tired, hanging from his shoulders in baggy, dispirited folds. I also knew, even before he opened his mouth, that he'd be in charge. It was there in the certainty of his bearing and the deference shown by the portly town police chief and the younger state cop with him.

"Gary Bushnell," he said, pushing his glasses up his nose and looking at us expectantly. "Why don't you all introduce yourselves, give me names, titles, phone numbers, and then I'd like to get some background about ..."

"Hold on a minute there, Detective," MacGregor said. "These people," he glared disdainfully around the table, "say that my grandson has been killed. I want to know just what evidence you have that your victim really is my grandson."

Bushnell cocked an eyebrow at him. "And you are?"

"Gregor MacGregor." Pronounced as though the name was a more than sufficient resume.

"It's a valid question, Mr. MacGregor, and we'll get to it due course." He looked at the rest of us. "Now, if I could get your..."

"Look," MacGregor said, "I asked you a question. Now, I've been trying to get some answers here for over an hour. I think I've waited long enough."

"In due course," Bushnell repeated. His eyes circled the table. "Your names?"

Maybe MacGregor recognized the voice of authority, or maybe he was just biding his time, but for the moment, he held his peace. I reminded myself that despite his bluster and bombast, he was an old man and he'd just had an awful shock. We went around the table and gave up our information. Bushnell made notes, and when I added, "EDGE Consulting," I got a curious glance as well.

The local chief's name was Dennis Porter and the dewy young cop, the only one among us who didn't look slightly gnawed by rats, was Gabriel Lavigne. Once he'd gotten us labeled, Bushnell went to work, diving, with his very first question, right to the heart of the matter. "Where is Todd Chambers?" he asked.

Dunham looked at Argenti, who shrugged, so he took the question. "He may be at his house. I really don't...He...there was a problem with...something about his wife." Dunham looked down at his hands.

"And his house is here on the campus?" Dunham nodded. "Where?"

Dunham uttered directions so fumbling they suggested an

inability to find his own ass in a dark room. Sure, cops make us all nervous, but we were supposed to be the grown-ups here, with a job to do. I pulled out my campus map, set it in front of Bushnell, pointed to where we were, and circled Chambers' house. "Here." If someone didn't move this along, we were going to be in this room all day and there were a dozen tasks waiting.

"Thanks." The detective handed the map to Lavigne. "Gabe, you want to scoot over there and find Mr. Chambers for us?"

Lavigne was out the door like a shot. It looked like what Lt. Bushnell wanted, Lt. Bushnell got. He smiled at the rest of us. "Best, I thought. Save time in the long run, not having to go over everything twice. Now, Mr. Dunham, what was the relationship between Alasdair MacGregor and Jamison Jones?"

"There wasn't one, to the best of my knowledge," Dunham said. "They traveled in different circles."

"So I understand. But I also understand the two of them had a fight last Monday. Is that right?" Dunham nodded. "Can you tell me what they were fighting about?"

I wanted to see how much truth—or how much story—Dunham would be willing to reveal. It was criminally unfair of Todd Chambers to leave his staff struggling with this when the calls about what to say were his.

I was sitting next to Bushnell, and the audible rumbling of his stomach reminded me that the sandwiches I'd asked Wendy for had never materialized. The cops were hungry. The staff was hungry, and even though this meeting was pure business, a little courteous hospitality wouldn't hurt.

"Excuse me," I said, pushing my chair back.

"Leaving us already, Ms. Kozak?" Bushnell asked.

"Just to see about coffee and sandwiches, Lieutenant, unless you'd rather I didn't?"

"Go right ahead." His smile was genuine. "I think we'd all be grateful."

Dunham looked as though he wasn't sure he approved since he hadn't suggested it, but Argenti was nodding, so he held his tongue. I hurried to Wendy Grimm's desk. "Mr. Argenti would like coffee and sandwiches in the Trustees' Room as soon as possible."

She was hunched behind her desk like she was under attack. All around her, phones were ringing and a confetti of pink message slips littered the desktop. She looked miserable and confused, which, under the circumstances was understandable. No one was giving her direction or support.

"Oh dear. I forgot all about…I guess you'd never believe I'm usually efficient."

"A situation like this is hard on everyone," I said. "But I think things will go better with the cops if we feed everyone, don't you?"

She was so relieved that I didn't yell that I wondered if she'd been conditioned by Chambers' wife into expecting abuse. "Twenty minutes, max," she said. "You want chips and fruit and cookies?"

"And sodas, if you can. That would be fabulous."

"Food I can handle." She waved a hand at her cluttered desk. "It's the rest of this…that poor boy dead and that other one locked up, and everyone calling and needing things and an-swers, and all these reporters…and I don't know what I'm supposed to do."

EDGE could have helped with this, but Suzanne still hadn't called. "Grab some people to help with the phones. Dean Iverson's secretary, maybe? As soon as we're done with this meeting, we can help you. Meanwhile, explain that everyone's in a meeting and take messages. Don't give out any information until we agree on what we will release."

Damn! Things were slipping through the cracks already. I was sure, in the pre-dawn list I'd given Dunham, that I'd told him what to do about the press, but no one had been on hand when I arrived.

"Is there a press office, or someone who does PR?" She nodded. "Get them over here, then, let them handle the calls. I'll need to see them as soon as we're done."

She hesitated. I couldn't blame her. She didn't know who was supposed to be in charge. Well, no one had told me, either, but where there's a void, I fill it. "We need to control this, Wendy, okay?" She nodded, overwhelmed but still agreeable.

Reluctantly, I ducked back into the conference room and mouthed twenty minutes at Argenti. This was so frustrating. I needed to be in here, but I also needed to be out there, making sure no one talked with the press, making sure Security was keeping reporters off the campus. I took a deep breath and tried to concentrate on the discussion. I hadn't missed much. Bushnell was still walking Dunham and Frank Woodson, the campus security chief, through a description of the fight.

"Why were they fighting?"

"Jones thought MacGregor had been bothering his sister," Woodson said.

"My grandson wouldn't ..." MacGregor began.

Bushnell held up a hand. "Tell me about that. The sister, she's a student here?"

"A junior," Dunham said.

"Her name?"

"Shondra. Shondra Jones."

"Was there a relationship between Shondra Jones and Alasdair MacGregor?"

"None that we know of," Dunham said, sliding his eyes at me. Bushnell didn't miss the look.

"As far as you know, had Alasdair MacGregor said or done anything insulting toward Shondra Jones?"

Under the circumstances, it was a question my father, the lawyer, could have parsed for hours. I was curious to see how Dunham would answer, but before he could, we were interrupted by the return of Gabriel Lavigne, herding Todd Chambers before him like a wayward sheep.

"Todd. How nice you could join us," Argenti said.

Bushnell waited for Chambers to sit. "Lt. Gary Bushnell, New Hampshire State Police," he said. "You are the headmaster?"

Chambers nodded. He looked like hell. He hadn't shaved, and the white-blond stubble made him look seedy. Coupled with his rumpled clothes and shaking hands, he looked more like an alkie coming off a bender than the preppie head of a prestigious New England boarding school.

"We're talking about the fight last Monday between MacGregor and Jones," the detective said. "Mr. Woodson says the cause of the fight was that MacGregor was bothering Jones' sister. My question is, as far as you know," his eyes circled the room, "and by you, I mean everyone here, of course, did Alasdair MacGregor say or do anything insulting toward Shondra Jones? Was he bothering her?"

The air was electric. Chambers shot a worried look at MacGregor and said, "As far as I know, there was no relationship of any sort between Alasdair and Shondra."

It was an interesting answer. I supposed that as he interpreted "relationship," stalking didn't constitute one; it was Dunham who thought stalking was one way a guy pursued a relationship. Surely, Chambers understood that the police needed to know what had been going on. One young man was dead, another arrested for murder, and it was all about Shondra Jones and her accusations. I struggled to keep my mouth shut and practiced Andre's skill of keeping my thoughts off my face. To me, violent death changed the rules and mandated truth-telling, but it was up to my clients how they wanted to tell their story.

"Then do you have any idea why Jamison Jones thought he needed to intervene on his sister's behalf?"

"No."

That was an outright lie. I forced my muscles to relax. If Bushnell was a good detective, he was reading the room, not just listening to what people said.

"Was Jones very touchy? In the habit of picking fights for no reason?"

"No. This was quite out of character. He's usually a pretty easy-going guy. Very popular. Very social."

"And what kind of relationship did Jones have with his

sister? Were they close?"

Chambers did answer this one. "Very close. And he worried about her. He was after us almost daily until we agreed to admit her."

"Did any of you speak with him after the fight?"

I knew the security guys had. But would their boss admit it. What would he say?

"Yeah," Woodson said. He was a spare man with a wrinkled, Clint Eastwood face and unrevealing hazel eyes. "We talked to him. Took four men to haul him away. You've seen Jamison. He's a big kid. But once they got him in the car, he calmed right down. Said he'd gone to ask MacGregor to stop bothering his sister, that MacGregor had said some filthy things about Shondra, and he'd lost his temper. He said he should have known better, MacGregor was a predatory bastard and mean straight through and it would take more than asking to get him stop."

I watched Bushnell write down that damning statement. Watched the senior MacGregor decide not to interrupt.

"But you have no idea why he believed MacGregor was bothering his sister, or what form that bothering took?"

"Just what he said at the time."

"Anyone else have any idea? Or anything to add?" Bushnell shifted his eyes to the others. Chambers had every idea. So did several other people at this table. The tension level was climbing with every question. By now, it was almost visible in the room. Chambers looked at Dunham, then at Argenti, and tugged a few times on his ear. Bushnell wasn't the only one who was reading the room, and I read that he was running short on patience.

"Do you have rules against fighting?" Chambers nodded. "Then I expect you spoke with both parties after the fight?" Another nod.

"Then tell me, Mr. Chambers," his voice boomed in the quiet room, "this is a simple question and we have a lot of questions to get through. Why did Jamison Jones believe MacGregor was bothering his sister?"

Chambers was not used to being yelled at. Especially not in

front of his staff, his trustees, and his most valuable alum. His pale face reddened in a blotchy, schoolboy way. He swallowed and stared down at the table for a minute. When he raised his head, he was back in Headmaster mode. Calm. Confident. In charge.

"You've got to understand, Lieutenant. We believe Shondra Jones, who is one of our minority scholarship students, is a deeply disturbed young woman. When she first came to St. Matthews, it turned out that she was a thief. We dealt with that, thought we'd gotten her straightened out."

He circled the room with his eyes and launched into the party line. "More recently, she has been coming to us with allegations that Alasdair MacGregor was stalking her, harassing her, disturbing her peace of mind by invading her room and leaving her obscene pictures. We looked into the matter and determined that this was not so. When we told her that we didn't believe Alasdair was stalking her, she became extremely angry and announced she'd handle it her own way."

I was trying to remember if I'd told Chambers about the conversation in which Shondra had said she'd handle this herself, and almost missed his next statement. "So we think she then went to her brother with these absurd claims and got him inflamed with some misguided need to defend the family honor. And now it's come to this." He bowed his head.

The man ought to bow his head, in shame, after a statement like that. In a few sentences, he'd lied to the cops, dismissed all the things I had learned including the evidence of his own records, disclaimed any responsibility for letting the situation get so out of hand, and placed the blame on two of his most vulnerable students. Seeing him puffed up with satisfaction at having gotten his balance back, I wanted to grab him by the scruff of his neck and give a good, hard shake.

Bushnell's questions went on, and Chambers and Dunham took turns providing answers that marginalized and disparaged Shondra and Jamison, laying the blame for the whole incident on her desire for revenge because of Alasdair MacGregor's white supremacist posturing, and Jamison's inability to shake his primitive, inner-city boy's need to ensure that no one showed disrespect for his sister.

There wasn't a hint of understanding or compassion for any of the parties—not for Jamison, or Shondra, or even for Alasdair, in their responses. No attempt to put any of it in context—to place Alasdair, Shondra or Jamison in social groups or explain their interactions, no effort to put faces on the three. No details of their thorough investigation and no acceptance of responsibility for letting the situation get so bad. Chambers was so busy with his destruction of Shondra and Jamison that he showed no signs of recognizing the tragedy that had brought us all to this room.

I thought about the obscene pictures Shondra had found in her bed. Did they still exist or had Miriam Chambers made good on her threat and purged the records? I saw Shondra's fierce, set face as she'd sat in my car, declaring that this was all her fault, that she should have let the harassment go on rather than involving her brother. Her certainty that Jamison would never have done what was done.

The past few minutes had given me a better understanding of her anger and disbelief when I'd said that I'd come to do a job and I would get back to her when I had time. No wonder she hadn't believed me. This slick denial and shallow, lazy characterization, this rewriting of the facts to suit their agenda, was what she was used to. People who would never get back to her and never had the time.

I thought about Jamison Jones in a police lock-up. How did it feel to be scared and alone, charged with murder? The only people he knew were the St. Matthews' people, who'd enticed him to leave his family and his neighborhood and come be their superstar basketball player. Come here and put St. Matts on the map, and we will be your family. Until you really need us. Then we'll flap our hands dismissively and disclaim any responsibility, labeling you a hopeless ghetto kid with an uncontrollable temper.

I thought about beautiful, troubled, and trouble-making Alasdair MacGregor, lacking the rules and appropriate adult guidance he needed to figure out his place in this world. Forgiven too much. Indulged and excused too readily. The horrible result when he finally tangled with someone more than his match.

The arrogance of these people, believing the situation could be explained away with glib answers. Their complete indifference to the reality of this tragedy and their responsibilities as the grownups in charge enveloped me in a sudden chill. Didn't they understand that someone was dead and three lives ruined?

Driving here, I'd resolved not to let this become personal. This was a job. The client school needed help and I knew how to provide it. Now, less than half a day into it, I was thinking about Alasdair, Shondra, and Jamison and not about my clients at all.

I clenched my fingers around my pen to still their shaking, but it didn't help. If I was going to deal effectively with the rapidly growing list in front of me, I had to get myself back under control. Without asking Bushnell's permission, I shoved back my chair and left the room.

## CHAPTER THIRTEEN

My attempt to leave quietly had been as subtle as an elephant at a tea party. When I paused in the hall, eyes determinedly shut against my tears, my whole tough girl persona collapsing, a firm hand took my arm, steered me into Chambers' office, and into a chair. Bushnell pulled another chair close and sat down beside me.

"Are you all right?" he asked in a quiet voice.

"Fine," I said. "It's just that …" My voice was embarrassingly shaky.

"Just that what?"

I wished he'd go back in there, conduct his business, and leave me alone. I knew he wouldn't. He was a cop and cops go where the chinks are.

"That none of them seem to understand, or care, about what's going on here."

"And what would you say is going on here?"

It was the cop equivalent of the shrink's infuriating, 'how do you feel about that?' but I answered him anyway. "That one child is dead, and two other children… students…whatever you want to call them, are in serious trouble and the people in there act like it doesn't matter, like the circumstances are insignificant instead of profound and this is just another meeting to get through before they can get back to business as usual."

I was running on at the mouth just like he wanted me to. "They've completely marginalized Shondra and Jamison and ignored the fact that other kids out there are scared and hurting, too. They're talking like there's only one side to this. Like Alasdair's death is tragic without recognizing Jamison's life is ruined, too, and like Shondra is some bad actor who made it all up and now look at all the trouble she's caused."

I shrugged. "I don't mind helping them deal with trouble—that's what I do, but I'd like to see some appropriate responses. Grief, guilt, regret. Something to show they appreciate the magnitude of what's happened."

What was I thinking, criticizing my clients like this? I was being a total fool and doing them a grave disservice. I shut my mouth, and clasped one hand firmly in the other, concentrating on squeezing. If I had concerns, I should discuss them with Argenti, not tattle to a sharp-eyed cop. What about issues like confidentiality and boundaries or the fact that my feelings were irrelevant?

"Look, forget about me, please," I said. "You've got a murder to solve and I'm blithering on like callous behavior shocks me, or the awful things people do to each other. Like I've never seen anything like this before."

"You have?"

I picked up my head and straightened my shoulders. Breathe in. Breathe out. "I told you I was a consultant, right? Well, what I do is deal with serious campus situations like this. So, yes. I mean no, this isn't the first time I've dealt with the sudden, violent death of a student."

His eyebrows rose. "And what's your take on what is going on in there? You said what? They're acting like Shondra made it all up. So you don't think she did?"

"Lieutenant, I'm sorry. These people are my clients."

"Are your clients telling me the truth?"

I squirmed again. Interrogation is very different when you're the subject. There's a sudden feeling of panic and an ugly, squirrelly desire to shade the truth. But R2-D2 was beaming Andre's fiercest face onto the wall, and his message was simple and to the point—tell the truth. Bushnell will know what to do with it.

"Yes," I said. "And no. I believe Alasdair was bothering Shondra and his family has big bucks so they're trying to protect him."

I burrowed deeper into my chair, wishing he'd go back in

there, wring what he could from my obfuscating clients, and then go see Jamison and Shondra. At least he'd get both sides. Then I could get to back to work and make myself so busy handling this mess that I'd have no time to think about all the bad stuff this death was bringing back.

"Big surprise," he said. "Guess we'll have to talk further. You coming back in?"

"I have to."

He patted me on the shoulder, which usually raises my feminist hackles. Today, it felt reassuring. "Take your time," he said.

"It's not my time." Maybe he wasn't going to ask questions, but I had some of my own. "Lieutenant, have you talked with Jamison Jones?" He gave me a coolly amused look and didn't answer.

That's how it was with cops—a one-way street. They could ask us all the questions they wanted, but we were only supposed to speak when spoken to.

In Bushnell's absence, Argenti and MacGregor had been having a go at Chambers. If he'd looked bad before, he looked a lot worse now. The blotchy way that anger took him was seriously unattractive. But so was the rest of his behavior, and, to a great extent, he'd brought it on himself. Still, it was hard to think you were king of the castle, building elaborate additions to it in the air, only to find yourself being questioned by people who thought you worked for them and expected you to please.

As I entered, Chambers was saying, "Well, neither did I. Who the hell who could have anticipated it would come to this? We thought, and it was a perfectly reasonable assumption, that concern for his college recommendations would keep Jamison in line. It's not exactly normal to find some nutcake Amazon's accusations leading to murder."

He turned to Craig Dunham. "We had Jamison under control, didn't we, Craig?"

Then, almost as an afterthought, to Ivers. "Didn't we?"

Her blank look, followed by the facial expressions

accompanying her mental scrambling, told me she hadn't been in the loop. Not a part of the old boy's network. Once again, I wondered about Chambers' approach to returning the school to a more conservative mode. Was he also trying to return to a day when all the principal administrative positions were male? How had Christabel Ivers reacted to that? Other than the subtle twitchings of confusion, her carefully painted face gave little away.

Bushnell cleared his throat. "So, to the best of your knowledge, there was no relationship between Alasdair MacGregor and Shondra Jones, except in her mind. Is that right?" He looked at Dean Ivers.

"I'm sorry," she said. "I'm the academic dean. If you'd like me to comment on their academic performance, I'd be glad to. I can tell you that she's been struggling this fall, and we've been watching her closely. But in terms of residential and social life, I'm afraid you'll have to ask Dean Dunham or Mr. Margolin. And the residential advisors in her dorm, of course." She looked at Dunham. "Who are they, Craig?"

A neat pass he had to scramble to catch. "Mrs. Leverett and...and...and...uh Maria Santoro."

"And where would I find them?"

"Cabot Hall," Dunham said.

"And that's where I'll find Shondra Jones?" Lavigne passed him the map. He studied it, then pointed. It was my map and Cabot was already circled. So was Pearson. He got it at once. Pointed to Pearson and said, "And this was MacGregor's dorm?"

"That's right," Dunham said.

"Can I assume, from these marking on Ms. Kozak's map, that you've been looking into Shondra's allegations?"

But MacGregor had waited long enough. Longer than I'd expected. "*Was* Alasdair's dorm?" he thundered. "I've asked you before, and I'm asking again, and this time I want a Goddamned answer. What on earth makes you so sure your victim is my grandson?" We all knew he hoped the cops were wrong. He'd probably half-convinced himself that this was so. It explained why he was bombastic rather than sad.

Bushnell shuffled through his notebook, consulted it, and looked at MacGregor. "It's a fair question," he agreed. "We don't have a positive identification. Unfortunately, the victim's...uh...face was both burned and battered, making a visual identification difficult. You're welcome to...uh...of course we'll take you to see him if you'd like. The morgue's not far...but we're expecting to have to use dental records."

"What about fingerprints?" MacGregor interrupted. "Wouldn't that be easier?"

"We're still working on that. Unfortunately, his hands were also rather badly burned."

"If he was so badly burned," MacGregor said, "then how in hell do you have any idea who the victim is?"

"Clothing," Bushnell said. "And his wallet. And also this." Bushnell pulled a plastic envelope out of his pocket, set it on the table with a heavy thump, and pushed it across the table. "We understand he always wore it."

MacGregor snatched up the envelope, unzipped it, and dumped the contents into the palm of his hand. It was a heavy gold ring. He stared at it a long while, then picked it up and studied it more closely, turning it so that he could see the inside. He pulled out a pair of reading glasses, set them on his nose and bent forward, apparently reading an inscription. Everyone else was silent. Finally, he put the ring back in the bag and dropped it heavily on the table.

"My grandfather's ring," he said. "I gave it to Alasdair on his sixteenth birthday."

He shoved his chair back with such force it slammed into the wall, supporting himself with shaky arms planted on the edge of the table. "Excuse me," he said. "I'm afraid...I don't...didn't. I was so certain. Alasdair was too clever, too manipulative, too sure of himself. He isn't...wasn't the type to be a victim."

He lurched toward the door on unsteady legs. Part way there, he had to stop to rest, leaning against the wall, his huge hand flattened against his chest. Chambers stared with horror at his prize donor, in obvious pain, his high color fading to a putty gray.

I snatched up the receiver of the phone on the table in front of me and handed it to Frank Woodson. "Call 911 or whatever you need to call, and get him an ambulance."

The door opened and Wendy Grimm came through, pushing a cart of food and drinks. "Well now," she asked in a falsely cheerful voice, "Who's hungry?"

## CHAPTER FOURTEEN

The next several hours flew by in the blur I'd longed for. We packed Gregor MacGregor off to the hospital and gulped our sandwiches while Bushnell gathered information. Eventually, given the pressures of our own work, Cullin Margolin was assigned to assist Bushnell, and the rest of us buckled down to managing St. Matthews' crisis. In the midst of the chaos, Suzanne finally called to say that she couldn't come and Bobby was on his way.

We'd had a couple pieces of good luck when we decided to move the business to Maine, and Bobby was one of them. Bobby's significant other, Quinn, who was a chef, had gotten a job at a restaurant not far from where we were setting up shop. Life would have been difficult without him. His good nature balanced Suzanne's mood swings and both of our workaholism. Not that he was a slacker—he had an enormous capacity for work—it was just that he was unflappable and sweet-tempered.

Bobby arrived right after I put down the phone, gathered up the faculty and staff chosen to make phone calls to parents, and herded them back into the Trustee's Room to give them their marching orders. I sat down with Todd Chambers and his publicity staff, went over information control strategies, and drafted a press release.

Then Chambers wanted me with him to meet his faculty. That meeting was long and grueling. The faculty were tense and demanding, looking to us to fill an information gap we were hard-pressed to fill. Chambers' unresponsiveness reminded me that he'd missed our preparation for the morning's assembly. Luckily, Craig Dunham was there.

The recurring theme from the faculty, under pressure from their anxious students, was, "What do we tell them?" They passed along the questions they'd been getting. What's the news? How was Alasdair killed and why would Jamison do such a thing? What was happening with Jamison Jones? Was he okay? Did he really do it? Could they visit him? Would there be a funeral? A memorial service? How could we explain one student killing another and still keep them calm and secure?

We repeated the advice we'd given at the morning's assembly, advised them to keep their doors open and stay available to students, and then tried to address their questions. They found, "We really don't know very much yet, but we promise to share it with you when we do," unsatisfactory and were confused by Chambers' insistence that they try to limit contacts—the students and their own—with the outside.

We were trying to strike a delicate balance. We couldn't control the phones, of course. Even if we could have shut down outgoing calls through the campus system, we wouldn't have. We wanted them to have access to their parents under such stressful circumstances, and their parents to have access to them. Although their use was strictly regulated, half the students had cell phones anyway. We knew when something bad happens, people like to diffuse the pressure by talking about it. But we wanted to prevent the press from doing an end-run around our security by trying to interview students.

Ellen Leverett, Shondra's housemother, inquired in a nasal, whiny voice, "What am I supposed to do about Shondra if she asks me to take her to see her brother?"

The answer was obvious. Shondra was the student most affected by all this. If she wanted to see her brother, someone should take her. But Chambers just shrugged, his response so many times today his shoulders must be getting sore. I didn't know if his wife was still missing or what was distracting him, but he wasn't acting like a leader. He was distracted and cranky, like a kid trying to wriggle off his chair and go play.

I was close to the point of taking him into the backroom and kicking him around, but not until he and Argenti had signed a contract. Luckily, Dunham stepped in and asked her to stay after the meeting to discuss Shondra.

As the faculty were filing out, I tapped Dunham's shoulder. "Find out how Shondra's doing, and if Mrs. Leverett is unwilling, tell her I'll take Shondra to see her brother as soon as I can get away." I resisted digging my fingers in and saying, 'make her do her job.'

The phones had rung incessantly and someone was always at my elbow with a question. It was the weekend. I'd given up part of my last weekend for St. Matthews, and worked a long, hard week. If all work and no play makes Jill a dull girl, I was getting duller by the minute, but there are no breaks in a crisis.

Leaving Dunham to deal with Mrs. Leverett, Chambers and I moved on to a sit-down with Jamison's and Shondra's coaches, a meeting they'd insisted on and Chambers had resisted. He was trying to get clear to go to the hospital and check on MacGregor.

Shondra's coach, Jenna Adams, was tall and strong, with a big jaw, calm gray eyes, and heavy, dark eyebrows that went strangely with her tawny ponytail. Her handshake was firm and direct. Jamison's coach, Al Sidaris, loped in behind her with the bent-kneed suggestion of a limp typical of the aging jock. He was an easy 6' 5", a lean, bald black man with a warm smile and worried eyes.

We'd barely settled in our chairs when he explained the worried look. "I know you're busy, Todd, but I've heard a rumor that's got me worried."

"What rumor, Al?" Chambers asked impatiently.

"You know, Todd. I hate to be adding to your troubles ..."

Outside, the misty gray afternoon was fading into a deeper gray dusk and a heavy rain was falling. The few students who could be seen through the windows were walking heads down with their hoods pulled up. Around us, the building hummed with voices and ringing phones. I looked at Chambers, expecting to find him bracing for more bad news. He was gazing absently over at the easel displaying the Arts Center plans.

Sidaris followed Chambers' gaze, dropped his eyes, then

cleared his throat, loudly. He looked at me, raised an eyebrow, and then back at Chambers, obviously wondering whether I ought to be hearing this.

When Chambers didn't respond, I said, "You can speak freely in front of me, Mr. Sidaris. I'm from EDGE Consulting, we're troubleshooters for campus crises." Sidaris still hesitated. "I'm working for St. Matthews."

He sighed, looked at Jenna Adams, then bent forward purposefully. "I know you know about Alasdair and his secret society, Todd." It wasn't a question. "I've heard the members may be planning some kind of revenge."

Secret society? I leaned forward, too, curious to hear more about this.

"What can they do, Al?" Chambers said. "Jones is in jail. They can't get at him."

Impatient with Chambers' obtuseness, Sidaris shifted his shoulders, his nylon jacket rustling. "That's right," he agreed, "and that's wrong. Use your head, Todd. What's the best way to get at Jamison Jones right now?"

I knew, and the sharp intake of her breath said Jenna Adams knew, but Chambers still looked blank. "Go after his sister," Sidaris said.

I waited a decent interval for Chambers to start asking questions or consider ways to head off further trouble. All he did was look at his watch. "What is this secret society?" I asked.

Chambers twitched impatiently. "Oh, just a silly idea of Alasdair's. Sort of a junior Skull and Bones, I suppose. He gathered together a group of legatees, boys like himself who are at least third generation St. Matthews. Their goal was to restore some of the old culture, the old dignity of St. Matthews. Things like wearing jackets and the school tie."

"And reintroducing hazing," Jenna Adams added. "And under the guise of free speech, encouraging behavior that made the lives of female and minority students miserable."

"You didn't mention this the other day, Todd." I looked at Chambers. "Is this the 'trouble' Alasdair was in? Has their behavior been out-of-bounds? Have they broken school rules?"

"They're just a bunch of high spirited kids," he said.

"They haven't broken any rules? You haven't had to discipline them?"

"It's never risen to that level."

Chambers was such a bad liar. For a moment, I felt infuriatingly helpless. This sounded like another problem with the potential to explode in our faces and once again he refused to deal with it. I wasn't here to sort Chambers out; I was here to help the school through a genuine crisis. What I didn't know was whether this could precipitate another crisis. That depended on what Sidaris and Adams revealed.

Jenna Adams was staring daggers at him. I kept my face bland and pleasant, directing my next question to Sidaris. "In your opinion, how much of a threat to Shondra Jones does this group represent?"

He shrugged. "Wish I could tell you, Ms. Kozak. The thing is, we don't know a whole lot about this group. They're pretty secretive. The Administration could identify potential members pretty easily, by looking at which students meet the legatee criteria, and who, among those, are friends or associates of Alasdair's."

He cleared his throat again, looking to Chambers for direction. Again Chambers didn't respond. "It's hard to predict what they might do. We only have a sketchy idea of who they are and what they've already done. It's likely that many of their victims haven't come forward. And it's hard to anticipate how they'll behave without their leader."

I wanted more details about this group and what they'd done to their existing victims, but Sidaris was speaking so reluctantly I decided to concentrate on Shondra. "This threat," I asked, "do you have any details, any names, any information to help us protect Shondra?"

"I got it from a confidential source."

"Mr. Sidaris, someone has been murdered. You must see that we can't take a chance on another violent event."

But did he understand the risks? Did Chambers? I'd been on campuses where they didn't. I decided to spell it out. "Two major underpinnings of the boarding school world are trust and safety. The parents who send their children here have to be able to trust that those in charge will keep their children safe. Another incident where a student is harmed, or even threatened with harm, and there could be a major exodus of students from this campus. We don't get a lot of chances to get this right."

Chambers was fiddling with something on his desk, biding his time until he could politely dismiss us and be gone. Trying to shake him, I added, "And you have to think about next year's class…about how it could affect your applicants if there's another incident." There was no response.

"Todd." I tried to make it sharp enough to get his attention. "If you ignore a threat to one of your students and she gets harmed, that could destroy your reputation. Not just the school's. Your own. We need to follow up on this threat."

"You're making a mountain out of a molehill," he said, looking at his watch. "And Shondra's a big girl. She can take care of herself."

A string of expletives tap danced through my brain. "Mr. Sidaris. Ms. Adams. Obviously you came forward because you believe this is something we should worry about. We can't protect Shondra Jones if we don't know where the threat is. You have to share what you know."

Sidaris, taking his cues from Chambers, wore a stubborn look. "If you have experience in these matters then you know," he said, "adolescents are skittish about sharing information. Right now, I'm in a position where they talk to me. If they think I'm not trustworthy, they'll stop."

I couldn't stand it. "They'll stop what? Telling you when the next girl is going to be assaulted? You think that makes any difference if bad acts aren't prevented? If something happens to Shondra Jones, there may be no next time. A school can only weather so many blows. Word gets around that students at St. Matthews aren't safe and the parents start pulling their kids out, you won't have to worry about your relationship with confidential sources because you won't have a job."

Jenna Adams shot Sidaris an "I told you so" look. He shrugged and studied the backs of his clasped hands.

This was like trying to reason with a bunch of Zombies. I tried another tack. "All right, Mr. Sidaris. You refuse to name your source or give any details. How about my earlier question. Based on what you know, is Shondra Jones at risk?"

He nodded.

"Can you suggest any reasonable way to protect her without revealing your sources?"

He had the grace to look embarrassed. "Well we...uh...Jenna and I...think that Shondra ought to stay with her. With Jenna, I mean. She's got a spare room. And it's not too likely that anyone would look for her there. Until this thing blows over, I mean."

God. These people were just so damned thick. Didn't they understand? Murder doesn't blow over. Dead is forever, loss is monumental, the emotional fallout extraordinary. No one knew that better than I did. She'd been dead three years and I still saw my sister Carrie in my dreams. Still thought of things I needed to tell her, expected her on the line when the phone rang at times when she used to call.

If Alasdair had had close friends, it might take them years, too. I didn't expect Jenna Adams planned to have Shondra live with her for years. Right now, the hurt and anger were very fresh, the need to respond and act urgent. What about classes? Meals? Sports practice? Crossing the campus? How would staying with Jenna protect her there?

"Let's think sensibly about this," I said. I wished Andre were here. I wanted a tough cop who was good at interrogation to extract the necessary information from these people and craft a safety plan for Shondra. Knowing her the little I did, I didn't expect she was going to be very receptive to anything we could think up. But I could easily believe she was at risk. "Todd, what do you suggest?"

"I think it's a mistake to take this too seriously," he said. "So far, it's been nothing but a bunch of pranks. There's no reason to think that will change."

This from the man who thought he had Jamison Jones contained. I remembered the note on my windshield. Ask about what Alasdair and them do to girls. Were we really talking about pranks or was Chambers covering up something more sinister? And what did it mean in terms of the threat to Shondra? Prank or serious violence?

"What about you, Jenna? Do you think this is a credible threat?"

These days, we Americans spend half our time reading news reports in which our government asks us to assess vague threats. Nationally, they've cried wolf so often I can imagine the level code entering the casual vocabulary of emotional assessment, as in, oh, yeah, I'm having kind of an orange day. This threat, on the other hand, was local and immediate. There's a big difference between worrying about every mall and airport in the country and one teenage girl.

"Of course I do. Otherwise we wouldn't be taking up your time, asking you to pay attention to this. It's not like we don't have things to do. You know how close sports teams get. We've both got nervous adolescents camped on our doorsteps, waiting for comfort and guidance, wanting to know how they're supposed to react."

I wanted to hug her. She, at least, got it. Sidaris seemed to be responding to some subtext I couldn't read, something that flowed between him and Chambers. I wondered what their conversation would have been like if I weren't here. But I had to deal with what I could – try to protect Shondra until we could investigate the threat and craft a long-term plan with or without Chambers' cooperation.

"Realistically, Jenna, what are the chances Shondra would stay with you?"

I had to ask. I had no way of gauging the depth of her relationship with Shondra. She shifted her shoulders, ducked her head slightly, and spread her hands. "Not great. But it's worth a try. I…we both…we care about those kids. Shondra's not the easiest person to deal with. But she's for real. She may hold back in class, but on the court, she's a leader. And she's just an incredible ballplayer. She has these fabulous instincts. You should see her handle the ball."

She dropped her hands. "Sorry. Guess you can see I'm her coach, huh?"

And a caring human being. "How was she, this morning, when you spoke with her?"

"You can imagine, if you've met her. The two of them are so tight. They're each practically the only family the other one has. To his little sister, Jamison walks on water. She was stricken. Sure it was all her fault. If only she were half as good with praise as she is with blame."

She slapped her palm on her knee. "There I go again. Wasting your time. Just let me know how I can help. Should I talk with her, see if I can persuade her?"

"Todd?" I wanted him making the call. So far, I had little respect for his decisions except the one to call us, but he had to keep making them. Ultimately, the way the school came out of this fell squarely on his shoulders. I'd try to keep his ass out of the fire, but I wasn't shoving him aside and sticking my own in.

"Whatever Jenna and Al think is best. I don't think it's a big deal but there's nothing wrong with erring on the side of caution. Now, if you'll excuse me." He grabbed his coat and headed for the door.

"You're going to the hospital?" I asked. He nodded. "Better give me your cell number, then. And don't stay too long. We need you here." I sounded like somebody's mother. He snapped out a string of numbers in a manner which made it clear that if I was someone's mother, he was someone's child.

The three of us watched the shiny black door close behind him. I tried one more time. "There's nothing else you can tell me? No names? Incidents? We've got a campus full of kids to protect here and Shondra may not be the only target. What about

144

Jamison's friends? Her friends? Their teammates?"

Al Sidaris had his troubled look back. "All I heard was about Shondra. But I guess you're right. It could be worse."

And he wasn't helping. "Is Woodson aware of this group?"

"I really don't know. Frank's a good guy. Capable. But he keeps his distance around the students, so who knows. And Chambers plays it kinda close to the vest when it comes to …"

He didn't need to finish. I knew Chambers would go a long way to protect Alasdair. But Alasdair was dead. So now who was he protecting? Was he willing to put Shondra Jones at risk to protect the dead boy's reputation, just to appease Grandfather MacGregor? It was a disgusting, if quite real, possibility.

I pulled away from conjecture and back to the present. "But there have been incidents?" I stared into Sidaris' sad brown eyes.

"Have there?" he asked.

There was nothing more to say. See no evil, hear no evil, speak no evil. It wasn't ignorance. Chambers had known what Sidaris was talking about. Was going back to the days of hazing and upperclassmen having license to misbehave and mistreat others part of Chambers' vision for the school? Was it possible he approved of secret societies that encouraged the harassment of women or minorities or had he simply been willing to tolerate a lot of inappropriate behavior from Alasdair if it meant building his arts center?

Sidaris seemed to be waiting for some direction. "Okay," I said, "so I guess you do as you've suggested. Jenna asks Shondra to stay with her for a few days." I hesitated. "Let's say for a few days. Until we've got a better handle on this. And if she refuses…I'd appreciate a call so I can think about what else we might do. And Al, would you tell Woodson you've heard rumors of a threat to Shondra, ask him to keep his eyes open?"

"Guess it can't hurt," he said.

Right. And what you're not telling me could help. I watched the two of them depart, considering his words. At this point, who knew what would hurt? And who even cared?

# CHAPTER FIFTEEN

Many meetings and phone calls later, including a disappointing one to Andre that produced no response, it was Saturday night. The campus calendar listed a number of possible activities—a movie, a concert, a student written and directed play, but as I crossed the campus, I didn't meet a soul. The rain had slackened to a light drizzle and the air was thick with fog that muffled sounds and created great halos of light around the streetlamps. The night had a soft loveliness but also a deep sense of desolation.

I wasn't feeling like a very cheery cowgirl myself. I might not yet have found the straw that broke the consultant's back, but my load was getting heavier. Every meeting made things worse. The PR people were under pressure from the media to hold a press conference but no one could move forward without Chambers. Shondra and Jamison's grandmother had called several times and no one wanted to return her call without checking with Chambers. He had disappeared after our meeting and either turned off his phone or was refusing to answer.

Chambers' continuing failure to disclose all the facts made any advice we gave unreliable, and his failure of leadership with respect to his faculty, staff and students threatened to render anything we did moot. I didn't see how we could reassure parents that their children were safe when it wasn't clear they were.

Chambers wasn't the only one not answering. I'd tried to reach both Shondra Jones and her housemother without success. It was that information void in a particularly vulnerable area that had sent me out on this nocturnal campus walk even though every hair on my body bristled.

It was a fearfully empty night. As I walked to Shondra Jones' dorm, my footsteps were the only sounds. There were none of the quick steps, giggles and voices of a normal night. The paths weren't well lit, though I supposed it was bright enough on an ordinary night. This was a kind of darkness that swallowed up light. I'd given my map to Bushnell and, navigating from memory, discovered that the rambling charm which made the paths pleasant by day made them difficult in the dark. After two wrong turns, I finally found Cabot Hall.

Unlike the other day, when I'd walked in freely, tonight I was relieved to find the door locked. I rang the bell and waited. After a few minutes, a nervous-looking girl opened it and peered out at me.

"Thea Kozak, from Headmaster Chambers' office, to see Mrs. Leverett," I said, afraid that using Shondra's name might alarm her.

Very slowly, she backed up enough to admit me. "Sorry," she said, in a little, breathy voice. "We're all kind of spooked after what happened, you know."

"I don't blame you," I said. "What happened last night is pretty awful."

I stepped up to Mrs. Leverett's door and knocked. After a few minutes, when there was no response, I knocked again. "I don't think she's there," my guide said. "I think she went out."

"Who's in charge, then?" I asked, "Ms. Santoro?"

"I guess so."

I thanked her, hiked up the stairs to Santoro's door, and knocked. Knocked a second time. And a third. It had been a long, miserable day and I was out of patience. If she didn't answer soon, I'd kick the door in. I do try to be balanced and keep my temper but right now I was feeling a little frayed.

I was warming up my leg with a few practice swings when a small voice asked, "Are you looking for Ms. Santoro?"

"Yes." I turned. It was the pastel blonde girl again. Cassie something.

"She went out about an hour ago. I saw her leave."

A whole dorm full of young girls left alone the night after a campus murder? Blood doesn't really boil, but right now, mine felt distinctly intemperate. I pulled out my phone and the list I'd providentially brought with me, and called Cullin Margolin.

At least he answered. "Mr. Margolin? Thea Kozak, from EDGE Consulting, I'm over here at …"

"I'm sorry," he said. "We've been instructed to refer all phone calls to …"

"Mr. Margolin," I snapped, cutting him off. "It's Thea Kozak. I'm the one who gave you that instruction, remember? Now listen. I'm over in Cabot Hall, looking for Shondra Jones. I don't know what's going on, but Mrs. Leverett and Maria Santoro have both gone out, leaving these students all alone."

"Gone out?" He sighed and muttered a few expletives. "Everything seems to be going to hell at once."

"You did make it clear that they had to be here?"

"Of course," he said, defensively. "All the advisors are supposed to be available throughout the weekend. We've called in some extra faculty as back-up. I'll find one of them and send her over immediately."

"I'd suggest you also find Mrs. Leverett and Ms. Santoro, explain to them what the word "fired" means, and get their asses back here pronto."

"You know," he said, as though we had all the time in the world, "you're not being very understanding. Located where we are, we have a lot of trouble finding reliable staff."

"Not nearly as much trouble as you'll have finding another job if you lose half your students because their parents don't think they're safe here."

I'm so perceptive. I can hear expletives across hundreds of feet of thickly treed campus, even when the speaker turns away from the phone. It wasn't unfair to be picking on him. He was in charge of this piece of the action—or, as it appeared, inaction. He had to start doing a better job. But I also had to be careful about sounding strident. As Andre often reminds me, you can be as angry as you want, just don't show it.

I gave him my number and asked for a call back when he'd

located Mrs. Leverett and Maria Santoro. Then I went to Shondra's door. I knocked once. Twice. No answer. No one was home to me on this campus. TV advertisers would have me believe it was my breath or my irritability. Maybe the social stigma of yellowed teeth. Something eminently treatable was causing my current social failure. But the voice over in my head was not about products, it was repeating what Al Sidaris had said. Alasdair's buddies were going to take revenge. Suddenly, it was very important to know whether Shondra was in her room, and if she wasn't, to find her.

"I think she's in there," a voice by my elbow said. The blonde girl again.

"You've seen her?"

"A couple hours ago. My room is right there." She pointed to the door across the hall. "I tried to tell her how sorry I was...about her brother and all...but she just did her Queen of Sheba thing and stalked by me like I was invisible. She's...I don't know. It's like I keep trying to be her friend and she just won't let me. Seriously, I don't know why I bother when she's so awful about it, but I guess I think she'd be interesting to know...if only I could only, like, get through her defenses."

She stopped, coloring slightly. "Do I sound like a real sap?"

"How did she seem, when you saw her?"

"Oh, she had that same cool exterior, but she also looked awful, you know. Like you'd expect, I guess, under the circumstances." She stuck out a small, white hand, as though we hadn't met before. "Cassie MacLeod."

"Thea Kozak."

"She might be asleep," Cassie offered. "I know she didn't get any sleep last night. She couldn't have. She was out all night."

Curiouser and curiouser. When the Administration tries to find anyone who knows whether Shondra's room and things have been tampered with, they can't find a soul. Yet here's someone who seems to have kept awfully good track of Shondra's comings and goings.

"Is she a heavy sleeper?"

Cassie shrugged, faking indifference, but curiosity gleamed in her eyes. "I wouldn't know. I just thought, you know, that if she was really tired, she might sleep through someone knocking on her door, that's all. I mean, like, she's always tired, but that, you know, with what's happened, it would get boosted up to another level, wouldn't it?"

She started toward the stairs. "Well. Good luck. I hope she's okay."

I tried the door again. If Shondra was asleep and I disturbed her, she wouldn't thank me, but she wouldn't thank me no matter what I did. I called, surprised that with all the noise I was making, no one looked out to see what was going on. Uncurious? Plugged into headphones? Out for the evening? It *was* Saturday night. I couldn't shake the unease Sidaris' words had caused. I needed to know what was on the other side of that door.

My phone rang. Cullin Margolin. "Ms. Kozak...I don't know what's going on around here." He sounded apologetic and uncertain. "After we spoke, I called around. Found Ellen Leverett and Maria Santoro waiting outside Todd Chambers' office. They say they got a phone call from my office, calling an emergency meeting with the Headmaster. But I didn't call and Todd isn't here. I don't know what this means."

I thought I did. "Tell them to get back here as quickly as possible...if they aren't already on their way. Do they have master keys which will open all the rooms?"

"Do they have what? Uh...oh...yes, they do. But why? What's going on?"

"I want to get into Shondra's room. She isn't answering her door and the girl across the hall is almost certain she's in there. Under the circumstances, I want to be sure she's all right."

"I'm not sure we should...there are privacy issues, here, and you know how touchy Shondra is."

"I guess I'm not making myself clear, Mr. Margolin," I said. "I'm trying to avoid another disaster for St. Matthews. I'm not worried about hard feelings. I want that door opened so I can see whether Shondra is alive."

His little, swallowed, "oh," was barely audible. In a stronger voice, he said, "Maybe I ought to send security along, too…just in case."

"That would be an excellent idea."

I checked my watch, wondering how long it would be before reinforcements arrived. It took ten minutes, max, for someone who didn't get lost to reach this dorm. Ten minutes with uncertainty on the other side of the door felt like eternity. Ten unnecessary minutes. Why hadn't he sent the residents back the minute he found them? I paced and fretted and bit my lip, picturing all manner of mayhem inside that room.

Eventually, footsteps on the stairs signaled their arrival. Santoro was her usual sulky self. Ellen Leverett wore a pinched, pruny look that made me want to mess with her, if only I'd had the time. She fished out a key, banged once for form's sake, and unlocked the door.

I stepped past her and switched on the light, holding my breath as the door swung inward. It was dreadful, but not what I'd been expecting. Shondra Jones wasn't there. Disaster was. Every book, paper and piece of clothing in the room had been shredded. The dresser drawers had been pulled out and smashed, the desk and chair smashed. Her eviscerated mattress leaned against the wall, grayish white tufts of stuffing oozing from the slashes. Shondra's underwear hung from hooks on the wall that had held pictures and bras dangled from the ends of empty curtain rods and the legs of the overturned chair.

Their shocked cries gathered the crowd my knocking and calling had not. Soon we were surrounded by gaping students, and moments later, the crowd was swelled by the arrival of two campus security guards and Cullin Margolin.

"I can't believe she did this," Ellen Leverett said. "I knew she was angry and upset, but these were her own things. A genuine case of cutting off her nose to spite her face. What was she thinking? That we'd just go out and buy her some more? Honestly, that girl."

It was such a compassionate remark. Just as she'd missed

everything else, she'd missed the symbolism of the carefully displayed underwear. I was sure Shondra hadn't. Even in death, Alasdair MacGregor could mess with her mind.

"When was the last time you saw her?"

"Dinner time, maybe? She came flying down the stairs and went past me without a word."

"She appeared to be very upset?"

"Of course. Upset and angry. But she was always angry, and naturally, after what her brother did, she was bound to be upset."

"You didn't try to speak with her? See if she wanted a counselor, anything like that?"

Maria Santoro gave her sharp laugh. "You're kidding, right? Offering Shondra help is like trying to pet a snapping turtle."

That was a hell of a line. I'd have to remember it.

"You've been in all day?"

"Of course."

"But you didn't hear anything?"

"I had my headphones on."

So much for making herself available. I looked around at the crowd of students. "All this destruction must have made a lot of noise. Did anyone hear anything?" Like sheep, they shook their heads.

Sweet Jesus, I thought, what is this place, anyway? The Stepford School? But there wasn't time to break their stories. I had to find Shondra. If Cassie was right, Shondra *had* seen this. If she'd been upset before, who knew what state she was in now?

"Do either of you have any idea where she might have gone?"

Santoro shrugged. Ellen Leverett considered. "Sometimes, when she's upset, she goes to the gym."

"The gym's open on a Saturday night?"

"Sure. Lot of the kids like to go there and work out."

I turned to Margolin and the security guys. "Let's check the gym."

One of the security guys demurred. "I dunno," he said. "I think we ought to stay and make out a report. Hell of a lotta damage here."

"Yes, and it's not going anywhere. Right now, we've got a distraught student out there and it's important to find her as soon as possible." I looked at Margolin and raised my eyebrows. Was he going to take charge or would I have to?

He pulled himself up. "Let's go," he said. "You guys have a car. It's faster if we drive."

# CHAPTER SIXTEEN

We swooped through the night on wet, twisty roads, siren blaring and blue lights flashing. Psychedelic coils of blue light and sound swirled around us, distorted by the fog, until we rocked to a stop in front of the gym. We piled out of the car and ran up the steps into the building, into a welter of gym smells— sweat and cleaner and chlorine—and the sounds of gym activities. Balls pounded, sneakers squeaked, weights clanged and water splashed, voices called and grunted.

This hive of activity suggested that Shondra wasn't alone here, and that if she wasn't alone, she couldn't be in trouble. But that was what I wanted to believe, not what I did believe. Anxiety made my stomach so tight it hurt. I was already wondering where we'd look next when we didn't find her here. We paused in the hallway, the other three looking to me for direction, even though they knew the place and I didn't. I shrugged. "Search the building, I guess."

I got the women's locker room and bathrooms, peering dutifully into toilet stalls and shower stalls, under benches and into dark corners. Twenty minutes later we were back in the hall again, empty handed except for the discovery that Jamison's locker had been broken into.

"Did you look everywhere?" I asked. "Basement? Closets? Coaches offices?"

The shorter, smarter security guard, whose badge read Dwight Cotton, looked at his companion. "You check the offices, Ron?"

"They were locked."

Cotton shook his head and started down the hall. "Might as well finish the job."

She was sprawled on the couch in Jenna Adams' office, feet

over the end, one arm folded across her chest, the other touching the floor, palm up, in what looked like a plea for help. She wore a tank top, tearaway pants and hightops. There were bruises on her arms. With her expressive eyes shuttered and her face relaxed, she looked touchingly young and vulnerable.

She appeared to be sleeping, but nothing we tried could wake her. Cotton checked her pulse and respiration, looked at her eyes, and shook his head. "Drugs, maybe? She's pretty far under, whatever it is. We'd better get her to the hospital." He looked at me. "You want us to drive her? It'd be a whole lot quieter. I don't think this place needs any more bad publicity."

"Do you think that's safe?"

"It's ten minutes away. Take that long for the ambulance to get here anyway."

I looked at Margolin. "It's your call."

"Go ahead and drive her," he said. "I'll get my car and meet you there."

"Could you let the Headmaster and Dean Dunham know what's happened?"

"I'll take care of it," he said

Ron pulled the car around to the back and we carried her out. Not an easy job, even with four of us. She was limp and heavy and so tall we had to fold her into the seat, arranging her on her side to be safe. Once she was in the car and the door shut, I pulled Cotton aside. "I know we don't want to draw attention to this, but I'm concerned about those bruises."

"She's an athlete," he said. "It happens."

"It can," I agreed. "Still, if you can manage it without too much fuss, I'd like the hospital to take pictures."

He gave me a funny look, but I've had plenty of those. I shrugged. There wasn't time to argue. "If you can."

The security guys drove off, and Margolin sprinted away to get his car so he could follow. I was left alone in the office. My car was fifteen minutes away across the campus and I wasn't eager to take another long walk in the dark. What was going on was too strange. Eventually, I'd have to, but I decided to stall

155

a little. Stay here where it was brightly lit and there were lots of people noises on the other side of the wall.

I looked around, wondering if there were clues here that could tell what had happened? If I should be careful not to touch anything. There were two things I knew I should do—call Lt. Bushnell and Jenna Adams.

I put Bushnell on a back burner, knowing he'd probably resent it and make my life miserable, and called Jenna Adams. She answered on the first ring, an expectant, hopeful "hello," like she'd been waiting for news.

"Coach Adams? It's Thea Kozak."

"Tell me you've found her," she said. "That she's okay. I've called and called. Gone by her room. Asked her friends. No one's seen her and I've been so worried."

"I'm here in your office," I said. "A few minutes ago, we got security to unlock the door and found her collapsed on your couch...unconscious...looks like it might be a drug overdose. Security officers have taken her to the hospital."

"The hospital? I'll get right over there."

"Hold on," I said. "I'm still in your office. It would be great if you could go to the hospital...she's going to need a friendly face, but I was hoping you could come by here first. Take a look around, see if anything unusual strikes you."

"Five minutes," she said, and put down the phone. No argument. No discussion. Too bad she wasn't running this school.

It was twenty minutes before she flew through the door with a red face and set jaw, followed by Al Sidaris. Her coat was unevenly buttoned. Sidaris wore track pants and his sweatshirt was wrong side out. She might have been waiting by the phone, but she hadn't been twiddling her thumbs.

"Sorry. I had a flat. Had to call Al to pick me up. If I ever get my hands on those stinkers ..." She halted, recalling her purpose. "You want me to look around and see if anything's amiss, huh?"

Despite the necessary clutter and the walls lined with photo-

156

graphs of herself and her players, it was a neat room. No papers on the desk, and where there were stacks along the wall, they were carefully aligned. She stayed rooted to the spot, her eyes circling the room in a scrutiny thorough enough to have satisfied a detective. Twice her eyes came back to the wastebasket, once to the window. Then she stepped behind her desk and surveyed the bank of drawers. Carefully, she hooked a fingertip under the center drawer and tugged. The drawer slid open.

Nodding, she stepped back, plucked a tissue from the box on the desk, wrapped it around her finger, and gently prised open the bottom drawer. Still keeping the tissue around her finger, she poked among the contents, then straightened up, nodding again.

"It's gone."

"What's gone?" Sidaris said.

But Jenna Adams was on a roll. She reached behind the door, pulled a yellow slicker off a hook and spread it out on the floor. She swept up the trash can and dumped the contents onto the raincoat. Nestled among the papers, apple cores, sandwich wrappers and other detritus was a small orange pill container. She used her finger to open the center drawer again, picked out a pencil, then knelt down and used the eraser to roll the container toward her and turn it so she could read the label.

"Vicodin. Better call the hospital so they'll know what they're dealing with."

I bent down and peered at the label on the bottle. Cassandra MacLeod. Cassie. The girl who seemed to be everywhere. "What's the story?" I asked.

Jenna Adams poked at the pill container a few times, sighed, and looked at me. "I wish I knew."

"You know something," I said. "You knew enough to look in the drawer, and in the trash. You knew the pills were there. Why?"

"Why shouldn't I know what's in the drawers of my desk?"

"Why suspect they might be missing or that Shondra might have taken them?"

"A hunch," she said. "Shonda knew I had them. She was there when they rolled out of Roland Shurcliff's pocket and I picked them up. And the wastebasket had been disturbed."

Just a sharp coach's eye or something more? She and Al knew a lot about what was going on around here. I only wished they'd tell me. Tell someone. How many bad things had to happen before people started sharing what they knew? And Roland Shurcliff was a new player in the game. "And Roland is?"

Al Sidaris answered. "On the basketball team."

"Quite briefly, Shondra's boyfriend. Currently, Cassie's boyfriend…and an FOA," Jenna added.

"Friend of Alasdair?" She nodded. "How would Shondra know they were in your desk?"

"I don't know. I don't know that she did. I don't know that anyone did. Maybe somebody was just looking to see what they could find, and this was it. Or maybe …" She didn't finish her speculation. "We should put this in a plastic bag…just in case."

"Just in case what?"

"I don't know. Just in case something happens to Shondra…just in case…oh, hell, Ms.Kozak, I don't really know. I only know things around here aren't right and we can't act as though they are." Her ponytail swished angrily. "That's all I'm saying."

"So would it be your guess that Shondra didn't break into your desk and swallow those pills because she was upset about her brother? Do you have an idea who else might have been involved? Cassie maybe, or this Roland Shurcliff?"

The ponytail swished again. "Don't make me speculate about any of this, okay? Not until I've had some time to think. Come on, Al. Let's go see about Shondra." She hesitated. "I just think you might want to put that thing in plastic, just in case."

"If you mean to preserve it as evidence, paper would be better. Plastic can ruin the prints."

Jenna Adams had appeared to be the one person who would step up. Now, having done her dramatic investigation act and mouthed concern for what was happening, she'd reverted to her earlier practice of speak no evil. I felt like I was in the middle of some silly gothic thing, where everyone trembled in fear of the unknown. The unknown what? Blackmail about their affair? The ghost of raises past?

"Could you finish the room. Anything else out of place or unusual?"

Reluctantly, she turned back. "The window's unlocked," she said, "and there's a soda can under the couch."

"You leave your office locked?"

"Yes."

"Any idea how Shondra got in? You think she used the window?"

"She's got a key." Adams hesitated. "I gave her one. Sometimes she needed a place to be alone. Sometimes ..." Another, longer hesitation. She was torn about telling me this. "Sometimes she slept here, to get away from the phone and...and the fact that her room didn't feel safe."

So she knew, too. I felt an impotent fury at all these adults willing to sacrifice Shondra, and who knew how many others, to Chambers' megalomania.

"What did Alasdair and his friends do to girls?"

"We're going," she said, bolting for the door.

"Maybe Mr. Sidaris would like to fix his clothes first."

"Good idea," he agreed. They hurried from the room.

I'd been going to hitch a ride back across campus with her but she was gone before I could ask. Reluctantly, I found a nice clean paper bag in her trash, used the pencil to roll the pill container into it, and added the soda can. I thought I already had enough jobs without adding evidence tech to the list, but unless it was some crazy form of playacting to point me in the wrong direction, her behavior had to mean something.

I tucked the bag into my briefcase, an item that's become so attached to me it's like another appendage, and left the office. I've done briefcases in the snow and briefcases in paradise and now I was doing briefcases in the London-thick fog. As I headed off across the dark campus, slithery tongues of fog crept like ghosts into the orbit of the few lights, and left a slick of wet across my face.

Fog distorts sounds, so that though I caught the occasional sound of someone else in the night, I couldn't tell where they were, and I couldn't see three feet in front of me. Somewhere in the distance, footsteps clattered and someone laughed. Then, closer, a branch snapped and I heard the slap of wet pants.

I stopped to listen. The slap stopped. When I started walking again, the slap followed. I stopped again. The slap stopped. I walked faster, heading toward some brighter lights I hoped were a building.

I'd be a fool not to be concerned. Someone had been killed here last night, and I'd been told people were looking for revenge. What if I'd foiled some plot by finding Shondra when she wasn't meant to be found? I gripped my case with both hands, swinging it in an arc in front of me, testing the heft. Ready to use it if necessary. It wasn't a great weapon, but swung forcefully, it might do some good.

I never had time to use it. There was a sudden, rapid, slap, slap, slap, the sound of something whipping through the air, and Chicken Little's sky came falling down on the back of my head. I tucked my briefcase under me as I fell, face first, onto the gritty path, scraping my out-thrust hand on the rough asphalt and burying my nose in a slimy mound of wet leaves.

## CHAPTER SEVENTEEN

I wasn't out for long. Even unconscious, I never lost my pitbull grip on the briefcase. Whoever had turned out the lights was trying to wrest it from my grasp when a voice yelled, "Hey, what's going on!"

My assailant turned and ran, departing with the same rapid slap of wet pants that had signaled his arrival. I knew it was a male both from the pungent sweat scent as he bent over me and because of the horrid aftershave or cologne he wore. It was a nauseating combination, and when my knight in shining vinyl hauled me to my feet, that smell plus my swimming head nearly made me heave.

I'm a fine detective, so I figured from the commanding voice, the neon orange vinyl and the shiny shoes that I was in the presence of security, even before he gripped my arm and asked, in a painfully loud voice, "What happened?" followed slowly, as though he'd had to turn a page in his mind, by "Are you all right?"

We needed to find someplace warm, dry and well-lit, and one that had a toilet, sink and mirror, before I was going to be able to answer the second question, so I took a stab at the first. "Guy jumped out of the bushes and hit me over the head," I said.

"You get a good look at him?"

"I got no look at him. He hit me from behind."

"I have a car over here," he said. "I'll drive you to the infirmary."

Where were you five minutes ago, I wondered, leaning on his arm and letting him lead me to his car. My head hurt. I was wet and dirty. I wanted to take a hot bath and crawl into a big soft bed. They had wonderful beds at The Swan. How long would I have to be polite to this man before I could excuse myself and go there? The constabulary, in my experience, liked to get every juicy detail of an attack. I had no juicy details. I couldn't even remember if I'd seen the bastard's shoes. I tested my aching head to see if it would divulge more information but the pathways were clogged.

"I'm fine, really...I think. I'd just like to get to my car. It's parked at the Administration Building."

"Students aren't allowed cars," he said firmly.

Ah, the wonders of a dark night. I was seventeen hours into my work day, ten hours since my last meal, and a couple years into my thirties. I felt a hundred long, dirty years old. "I'm glad to hear it, but I'm not a student. My name is Thea Kozak, and I'm a consultant working with Mr. Chambers on the Alasdair MacGregor killing."

"The infirmary," he repeated, as though my words were merely the confused mutterings of a crime victim. He took my briefcase in one hand, tucked a strong arm under mine, and propelled me to the car. I was in no shape to resist. He opened the door, handed me gently in, and closed it again, using his radio to call Security Central and report what had just happened.

With two guards off at the hospital with Shondra, and now this guy babysitting me, the campus was wide open for any evildoers who were out tonight. I hoped Chambers and Dunham had taken the fiasco at Cabot Hall seriously and made sure that all the dorm residents were in place and on guard, but I couldn't even count on them checking their messages.

The nurse on duty had a sweet face, a cloud of graying curls, and plenty of time on her hands to minister to my battered self. She directed me to a bathroom, where I washed my face, drank some mouthwash, and established that I didn't want to look at myself in the mirror. My barrette was back on the path and in the fog my hair had exploded in a wild tangle. Under fluorescent light, I was an unattractive shade of pale green. She checked the lump on my head, exclaimed in outrage at my story, then picked the gravel out of my oozing palm and wrapped it in gauze.

I listened politely to the lecture about possible concussion.

By this time, I probably could have written it. I was thinking of the luscious deep tubs at The Swan, my chances of begging a late night snack from the landlady, and the bliss of falling into bed. My dreams of delight were shoved abruptly to a back burner by the arrival of Todd Chambers.

Obviously, he hadn't come for any caretaking purpose. He looked far too aggrieved. The first words out of his mouth confirmed that he possessed all the compassion of a basking crocodile. "Look, are you going to be able to work tomorrow? Because we're up to our ass in this business and we need a consultant who can consult."

It was the most backbone he'd shown yet, but I wasn't exactly delighted that he'd decided to try it out on me. There were plenty of better venues to vent his wrath and plenty of more important projects that needed decisive energy. Still, I was supposed to be there for him, not he for me, so, in my new maturity, I didn't yell back, "Yeah, and the school needs a headmaster who can master." Instead, I unclenched my injured hand—I was only hurting myself—said of course I'd be able to work. "How is Mr. MacGregor?"

"Fortunately, it was a very minor event, and he's resting comfortably."

He cleared his throat, and I could see little lists ticking away behind his eyes. Suddenly, Todd Chambers was a man with an agenda. If I didn't cut him off before he got going, I'd never make it to that lovely soft bed. "And Shondra Jones? How is she doing?"

"What are you talking about?"

So he hadn't checked his messages. This was no way to run a railroad. In a situation like this, staying on top of things was crucial. I bit my lip and put a lid on my temper. "I'm talking about the message you didn't check. I'm talking about the fact that Cullin Margolin and I found her unconscious about half an hour ago in Coach Adams' office. Two of your security men have taken her to the hospital."

"Goddammit!" he said. "Isn't one of them in trouble enough?"

Like they were doing this to personally aggravate him. "Look, Todd, I'm dead tired and my head hurts. I need to rest so I can work in the morning. In the meantime, you have to pay more attention to what's going on. These are your students. This is your school and the buck stops at your door. You can't ignore messages or be out of touch for long periods of time. Being in charge means being informed."

I winced at my own words. They sounded like a t-shirt motto.

Maybe it was my imagination, but I thought he smiled. He didn't sound good-humored, though. "Look, I don't need a lecture about how to do my job from some self-important woman consultant, thank you very much. This is MY school." He turned on his heel and headed for the door.

I was sitting in a prep school infirmary, battered, gritty and wet. Exactly how the self-important behaved. But something about his conduct suggested he was trying to make me mad, so I ignored his pique. "Call the hospital," I told his back. "Show some concern. And while we're on the subject of concern, has anyone from St. Matthews been to see Jamison Jones?"

"I've been busy!" he snapped.

"That's why you have a staff, deans and assistant deans, and school attorneys. Has anyone been in touch with Jamison and Shondra's grandmother?"

"I told you …"

"I heard you, Todd." I waited until he'd turned to face me. I wasn't speaking to his back. "Maybe you've forgotten this, but while you were off wandering in the desert, looking for you lost wife, the Trustees hired me to help manage this crisis. My job is to see if I can keep you out of trouble and keep St. Matthews from losing students." Another tick on my own checklist. First thing tomorrow, get a contract signed.

"However pigheaded you choose to be, I'm still going to do my job as long as your trustees want me to."

I considered what else his careless indifference might have prevented him from knowing. "Both of the residents in Cabot Hall were lured away to a false meeting with you this evening,

164

leaving the dorm unattended. While they were gone, Shondra Jones' room was trashed. She's in the hospital. Someone attacked me while I was walking on the campus. I know all this seems overwhelming, but it has to be dealt with. You must pay attention to communication…have some strategy for your staff to determine whether phone calls have actually come from you. You may need to beef up your security staff, temporarily."

"My God. How does your husband stand you?" he said. "Nothing comes out of your mouth but criticism and orders."

"Luckily for both of us, I don't want you to marry me, only to pay attention and deal with things."

I didn't for a second believe his complaint was genuine. Was he trying to make me so mad I'd lose it and he could fire me? Did this pissant little Headmaster think he was a formidable opponent? What could possibly have happened in the last few hours that made him so cocky? Even if he'd been scarfing down his wife's antidepressants, they didn't work this fast.

I put on a fake smile. "I'm heading over to The Swan to get some sleep. What time do you want me in the morning?"

"I don't want you," he said, rude as a peevish child.

"Shall we say eight-thirty?" I was all sweetness and light.

My mother would have been so proud. I was as cheerful as Little Mary Sunshine. A Little Mary who didn't want to miss her breakfast at The Swan. I picked up my briefcase in my uninjured hand and headed for the door. Not as steady as I'd like to be and every step jarred my poor head, but getting away from him was relief enough to outweigh that.

The boor didn't even hold the door. Must not have had a nice mother. Lousy mother. Lousy wife. Wait a sec. Why not blame his father? It's fathers who teach their sons to hold doors.

I fired up the Saab, driving with gritted teeth the short distance to The Swan. I rang the bell, did the necessary paperwork, and was given a room. Mrs. Mitchell, the landlady, offered to bring me a tray of tea and sandwiches without my having to ask. As I started upstairs to my room, she called after me, "Would you like my husband to bring up your suitcase?"

165

It was such a contrast to Chambers' loutish behavior I almost went back and hugged her. She didn't seem like the hugging type, though, so I settled for a grateful "yes" and handed her my car keys.

I'd taken off my shoes, peeled off my socks, and dumped my jacket on a chair when there was a knock on the door. Luggage or sandwiches? Either would be fine. I walked carefully across the room—years of experience with knocks on the head have taught me caution—and opened the door.

Lt. Bushnell pushed past me, walked over to my arm chair, and sat down. Another contestant in today's rude man competition. "We've finally got a chance to have our little talk," he said.

"Why don't you make yourself comfortable," I said. I know cops act this way, but I was tired and Chambers had had a corrosive effect on my mood. Bushnell tipped his head back and closed his eyes. I instantly regretted being snappish. At least I'd gotten a few hours sleep last night. He'd gotten none.

"Mrs. Mitchell is bringing up some sandwiches. Are you hungry?"

His lids lifted slightly. "Coffee?" he asked.

"It could probably be arranged. I'm having tea."

Another knock on the door. This time the Mitchells arrived together, he with my suitcase and she with a tray. She slid it onto the coffee table in front of the fireplace, picked up a device that looked like a TV remote, and ignited the gas logs. "I brought along some coffee for the lieutenant," she said. "Can I get you anything else?"

"No. Thanks. This looks wonderful."

"Oh, before I forget. Your husband called. He said …" She tipped her head sideways, and placed one finger along her jaw, as though that helped her remember. "Oh, yes. He said to tell you he's sorry that he hasn't called…but the whole house is a crime scene…and he doesn't expect to be finished anytime soon. He says he's in cell hell, so you probably won't be able to reach him. He'll call in the morning." She tapped the finger twice. "Does that make sense to you? He said you'd understand."

"Perfect sense," I agreed. "Thanks."

The Mitchells departed, leaving me alone with Bushnell's funny look. I closed the door behind them and went and sat on the edge of the bed. It took willpower not to say, "nite, nite," and fall back against the fluffy pillows

"The whole house is a crime scene?" he said. "That some kind of inside joke?"

"Not exactly. He's working a homicide."

Bushnell gave me an appraising look that took in my bandaged hand and lousy color. "A homicide detective? What happened to you?"

"I assume those two sentences are unrelated?"

"What? Oh. Right." A smile creased his tired face. "I think I need some coffee." He poured himself a cup, then added cream and sugar.

"I think you need some sleep."

"You'd be right there," he agreed. "You were the last thing on my list."

"People are always saying that. I don't know what it is about me. Maybe this habit I have of telling people what to do."

"That's what you're here for, right? To tell people what to do?" He drained his cup, poured another, and reached for a sandwich.

I thought of the miles that separated me from Andre. Wondered if he had coffee and sandwiches, knowing he'd be as tired as Bushnell. Whether the case he was working was awful. The only good side to not being able to call him was that I didn't have to tell him what had happened. He respects what I do and who I am, but he worries. What husband wouldn't worry about a wife like me, always mixing it up with bad guys? I smiled at an image of the two of us in front of the mirror, comparing bruises and scars. We had to be one of the craziest couples in the history of the world.

"What's so funny?" Bushnell asked.

I tried to wipe the goony look off my face. "I was thinking about my husband," I said. I waggled my left hand. "We just got married last summer."

"Congratulations." He opened his notebook. "What happened to your hand?"

"I was walking across the campus and someone came up behind me and hit me in the head. I put out my hand to break the fall."

"You don't seem very upset about it."

What did he want, some teary, dithering female? "St. Matthews hired me because I'm calm in a crisis."

"Is that right? Even when the crisis extends to attacks on
• yourself?"

Was he trying to make me mad—it was a trick cops used— or was this just Make Thea Mad Day? I shrugged. "I don't see how that helps anything."

"Having the appropriate feelings when you're a victim of violence? Why not?"

Appropriate according to whose standards? "Look, Lieutenant, I'm happy to cooperate in any way I can with respect to the case you're investigating, but we're both tired and I, at least, intend to get some sleep. So can you ask whatever it is you want to ask and then go?"

Bushnell didn't like that. Probably one of those people who want me to act sweet and docile because I have a pretty face and a big chest. Or was that just my hang-up? Maybe he just liked to run the show and resented that I was trying to do that, too. Sometimes I got tired of trying to figure people out and wondered what profession I could try that was more solitary. Some days, hermit looked very appealing. Anything was bound to be safer than this. But then, say you're a consultant and few people imagine a life full of guns and knives and blows to the head.

"Sandwich?" he said, offering the tray.

"Sure." I leaned forward too quickly and the world blurred. "On second thought, no thanks." I closed my eyes and sank back against the pillows.

"I should take you to a hospital," he growled, bouncing from bully to protector in a breath. The cop, even the good one, is a bit of a two-headed monster.

"I'll be okay. Just...I mean...would you please ask your questions so we can both get some rest?"

So he did, still a little cranky because I wouldn't let him serve and protect. "What can you tell me about the relationship between Shondra Jones and Alasdair MacGregor?"

"Since sometime last spring, Shondra Jones has been the victim of a stalker. Back then, it took the form of harassing phone calls...obscene, sexual in nature, according to her. The school bought her an answering machine so she could screen calls, but then the machine got stolen and she didn't have the funds to buy another."

"There are people on the campus who can confirm this?"

I shook my head, realized my mistake, and held up my hand, waiting for it to clear before I answered. "Both her roommate and her advisor are gone, but the school knows how to reach them...and there were some records." Miriam Chambers might have made them disappear. I didn't say that, though. I was walking a fine line here between what he needed to know and what my client didn't want known. A fine, ugly, murky line that made me feel cheap.

"You've spoken with Shondra? And you believe she *was* being stalked, even though your clients don't agree?"

He made it sound like my clients' behavior was somehow my fault. I didn't take the bait. "Yes."

"Did she tell you her stalker was Alasdair MacGregor?"

"Yes."

"She tell you how she knew?"

"She said she recognized his voice. Look, why are you asking me these things? Why not ask Shondra?"

"I will," he said coldly, "just as soon as I can find her."

"You haven't spoken with Shondra at all?" I couldn't believe it. She was central to all this. What had he been doing

169

all day?"

I forgot that cops read minds. "I've tried to find her. No one seems to know where she is. I've talked with people in her dorm. People on her team. Friends of Alasdair's. Friends of Jamison's. People on his team. Trying to build a picture. You know how it works." His tone became accusatory. "You wouldn't happen to know where she is?"

"She's probably still at the hospital."

"The hospital?" Bushnell exploded out of his chair. "What the fuck is going on around here? Everyone knows I'm all over hell and gone, trying to find Shondra Jones and no one bothers to tell me where she is?" His volume hurt my head. Everyone at The Swan, awake or asleep, must have heard what he said.

"Lieutenant, please. We only just found ..."

But he was on a tear. "So, have you known all day? Have Chambers and Dunham?"

"She wasn't at the hospital all day." I said. "As far as I know, there's no conspiracy here, they're just a little disorganized."

"Like hell there isn't!" He set down his coffee cup with bang that should have broken it, marched over to the bed, and grabbed me by the shoulders. "I don't know what you people are up to, but I need some straight answers from someone and I'm not leaving until I get them."

Had I really been foolish enough to feel sympathy for this man? "Take your hands off me," I said. I didn't care if everyone in The Swan heard that, too.

"Don't you get it?" he said, leaning into my face and rattling my poor, fragile head. My stomach lurched and twisted. "Somebody is dead and everyone around here acts like they're at an effing tea party."

A fact of life he should know—you don't shake someone who's had a blow to the head. It's like shaking a bottle of Coke, with uglier results. I clamped a hand over my mouth, hoping I could make it to the bathroom.

"Let me go or watch out!" I said. I tried to wriggle out of his grasp, but he held on.

"All right. You were warned." I dropped my hand.

Some mind reader. Some smart cop. Maybe he was just too tired to be smart. I didn't care. Not about his mood or his pants or his shoes. I'd tried to play fair. He'd made it impossible. As I slammed the bathroom door behind me, he was treating The Swan's guests to curses that would have educated a bunch of stevedores.

## CHAPTER EIGHTEEN

Round Two was a lot like round one, except Bushnell wore a thick terry bathrobe while Mrs. Mitchell dried his pants and socks. "Where were we?" he began at full volume.

"You're making my head hurt." I took a swig from a bottle of seltzer, hoping it would help settle my stomach. He had horny, yellowish nails and pale, dry feet. Much too intimate. A married woman should know no bare feet but her husband's.

"Oh, your head hurts," he mimicked, but at least he used a softer voice. "All right, what's she doing at the hospital and how long have you known where she was?"

I wanted to yell back, but I'd only hurt myself. He had a right to know and I wanted to help—or I had until he was such a jerk. It was bad enough that he'd unfairly assumed I was colluding with my clients to keep information about Shondra from him. But grabbing me? I hated being grabbed. I was too weary to fight, though. I didn't feel like something the cat had dragged in, I felt like something the cat had played with for hours.

"Drug overdose, I think. I...we...Cullin Margolin and I found her in her coach's office about forty-five minutes ago. Maybe an hour, now. We thought she was asleep but we couldn't wake her. Security took her to the hospital."

"Damn. Excuse me." He dialed a number, gave some instructions, then brought his laser-sharp gaze back to me. "How did you know to look there?"

"Don't be so damned condescending, Lieutenant. I knew the same way you would. Common sense, experience, and asking the right questions. I went to her dorm and ..." How much of this should I tell? All of it, probably. He'd find it out sooner or later anyway. "There were no residents…no grown-ups in the place. They'd been lured away by phone calls. I made some calls and located them. We got Shondra's door unlocked and found her room had been completely trashed. Everything destroyed."

I stopped there, imagining what it must have been like for Shondra to come upon that mess, so deep into my own thoughts I almost missed his next remark.

"Yeah, I guess that's no surprise," he said. "I hear she has an incredible temper."

"She's pretty tough," I agreed, "but I don't think Shondra did this."

For anyone looking for the easy answer, it would look like Shondra had done it. She'd been mad and upset enough and she was capable of extremely impulsive behavior. But the residents had been lured away for some reason. She was poor, proud, and, according to Maria Santoro, compulsively neat. And that draped underwear was a red flag.

Then I wondered, was the destruction a cruel act, the revenge Sidaris had spoken of, or was it instead, or also, to cover up a search? If so, a search for what? Hadn't Shondra said something about pictures? Pictures of what? Once the questions started, they just kept coming.

"Oh, you don't. I suppose you have some theory about who did?"

I didn't think saying, 'can the sarcasm' would be helpful, and I didn't know what else to say. I didn't know who had done it. The closest I could come to a theory was the mysterious group Alasdair had formed which the two coaches had alluded to. And it wasn't a developed theory, it was half-baked speculation, gleaned from unhelpful witnesses and a note left on my windshield. It would be ludicrous to suggest it to Bushnell in his present mood. He'd only beat me over the head with more suspicious questions I couldn't answer.

"I'm afraid not."

He tried a few more probing questions to which I had no useful responses and moved on to other subjects. He asked several times, in different guises, what I thought was going on, and what my clients were trying to hide, and a bunch of questions about Jamison Jones and Alasdair MacGregor. I described my conversation with Jamison Jones and confessed to my inability to learn much about Alasdair. Beyond that, most of my answers were versions of "I don't know," which didn't please him much.

I was praying for Mrs. Mitchell to reappear with his clothes, when he circled back around to Shondra again. "So, you've spoken with the Administration, and with Shondra, with her brother, and with other people in her dorm. Based on all of that, did you reach any conclusions about whether Alasdair MacGregor was actually stalking Shondra Jones?"

"Someone was. But people around here are quick to defend Alasdair, so that's as far as I got before they sent me packing."

"Sent you packing?" He shook his head in exaggerated disbelief, studying my green face with hateful intensity. "You sure looked like a member of the team today."

I took another swig of seltzer, wishing it were bourbon instead. But much as I enjoyed Jack Daniels' company, he was even harder to take on a fragile stomach than Bushnell.

"This really isn't relevant," I said.

"Why don't you let me decide. Tell me about getting fired."

I sighed, shrugged, and told.

"So what Chambers said today, about Shondra making it all up…he knows that isn't true. Does he really think I'm so stupid that I wouldn't find out?"

It wasn't a real question. I stared down at his pale toes, wondering if this was going to come back around and bite me on the ass. It would be just like Chambers to fire me again for telling the truth to the police. Tonight's behavior suggested that either he still didn't get what was going on and why he needed me, or that he had some incomprehensible plan of his own which he believed justified shirking all the details of his job.

I wished Andre were here. I wanted to shove Bushnell into the hall, close the door, and ask what *he* thought was going on.

I'm pretty good at clues and cues, but everyone involved in this was an enigma. If Bushnell had some theory I was no better at deducing that than anything else. It could be as simple as that Jamison had done what he did because MacGregor really was messing with his sister.

Even if that was the solution to his murder, there was a lot more going on here. Things I didn't want to get involved in, things I couldn't avoid if part of my job was ensuring that the school's students were safe. Or was this just Thea the Crusader again? Maybe tomorrow, after I'd slept, I see all this more clearly.

At long last, Mrs. Mitchell knocked on the door, handed in the pants and socks, and beat a hasty retreat. Bushnell thanked me insincerely for my time and cooperation and went into the bathroom to change. When he'd dressed and the door had finally closed on his upright, narrow frame, I wanted to jump up in glee and make rude monkey faces. Instead, I climbed into bed, praying for a dreamless sleep.

Except in the dramatic clincher, when things do occasionally go right for me, I'm not the sort of person whose prayers are answered. My life is more Sisyphean and my dreams are horror shows. Tonight, my wooly brain didn't have the capacity for dreams, good or bad. I felt into heavy sleep which was almost immediately interrupted by the phone. Hoping it was Andre, I roused myself and grabbed it. It was Bobby Ryan, calling to see what time he and I were meeting in the morning and asking, by the way, what all the shouting had been about. I explained about Bushnell, agreed on seven to give us time to gear up for Chambers, and snuggled back into the pillows.

Half an hour later, the phone rang again. This time it had to be Andre. No one else would call this late. I rolled over and said "hello?" There was a long silence and a click. Well, he'd told me he was in cell hell, hadn't he. He'd try to find a place with a better signal and call again.

It was twenty minutes before the next call. Another silence and then click. And twenty minutes later, the same thing again.

175

It's a dastardly combination, being three-quarters asleep and a slow learner. I answered three more calls before I figured out this wasn't Andre. This was someone giving me a taste of what Shondra Jones had been living with.

I tried Andre's number once more, without success. I wanted to stay available, in case he did call. It was so difficult to reach him and I needed to hear his voice. For the next two hours, as regular as clockworks, the phone rang every twenty minutes. I always answered and there was never anyone there. Finally, I gave up, took the room phone off the hook, turned off my cell, and pulled the pillow over my head.

It took me a long while to fall asleep—my mind was full of Shondra, and St. Matts and the whole messy situation—but when I did, I slept like a rock. I didn't move again until my alarm, bleating like a sick sheep, dragged me back to reality. I woke with a blinding headache, a throbbing hand, a growling stomach, and the disposition of Ebenezer Scrooge. A message on my phone said I'd missed a call from Andre. Let me find the nasty little bastards who had kept me up all night and I'd pluck their little heads right off their shoulders.

# CHAPTER NINETEEN

Mrs. Mitchell's lavish breakfast should have ensured that The Swan was always full, but the breakfast room was empty except for me and Bobby. Maybe the rest of the guests got to sleep in. Bobby was chipper and smiling—the man has the nicest disposition of anyone I know—even though he was clutching a sheaf of papers daunting in its thickness. He took a look at my face and announced, "Not a word of business until you've eaten." Not just a nice man, but smart.

I heaped up my plate with waffles and topped them with strawberries and whipped cream, added a small mountain of crisp bacon, a cup or so of fluffy scrambled eggs, and got a bowl of thick oatmeal swimming in cream and brown sugar. An army marches on its stomach, after all, and I knew today would be a series of battles. It wasn't just a jaundiced view from too little sleep and a wounded head, it was reality. Dunham would still be thick, Chambers devious, and Argenti demanding. And that was before we got to Bushnell, who defied description, and the other assorted dysfunctional players.

My mouth was full of waffles when the phone rang. Andre, at last. I excused myself and carried the phone out into the hall. "I miss you," I said.

"I called. You didn't answer."

"I know. Someone called me every twenty minutes all night. I'd answer, hoping it was you, and there'd be no one there. Finally, I turned off the phone so I could get some sleep."

"Sounds like your situation is as crazy as mine."

"I'm so fed up with mine I could scream. I suppose I wouldn't have a job if these people were functional, but honestly! They're like hens in a thunderstorm. Piling up in corners and clucking madly."

"Hey," he said, "that's pretty good."

"I thought it was cranky."

"When my bride doesn't get enough sleep, she does get a bit cranky."

"And when the bad guys thwart my groom? Tell me about your night."

"It was lonely," he said. "You weren't there."

Go ahead, try to break my heart, Lemieux. You weren't there either. "And your case?"

"Big house on the water in Scarborough...leased by a couple drug dealers....night before last, well, early morning, actually, the neighbors heard gunshots...sounds of fighting. They called the Scarborough police. Local guys went and knocked, no one answered. They waited for first light, looked in the windows, saw knocked over furniture. Waited for a judge to give them a warrant, went in and found blood everywhere so they called us."

And so it went. The public thinks it's easy. You hear trouble, you call the cops, cops break down the door and get the bad guys. In real life, the cops can get there and if there's no sign of trouble and no one to answer the door or give permission to search, they may have to cool their heels for hours. "And what did you find inside?"

"Enough blood to tell us someone had been killed there, knife marks, bullet holes and no bodies, alive or dead."

"Sounds like almost as big a mystery as I've got. At least you get to be in charge. I've got this jerk of a state cop with a poker up his ass named Bushnell breathing down my neck and calling me a liar every time I open my mouth."

"Gary Bushnell?" he said. "Hey, he's a great guy."

I loved my own personal cop more than life itself. Goodness knew I'd gone to great, some might say foolish, lengths to prove it. But sometimes the brotherhood—and for the most part it still was a brotherhood—got me down. He knew Bushnell. Dammit! Would his opinion of the great Gary Bushnell change if he knew the man had grabbed his wife and shaken her until he'd made

178

her sick? I decided not to ask. Andre didn't need more things to worry about. I could tell from his voice he was exhausted.

Husband. Wife. Such new, unfamiliar words. How long would it take for them to become old hat? Andre the old hat. Old white hat? But the old hat was talking again. "What? You didn't like him? Hey, did he give you a hard time?" His voice dropped to a growl. "You want me to talk to him?"

Just what I needed—my hero with a badge and a gun, calling up and telling Bushnell to leave his wife alone. All credibility gone, little woman status confirmed. "No. Sweetie pie, honey-dew, darling, I do not want you to talk to him. I think he's a jerk. In fact, he went out of his way to prove he was. But I'm a big girl and I can take care of myself, thank you very much."

"Uh oh," he said. "Sounds like I trod on some very tender feet."

It was a tender head, actually, but I wasn't mentioning that. If our positions were reversed, he wouldn't tell me, either. "You had any breakfast?" I asked.

"Oh, yeah." He brightened right up. "Biggest damned lumberjack breakfast you ever saw." My honey really loves to eat. "Whoops," he said. "Gotta run. There's a local cop over there waving at me kinda frantically. Maybe they've found some body parts or something. I'll call tonight, so leave the phone on, okay?" He was gone without even a hearty Hi Ho, Silver, away.

I headed back to my waffles, purposeful and hungry. But no more purposeful than the two girls who'd just come through the door, sighted on me, and headed in my direction. Their wide, squared shoulders and easy gait said athletes. Their eyes said seeking. Their worried faces said Shondra. And my waffles were getting cold. I headed back into the breakfast room. They'd have to follow if they wanted to talk.

Bobby smiled at me, frowned slightly at them, and rattled his papers softly, reminding me we didn't have time for diversions. "Sorry," I said. I dropped into my seat, grabbed my fork, and shoved a bite of waffle into my mouth.

The girls weren't shy. They took the other two seats at the

table and waited for my attention. Whatever the current debate on girls and self-esteem may be, and like so many other aspects of popular psychology, it has a 'flavor of the month' quality, Title IX and the resulting access to competitive athletics has done wonders for young women in the assertiveness department. Even when I wasn't keen to be aggressed on, like now, I had to applaud the improvement. I'd been a teenage female athlete back when being strong and tall and competitive hadn't been so well received.

The girls exchanged glances and the bigger one took the lead. "You're the consultant working with Mr. Chambers on this...uh...on Alasdair's...uh...murder, aren't you." She stuck out a hand. "I'm Lindsay Davis. This is Jennifer Reilly. We're on the team with Shondra and we're here to ..." She faltered and looked at her companion. "Help me out here, Jen."

Lindsay had copper-colored hair, cut sensibly short, freckles dusting lily skin, and smart gray eyes. Jen Reilly was dark, with hair at least as curly as mine, bright brown eyes, and unnaturally straight, unnaturally white teeth. Now she showed all those teeth in a nervous smile. "We think...someone needs to know...uh...something strange is going on here."

She searched for a way to explain. "I know what we've been told that Shondra targeted Alasdair because of his views...and that there was no stalking going on, it was all just a misunderstanding on her part. But it's, well, kind of a scary thing to call Mr. Chambers a liar, but I...we...that's just seriously not true."

The clock was running and Bobby and I had to talk before we met with the St. Matthews people again but I needed to hear this. I might not get a second chance. I introduced myself and Bobby and apologized for eating while we talked. I'd learned from my cop to eat when I got the chance.

"So you believe Shondra was being stalked and Alasdair was doing it?" They nodded.

"Well, sure," Lindsay said. "Once he'd asked her out and she'd shot him down. That's Alasdair...that was, I mean. If he couldn't have what he wanted, he had to destroy it. They called it high spirits...or youthful pranks...but the truth was...he was just plain crazy. Not funny crazy, either. Bad crazy. Mean and scary crazy."

"Alasdair was dangerous and vicious," Jen said. "Kids were afraid of him...of what he'd do, because they knew the Administration wouldn't do anything to him. Things other kids got in trouble for, Alasdair just skated." She shrugged. "His family was just too big a deal around here. Headmaster Chambers...he...well, it was kind of pathetic, if you know what I mean...he'd like practically kiss Alasdair's feet."

"His ass," Lindsay corrected.

"Whatever...but we didn't come here about that. Not exactly, I mean. We're...well...I guess there's two things, really." Jen stopped and looked at Lindsay.

"I know it was hard for you to come," I said. "It must be important, or you wouldn't have bothered."

"It's going to sound crazy," Lindsay said. "That's why she...why we...haven't said anything to anyone...like our advisors or anything. Not even to Coach Adams, and she's pretty cool. Only...it's hard to know who you can trust around here, you know?"

She gave me a close, nervous scrutiny. "I mean, I'm here and everything, but I don't even know if I can trust you."

There was so much wrong with a campus where the students felt unsafe talking about what scared them and unsure who was a trustworthy adult. "What made you think you could?"

"Shondra," Jen said. "That is, she didn't trust you exactly, but she said you were kind of cool, and that you, like...well, that maybe you believed her?" She shrugged. "That's more than anyone else did, isn't it?"

"You believed her."

"Well, yeah," Jen said, "but I knew Alasdair, didn't I, like what he does and stuff." I raised an eyebrow. "Well, not that anyone would care or anything...I mean, like who'd listen to me, right? But I had my own run in with him, didn't I, Lindsay?"

Lindsay nodded. Bobby gave up and set his stack of papers

back down on the table. This wasn't going to be a quickie. They had a story to tell but getting it would take time. Since we were in for the long haul, I offered the girls breakfast. They were hungry teenage athletes. They didn't say no. Bobby got up to get us both more coffee.

Over her waffles, Jen elaborated. "Back when I was a freshman…I'm a junior now, like Shondra…Lindsay's a senior…Alasdair asked me out. Well, he was cute, even then, and he had that swagger…that confidence that most freshman boys lack…so I said sure, and we went out a few times. He was weird, but we were all new at this. And anyway, I hadn't dated before, so what did I know?"

She set down her fork and clasped her hands tightly together. "So this one night we're up in his room and he says that he thinks we ought to have sex…just like that…and I was like, no way was I ready for that. So that's what I told him. I thought, well, he might be kinda put out, but he'd understand, only he, like, took it really badly…yelling at me. Said I'd led him on. He started throwing things."

One thumb stroked the other in a steady, nervous rhythm. "I started crying and he got all apologetic and I thought we were okay. But the next time we were together, he tried again. It got to be like a wrestling match and I was thinking I'd better just break up with him."

She stared down at the busy thumbs. "And then he…one night, he said he had some vodka and did I want to try it, and I…well…I guess I was just dumb in those days, or too naïve or something…because I said sure, and we drank some, and I got all dizzy and woozy, and then Alasdair tried to …" She shot an embarrassed look at Bobby and wouldn't go on.

"He tried to force her," Lindsay said. "She got away and staggered out into the hall, and luckily the resident was walking by, so she got rescued. But when she wanted to complain about Alasdair, they all told her it would get around the campus and hurt her more than it hurt him, and she believed them."

"But he told everyone that I'd brought the vodka, and gotten drunk, and let him…you know…and then made a fuss after, and that got all over campus." Two years later, her voice was still raw with the pain of it. "When I went back to the administration and said I wanted to file that complaint, they told me it was too late. It took a year with no guys, no dates, and all my friends standing up for me…before it died down. I felt so…so betrayed. By him, but even more by the school. By the way they let me down."

"Did Shondra know about this?"

"I don't know. She wasn't here when it happened. I never told her my version, so maybe all she knew was the gossip. Alasdair's lies. The thing is, see…it's not so much that we are Shondra's friends, as that we'd like to be. Sometimes she tells us stuff…like she did about you…but she's so difficult that we can't be the kind of friends we'd like to be. We try, sometimes, but then she's all prickly and impossible, and we back off. It's…I don't know…I was talking to my mom about it last night…it's so sad, really. I mean, who doesn't need friends?"

"Shondra sure does," I agreed. "That's an awful story. I'm sorry to hear the school let you down like that. I like to think things are getting better, but what happened to you happens a lot…they think they're protecting your reputation and what they're doing is silencing you and making you feel even more guilty."

Feeling guilty myself, I checked my watch. Bobby and I had an eight-thirty meeting with Chambers to prepare for. I wished we had more time. There were so many questions I needed to ask. Maybe I could arrange to meet them later.

"Lindsay, you said there were two specific things you wanted to see me about?"

"Well, the first was what we said…that we believe Alasdair was stalking Shondra. I mean, that we thought you ought to know how he lies…lied…so that maybe what Jamison did makes more sense, like maybe it was self-defense or manslaughter or something. I mean, seriously, you saw that fight. I know 'cuz I saw you there, and Alasdair, he was like trying to

183

make Jamison mad."

Lindsay looked down at her plate, unsure about how much she wanted to say. "They were all there, baiting Jamison, Alasdair, Justin Palmer, Roland Shurcliff, Tommy McLeod and Jared Sole...but where you were, you couldn't hear the stuff they were saying. They're monsters. Filthy monsters, they..." But whether it was the pressure of my deadline or her own reluctance, Lindsay stopped talking.

"Yeah," Jen added, "and they're doing to Shondra what they did to me, making it all her fault. And she was just trying to protect herself. They're just like saying she's a crazy liar and she's not."

"And the other thing," Lindsay interrupted, trying to be considerate of my time bind, "is we were hoping you could tell us what's going on with Shondra. She's disappeared."

"Have you spoken with Coach Adams?" They shook their heads. I wasn't sure what to tell them, I wasn't up to speed yet. I tried to put it as neutrally as I could. "There was a problem with an overdose last night...she had to go to the hospital."

They exchanged scared looks. "Is she going to be okay?" Lindsay asked.

"We've got an important game on Wednesday," Jen added. "Will she be able to play? Because she's like...well, she's wonderful. She's got this thing where...I don't know how to describe it...she makes us all better players when we're around her."

"I hope she'll be able to play. We'll know more later this morning. Probably your coach can tell you, but if you'd like to give me your phone numbers, I can at least leave you a message when I know more?" Bobby, who had his pen ready, wrote them down. "Is that it?"

They looked at each other. At the floor, the ceiling, the buffet, and back at each other again. Never at me or Bobby. Finally, Lindsay caught a breath and said, in a surprisingly small voice, "You tell them, Jen...you're the one who...it was your idea."

Jen's thumbs began their dance again. She hesitated and then I saw her decide to trust me. "Maybe you'll think I'm completely crazy for saying this. Only Lindsay didn't, which was what gave me the courage to come tell you. I know what the cops are saying and I know what Mr. Chambers and Dean Dunham and all of them are saying...but I think...that is I don't believe...I mean ..."

She raised her head and looked at me, tears filling her nice brown eyes. "Yes, of course you'll think I'm crazy, but I don't believe that Alasdair is dead."

## CHAPTER TWENTY

She would have run away if I hadn't gotten between her and the door. She was already out of her chair, heading fast in that direction. Luckily, I've logged my time in Coach Lemieux's Fitness Camp—Andre loves all sport and outdoor activities—so I was just able to beat her to the door. Even at a distance, I could feel the nervous vibrations of her body. Her fear was every bit as strong as her sense of duty.

"Look," I said, "You can't drop a bombshell like that and then run for it. You came here to help Shondra. You haven't done that if you bolt and run."

I took a breath, stepping back to give her more space. "Why do you think Alasdair isn't dead?"

But she was too upset. "I need to go," she said. "Please. Lindsay will tell you." It was predictable teenage behavior, demand time and attention for something important, then panic and flee. She stared at my immovable chest and blurted, "Maybe it's hateful but I was so glad he was dead and I could stop looking over my shoulder. Please," she repeated. "Let me go." I stood aside and she ran.

Lindsay, right behind her, paused only long enough to whisper, "She says she saw him last night."

Dammit, this was not what I needed right now. What on earth was really going on on this campus? They ought to rename the place St. Matthews Asylum for the Intermittently Insane. Too many strange things had happened since I took this job. I hoped I never had another one like it. But it was a job, and Bobby was staring at me with a look of desperation so I shoved Jen and Lindsay's suggestions that the administration condoned abuse of female students to a back burner.

186

"Is it just me," he said, "or is everyone in this place crazy?"

"It's not you."

He smiled. "That's what I thought, but it's so easy to doubt yourself when everything seems wrong. This place…it's like no one is in charge. Or like we are. Everyone's waiting for direction and when I tell them what to do…well, first they're cautious, like I'm supposed to be yelling instead of speaking, and then when they're sure I'm not going to yell…they just get so grateful and go do what I tell them."

He shrugged his broad shoulders. "Most places, we're walking a fine line, trying to do our job without stepping on any toes." Another endearing Bobby smile. "These people don't seem to have any toes."

"Chambers has toes enough for the lot of 'em. And you haven't met her yet, but his wife is a tyrant who made everyone's life miserable. Apparently, she's had a breakdown or something. But part of his failure of leadership stems from allowing her play a role in management. When she fell apart, he was so distracted he didn't step up when the crisis occurred."

"That explains some things."

I dashed to the buffet for more food. I'd had enough experience with St. Matts hospitality to know this might be our only meal. "How'd it go yesterday?" I said. "And what's on our agenda for today?"

Bobby extracted some sheets and passed them to me. "We had a fairly good success rate yesterday, reaching the parents, and they took the news pretty well. There were some we couldn't reach, of course, and a few concerned enough to be flying in." He shrugged. "You always get that. We worked until pretty late in the evening, and Dean Dunham was going to try some of them again this morning. We promised them a written update as soon as we can prepare one. A letter from the Headmaster."

He shook his head. "Only I'm damned if I know what to tell them. Do you?"

I was the partner, so I was where the buck stopped. But like

Bobby, I had no idea what the police knew or whether the investigation had made any progress. I had no idea what Jamison Jones' side of the story was or whether there would be some new set of questions or level of crisis raised by his defense. As for what was going on on this campus? My experience so far suggested we ought to contact all the parents, tell them to come get their kids and take them somewhere safe.

I shook my head. "Truthfully, Bobby, I have no idea what's going on, nor any idea how to find out. That's the first priority on my list today. What's on your agenda?"

"Same as yours—figure out what's going on—at least, the official position." He glanced toward the door. "Never mind what the truth may be...and start working on a letter to the parents. Draft another press release, probably, something about the students and faculty mourning the loss of a fellow student and pulling together in a supportive community in this time of shock and grief."

He glanced toward the ceiling, as if seeking heavenly for-giveness for taking liberties with the truth. "Brief the faculty and staff about the status of things. Get feedback from them about the emotional state of the student population. You?"

"I've got to work on security issues with Chambers. I don't know if you heard, but last night the resident advisors were lured out of Cabot Hall, where Shondra Jones lives, and her room was trashed. I've also got to work on communication. There are no systems for keeping in touch and no one's checking their messages. It's hard to convince them of anything when I can't get them to listen."

"Badly trashed?" he interrupted.

"Destroyed."

"They'll say she did that."

"Right. That's how it's supposed to look. But I don't think she did. When we couldn't find her at the dorm, Cullin Margolin, some security guys, and I went to the gym looking for her. We found her unconscious on a couch in her coach's office. Looked like an overdose. Security took her off to the hospital. That's something else we need to deal with. Students will have heard about that and want to know the story. About which I have no clue. Nor any idea who hit me over the head. Or why."

Bobby wore his worried look. He's been through enough disasters with me to be wary. "Maybe we should reconsider this whole project, Thea. Seriously. No matter how good we are, we can't do a decent job without our client's cooperation. Without something at least vaguely resembling the truth. And I think ..."

He held up a hand to stop my protests. "Look, we've been through a lot together. You and me, Suzanne, all of us at EDGE. Our reputation won't suffer if we back away from one difficult client. It might if we don't. I watched Chambers yesterday. Not only does he have no idea how to handle this, he doesn't care. I don't see how we can make him care. We need to trust our instincts. Mine says we're perched on the edge of a tar pit."

I thought we were already in the tar pit. I just hoped we could still get back to solid ground. But much as I wanted to pack and go home, I was a sucker for people in trouble. Not Chambers and Dunham and the St. Matthews trustees. Much of the trouble they were in was of their own making. I worried about Gregor MacGregor, who, despite his bombast, had suffered a terrible loss. I worried about Shondra and Jamison, and young girls like Lindsay and Jennifer who clearly weren't living in a safe environment.

Yeah. I know. The world's a hard place and everyone—even vulnerable students—needs to learn to live in it. But there are many ways to learn. Getting fed alcohol and attacked was pretty far down my list of appropriate learning experiences. Being further betrayed by the responsible adults was even lower on the list. And getting seduced into leaving your home and coming to an institution that promised to serve *in loco parentis*, only to find yourself abandoned, was an outright breach of contract.

So I didn't want to give up. But Bobby wasn't giving up, either. "Let's call Suzanne and see what she says. Get a third party involved," he suggested cautiously, knowing how prickly I can be. "Someone who isn't so close to the situation."

We were a business, not a democracy, but I didn't want Bobby to feel like he didn't have a voice and I certainly didn't want him to think about quitting. We were already short on staff, with no noticeable diminution in work. He pulled out his phone and dialed Suzanne's home number, got her voicemail, and left a message for her to call us as soon as possible.

"When she calls, we'll both take a break and discuss this with her," I said. "Until then, we soldier on, okay?"

Soldier on. More battle imagery. What was it with our language? Sports and war, sports and war. Motherhood is an unending twenty year commitment, at a minimum, but no one ever says "mother on," even though soldiers are more likely to get a night's sleep. Oh well. I was the one who'd used it. "You want to ride together?"

He gave a non-committal shrug. Not a happy camper. Well, I wasn't a happy camper, either. I had a bruised head and had missed a night's sleep. Like Shondra Jones, I don't take well to being messed with.

I shrugged, too. It seemed like the gesture which fit this situation best. "I don't like this place...this situation...any more than you do, Bobby, but I'm worried about these kids. The ones who were just here, and the rest of the student body. As you pointed out, no one's taking charge. They're trying to work under stress and in an information void. That's not a good place to be when you're trying to learn."

He started to shake his head, but I pressed on. "At least we know what's supposed to be done. We can try to make it happen. If we fold our tents and go home, it's the students who'll suffer. I don't want to leave without trying to put things in better shape than they are now."

I stopped there, knowing the rest of my motivation would worry Bobby. I wanted to know who'd attacked me. And why.

"Okay," he said. "Want me to drive?"

"You know what? I think I'd better drive myself. If we can get things under control, I'd like to visit Jamison Jones."

"As long as it's not because of my car."

"How likely is that?" He just grinned and thumped away up the stairs. Bobby has a powder blue 1968 Mustang he's totally in love with.

The rustling paper bag in my briefcase reminded me I should have given the pill container and empty can to Bushnell. I probably would have if he hadn't been such a big jerk. Well, I wasn't carrying them around all day, and given the nocturnal phone calls, and the damage to Shondra's room, I wasn't leaving them here. That meant the trunk of my car. My traveling closet. I'd once hidden a controversial briefcase in there and a nosy cop, after picking through the empty coffee cups and donut bags, assorted dry cleaning, beach chairs, and other items, had glanced at it without interest and moved on.

I stopped to tell Mrs. Mitchell we'd want the rooms for another night. She looked a little worried, checked on her computer, and then smiled. "Not a problem," she said, despite Bushnell's rude behavior. She was a very forgiving woman.

I wasn't optimistic that we'd finish today. There were too many undercurrents we hadn't explored. Too many things happening. Maybe, if we were lucky, Bobby could leave. But I wasn't leaving until I'd figured out what was really going on, even if it meant another day away from Andre.

"*She's* in there," Wendy Grimm whispered, as I passed her desk.

I thought twice, in my guise of Thea the Human Towtruck, about putting myself into reverse and backing right out when I saw the line-up that awaited me. Along with Chambers' and Dunham's gloomy faces, the resurrected Miriam Chambers was there, coiffed and swathed in designer garb, and she looked like whatever she'd had for breakfast didn't agree with her. The only person who looked even vaguely welcoming was Frank Woodson, and that could have been because his face was hidden behind a cup of Dunkin Donuts coffee.

I set down my briefcase and pulled out a chair. "All right." I forced a bright, unnatural smile. "Where would you like to begin?"

"Why don't you tell us?" Miriam Chambers said, running a riff with her bright red nails down her chair arm. "Isn't that what we hired you for? Managing the situation?"

*Lady, you didn't hire me for anything. Last I saw you, you were trying to fire me.* No one bothered to ask how I was, but I hadn't expected them to. I looked at Chambers. "What's the news on Shondra Jones?"

Chambers looked to Woodson for the answer. "She's okay," Woodson said. "Not a happy camper, but getting your stomach pumped is never pleasant. They'll let her go later today. But I guess we won't know what she took until they get the tox screen back."

I thought we already knew what she'd taken, but maybe this was another failure of communication. "They are running some tests?"

Woodson shrugged. "Said they would."

I felt like I was nickel and diming the day away, but these questions needed to be asked and answered. "What about her room?" I directed this one to Craig Dunham. "Right now, she's got no place to come back to."

"Well, what does she expect?" Miriam Chambers sniffed. "She did it to herself, after all."

"We don't know that." I wasn't getting into a pissing contest with her. Not with so much work to be done. "Maybe you could get Jenna Adams and her teammates working on that? I bet they'd like to do something to help. And you must have spare furniture."

"Good idea." He shoved back his chair. "If you'll excuse me, I'll take care of that."

"Get Margolin to help. And remind Coach Adams that Shondra will need clothes. Maybe there are some tall teammates who can help." I knew how difficult it was to find clothes when you were tall.

I turned to Woodson. "Are Bushnell and his people still nosing around?" Whatever Andre said, Bushnell would have to do something spectacularly good to revise my opinion of him.

Woodson's grim nod suggested his opinion of Bushnell wasn't much higher than mine. "Any idea what they're looking for?"

"Clues?" he suggested. "What I hear is, Jones won't say a word. Not one damned word. Kid lawyered up soon as the cops grabbed him...guess that's no surprise, given his background. Most of the kids here wouldn't know the rules 'til they called Daddy and Mommy, but Jones, he just said he wanted a lawyer and wasn't a damned thing they could do." He sounded proud of Jamison, which made me wonder whether they knew each other, maybe had some kind of relationship.

"Do we know anything about the cause of death yet? Any autopsy results?"

"I think they did that yesterday, but Bushnell is being pretty close-mouthed. Damned frustrated, too. I guess they thought they'd gotten one possible identifier fingerprint, and then it turned out they couldn't find a single one in MacGregor's room to match it to."

"Sounds like even if Bushnell is being close-mouthed, someone is talking. Maybe they ought to look for prints in Shondra's room." It felt like something zinged rapidly among them, but it was nothing I could read on their faces. "Does Jamison have a lawyer?"

"Oh, yeah," Woodson said. "Hotshot named Tamora Fleming, comes from the biggest firm in New Hampshire. I hear she does mostly white collar crime." His lined face lifted in a passing smile. "Course, given our population, and the identity of the victim, I guess you might call it a white collar crime." Chambers and Dunham, both white collar types themselves, didn't look amused. But Woodson wasn't done. "And I hear she eats prosecutors for breakfast."

Chambers grimaced. Miriam gave a restless shift that in a younger woman would have been a flounce. "Frank, given how nervous our students are, maybe you ought to get out there and kind of...well, just be around," Chambers said. "Don't you think?"

Woodson shrugged. "If you're done with me." He shifted his

eyes to me and I thought I detected sympathy. "Before I go, young lady. I hear you got kind of banged up last night. Donnie, that's the guy who found you, filed kind of an incoherent report. I thought maybe we could take a few minutes," his hesitation was deliberate, "when you've got some time, and try to write something a little more organized? Be kinda nice to figure out who the bastard was."

"I don't know how much help I can be, Mr. Woodson. I didn't see much. But I'll be glad to try. It is upsetting to think something like that could happen on this campus." I deliberately shifted my own eyes to Todd Chambers. "Especially when we're making such a big effort to reassure the students and their families that they're safe."

"Exactly," he agreed. "Well. Better get out there and act reassuring, huh? I'm at 774-1202. Give a call when you're free."

Dunham was gone and Woodson was leaving. Where the heck was Argenti? Soon I'd be all alone here with the Chambers. Sure enough, the door had barely closed behind him when Miriam Chambers pounced. "You have got to help us out here," she said in her low, husky voice. "Keeping the parents calm is all important."

Wasn't that what we'd all spent yesterday working on?

"I told Todd we should expel Jamison and Shondra, make it clear we were taking appropriate steps to rid the place of trouble-making elements. What do you think?"

The words just tumbled out. "I think you must be out of your mind. And I think you should stop trying to meddle in the affairs of this school, because your judgment is awful."

"You're the one who meddles," she said. "I'm not at all sorry about what happened last night. And now that we've got things back under control, I can't allow you to do anything which will interfere with Todd's legacy."

She gave me a slightly loopy smile, picked up the heavy vase of flowers from the table beside her, and flung it at my head.

## CHAPTER TWENTY-ONE

Having amply demonstrated how good her judgment was, she gave her husband a melting smile, mouthed, "Now she'll leave," and glided from the room. Chambers took a step toward me, a step toward the door, then flung out his arms and simply stood there. "I'm sorry...I...you know that...well...Miriam isn't well...and sometimes she...that is, she didn't mean anything by all that."

He gave up his pathetically inadequate explanation. "Are you all right?"

I was wet and bruised, decked with and surrounded by mangled posies, and all I could think of to say was so inappropriate it was perfect. "She's got a hell of an arm."

"Yes. Well. Miriam works out."

I thought she wasn't working out, or at least, that she was working out very badly. But if he didn't already know this, he didn't need to hear it from me. Or couldn't. People have funny receptors where relationships are concerned. Luckily, I hadn't taken off my coat. And being a spiller, I tended to wear dark colors, so the front of my dark green sweater didn't look wet and neither did my long black skirt. Dressing for success, Thea Kozak style.

If I'd had more time, I could have entertained myself designing a line of work clothes for women in challenging professions. Chic Tyvek blouses topped by Kevlar vests in feminine colors. Bullet proof, control top panty hose. Belts with pockets for PDAs and holsters for guns. Steel-toed pumps. But Chambers was waiting.

So far, I had successfully survived both nocturnal and diurnal attacks, and kept my temper, a feat my mother would have marveled at. I stepped out of the circle of flowers, pulled

195

off my raincoat, and dropped it over the back of a chair. The bone in my wrist, which had deflected the vase, was stinging. Otherwise, it was just another small incident in the life of Thea Kozak, educational consultant. I opened my briefcase and pulled out my notes. Neither rain nor sleet, nor snow nor thugs nor flying flowers were deterring me from my appointed rounds.

"Sit down," I said. "We've got work to do."

"I should check on Miriam," he said.

You do and I quit. I didn't say it aloud. Mentally, I already had one foot out the door. I wasn't walking through it, though, until I'd done what I could to stabilize things. Nor was I giving him the satisfaction of sending me packing. I wanted to be in charge of time and place. "Not now. You have to think about your students, Todd. They're all out there wondering what the hell's going on. It's your job to give them some answers."

"But there's nothing to tell them. We don't know anything."

"Then start finding out. You know that their parents have been contacted, right? And that Shondra is okay? That the police are proceeding with their investigations? And what about funeral arrangements? A memorial service? Have you thought about any of that?"

He had that sullen little boy look again. "It wouldn't hurt to simply reassure them that life is going on as usual," I said, "or to tell them that counselors will continue to be available. Treat it like a reassuring daily update, putting the best spin on it that you can."

Instead of responding, he walked over to the window. I went on anyway. "I doubt if many of them will have heard about the attack on me, so we won't mention that."

"They don't know you anyhow," he said.

"Oh, get real, Todd." I wanted to shake him until some sense rattled loose. "You honestly think it's more reassuring to them, the day after a campus murder, that a stranger is attacked on the campus? How is that supposed to be comforting? You can't have a very high opinion of your student body if you think they're indifferent to the welfare of strangers. Or that they can't see the relevance of such an incident to themselves."

"I just meant …"

"Sit down, will you please," I said. It was making me crazy the way he hovered there, like any moment he was going to stop listening altogether and drift out the door. "I know exactly what you meant. What I'm saying is that you have to start thinking before you open your mouth, because not everyone is going to give you the benefit of the doubt."

He might be indecisive, but I was clicking into gear. "You have to start thinking about covering your ass. Indifference to me is one thing, a failure to warn, or to take appropriate steps to beef up security could land you in a heap of trouble. You don't want to risk being accused of providing an inadequately safe environment. What if we hadn't found Shondra? What if it wasn't accidental overdose or even a deliberate one on her part? What if she's a victim?"

His face hardened. Shondra Jones as a victim was something he refused to consider. I climbed down off my soapbox. We didn't have time for an argument. "Look…what if it hadn't been Shondra? Last night, someone lured the residential adults out of that dorm, leaving all the girls vulnerable. Can you imagine the consequences if something had happened to one of them—a fire, some injury or assault? We can hope that word of that hasn't gotten around. But you have to take steps to ensure that it won't happen again."

I felt like I was talking to a wall. But he wasn't the first wall I'd spoken to. It was one of my specialties—I was the woman who talked to walls. "Look, I know you're distracted by concerns about your wife and the principal donor of your new arts center. And it is the most awful thing that can happen to a headmaster, having one student accused of killing another. But that's your reality right now. You have to deal with it. Getting your school sued and yourself fired won't look great on your resume."

"I don't know," he said, finally sitting down. "I don't know what to do. Miriam says if I get rid of the troublemakers, the parents will respect me for being tough and putting St. Matthews back on track."

No sense fighting him on this. "In the long run, she may be right. If you do have troublemakers, and they are removed from the school with strict adherence to your own rules and procedures, that's fine. But your situation won't be improved by a sudden purge without due process. If anything, that will make your students more nervous, which is the last thing you need."

"So I can get rid of them, I just need to hold some kind of hearing, is that it?"

"According to your rules." Trying to draw him back to more immediate issues, I asked, "Do you have any idea who might have been behind last night's shenanigans?"

He looked blank. Maybe 'shenanigans' was not in his vocabulary. "Who lured your resident advisors away from the dorm?"

"No idea." He was about as convincing as the four-year-old saying he didn't take the cookies. Now, I've had the benefit, if you can call it that, of being interrogated by some of the meanest guys in the business. I could have tried those lessons on Todd Chambers. But I didn't have my gun or my back up thugs, and anyway, what was the point? I was trying to help him limp through this crisis. Once things were stable, EDGE could make a gracious departure and he could shoot himself in as many feet as he wanted.

"Maybe you and Frank Woodson can put your heads together and come up with a plan to ensure that it doesn't happen again. Maybe he has an opinion about whether security needs to be beefed up, too. He seems like an okay guy." I'd met security directors who weren't.

"Frank's okay," he agreed. Except it didn't seem much like agreement. "You know...I think we talked about this before...I'm not too happy having some outsider coming in like this and telling me what to do."

For a minute, it had looked like he was going to work with

me. Now he was back to being defiant. I was getting close to my wit's end. Maybe it was only my temper's end. My wits still seemed to be about me. There was something not quite believable in his behavior. Last night at the infirmary and again today, there was an insolent quality to his responses, as though someone or something was encouraging him in his indifference.

I was pondering what to do or say that didn't sound like an order yet might move him off the mark, when the door banged open. Charles Argenti strode in, nodded at me, and helped himself to a chair. Like Woodson, he had a Dunkin Donuts coffee. I wanted one, too. I'm pretty well addicted to DD's coffee. I guessed their mothers hadn't told them not to eat or drink in front of others if they weren't willing to share.

"So," Argenti said, "how is everyone this morning?"

Something else mothers will tell you—if you can't say anything good, don't say anything. Besides, Chambers didn't want me running things. I held my tongue and let him respond. What he said nearly blew my socks off. "At least there haven't been any more problems."

Could I assume that he and Argenti had exchanged information after I saw him last night? It didn't make sense to assume anything, did it? I waited for Argenti's sharp eyes to turn to me. "And how are you, Thea?"

"My head still hurts, and someone made hang-up calls to my room every twenty minutes all night, so I didn't get much sleep. Otherwise, I'm fine."

He studied me curiously. "Something happened to your head?"

Chambers was staring daggers at me, but I didn't care. If looks could kill, the human race wouldn't have survived this long. I told Argenti about my nocturnal assailant, and then, in case he was in the dark, I told him about Shondra's overdose, the trashing of her room and the missing dorm residents. Argenti had hired me and he needed to know this stuff.

When I was done, he slid his eyes back to Todd Chambers.

He had hawk's eyes, penetrating and a little scary, and a slightly hawkish nose as well, which made his face, when he wasn't smiling, quite fierce. "This is your version of nothing happening?" When Chambers didn't answer, he said, "And how is Miriam?"

"Doing much better."

Able to leap small buildings in a single bound. Cause more trouble than a truckload of monkeys. Maybe Miriam had hit me last night. She certainly didn't like me. But I was sure my attacker had been male.

"Todd, let's start planning what you're going to tell your students, shall we?" I was trying to nudge him gently. I might as well have whacked him with a 2x4.

"Look," he said, getting to his feet so abruptly I was grateful there weren't more flowers to be flung, "who is in charge here, you or me?" I wasn't about to dignify that with an answer. "You can't just barge in here and try to take over."

I had no idea why he was being so absurd, although I suspected it was about driving me away. "Believe me, I am not interested in doing your job, Todd. I'm here to help *you* do it. I'm here because I've had more experience than you at dealing with situations like this. I can identify the issues and areas of concern and suggest methods for dealing with them. Ultimately, whether you take that advice lies with you. It appears that you are choosing not to."

I put the papers back in my briefcase and faced Argenti. "I'm sorry. You have a very difficult situation here. However, as long as Mr. Chambers persists in being hostile and combative and rejecting my advice, my remaining here is a waste of everyone's time."

I picked up my wet raincoat, shook it, and draped it over my arm. "For the sake of the students, I hope someone will step up and act like a responsible adult. As I've told Mr. Chambers...St. Matthews leaves itself open to major problems by allowing such an unsafe campus situation."

"Thea...wait...please." Argenti followed me into the hall,

200

closing the door behind him. "We couldn't have gotten through yesterday without you, and we're not out of the woods yet. I know Todd's being a horse's ass, but please don't quit on us. Let me sit down with him and see what I can do. Give me an hour."

"You're his boss, but I don't know what you could do or say that's going to change his attitude, Charlie. He seems determined not to do anything that will improve the situation. It makes no sense to me."

"Give me an hour," he repeated.

"All right. An hour." I handed him a card with my cell phone number. "Call me and let me know what's going on."

Wendy Grimm was hovering several feet away. When Argenti and I moved apart, she looked at us nervously. "The hospital called wanting to know when we were going to pick up Shondra," she said. "I…I didn't know what to tell them."

I looked at Argenti and shrugged. "It's as good a way as any to spend an hour, I guess. What shall I do about Bobby Ryan?"

"Let him keep working," Argenti said. "I'll call you."

I got directions from Wendy and headed to my car, wishing I were going home. It would be a wonderful moment when I finally saw the last of St. Matthews in my rearview mirror. This was about as much fun as rubbing myself with sandpaper.

I blame my parents for my inability to walk away from things. Dad's a sweetheart at home, but the most tenacious lawyer imaginable when clients are involved, and my mom, for all that she sighs and whines about my overworked, dangerous life, modeled overwork and compulsive behavior for me every day of my youth.

I was pleased to see that there was security at the gate, checking people out as well as in, although the gray car leaving right behind me didn't stop for the waving guard and almost ran him down. The world is so full of impatient drivers. No wonder there's road rage. The idiots endanger us all.

I drove to the local hospital knowing that I was just trading one unpleasant situation for another. Shondra wouldn't welcome me with open arms or an open mind. And I was not feeling especially resilient. I think I'm wearing out faster than most people. As Indiana Jones says, "It's not the years, it's the mileage."

I took a few minutes in the parking garage to dredge up some compassion and patience. No sense in preaching it to others if I wasn't going to practice it myself.

The impatient gray car that had followed me from St. Matthews had gone past when I took the turn to the hospital, so I filed that one under paranoia and let it go.

She was waiting in a wheelchair in an empty, sterile room. She looked awful, gray-skinned and dishrag limp. Not what I would have expected from an athlete. But I didn't know what effect the drugs she'd taken could have, nor how much of this was the result of her brother's troubles. Her greeting was, "What the fuck are you doing here?" in a harsh, whispery voice.

"They sent me." She shrugged and that was the end of it.

I signed the offered paperwork on behalf of St. Matts—it was easier than denying responsibility or trying to explain my situation—and sprang her from the cold bright lights and antiseptic halls as quickly as I could. Hospitals give me the heebie-jeebies. I only have to walk through the doors and every broken bone and bit of scar tissue on my body starts to throb.

She didn't speak again until the car was moving. "I don't want to go back there," she said. "I want to go home."

I didn't blame her. "Be good if you could finish the semester. And the basketball season. Your teammates are counting on you."

"Yeah, right. Like they care."

"You know them better than I do, so maybe they don't, but two of them hiked over to The Swan first thing this morning to ask me if you were all right and if there was anything they could do."

"Which two?" Did I only imagine that she sounded slightly less sullen?

"Lindsay and Jen."

"Oh. Them." A long silence. "They're okay. But ..." Another silence.

I left her alone, figuring she'd get to what she wanted to say in her own good time. I drove slowly, because the trip wasn't very long, checking my mirror for the gray car. I didn't see it. It was only when we turned onto the road leading to St. Matts that I realized that I didn't know what I was bringing her back to. If she was coming back to chaos and destruction, an empty room, or something a bit more welcoming. I'd sent Craig Dunham off to put things right but I had no idea if he'd actually done it.

"Where do St. Matthews students go when they want to shop for clothes?"

"Home."

"What if they need a pair of shoes in the middle of the term? Or new underwear?"

"There's a bus to the Mall. Why, you need new underwear?"

"No. But I think you do."

"My grandmamma ..." She made a sound somewhere between a giggle and a sob, "...says clean underwear is important because a person never knows when they gonna...when they're going to...be taken to the hospital. Guess you saw my room, huh?"

"Did you do that?"

"What do you think?"

"I think you value a nice, neat space and whoever did it knew that about you."

"You can't be for real," Shondra snorted. "That is just way too close to the truth."

"And what is the truth?"

"They done it to get to me, yeah. That's the way things have been all along. But they were also looking for something."

"Any idea who 'they' are?"

"Everyone knows who they are. Alasdair's friends."

"And what were they looking for?"

"Something they didn't find." Triumph momentarily replaced the weariness in her voice.

"Which was?"

"A tiny surveillance camera that proved Alasdair had been in my room."

I'd seen 'nanny cams' advertised on late-night TV, but I'd never known anyone who'd used one. "If it wasn't in your room, where was it?"

"I don't know. I gave it to Jamison."

I almost drove the car off the road as a dozen questions flooded my mind. Where had he gotten it? Was it still around? How had Alasdair known and who were these friends of his who were still acting on his behalf? It was an 'ah ha, the plot thickens' moment. "And you don't know where he put it?"

"Nope. I guess we'll just have to ask him."

It looked like underwear was going to be postponed. We were taking a field trip to the jail.

## CHAPTER TWENTY-TWO

I made a u-turn and headed back toward town. Then, realizing I had no idea where I was going, I pulled over, got out my phone, and dialed Frank Woodson's number. "It's Thea Kozak," I said, when he answered. "I've got Shondra Jones here. We want to see her brother."

"And you don't know where you're going?"

"Nor what our chances of success are."

"So you called me." He sounded pleased. He started reeling off directions until I stopped him. I'm a competent navigator, but I can't hold more than three turns in my head. After that, I need to write things down.

I fished out a pencil. "Go ahead."

"It's easy," he said, going over it again. "When you get there, ask for Billy Turner. He used to be one of my guys. Works there Sundays. Tell him you're working with me over here at St. Matthews." Brisk and to the point. I thought he was finished, when he surprised me by asking, "How's she doing?"'

"She's okay. Quiet. You want to talk to her?"

"That's okay. She spilling her guts into your welcoming ear?"

"How likely is that?"

He laughed. "Don't forget about me, okay? Tell Jamison I said hello."

So my instinct had been right. There was some relationship. Enough so he wasn't distancing himself when Jamison was in trouble like everyone else was.

"That Woodson?" Shondra mumbled. She made a face when I nodded.

I handed her my scribbled notes. "You're the navigator." I shot away from the curb, glad to finally be doing something. I'm an active fixer, and so far, I'd spent too much of my time here arguing about whether I'd be allowed to do my job. I thought I caught of a glimpse of a gray car, but gray cars are common, and it didn't get close enough for me to be sure.

At the jail, Billy Turner's name greased the skids, and after only half a mountain of bureaucracy, we were ushered into a room where we could speak with Jamison. He arrived looking weary, the jail-issued jumpsuit so meager on his big frame he looked like a kid who'd outgrown his clothes. And he looked as much like the killer of another human being as I did. But then, I was, wasn't I? I put that thought back in the locked box where I keep the baddest stuff and brought my attention back to here and now.

Despite his own plight, his first words were, "Hey, Shonny, what happened to you?"

"Something I drank," she said. "Might ask you the same thing."

"Still tryin' to figure that out," he said. "Me and my lawyer. I get a call to meet Alasdair and talk things over and the next thing I know, I'm in here."

"He any good?" Shondra interrupted. "Your lawyer?"

"I hear *she's* the best in New Hampshire." He stopped, staring at me as though he'd just realized who I was. "What's she doing here?"

"She drove me."

"I wonder why?" His handsome face went tight and unfriendly. "She works for them, Shonny. You know that. I'm not sayin' shit in front of her."

I wasn't surprised he was wary, after what had happened, plus, he'd probably been warned by his lawyer not to speak to anyone. And I couldn't deny it. I did work for them. I wanted to hang around and listen to their talk. I wanted to ask him a dozen questions of my own. But Jamison was strong-willed. If I stayed, he wouldn't talk, and I'd brought her here so they could talk.

"That's okay," I said. "I'll leave. I know you two need some time."

"Appreciate it," he said. More manners and poise after two nights in jail than Todd Chambers would ever have.

The guard let me out and I went back to a depressing vanilla waiting room. I hadn't brought my briefcase and the only reading materials that weren't tattered with half the pages ripped out were a fishing magazine and yesterday's local paper. Though this whole job felt like a fishing expedition, I didn't see how flies and lures and waders and bass boats would help, so I chose the paper.

I skimmed through the predictable stories, mostly puff and speculation, about Alasdair's death. When I'd exhausted those, I wandered through zoning flaps, tedious reports of the state legislature, local who's who, fender-benders, two small robberies, a dramatic domestic stand-off, and a bunch of people gone missing. The missing included an eighty-five year old with Alzheimer's, two experienced hikers lost in the woods, a rebellious thirteen-year-old girl who had failed to come home from school, and a seventeen-year-old boy who'd gone out to a party and never come home.

It looked like the cops had had a busy weekend looking for all these strays, even without the complications of Alasdair's death. It's always a surprise to read the police blotters in local papers and realize how much goes on we're unaware of. Not me, though. I've become too aware. An empty car by the roadside, a snatch of overheard conversation, someone giving me a funny look, even a car that stays behind me too long—they all get me wondering. Which was why I noticed gray cars.

It felt like I'd been waiting for hours, but when I checked my watch, they'd only had about forty minutes. I shifted impatiently, staring at the door. Argenti still hadn't called. It was time for me to get back to St. Matts and see if I had a job. I was half-hoping I didn't.

It would be a first, though, getting canned twice by the same client. A first, and a last time I let myself get in so deep without a clearer set of ground rules and a more malleable client.

Chambers was as responsive as a bucket of wet cement. Still, my ego was bruised. I'd gotten pretty confident that I was good at this, and I was doing such a bad job here. I couldn't get anyone to listen, or to talk. I couldn't even get them to acknowledge that they had a job to do, let alone get them to do it.

I sighed, folded up the newspaper, and checked my phone for messages, just in case Argenti had called and it hadn't gotten through. There were no messages, not even one from Suzanne. That was another problem. Not only were things going badly here, they seemed to be going pretty badly back at the office. I couldn't think of another time when Suzanne hadn't been right on the ball. Yes, she had a lot on her plate, with Paul's new job and a child, but plenty of women had full plates and still returned phone calls. It made me wonder if things were okay with her.

I was trying to call Suzanne when a droopy, teary-eyed Shondra shuffled through the door, looking like she'd been the one in jail. "Can we go now?" she asked.

"Think you can make it to the car?"

"I'll make it," she said, grimly. "Gotta get back there. I've got stuff to do."

So she'd changed her mind about going home. "Stuff for Jamison?"

"Maybe."

"Maybe you should let me help you, Shondra. You're in no shape to be doing anything but rest right now."

"I got no time to rest," she said. "Got things to do."

"Like?"

"Like none of your business."

Maybe it was something in the school's water that made them all so difficult. Maybe they weren't to blame. Maybe they were innocent victims of some subtle poison. Or lead. It would be great to have it all explained so easily. Test the water, fix the problem, explain away Chambers' miserable attitude, his wife's craziness, Jamison's crime, the dark deeds everyone hinted at and refused to describe, and Alasdair's evil, manipulative

208

behavior. It was a pleasing, if totally unrealistic thought.

"Sometimes you can't do it alone, you know. Sometimes you have to let people help." My phone rang. I ignored it. "You told Jamison it was something you drank that sent you to the hospital. What was it? Where did you drink it?" She ignored me. "Look, Shondra, I may not be your friend, but I'm not your enemy. I want to help you and I want to keep you safe. I know that's not the message you've been getting from the Administration at St. Matts, but that's what I'm here for."

"They hired you to make sure I'm safe?" She gave a bitter little laugh. "You really think I'm dumb enough to believe that, after how they been? Girl, you believe anything they's telling you, and you're the one who's dumb around here. The only thing they want from me is I should be gone and stop botherin' them."

"If you think I'm working for them, you have no reason to trust me. Try looking at it this way. I don't work for Mr. Chambers or Mr. Dunham or any other individual in the administration. I work for the school. And St. Matthews' School is you and your brother and all the other students who have a right to a safe and supportive environment."

She gave me one of those devastating teenage looks, packed with cynicism and disbelief. "Sound like you readin' from some brochure," she said, making 'brochure' obscenely long and unsavory.

"It does," I agreed, "but that's why I'm here. To help them make things normal and safe. Part of that is learning the truth. This whole mess happened because they didn't want to know the truth. They wanted to believe in their own reality—that Alasdair was a good kid, you were a troublemaker, and that there wasn't a predatory atmosphere on the campus. They disciplined and let things go based on their desire to preserve that reality. But it can't go on. You and Jamison and Alasdair aren't the only ones affected here. There are other students at risk, others who aren't heard or believed."

Something flickered in her eyes. Recognition? Curiosity?

She wasn't about to let me find out. "I don't care," she said. "I've got to think about me and Jamison. Gotta figure out what I can do to help him."

"And I'm trying to help you."

"Don't want your help," she said.

I felt ten years old again, arguing with my brother. "Maybe you don't want it, but maybe you need it. And maybe, just maybe, and I'll bet you haven't considered this—I need your help. I need to figure out what's going on at St. Matthews and you can help me do that."

"Like I care about any of that."

I stopped the car so abruptly she gasped, the car behind me whipping around with an angry blast of its horn. "Goddammit, Shondra, get over yourself. You care about helping your brother, don't you, after he got into this mess trying to help you? Maybe you're so busy being stubborn and proud you're missing the point here. Your brother is accused of murder, plain and simple. Whether it's murder one, murder two, or manslaughter, he's looking at spending a substantial portion of the rest of his life behind bars. That's his reality right now. He can have the best lawyer in the world, but unless she's got something to work with, she can't help him."

Maybe I needed to get over myself, too. Here I was, a professional adult, sitting in my car yelling at a pathetic, sick, scared silly sixteen-year-old girl only an hour out of the hospital. Modeling both impulse control and compassionate behavior. I was formulating an apology when she started to cry and my phone rang.

It was Suzanne, practically my best friend in all the world, the woman who knows me better than anyone except Andre. Without preamble, she announced, in a peremptory tone she hadn't used with me since I was her novice employee, that after consultation with Charles Argenti, they had decided she needed to join the team. She'd be leaving soon and we'd all be getting together this evening for a conference about how to proceed.

She didn't use the word "replace" but that's what she meant.

It represented failure on a scale I couldn't ever recall experiencing and the triumph of Todd Chambers' misguided notion that Suzanne, because she understood the plight of the headmaster and his wife, would be more willing to accept their plans and suggestions without probing beneath the surface than an abrasive, suspicious person like me.

"We'll need to talk before the meeting," I said, "so you'll know what you're getting into."

"Mr. Argenti gave me a pretty good idea," she said.

"He may have given you a pretty good idea of the party line," I countered, "but there's a lot more going on here than they'll be willing to tell you, and you are going to need to know it."

"You sound positively paranoid, Thea."

"Negatively paranoid, actually. Or at least negative. Before you try to deal with Curly, Larry, and Moe, I'm going to do my best to explain who's on first and when to duck. Let's plan on dinner at The Swan…that's the bed and breakfast where you'll be staying. What time is good for you?"

"Actually …" She sounded reluctant to tell me this. "The Chambers invited me to stay with them." Something they had not done for me. Back then, they hadn't recognized how important it was to control the information flow. It wasn't uncommon for campus visitors to stay at the Headmaster's house.

"Decide for yourself," I said, "but I wouldn't recommend it. For one thing, you'll starve. She's the world's worst cook. You'll also lose the opportunity to get some distance from the situation, as well as losing privacy and a chance to meet with Bobby alone. Believe me, you'll need space and objectivity to deal with this group."

"We'll see," she said, temporizing. I had a sudden panicked moment, wondering what had been said about me and whether she might have actually believed it. We're all subject to moments when our self-confidence suddenly fails. A frustrating two days, a head injury, being attacked verbally and by flying flowers, and now this.

"Dinner at The Swan at six, and we'll take it from there," she said.

I agreed, bit my lip, and didn't tell her to bring a portable polygraph machine. Suzanne is a competent grown-up. Instead, I fished a packet of tissues out of my bag and handed it to Shondra. "How would you feel about some lunch?" I asked.

"Dining hall slop?"

"I was thinking about burgers and fries. Maybe a milkshake?" Was I making a mistake? This girl had just had her stomach pumped. I based the offer on my own experience. Generally, whatever has happened to me, the instant I'm sprung from the hospital, I want to go someplace where there is real food and stuff my face.

I pointed at the big red and white sign looming just ahead. "Friendly's?"

"I guess." I flicked on my signal and turned into the parking lot.

We were halfway to the door when she put on the brakes, planted her hands on her hips and turned toward me. "Just so's we're clear," she said. "Don't you be thinking you can buy me a burger and get me to spill my guts."

"I was kind of hoping you wouldn't spill your guts. Maybe we should go for tea and toast."

"Talk," she amended, but she smiled. "I hate tea and toast. Who was that on the phone? You didn't sound too happy."

"My partner, Suzanne. It seems that the St. Matthews administration has decided my working style is too abrasive and they want to bring in someone more malleable."

"They'se getting rid of you?"

I shrugged. "Not easily."

"So you be leaving," she said, as though I hadn't spoken. "Your partner...she's gonna go along with them and their lies?" Another long pause. "Not that I like you or anything. But, other than Coach Adams, you're 'bout the only person I've met around here gives a damn 'bout me and Jamison."

We ordered and sat silently until the food came. She slowly

212

picked up a dozen fries, one by one, and ate them without looking at me. "I sure wish Jamison was here. Wish I knowed if it was safe to talk to you."

"Why don't you try me and see?" I watched her face closely, hoping my eagerness wasn't showing. There had been so many veiled hints of sinister undercurrents at St. Matts. Shondra might pose as a loner, but I'd bet she knew plenty from her teammates, from her brother, and from the serious listening she'd done once she knew she had to handle her problems herself.

She studied me with wide, uncertain eyes, as though, if she stared hard enough, she could see right into me and find some answers. She was desperate to talk and so unwilling to trust.

"You can stop any time you feel uncomfortable, Shondra. Maybe you could start by telling me what happened last night?"

"No." It was a considering no, not a dismissive one. "No, let's talk about that camera," she said, staring down at her long, flexing fingers. "About what we do with what's on it. I know where it's hid."

# CHAPTER TWENTY-THREE

Not wanting to seem too eager, I picked at my own fries, waiting to see where she'd go with this. "Yeah. I guess. I mean, I guess it wouldn't hurt, you knowin' that, seeing as you know about Alasdair anyway."

I poured the rest of my milkshake into my glass, wondering how quickly the ill-effects of not spending time in the gym began to show. I'd read somewhere muscle starts breaking down after forty-eight hours. A year to build it, two days to lose it. It seemed perfectly in keeping with the rest of my life. Seven years to build a career where I could come in and take charge and effectively help schools in trouble; a single week to get canned and sent packing twice.

To hell with my muscles. My spirit needed this chocolate. I was torn, though, whether to consume it or just smear it on my thighs and be done. I'm a big believer in efficiency.

"Hey," she said suspiciously, "what are you smiling about?"

"Chocolate."

"Oh." She gave me a puzzled look and went back to her fries.

"You about ready to go?"

"I guess. Don't exactly know what I'm going back to. You seen…saw…my room. Those motherfuckers don't do anything by halves. Ever."

"You know who did it?"

Another scathing teenage look. "Everybody does."

Was this just Shondra, or another ugly truth about the St. Matthews community? "What does that mean?"

"I mean, it's no secret Alasdair had this group he called the Neo-Skulls. Numb skulls, Jamison always said. Or that they targeted minorities. Chinks, Spics and Nigs, Alasdair used to say. He said it a lot 'til Mr. Sidaris got on him and threatened him with a month of early curfew. Alasdair used to say lots of ugly stuff. The coaches did what they could, but Mr. Chambers, he always let Alasdair off."

"Everybody knew about this? It was common knowledge on campus?"

"What do you think?"

"I think I want you to answer my question. I don't like to be guessing about things that may be important."

She dropped the fry she was holding and slid out of the booth. "Can we go now? I don't want to be talkin' 'bout this here. Someone might be listening."

More sensible than I, wasn't she? "Fine. Let's go." I pulled bills out of my wallet and dropped them on the table. She was already moving away. Fast. There was nothing like the reviving power of meat. It might not be PC, or whatever the term is for nutritionally correct. NC? But Andre and I were fervent believers in the restorative power of a good burger. Burgers. Chocolate. Hot bread. Red wine. Good bourbon. Yeah. We ate salads too. Plenty of salads. But after a hard day fighting bad guys, there was nothing like steak on the grill, baked potatoes, and a roll in the hay.

"You're smiling again." She'd stopped to wait for me. Hurrying to catch up, I almost mowed her down. Around us, people were staring. I'd forgotten what a sight we were. I was tall enough to draw subtle stares, while Shondra drew outright gapes.

"Thinking about my husband," I said, pushing her gently ahead of me down the aisle. She'd started talking and I didn't want to lose momentum.

"He a hunk?"

"I think so."

"How long you been married?"

"Three months."

"You'll get over it."

I doubted it. I'd worked too hard to get the man to grow tired of him anytime soon. Lots of women diet or dress-up, fix their hair or wear make-up, hoping to snag the man of their dreams. I'd gone undercover as a waitress in the restaurant from hell and tangled with some very bad guys. Stand by your man, Kozak style.

We went back out into the gray afternoon. The air had a real bite today, a damp chill that worked its way under my raincoat and raised goosebumps. Even from across the parking lot, my car didn't look right. When we got closer, I saw why. The two front tires were flat as pancakes. One tire I could have handled—changed it myself or called the folks at triple A, those tattooed, cigarette smoking young guys who look scary but are usually so nice. But two flats required a tow truck.

Sometimes bad guys could be so dumb. If they wanted me to leave, why strand me here with a defunct car? But maybe this wasn't about me. What if it was aimed at Shondra? Then I had to get her out of here. But to where? I didn't believe the campus was safe.

She stared at the car, uttered a few of the expletives I'd been thinking, and kicked one of the poor, slack tires. "Now what we gonna do?"

I brandished my phone. These days, help is just a fingertip away, assuming you're not in a black hole or some other form of cell hell. I called AAA to have the car towed and then called Bobby to come and get us. Very efficient. I wasn't even upset. The only trouble was that Shondra and I *had* lost our momentum. I didn't know if I could get her talking again.

"Help is on the way," I told her.

"I don't like this," she said, taking a long, slow look around the parking lot. "It's creepy. Who knew we were here?"

I'd told no one. But someone had found us. Maybe it was time for me to start driving a mud-colored car instead of a bright red Saab. Take one of those cop courses in defensive driving techniques. Learn to sweep my car for tracking devices. But I was a consultant, dammit. People weren't supposed to be following me. They were supposed to be asking me for advice. And not about how to dodge a tail.

We could have gotten in the car, but it was too weird to sit in a car with two flat tires. We leaned against my trunk, waiting for the AAA man who'd said fifteen minutes, and I tried to get the conversation going again. "This camera…is it hidden securely? Somewhere Alasdair's friends won't think to look?"

"I hope so."

"How do they know about it?"

Her shoulders slumped. She had an amazing ability to look dejected. I liked her better proud and angry. She was good at that, too. "That's my fault. Thursday night, see, he made one of his calls. He hadn't called for a while…not since I got things so stirred up. I guess maybe Chambers and them leaned on him to stop, never mind that they said he wasn't doing it. They knew he was. Or maybe he just thought if he stopped for a while, I'd relax and then, when he'd start doing it again, it would be worse. That was the way he worked."

She shuffled her feet, studying them as they moved, considering what she'd say. "So I was mad, you know, and I told him, straight out, that I knew it was him, Alasdair, and he'd better quit, because I had him on camera, in my room, going through my things, leavin' one of his nasty pictures. I said if he ever called me again I wasn't going to bother with the Administration, I was going to give what was on that to the press and a lawyer. I told him I'd sue his ass and St. Matthews' ass and to hell with all of 'em."

Her feet shuffled. Her hands flexed. When she spoke again, her voice was almost a whisper. "He said like hell I would. That no one had better ever see those pictures or I'd be sorrier than I could ever imagine. Not just me but my whole family would be sorry. He said he knew I was too smart to make a mistake like that. Then he laughed and hung up."

Her brown eyes filled with tears. "I didn't listen. I didn't believe him, when I know I should have. Alasdair always get his way, him and those friends of his are always hurting girls and getting away with it. But I was so mad, I wasn't going to let him do it any longer. I called that reporter, and now look what's happened."

"What reporter? You've never mentioned a reporter, Shondra." Someone had, hadn't they? One of the girls in her dorm? And what was this about a lawyer? "I need to know who you've spoken with, Shondra, and what you've told them."

"The reporter…well, actually, you know…he called me. I think he's a friend of Jen's father or something, so maybe she got on to him somehow. Anyway. He called me and we met."

"Did you give him the pictures?"

"No. Not yet. I …"

An engine roared. A gray car leaped out of a parking space, hurtling straight at us.

"Watch out!" I shoved Shondra backward, pushing her between my car and the next, her eyes widening in surprise and indignation as she found herself falling. I was in mid-jump myself when the gray car caught my foot, propelling me onto my trunk and slamming me hard against the rear window. The glass disintegrated under my head.

There was a loud thud and the crunch of metal on metal. The car beneath me shuddered as the gray car reversed in a clash of metal and falling glass and raced off.

I lay there amidst the chunks of glass on the window ledge, waiting for my head to clear, unhappily aware that I hurt in a lot of places. What the heck was I doing here?

Dizzily, I lifted my head and squinted at the gathering crowd. "Could someone call 911?"

They all stared without speaking, which unnerved me. I was afraid when I moved I'd discover a missing limb, or that I'd somehow become disrobed. Cautiously, I checked my arms and legs. Aside from a rucked up skirt, revealing sprawled limbs decently covered by black tights, I was intact and dressed. It was simply crowd mentality. Being in groups makes people stupid.

It was Shondra who took charge. She barked at the crowd to back up, give us space, and call the cops, then leaned in to tug down my skirt. I was grateful. I could have called, but my swimming head wanted to rest there quietly among the shattered glass a little longer.

Swimming head or no swimming head, I wanted those bastards caught, so I sifted through those last moments, piecing together what I knew about the gray car and who had been in it. At least two men. Young. The driver blond and the other dark. Despite the gray day, the driver had worn sunglasses. His companion had worn a baseball cap. They had both been above medium height, given the proximity of their heads to the ceiling. They had both been smiling. The car had been a Honda.

Bastards.

It's a game Andre and I play. Walking down the street. Driving. Sitting in restaurants. Take a quick look, look away, and describe what you've seen—clothes, hair, gait, age, distinctive characteristics. At first I was awful at it. I got things so wrong. I wasn't so much observing as inventing. But under his tutelage, I've gotten pretty good.

"Mrs. Kozak. Mrs. Kozak?" Shondra sounded scared.

Time to stop wallowing in self-pity and act grown-up. Wasn't that the job I'd signed up for? I opened my eyes again. Oh, man, did I hurt. I never wanted to move again, even though the prospect of lying here forever wasn't pleasant. I pictured them towing the car away with me still sprawled on the back like a fresh-killed deer.

"Are you okay?" I felt her breath on my cheek as she leaned over me.

"Nothing a week at a spa won't cure."

Carefully, I raised my head. The clatter of dropping glass sounded like my skull was coming apart. I knew glass would be caught in my hair. I probably looked like a rhinestone Medusa. Auto glass is designed to shatter in chunks rather than spears, but it's still glass. I felt the sting of small cuts on my cheek and neck. Touched them and my hand came away bloody. Another good reason for wearing dark clothes. To my list of designer clothes for the adventurous businesswoman I add the hard hat cloche.

"You're bleeding," she said accusingly.

219

"Are you all right?"

"Thanks to you."

Now that it was clear I wasn't dead, people were hurling questions at me like reporters at a press conference. "You want to shut them up, please?" Shondra barked again and they quieted down. Sometimes there are real advantages to being 6' 3" and trained to be aggressive.

But she was a scared kid and someone had just tried to kill her, or at least scare her in a way that said they didn't care if she was hurt in the process. I've met my share of people indifferent to their fellow humans, but they still astonish me. My little sister, Carrie, used to plant her hands on her hips and swish her tiny butt and declare, "You aren't the boss of me." That image appears when I encounter people who are so sure they're the boss and have the right to make life and death decisions about others. Like Carrie, I get mad.

In a way, I was here today because of Carrie, my little sister who was murdered. That was what set me on this path. Not the path of being a consultant, the path of being willing to go into hard situations and look for the truth. Of being someone who doesn't back down when the going gets tough, who feels the need to protect the vulnerable.

If I'd backed down, Carrie's killer would have gotten away with murder. I wasn't letting that happen. Not to Carrie, not to Andre. Not even to people I didn't like that much, like my client Martina Pullman, strangled with a stocking and left grotesquely dead. Whether she liked it or not, I wasn't sitting around like everyone else playing 'see no evil' while something bad happened to Shondra Jones.

## CHAPTER TWENTY-FOUR

The first person to arrive was Frank Woodson, which surprised me. It ought to have been Bobby. As Woodson stopped with a jerk and hurried up to us, I heard the distant sound of sirens, and my phone rang. All the bells and whistles to go with the ringing in my head. I raised the receiver cautiously to my face, not wanting to hurt any tender places. "Hello?"

"Thea, I'm sorry." It was Bobby. "I couldn't get away before. I'm just heading down to the car now."

"It's all right," I said. "Frank Woodson's here. We can hitch a ride back with him. I can't leave yet anyway. It's not just a flat tire anymore. Someone just deliberately slammed into my car."

"I told you we should leave," he said. "Are you okay? You sound a little shaky?"

"I am shaky, Bobby. I got knocked through the rear window and my car is a wreck."

"Do you want me to call your husband?" Bobby knows my habit of pretending I'm fine when I'm one of the walking wounded.

"Don't you dare, Bobby. It's just a few scratches. I don't want him worried."

"Maybe someone should worry about you. You don't take care of yourself."

"Bobby, you know I love you dearly, but I do not need another mother."

"Friend," he said. "And everyone needs friends."

How could I argue with that? I gave up. My head was woozy, Woodson was staring, and the cops had arrived. "You're right. Look, I've got to deal with the cops. I'll call you when I'm done, okay? And don't worry. It really is just cuts and bruises." He didn't need to know that I wanted to walk away from this chaos,

221

fold up in a little ball, and weep. Neither did Shondra. I was supposed to be in charge. "You know Suzanne's coming?"

"I know." Somehow, he got understanding and sympathy into those two words.

Two local cops were striding toward me. Woodson was beside me, about to say something. Shondra had backed away, watching all of us nervously. An old man in a flannel shirt and baggy jeans held up with suspenders hovered nearby, waiting for a chance to speak. Then everyone began talking.

As if there weren't enough people at the party, a state police cruiser flew into the parking lot and jolted to a stop beside us. Lt. Bushnell leaned out, looking so disagreeable you'd have thought I'd staged all this just to avoid him. "Ms. Kozak," he began.

My knees buckled. I grabbed Woodson's arm and closed my eyes, leaning heavily against him. "I have to sit down."

He was steering me toward his car when one of the local cops interrupted. "Excuse me, ma'am. Is it your car that was just run into?"

"Yes."

"Then we need to speak with you."

"She's dizzy," Woodson said. "She needs to sit down."

"Ma'am? Should we call an ambulance?"

I thought they ought to call out the militia, declare martial law, and take over the St. Matthews campus. I thought Shondra and I should retreat to Rapunzel's tower and refuse to let down our hair. I shared neither of these thoughts with him.

"No ambulance, please, Officer. I'm just a little shaken. The car that hit mine...deliberately hit mine...caught my foot and knocked me through the rear window." If they'd only leave me alone, I could get my thoughts together.

"If it will help, I saw it." It was a gruff country voice. The old man with suspenders. "And I've got the license number of that car right here."

Such an unlikely hero. If I hadn't been so dizzy I might have hugged him. "Did you see the accident?" the local cop asked.

"Worn't no accident," the old man said.

The cop looked at his partner. "You want to take him, I'll take the vic?"

That was me. I had a hard time being a victim. Right now, I was having a hard time standing up. "You can pick your spot, Officer," I said, "but it has to be somewhere I can sit."

"You and Shondra come with me," Woodson said. "When we're done, I can drive you back to school." He took a firmer grip on my arm.

"My car's right here," the cop said.

"We'll put her in my car," Bushnell said firmly. He gestured toward Shondra, who was staring daggers at him. I figured that meant he'd visited her in the hospital and been his usual charming self. "Better get Ms. Jones, too, before she takes off again. She's a hard young woman to pin down." He took a firm grip on my other arm.

It was all I could do to keep from waving a vague hand in the air and saying in mock-southern, "All of you boys arguin' over little ole me." It would have puzzled the local cop and really pissed off Bushnell, which would have been my purpose. But all this wrangling made my head spin.

We ended up one big, happy family, squeezed into Bushnell's Crown Vic, Woodson and I and the local officer in back, Bushnell and Shondra in the front. Woodson looked unhappy, but whether it was dislike of the state cop, losing the battle for control of Shondra and me, or something else, I couldn't tell.

Shondra, bless her heart, had brought my briefcase and my purse. I searched my purse without success for a tissue before remembering I'd given them to Shondra in the car. It was Woodson who finally realized what I was doing and handed me a handkerchief. I dabbed cautiously at the stinging spots on my cheek. The local cop, sandy haired, sandy mustached and beefy, sat poised on the edge of the seat, one thick thigh in the car, the other out the door. He identified himself as Lehane, dug out a notebook and began to collect my story.

It was simple and straightforward, if having someone drive

a car straight at you can ever be called simple. Simple act, I supposed, powerful reaction. Before I'd finished, Shondra, who'd been a rock while it was happening, was in tears again, and I was experiencing the limp aftermath of an adrenaline rush. He wrote it all down, asked some questions, reminded me to call my insurance company, and climbed out of the car. "I'll just get some pictures."

His partner, who'd been talking with the older man and some other people who said they'd witnessed the incident, strolled up and divulged, in a confidential tone I heard clearly, that the car involved in the incident belonged to a local kid who'd taken off on Friday. That didn't square with what I suspected, which was that Alasdair's numbskulls were somehow involved, but maybe the kid was a day student at St. Matts or his car had been borrowed or stolen.

When Lehane finished, I was ready to crawl off to The Swan and climb into a nice hot bath. There were a few problems. I wasn't finished with Shondra. I wanted to see those nannycam pictures and get her settled. I felt maternal enough to want to see that her room had a bed and furniture, and I wanted to hand her over to someone who would pay attention, like Coach Adams. My more immediate problem was transportation. I needed to rent a car.

Whatever my agenda was, it didn't look like it would mesh well with those of the other occupants of this car. Woodson's expectant look reminded me that he was still looking for a report of last night's assault, and Bushnell was giving Shondra the same look. If these guys got their way, Shondra and I would be split up and interrogated and who knew what would happen then.

"Look," I said, "I know you guys have questions for us, but we're neither of us up to it right now. I'm pretty shaken up and Shondra's just out of the hospital."

Sometimes talking to cops is like talking to my foot. Same level of response, same amount of interest. Actually, my foot is friendlier. It responds when I ask it to. Woodson and Bushnell both shook their heads in such a synchronized fashion it looked rehearsed and came out with similar versions of "I don't think so."

"Tell you what," Bushnell said. "Why doesn't Frank take Ms. Kozak over to his car for their little chat, and Ms. Jones can stay here with me."

"Not so fast," Woodson said. "I should get them both back."

"Tell *you* what," Shondra said. "I am a minor, being as I'm sixteen, and you aren't supposed to talk with me unless an adult is present."

Bushnell looked slightly stupefied, then snapped, "Under the circumstances, an adult isn't required." No matter. I was so proud I could have hugged her. He should have known, after Jamison invoked his rights from the get-go, that the Jones kids might be babes in the woods in the academic forest of St. Matthews, but they knew their way around cops. They didn't need to know it from experience; it could have been part of their neighborhood lore.

Shondra looked over the seat at me. "You will stay with me, won't you?"

I think Woodson actually growled, which seemed strange, since earlier I'd thought he was protective towards Jamison and Shondra, and what he and I had to discuss wasn't very important. But that was based on my own intuition, which was usually right and occasionally somewhere out in left field. Another sports image. He might have been growling at Bushnell. Cops are very territorial.

"If you want me to."

"Oh, I do," she said. "Since Grandmamma isn't here, I need someone from the Administration with me. Since you work for them, I'd guess you count." I could swear she tipped me a wink.

I was operating at a less than optimum level. If Bushnell's goal was to solicit information in his case against Jamison, she probably should have a lawyer of her own, or maybe Jamison's lawyer, or one from St. Matthews. But it didn't look like Bushnell was going to be deterred. I'd already discovered how charming he could be. I wasn't letting her handle this alone.

"You mind if I sit in?" Woodson asked. Representing the school in a different way, perhaps. Would he carry whatever was said back to Todd Chambers?

Bushnell shrugged. "Suit yourself." Without further preliminaries, he launched into his questions. Going over what Chambers and the rest of the St. Matthews administration had told him, along with what I'd said and information he must have gotten from other students and faculty.

There are times I've wished I'd gone to law school and this was one of them. I wished I knew the underlying law better so I could figure out what he was trying to establish. Motive? A propensity for violence or impulsive behavior on Jamison's part? It was more than the basic story. The sneaky way he kept coming back to things, approaching them with slightly different questions, told me that.

Shondra did a good job of holding her own, but she was young, she was tired, and she had a temper he was doing his best to make her lose. Once or twice, I put a hand on her shoulder, cautioning her to think before she spoke, until he outright told me to stop doing that.

"She asked me to stay and help her out," I said.

"I'd say it's more like you're controlling her," he said.

"She doesn't have to talk to you," I said. "She can leave anytime she wants."

"And how does that help her brother? I'm only trying to figure out what the truth is. He's not talking. If she's not talking, either, than all we've got is Alasdair's side of the story...up until the time he died, together with the story the Administration and his friends are telling me, about Ms. Jones targeting Alasdair because of his racial views, and when he objects and stands up to her, she makes up this story about being stalked and gets her big brother to play avenging angel. Viewed that way, Jamison Jones looks like a very deliberate killer."

Bushnell paused for effect, then added, "You know that MacGregor's face was battered beyond recognition. That's a

226

very personal kind of killing."

He said it like he'd bought the party line. I thought it was just deliberate provocation.

"Jamison didn't kill anyone," Shondra began. I put a warning hand on her shoulder.

She shook it off. "You're just trying to make it look like he did. He's your scapegoat, is all. Alasdair got into some kind of trouble. Maybe with his crazy, preppy friends, I don't know. His secret society. Maybe he finally went too far." She said it with such loathing. "Or maybe his trouble was with those drug dealers he was so friendly with. Maybe he pissed someone off real good, got hisself killed, and now you blamin' my brother because it's easier to blame some black kid with no family or connections than conduct a real investigation where you might upset some big shot alumni donor."

She shook her head vigorously, uncurled her clenched fists, and stabbed one sharp finger into Bushnell's chest. "You believe the crap they're feeding you over at St. Matts, and you too stupid to be a cop."

Bushnell stared at the stabbing finger until she pulled it back. "You disliked Alasdair MacGregor, didn't you?"

"You damned right I did."

"And Jamison would do anything for his little sister, wouldn't he?" Shondra didn't answer.

"I know your brother used to get into fights in the neighborhood. I know it was just luck, and some people pulling for him, that kept him from being arrested. I know the kind of boys he used to hang around with."

"You don't know shit."

"I know your brother has had counseling about how to manage his temper."

"He worked real hard," she snapped, "and anyway, that's not your business."

"Everything about you and your brother is my business. I know that neither one of you would be at St. Matthews if it weren't for basketball."

227

"So?"

"So maybe Alasdair was right that you really didn't belong there. And maybe that made you and your brother mad. Mad enough to kill."

I wondered what was behind her remarks about drug dealers, or whether Alasdair might have done something sufficiently offensive to his ugly little clique to make them kill him—if, as Bushnell had said, this was a personal crime. I could tell that Shondra was becoming explosive. I was considering how to stop this interview when Shondra grabbed her door handle, jumped out, and took off running.

I grabbed my own door handle, meaning to go after her, and came up against a hard reality. I was sitting in the back seat of a police car. The door wouldn't open.

Bushnell took off after her, leaving me and Woodson stuck in the car, staring at each other glumly. Oh well. He'd never catch Shondra. She was taller, younger, and fitter. And very angry. Bushnell would be back pretty soon.

# CHAPTER TWENTY-FIVE

Bushnell came limping back, red and sweaty, got in and slammed the door. "If it weren't for you ..." he said.

"Oh, please, Lieutenant, this is your fault and you know it. You knew she was prickly, and if you were listening at St. Matthews, you also know she was up to her ears in lying and untrustworthy adults. You're supposed to be a pro...you must know there's more than one way to skin a cat."

"I'm investigating a murder," he said truculently.

"And you're an experienced detective. You're supposed to know how to deal with people."

"I'd like to deal with you," he muttered.

Woodson had been silent long enough. "You want to let us out of here?" he said. His quiet voice had an edge to it. They were both in the public safety business, yet Bushnell treated him no better than he treated me. Or worse. He ignored Woodson.

"Oh. Yeah. Right." Bushnell got out and opened the rear door. As we climbed out, he studied me with his cold eyes. "You got any idea where that girl will go?"

"No."

"I'll bet you do."

I wished he were right. "I might have gotten one, given a little more time. I was just starting to make a connection...then that asshole drives into my car, which shakes her up, then you come along and finish the job."

I fixed him with my own cold stare. He shouldn't be allowed to get away with being such a jerk. "You have any idea how upsetting it is to have someone try and run you down? Ever been knocked through the window of a car?" He didn't respond.

"Something that puzzles me," I said. "My husband thinks

you're a pretty decent guy. I wonder where he gets that from?"

"Your husband says he knows me?" Suspicious, like I was trying to get some kind of an edge.

As if I cared. The moment when decent behavior might have gotten him better cooperation had long passed. I'd been badly shaken and I was losing my famous little temper. "Are you married?" I asked. He stared, then nodded. "Well, I'll bet you'd be royally pissed off if my husband treated your wife half as badly as you treat me. Maybe you can ask him sometime, when all you New England homicide detectives get together for some bonding thing. Andre's usually a good judge of people, but this time, he's got his head wedged."

If I were a spitter, this would have been the moment to drop a little derogatory drool, but though it would have been the perfect gesture, I think spitting is revolting. I turned to Woodson. "Let's do that follow-up interview, and then maybe you could drive me somewhere to rent a car?"

"Sure thing." He gestured at my poor mutilated auto. "But what about your car? You call a tow truck?"

"Yeah, Triple A. They said fifteen minutes." But Triple A was not famous for speed. "If you don't want to wait, that's okay. Once the tow guy comes, I can call a cab."

"Who knows how long they'll be." He looked at his watch, then regretfully back at me. "I'd like to stay 'til they turn up, but you know how things are on the campus right now. I ought to be getting back," he said. "Maybe the lieutenant could give you a lift."

I looked at Bushnell. "I'd rather walk."

Bushnell shook his head and turned his back, but he still didn't leave. I turned back to Woodson. "I should get back," he said. "Maybe we can do it by phone."

I couldn't really blame him. Security was an issue right now. I wished I could drive away, too. But first I needed some wheels. "Where can I go to rent a car?"

Because I was feeling fragmented, I got out my Blackberry and tapped in his directions, then watched forlornly as he drove away. It's true that I like to rescue myself and am fiercely independent, but I was feeling pretty battered. I wouldn't have minded a polite, well-behaved knight in shiny armor. Instead, I had that abrasive bully Bushnell.

As soon as Woodson left, Bushnell stalked back. "Who is your husband, anyway? I don't know any cops named Andre Kozak."

"Neither do I," I said. "*My* name is Kozak."

"You don't have to make everything so damned hard."

"As I recall, I didn't grab you and shake you until you were sick."

"Look, I'm sorry about that."

"And what? It would have killed you to say that? You might have lost your investigative edge? It's not like I was a suspect." I could have gone on playing this edgy, bitter game but it was such a waste of time and energy. I wished he'd investigate his crime, find out the real story, and leave me alone. Standing made me tired. It was chilly and I hurt. "I wish you'd go away," I said. "I have to sit down."

"You can sit in my car."

"I could also try walking on hot coals, but I bet that would be painful, too."

"Everybody makes mistakes," he said. "So, who's your husband?"

He was a detective. He could have found out easily. But as I said, I was tired of the game. "Detective Andre Lemieux. Maine State Police."

"Oh. Hell." He turned away. Turned back wearing a 'looks like I've really stepped in it' expression. Except for the bad guys, people who meet Andre really like him. "Mrs. Lemieux...I'm really sorry."

"Goddammit, Lieutenant...my name hasn't changed in the last minute."

Andre is always telling me to lighten up, when he's not telling me to put a cork in it. He thinks I take this business of standing on my feminist principles too far. He thinks I have too

231

great a need to be right. He says I should try to be more flexible and forgiving. Sometimes I think he's the one who should put a cork in it, but he's not always wrong.

I took a deep breath. "I'm sorry. I'm frustrated by this whole situation. I don't think I'm hearing the truth and I don't think you're hearing the truth from the St. Matthews administration. And I think the truth about what has been going on among the parties—and at St. Matthews generally—is at the core of this. I've been the victim of physical attacks twice in two days, for no reason that I can understand. And I'm very concerned about Shondra's safety. I think *this* attack may have been directed at her."

I looked over at my mangled car, bumper on the ground, taillight glass scattered everywhere, trunk hood buckled, rear window gone. It felt like a very personal violation. "I really like my car. My head hurts, I'm bleeding. I've got glass in my hair...I'm unnerved and upset and...well...I'm afraid I've been taking out some of that on you."

He looked as surprised as if I'd slammed him upside the head with a big, wet fish, a slightly goggle-eyed look that was endearing in its vulnerability. I'm so perverse. I love it when cops prove they're human. Then his eyes narrowed. "Is this some kind of a game?"

"You're the one who plays games, Bushnell. I guess I can, when I have to, but what would be the point?"

"People play games for lots of reasons."

He reached toward me, then pulled back his hand. "You look like you're about to fall over. Come sit in the car. I promise I won't say a word, if that's what you want."

"What I want is Triple A to come so I can hand over my car, go rent another one, and then go back to The Swan." I didn't share my fantasy about a warm tub and a small rest. He might have found my longing to collapse far too feminine.

With a roar, a huge flat-bed black tow truck, decorated with pink and baby blue swirls and Jose's Towing in gaudy silver letters, charged into the lot and rocked to a stop beside us. A round-faced guy with three-day stubble leaned out. "You the lady needs a tow?"

I was. I was ready for him to hook me up and drive me away. But he meant the car. I pointed. He stared and shook his head. "How did that happen?"

"Just what I was wondering." I unzipped my wallet and got out my AAA card. "Guess you'd better take it to the Saab dealer. I understand they've got a body shop."

"Pretty good one," he agreed. He hopped down from the truck, stuck a cigarette in his mouth, lit it, and started working on his clipboard. After I'd given him the relevant information, he jockeyed his truck into position, hooked onto the car, and winched it onto the truck, bits of glass and metal dropping off and rolling down the ramp. A bright red car looks so vulnerable when it's wounded. He handed me a receipt and roared away.

Once again, I was alone with Bushnell. "Let's go rent you a car," he said.

The adrenaline had subsided and my bruises were making themselves known. I walked stiffly around the Crown Vic and gingerly lowered myself onto the seat, closing my eyes and letting him take me away from all this.

The skinny man behind the rental desk stared disapprovingly at my cut face and Medusa hair. "What happened to you?"

"Madman ran into my car. I need to rent another."

"Compact? Mid-size?"

"What have you got in a full-sized car?" I wasn't interested in squeezing myself into a sardine can just to save a few bucks and my bad mood needed a lot of space.

"Let's see." He tapped some keys, stared at the screen, tapped some more. "Got a Lincoln."

I hated the mushy way big American sedans drove. It was like piloting a whale down the street. No sense of the road. "Anything else? An SUV maybe?"

"Jeep Cherokee?"

"That's fine." And hurry it up. The day is slipping away.

"There's a surcharge," he said ominously, tapping his keys

again.

"That's okay." I waited. He tapped. Tapped. Tapped. By now he could have written chapter one of the Great American Novel. Eventually he raised his eyes briefly, lowered them again at the sight of my face, and elicited vital information. I handed over my license and a credit card, and he rather grudgingly gave me the keys and told me where to find the car. All the time, Bushnell hovered by the door.

By the time I'd signed the final paper and pocketed the keys, I'd had it with the human race. I needed to get to a place where I could shut the door, scream, and then spend an hour getting the glass out of my hair. I thanked the man. I thanked Bushnell. Then I levered myself up onto the high seat, slammed the door, and Trigger—the name I'd instantly given the Jeep—reared up, the big V-8 rumbling happily, and took off so fast I almost had another accident. Yee ha!

As I zipped toward The Swan, I was glad Bushnell was behind me. I didn't want to see the look on his face.

No one at The Swan even blinked when I returned with a scratched face and a different car. I dragged my battered body up the stairs, dumped my briefcase and purse on the bed, spread a towel over the pillow to catch wayward glass and lay down, closing my eyes and practicing relaxation breathing. I thought calm thoughts. Clear blue skies. Billowing waves. The warmth of sunshine. It didn't work. The puzzling situation at St. Matts was as persistent and intrusive as a mosquito in the dark. I couldn't relax until I'd sorted things out.

I sat up and dug out my phone. First I tried Jenna Adams. I got her voice mail so I left a message that Shondra was out of the hospital but had bolted before I could get her back to St. Matts, told her to be on the look-out, and asked her to call to discuss plans for Shondra's safety. As a nod to private school protocol, I made a courtesy call with similar information to Shondra's advisor. Funny how "courtesy call" has become the new euphemism for annoying phone call.

Then, without too much hope of a positive response, I called

Craig Dunham. Before I got to the subject of my call, he said, "I heard about the…uh…accident…are you all right?"

"Fine. Thank you. I'm calling about Shondra. She …"

"I heard you took her to see her brother. That was good of you. How'd it go?"

"I can't really say. I waited outside."

"Oh." He sounded disappointed. "So how's she doing?"

"About like you'd expect. Edgy. Upset. Less than 100%. Has she shown up anywhere at St. Matthews yet?"

"What are you talking about? You didn't bring her back to the dorm?"

Funny that he'd heard about the jail visit and the accident but not that Shondra had taken off. "She ran away while the police were there taking a report of the accident. That state cop, Bushnell, was talking to her. He got pushy and she bolted. Bushnell went after her, but you know Shondra. She's fast."

I decided I could conduct this business lying down. Gingerly, I settled my head back on the pillow and closed my eyes. "How did you hear about the accident but not about Shondra running away? Woodson only told you half the story?"

"Woodson? I've been looking for Frank for hours. Haven't been able to find him. He was with you? Excuse me." There was a commotion as someone came into his office and distracted him, then he was back with me. "I heard about the accident from your guy. Bobby Ryan. He was all upset about his car. Maybe he sent Woodson."

Now I was confused. Woodson showed up before Bobby called to say he'd been delayed and was finally on his way. But maybe there was a piece I was missing. Maybe there was a universe of car troubles today. Maybe Bobby had had car trouble and then gotten it fixed, and while he was fretting about that, he'd spoken with Woodson who'd headed over to see what was up. I'd also assumed Woodson had come right back to St. Matthews and reported our latest problem with Shondra. It was important information. But why did I assume he'd do that? Failing to share information was business as usual around here.

"You got Shondra's room fixed up?" I asked.

"Did the best we could," he said. "What a mess."

"And otherwise? Any problems with difficult parents? Upset students? Intrusive press? Any further developments in the investigation?" I wanted to ask about Alasdair's Neo-Skulls, and how they might fit into this, but that I needed to do face-to-face.

"I'm working on a memo about all that," he said, "for your partner." Stiff and a little smug. It was so foolish. They had little to be smug about. This mess was far from over. Besides, they might not work like a partnership on their side, but we did on ours.

"That's good," I said, deciding to needle right back, "because Shondra mentioned talking to some black reporter about having proof that Alasdair had been in her room, and I wasn't clear when that happened."

"She what?"

"She didn't elaborate. Bushnell scared her off before we finished talking." I decided not to elaborate, either. "Can you ask Mrs. Leverett to call me if Shondra turns up?" He allowed that he would, and we parted telephonic company. I was still uneasy about Shondra, both her whereabouts and her safety, but I'd done what I could.

I tried to call Bobby, but couldn't reach him. Since Bobby always answered his phone, I imagined a dozen awful things that might be happening. Crises occurring without me. Random attacks. But Dunham had said Bobby was having car trouble. Most likely, he was dealing with an AAA guy himself and would call when he was finished.

In the midst of these speculations, my sleepless night and stressful day caught up with me. My eyelids slammed down, my brain went into energy-conservation mode, and I went night-night.

## CHAPTER TWENTY-SIX

I woke because someone was in my room. I heard the faint thud of footsteps, the rustling of clothes, the sounds of someone breathing. Too many years among the bad guys have conditioned me to be cautious. I held my own breath and listened. Without opening my eyes, I said, "Bobby called you, didn't he?"

"No."

"Don't tell me it was that damned Gary Bushnell."

"Yeah. He said he thought maybe you didn't like him."

"Very perceptive fellow, that. It was nice of him to call you, but he's still a world-class jerk." I opened my eyes and held out my arms. "I'm awfully glad to see you, detective, but aren't you supposed to be working?"

"Am working," he grunted. "Working at keeping my marriage, and my bride, intact." He touched my hair. "Ouch.!" He pulled back his hand, inspected it, and sucked on his finger, where a bubble of blood had risen. "Gary said something about you needing help combing glass out of your hair?"

"I do," I agreed. "What time is it?"

"Why? You got a date?"

"Dinner meeting with Suzanne at six."

"It's not even four. We've got plenty of time."

"Never enough." I looked up at him, sitting there on the edge of the bed, hovering over me protectively. Would other women think he was handsome, or would they find his firm-jawed face too hard, that bristly dark hair too military short? Would they look at his broad, solid body and wish it lithe and slender? I loved having some bulk to brace myself against. He was only two inches taller, but in the weight and muscle departments, despite my faithful attendance at the gym, he dwarfed me.

Broad, solid, commanding. He could be such a cop. But the bad guys, and the public, rarely got to see his wicked, dancing eyes.

"First, a nice, hot shower," he said, "then I'll comb the glass out. How's that sound?"

"It's a great big shower."

"That an invitation?"

"Did you need one?"

"Everyone wants to be wanted." He raised a quizzical eyebrow. "What does that expression mean?"

"I'm trying to remember if there was ever a time when I didn't want you."

"When we first met, I believe."

"You were a jerk," I agreed. "Other than that?"

He shook his head, grinning. "Not that I recall." He stood and offered a hand to help me up. "I'm so pleased to find you're being your usual careful self."

"It ain't me, Black Bart. I'm just a patient little consultant, going about her business. It's those bad guys." I let him pull me to my feet, closing the space between us.

"Right," he said. "I've noticed how Suzanne and Bobby are always getting battered about."

"That's why they send the big gal in first, to draw the enemy fire. I'm EDGE's special ops person. They come in when it's safe."

"So you think it's safe now?"

"Damned if I know, Lemieux." I stepped back, pulled my sweater over my head, dropped it on a chair, and unzipped my skirt. I peeled off my panty hose, an act so unaesthetic I turned so he could enjoy my cleavage instead. There's a reason why strippers and porno flicks use thigh-high stockings or stockings and garter belts—so the women undressing don't have to hop around on one foot, all bent over and awkward. "So. You joining me in the shower or what?"

"What would you do if I said 'or what'?"

"Shower alone, I guess."

I tried to sound morose, but Andre was here, and battered and bruised as I was, I felt like singing. Not the wistful "Someday my prince will come," I'd been thinking earlier, but something thumping and righteous. Maybe Shondra was right and eventually I'd get sick of him, but I didn't see it happening anytime soon. I can keep my nose to the grindstone, deal with difficult clients and danger, do whatever needs to be done, without too much self-pity. Partly that's my workaholic genes, but a major part comes from having the cushion of Andre's presence.

I peeled the stockings over my toes and tossed them on top of the rest of my clothes. "Nice feet," he said, starting to unbutton his shirt.

"Nice feet?"

Instead of answering, he slid one of his own bare feet over mine. He took off his shirt, his tee-shirt, and squared his shoulders. I rested my face against his chest, inhaling him. "You've been with smokers."

"One reason we're on our way to the shower."

Like the rest of the amenities at The Swan, it was wonderful. None of those wimpy, water-saver showerheads that make you feel like you're standing under a watering can. This shower had four heads, serious hot water, and plenty of room for making whoopee. Darned good thing. We'd spent a night apart and were behind on our whoopee. By the time we rolled out into the steamy bathroom, all pink and rosy, we'd made up for lost time.

We wrapped up in thick white terry robes, and I sat on the toilet seat while Monsieur Andre combed me out. It took part of a bottle of spray detangler, a number of choice curse words on his part, and the better part of twenty minutes, but in the end, the glass was dislodged and Medusa tamed. To celebrate the restoration of order to the world, we decided to go to bed. Another notch in our belts and we fell into sated sleep.

At 5:45, Andre the Efficient's watch alarm roused us from log-deep sleep. I muttered for it to shut up and burrowed back into the warm space between his shoulder and his neck, the most secure space I know. His arms tightened around me. We had a minute of grace to savor before duty called and we had to start pulling on clothes. Some minutes are shorter than others. This passed in the space of two breaths, and he was whispering in my ear, "Time to get up. You've got a meeting."

I rolled over onto my back and stared up at the ceiling. "Maybe it's time to think about a new job."

"Like what? Can you honestly think of anything else you'd be interested in doing?"

"This."

"Hard to make a living at it," he said, his voice a deep rumble in his chest, "with just one customer. Besides…even if you'd been home, I wouldn't have been there. And you're good at your job."

"You wouldn't think that with what's going on here."

"You can't win 'em all," he said. "That's not you, it's the client,"

I needed some sympathy and an objective ear. I was about to launch into a description of the whole nasty business when someone knocked. I grabbed my robe and padded across the room. Suzanne was a vision in sapphire blue suede, every blonde hair in place. She took in the robe and wild hair, converted a reflexive frown into a smile, and peered around me. "Hi, Andre," she said. "Trying to keep my partner out of trouble?"

Andre reclined on his side, hairy chest exposed, loins draped with a velvety green blanket. It was enough to make a strong woman swoon. "Trying to get her in trouble," he said.

"Well, good luck. See you downstairs." She paused. "Ten minutes, right?"

"Plenty of time," he said.

"I expected to find Thea propped up on pillows with an ice bag and Bandaids." Suzanne shook her head. "You two are something else."

"We do our best."

She smiled, shrugged, and turned away. Seemed like the same old Suzanne. Maybe I'd only imagined that distance and reserve on the phone. I had a pretty good imagination, and St.

240

Matthews' collection of liars and looneys could really get it going.

I dropped the robe, looked at the pile of clothes in the chair, and went to my suitcase instead, challenged by Suzanne's sapphire splendor. Just because I hate shopping doesn't mean I don't care what I wear, it only means that finding clothes is difficult. Short women complain that clothes aren't made for them. Tall women have the same complaint. I don't know who they're designing for. Not for short arms and legs, nor for long arms and legs. Not for large chests. Medium tall, medium-sized women with boyish hips and wide shoulders. No surprise, if the designers are male. They design for the body most like their own.

I dressed my womanly body in slim black pants and a gray-green sweater that made my eyes glitter. I put on soft black cashmere socks and shoes that looked professional but had quiet rubber soles for sneaking and traction. I pulled my hair back and clipped it. Looked at my honey. He had a hungry look.

"You want to have dinner with us?"

"Thought this was business?"

"I wouldn't mind hearing your reactions. And the food here is great."

"Well…if you think Suzanne won't mind. I am a little hungry." The man is as bad as I am about getting to regular meals when he's working—that's kind of a given in the cop's life—and he has twice the appetite.

She didn't even blink when we appeared together. Just smiled at Andre and offered her cheek for a kiss. "I take it we're getting some professional advice?"

"We can try."

"Look, Thea …" She modulated her voice, and went on. "I know you're not pleased with the way things are going here, and I'm sorry. But our first duty is to the client. If they think they can work better with me, we have to go with that."

"As long as you don't let them bamboozle you."

"Don't tell me you think I'm as naïve as they obviously do."

241

I figured truth was the only way to go. No sense in finessing with Suzanne, in trying to figure out approaches and strategies. If we couldn't let it all out with each other, this partnership wouldn't work. "You sounded pretty damned censorious on the phone."

"I did?" She rubbed her forehead wearily. "Then I'm sorry." She looked at Andre. "This business of trying to be a wife, especially a wife to someone in Paul's job, is harder than I expected. I'm always feeling torn in two directions, inadequate at both. When I spoke with you, I'd just had a ridiculous conversation with Todd Chambers followed by a ridiculous conversation with Paul's executive assistant about when she could schedule a series of small student-faculty gatherings. They were both so whiny and petulant I wanted to yell at them both to leave me alone because I had a job to do—but the truth was, they were both talking to me about doing my jobs."

She sighed, shrugged, and folded her hands in her lap. "I think I need a vacation. All by myself. Somewhere with no phones. No Blackberry. No e-mail."

When Andre showed up, I'd felt like singing. Now I felt like standing on my chair and belting it out. But that, as my mother would have been quick to advise, would have been unladylike and anyway, I sing like a crow. I contented myself with a smile and concentrated on the menu. I'd had a big lunch and a quiet afternoon, so why was I so hungry? I ordered soup and salad and a big chunk of swordfish. I might even have dessert. Andre went for the filet and a baked potato. Suzanne had salad and fish.

"You don't eat enough to keep a bird alive," I said.

"In case you haven't noticed," my petite partner pointed out, "I'm considerably smaller than you two. And being middle-aged has ruined my metabolism."

Middle-aged? She was four years older. Thirty-six. Was thirty-six really middle-aged? I looked at Andre, who was also thirty-six. He didn't miss the scrutiny. "Don't worry," he said. "Guys don't worry about their metabolisms and anyway, I'm barely out of adolescence."

"That's for sure," she said. "Imagine driving two and a half hours because you miss your wife when she's going to be home later on anyway." It sounded like she no longer believed Paul would do that for her. My partner was worn down, and I'd been so wrapped up in the craziness of my own life, I hadn't even noticed."

"Yeah, it's a funny thing," Andre agreed. "First someone hits her over the head. Then some jerk tries to run my wife down, knocks her through her car window and smashes the car, and I actually get concerned."

"Someone tried to run her down?" A flush rose in Suzanne's face. "Thea didn't tell me that."

"The original stoic," Andre said.

"Not," I raised my eyebrows significantly at my doting husband, "that I told Andre, either. He heard it through the old cop's network. And," I said, trying to smooth things over, "I hadn't told Andre I was coming home because I wasn't sure what the situation here would be, or what his situation was. Not that I wasn't glad to see him."

"That was pretty obvious." No. Suzanne was not herself.

"Hey," he said. "Watch who you're calling an old cop."

"If you want to eat with us, you have to be quiet and concentrate on your dinner. This is a business meeting."

"You see what kind of mother she's going to be?" He looked to Suzanne for sympathy.

It was a subject I wouldn't have touched with a barge pole. After my awful experiences last summer, motherhood was something I was doubtful of ever achieving. It sure wasn't something to joke about. But he knew that. I wondered what he was up to.

"She'll be a great mother." Suzanne glared at him and put her hand over mine.

"And she's a great partner," he said. "Now I'll shut up, eat my dinner, and let you two get down to business."

Suzanne put her other hand over his. "You're a great partner, too."

An efficient teenage girl took away our soups and brought salads. As soon as the girl had gone, I launched into my agenda, filling Suzanne in on how Chambers and Dunham had been behaving; on the incredible security lapses in Shondra's dorm and probably on the entire campus; on the rumors about a group called Neo-Skulls formed by Alasdair, who might still be bent on taking revenge, and how Chambers insisted on ignoring their existence. About the veiled hints of harassment and injuries caused by this group, which the Administration seemed to have condoned.

"I keep trying to explain that these are things he can't ignore, or that he ignores at his peril if someone else gets hurt...and he blows up and tells me he's the headmaster and he gets to make the decisions. He calls me an uppity woman trying to give him orders, when I'm only doing what he's hired me to do."

"Except that Argenti hired us," Suzanne said. "How is he fitting into all this?"

"I thought you might know. The last time I spoke with him, Chambers was trying to fire me and Argenti begged me not to go and asked for an hour to work on things. He said he'd call. I went off to the hospital to pick up their wayward student. Next I heard, I was out and you were coming in to replace me. Argenti never did call."

"It's just business," she said. "It's not personal."

"Oh, it's very personal. Chambers' wife told me they wanted you here because, being a headmaster's wife yourself, you'd understand their situation and help them do what they want to do instead of arguing with them."

"That seems pretty reasonable."

"What does?" I tried not to raise my voice. "Rubberstamping a dishonest letter that misrepresents the facts? Letting them pretend they don't have a duty to all their students? Or that they can disregard their own written procedures whenever it suits them? Agreeing that it's okay to destroy documents in a student's file if they might be damaging to the administration's position...and possibly even allowing a gang of conservative students to terrorize and abuse women and minorities?"

"Of course not. We both know those things are unacceptable. I meant it's reasonable to ask for someone they can work with more easily. Sometimes it's not the content of the advice, Thea, it's the approach. You're making them feel attacked and threatened."

I knew better than to be snappish, but I wasn't in the mood for a lecture. "And you think what, Suzanne? That you can come in and charm them into doing what they have to do?"

"I can certainly try."

"Well, I wish you luck. Better get them to sign a contract before they decide to sack you, too." I hurried on before she could interrupt. "Now, there are a few other things you should know." I told her about Shondra's overdose and disappearance, the trashing of her room. My visit from Lindsay and Jen, and their stories about Alasdair. I hesitated about reporting their parting remarks, but I was in the presence of a homicide detective.

"You're holding something back," he said.

I looked at him curiously, but his face was blank. Professionally blank. Still, I thought his comment meant he believed I shouldn't hold anything back from Suzanne. "Here's one of those things you might as well hear, but take with several grains of salt," I said. "Those same girls, the ones who told me about the attempted date rape and the administration's response? They say they saw Alasdair…or, one of them did, last night."

Suzanne shook her head wearily. I wasn't making this easy for her. She wanted a set of manageable facts, not a bunch of speculation. "Thanks for telling me." She contemplated the wisps of salad on her plate. "Who have you found to be most credible?"

"Dunham's not too bad. A little thick, but he means well. Blows hot and cold, depending on the cues he's taking from Chambers. And the coaches, Jenna Adams and Al Sideris, are helpful, but they're employees. I don't know whether their jobs have been threatened or it's just the party line, but they balk at sharing too much information—such as the names of their sources or the details of what these Neo-Skulls have done. Chambers is purposely opaque, sometimes deliberately unresponsive, and occasionally rudely aggressive. Argenti is trying to run things, and he's certainly decisive, but he's been so hands-off that he doesn't really know what's going on."

"What does Bobby say?" Suzanne asked.

"Where is Bobby?" I'd been so wrapped up in myself I'd forgotten that he was supposed to be here, too.

"When I spoke with him this morning, he said he'd join us, but I called just before I came downstairs and I couldn't reach him," she said.

It wasn't like Bobby not to return calls. His reliability was part of what made him an ideal employee. Like everything else around here, it made me uneasy.

The waitress arrived with our entrees, and there was a pause in the hostilities while we ate. Hostilities was the wrong word, but there was certainly something going on. It wasn't like Bobby not to answer his phone, and it wasn't like Suzanne not to listen to me carefully and trust what I was saying. I wanted to drag Andre out of the room and ask him what he thought was going on, but I was supposed to be able to work with my partner without running for help. Maybe I was just suffering from post-concussion syndrome and things would seem fine in the morning.

I decided to declare a truce. "I hope you can work with them. They really need the help, whether they think so or not."

"We'll see. I'm meeting with Todd Chambers at his house in half an hour. He's supposed to have had his staff prepare briefing memos for me."

She hesitated. "If you're not in a hurry to leave…since you don't need to rush back to your husband," she smiled at Andre, "it would be great if we could go over them later."

Andre set his fork down on his empty plate, pushed back his chair and stood up. "Guess I'll mosey upstairs and leave you girls to talk." He winked at me. Neither Suzanne nor I liked

246

being called girls. "I'd be grateful if you'd bring a piece of that chocolate fudge cake when you come up."

Suzanne watched his broad back departing and sighed. "Chocolate cake. I only have to look at a piece to gain five pounds."

"Yeah, the wonderboy really can put away food. But he also hits the gym four times a week, unless he's stuck in the field."

"Paul's on the Atkins diet," she said. "One more thing to worry about. I'm getting so I can give you the carb count of a marble."

"Marbles have carbohydrates?"

"No. That's why we can eat them." She pulled out her phone. "I think I'll try Bobby again." She dialed and got no answer. "I'm beginning to worry," she said. "He's supposed to be here."

I set down my fork. The fish was delicious but suddenly I wasn't hungry. I could see no reason why someone would go after Bobby, but this place didn't operate on reason. "Maybe the phantom attacker got him, too."

"Don't even joke about it, Thea."

I looked at my partner. She looked so untainted and optimistic. So neat and lovely and intact. I wanted to walk her to her car and send her back home to her husband and son, safe from the lurking ugliness of this place. She had enough on her plate already. She didn't need the subtle pit-of-the-stomach anxiety that underlay every encounter here. "Suzanne, I wasn't joking. Maybe I'll grab Andre, drive over to the administration building, and see if I can find him."

"Whatever. Let me know if you do." She shrugged in all her blissful innocence, gathered her things, and left.

# CHAPTER TWENTY-SEVEN

When I came into the room carrying a tray of coffee and chocolate cake, Andre had turned on the fire. I looked at the licking flames, the lovely room and my handsome husband. It was Sunday night, when we should be curled up together, enjoying some leisure time. Unwinding from the week and winding up again for the next one. We had chocolate and coffee and a big, soft couch. This was life the way it should be.

He smiled at the tray. "You're such a good wife," he said.

"Doesn't take much, does it?"

"Considering that I swore I'd never get married again, I'd say it took quite a lot. Come, sit down, and tell me about your week." He dropped onto the couch and patted the space beside him. "I know you're anxious to dive back into your work, but let's take an hour and pretend we're a normal couple on a normal Sunday night." He patted the space again.

"I'm worried about Bobby."

"Just an hour, Thea. Something I've learned over the years, you have to draw lines and learn to shut things out. Otherwise, there would never be any normal life. There's always something else to be done, someone to worry about. Some ugly thing that sticks in your head." He held out his hand. I took it and let him draw me down beside him. "Cake and coffee," he said. "Watching the fire. Then we can go back to worrying about Bobby and Shondra and anyone else who needs to be worried about. Okay?"

"Okay." The compulsive in me reluctantly yielded to his greater experience, as well as to the temptations of comfort and his company. I nuzzled his shoulder with my chin. "So. What about your week? You find any bodies yet?"

"Sort of. Found a head. Actually, a head and one leg."

"Body parts, body parts, who's got the body parts," I murmured. "Are there still guys out there looking for the rest?"

"Of course. Don't you want to know where we found them?"

"Dying to know."

"That's an unfortunate choice of words."

"Eager," I amended.

"In the landlord's freezer. Wrapped in freezer paper and neatly taped. We opened every other goddamned thing in that freezer. All the stuff labeled moose and bear and venison."

"Souvenirs?"

He shrugged. "Could be. We don't know yet. Sometimes it gets hard to tell weird and crazy from deliberate." He poured cream into my coffee, handed it to me, and lifted his. "This is good. You were right. This is a great place. Good bed. Excellent shower. Fine food."

"Good company. When do you have to go back?"

"Let's not talk about that yet," he said. "This is our hour."

Meaning soon. I fought my impulse to beg him to stay and tried to follow his advice. Compartmentalize. Shut the door on everything but the here and now so I wouldn't spoil this. "So what do we talk about? Body parts?"

"Whatever we want."

"Body parts," I said. "Then what happened?"

"We brought in a couple extra guys to go check freezers, dumpsters, car trunks. Got a bolo out on the landlord. And I got some time off. Told 'em I had a hot date."

I yawned. "Sleepy date."

"That's marriage for you," he said. "It's like they always say. When you're dating, women are so eager for your company and to sleep with you, then you get married, and bam! It's all not tonight dear, I'm tired."

"Not again tonight," I corrected. "Aren't you tired, Superman?"

"Day I get tired of you, Mrs. Superman, they plant me."

"But you're work tired?" He nodded. "And tired of the messes I get into?"

249

"Tired of having you hurt, you mean? Of course I am. Well, not tired. Worried. Makes me want to lock you up somewhere and keep you safe. I have to keep reminding myself that I like *you*. You the way you are, not you in some idealized form. I can't quite imagine what a precious, coddled, normal life Thea would be like. Not rescuing the downtrodden or sweeping ahead with righteous anger. I don't imagine that I'd like her as well. Not enough hooks and edges."

He picked up his cake, tapping the plate with his fork. "Just like I could give up chocolate cake and eat fruit. Delightful, healthy fruit. But it wouldn't have the same rich, sinful essence. It wouldn't be dense and complicated and compelling. Like you."

"I'm dense?"

"Well, you're being dense right now."

"Give me twenty or thirty years. I'll learn to take a compliment."

"A guy can hope." He touched the ring on his left hand. "Look how far hope has brought us."

Like Andre, after my husband David died, I'd sworn never to get into a relationship again, but here I was. Worried sick when he was out on a case, always struggling to accept the reality of his dangerous life and the way my heart stopped when the phone rang, and unwilling to change what was so essentially him. But it always amazed me to get the same things back.

We relished every second of our stolen hour, sitting side-by-side watching the licking flames. Talking about mundane subjects like when we'd find time to go house-hunting and how we'd manage Thanksgiving and Christmas with two such possessive mothers. About finalizing our wedding album so my mother would stop complaining. How scary it had been for me to fire that gun. Breathing in warm silences, comfortably shoulder to shoulder.

"About Suzanne," he said. "I think she's going to be okay. You're the target, I admit, but I don't think this is about you. I think it's about her struggle to manage her life. She's afraid she's not going to be able to do it and she needs someplace to put those feelings. A best friend is always a good target. You know she respects you."

I hoped he was right. Working at St. Matthews had undermined my confidence. I wasn't feeling my usual tough-as-nails self. Getting assaulted can do that. I'd left the dinner table ready to go slay dragons but now I was content to sit here in front of the fire and let George do it. St. George, I suppose, since dragon slaying was involved. I rested my head on Andre's shoulder and closed my eyes.

The phone rang. Jenna Adams, wanting to know if I'd seen Shondra, worried that she hadn't. And it all came rushing back. "Did you try her room?"

"She's not answering the phone."

"I meant go over there. After her history with Alasdair, I can see why she might not answer her phone."

"I've been busy," she said defensively.

She disappointed me. I'd counted on her for follow-through. "Maybe you could do that now?"

"Maybe in a while."

When, I wondered? Midnight? Yelling at her wouldn't do any good. I didn't have the authority and, apparently, she didn't have the commitment. I couldn't think of another suitable response, so I made some noncommittal sound and put down the phone.

"Guess that's it for our hour," Andre said, looking at his watch.

Nodding, I picked up the phone again and tried Bobby's number. No answer. I left a message, then scrolled through my list until I found his home number. His significant other, Quinn, answered. Odd, because Quinn was a chef. I would have expected him to be at work.

"Quinn, it's Thea. Is Bobby there? I've been trying to reach him on his cell phone and he isn't answering."

There was a puzzling silence, then Quinn said, "He's here, but he can't talk right now."

My stomach sank to my toes. Bobby would never leave without a word in the middle of a job. He was too responsible. Suzanne and now Bobby. I felt an eerie, crumbling sensation. A jet of panic. "Quinn, is he okay? Is he hurt?"

"He's okay physically. Emotionally, he's a wreck."

Quinn was a charmer who loved to talk. His reticence was alarming. Was something seriously wrong between them? Had something happened to Bobby's family? "What's going on?" I asked.

"It's Peggy Sue," he said. I was trying to remember who Peggy Sue was when he added, "The car. Someone at that stupid school really trashed it." There was a pause, and I heard him speaking to Bobby, explaining I was on the phone. Then he was back. "He's sorry, but he really can't talk right now."

"Trashed it how? When did this happen?" The car was Bobby's baby—he'd done all the work himself, reviving it practically from the scrapheap, but it still wasn't like Bobby to leave without a note or a word of explanation.

"Oh, Thea, such devastation. And after all Bobby's hard work. The engine was trashed. Hoses cut, pieces removed, sparkplug wires cut. It was just savaged. The outside is fine, thankfully. But it will take days to make it right, and that's if he can find the parts. And he's just...well, you know how he feels about that car. I'm...We're ... What can I say? Devastated."

Another pause, filled with the sounds of indignant breathing. "Oh, you had another question, didn't you. When? It must have been around one or two? I'm not sure. It was about 2:30 when he called me, in tears, and said I had to come get him. I got my assistant to cover for me and drove right over. We had a tow-truck bring the car back. Look, Thea, this isn't a good time, okay? We're just...you know...struggling to deal with this. Why doesn't he call you tomorrow?"

"Wait, Quinn. Don't hang up." I needed to understand this better. When had I spoken with Bobby? A little earlier than that. I'd called him for a ride and then later he'd called to say he'd been delayed but was on his way. He hadn't seemed upset then.

I felt like I was working a jigsaw puzzle and none of the pieces fit.

"This is not a good time," Quinn repeated. "We're upset. I have to go."

"Will you ask Bobby one question for me? Ask him who he told about the accident...about my car."

"Thea. Darling. You don't understand what I'm dealing with here. He's just gone to take a hot bath. If he's feeling up to it, I'll ask when he gets out." Quinn put down the phone. If I called back, I knew he wouldn't answer. Quinn reminded me of my mother. She was convinced Suzanne worked me too hard; Quinn believed I worked Bobby too hard. Impossible to make them understand that we worked hard because we chose to.

I put down the phone. "Curiouser and curiouser." I poured some lukewarm coffee into my cup, and stared at the too perfect artificial fire. Nothing that had happened since I took this job made sense. Not professional, reasonable way to run a school sense and not logical, interpersonal sense. There was a level of game playing going on here that I couldn't get a handle on. "None of this makes any sense."

"Maybe you could be more specific?" Andre said.

"I don't know if I can. Maybe it will help if I start at the beginning. You know about that. Todd Chambers called us for help with a campus problem. His version of the campus problem was that a minority student, Shondra Jones, had, for either irrational or vindictive reasons, accused a fellow student, known for his conservative, practically white supremacist views, of stalking her. Her accusations had inflamed the campus and upset other female students. He wanted us to approve a letter to the parents, assuring them that there was no stalking problem."

I stared at the tongues of yellow and blue gas flame, feeling pretty out-of-gas myself. "Have you got time for this? You don't need to be back?"

"I need to get back, but I've got some time."

A little bit of time. I hated to waste it on St. Matthews, but

I wanted Andre's advice. "I refused to approve the letter without asking some questions, and discovered that the student *was* being harassed, that the school had failed to follow its own rules and procedures by not questioning the alleged stalker or holding a hearing, that they didn't get the concept of stalking at all. When I suggested a different letter and some systemic changes, I was sent packing. With me so far?"

"Of course." He nodded impatiently.

"It was Suzanne they wanted all along, not me. Chambers believed she would avoid asking hard questions and support his agenda, which appears to have been calm the parents and go back to business as usual, a business which mostly seems to have revolved around the Headmaster's desire to raise money for a fancy new building rather than running a quality school. Then they had the murder, where apparently the harassed girl's brother, Jamison Jones, beat Alasdair MacGregor, the boy who was harassing her, to death and tried to burn his body in a fire."

I grabbed a breath, knowing I was racing through this. "The head of the Trustees, Charles Argenti, called us back in and we started doing our thing. Not far into the first day, we discovered that the dead boy, Alasdair, had formed the Neo-Skulls, a group of legatee boys who specialized in harassing women and minorities, but who were never disciplined for it because their families were big donors."

Andre put a hand on my arm. "Easy, Thea," he said. "I don't have a plane to catch."

"Okay. Sorry. This gets me all wound up. So this group had threatened to revenge Alasdair's murder, which we…or I…took as a threat to Shondra Jones…but the coaches who reported the threat stonewalled about giving any details, and Chambers refused to take the threat seriously. All along, they've refused to listen to our advice, and Chambers and his staff are still doing their best to avoid telling the truth about what is going on on this campus."

I sucked in a breath. "I don't understand why they're behaving this way. There are other things that don't make sense.

254

When we found Shondra unconscious from an overdose, and her room completely trashed, Chambers hardly blinked, even when we learned that the dorm residents had been lured away by a bogus phone call. And Chambers' behavior last night was so smug and so indifferent, like nothing was happening here that he needed to pay attention to…like his crisis was over and it was okay to act insulting again."

"Remember to breathe," he said. "This isn't your problem anymore. It's their problem, Suzanne's problem."

"It *was* their problem, before someone attacked me. Before they trashed my car. Before they tried so hard to get me out of the way again. Now, their problem is that I'm not leaving until I understand what's happening and why it's happening, why someone is so desperate to have me gone. And I can't go until I know that Shondra is safe."

"Shondra is your latest waif?"

"If a 6' 3" tough, fit female basketball player can be characterized as a waif." I checked my watch. "And the first item on my agenda is to see if I can find her. I thought her coach would be taking care of that, but it seems that she's too busy."

"And someone's got to do it, right?" He looked like he wanted to argue. As he'd said, it wasn't supposed to be my problem anymore. Then he sat down beside me and picked up my hand. "Where would I be today if you weren't so determined?" I squeezed back, the flames blurred to a kaleidoscope of blue and gold by my tears. It was something we would never know.

Abruptly, he dropped my hand and stood up. "I have to go."

"I know," I said. "I wish …"

"We both wish. Look, will you do something for me? Something you aren't going to like much?"

Here came the 'be careful' speech, or the 'get out of town' one, some form of protective behavior. But it was natural for him to be protective. He was a cop. He held out his hand. "Give me your phone."

I gave it to him.

"You got Gary Bushnell's number?" I dug out Bushnell's card and handed it to him. He programmed the number into my phone, first on the list of automatic numbers, and gave it back. "I hope you won't need to use it."

"Better safe than sorry, right?"

"You got it."

We shared one last hug, then he dropped his arms and reached for his coat. "You be careful out there," I said. "I don't want to be finding parts of you in people's freezers."

"How likely is that?"

"You're the detective. You tell me."

"You're the one who needs to be careful. In fact, when you get home, I'm getting you a helmet like the ones skiers wear. You can decorate it any way you want. Ribbons, beads, flowers, pompoms…but you have to wear it all the time, just in case."

"Maybe I'll get a bright red one. Stencil EDGE Consulting on it. Get me some of those shoulder pads like football players wear. That would really make people sit up and pay attention."

"I think you've got people paying attention," he said quietly. "That's why they're trying to get you out of here. You scare them."

"Yeah, right."

He gave me a look, one of his 'believe me, I know bad guys' looks. "Right. So you be careful." Then my handsome husband walked out the door. I heard him thumping down the stairs, resisting the impulse to run after him and tell him he couldn't go. He had to go, and so did I. Back to the St. Matthews campus.

# CHAPTER TWENTY-EIGHT

I was stiff and sore from battling the forces of evil, and sleepy from good food and sitting by the fire. Gearing up to go back out into a chilly night wasn't easy. But then, no one said life would be easy. I'd had my hour with Andre. It was time to get back to work. I changed into sleuthing clothes, black sweater and pants and charcoal trail runners, stuck a tiny flashlight and my pepper spray in my pocket, and went down to the Jeep.

I parked in the lot behind Shondra's dorm, then sailed right in through the unlocked door, unchallenged and unobserved all the way to Shondra's door. They had awfully short memories around this place. If I'd been an axe murderer—these days, in films, the guy who wants to be thought good always declares he's no axe murderer, so society must be rife with them—I'd have reached my quarry easily. I knocked on her door, not expecting a response, waited a minute, and knocked again.

The slight shuffle of feet told me I was being observed. I turned to find Cassie the pastel blonde watching me from a doorway across the hall. She widened her eyes as I turned. "Oh, good. So Shondra's back?" she said.

A wise friend once told me that if something's too good to be true, assume it isn't. If someone who appears to be a sweet, innocent friend wannabe is always on hand but never actually seems to perform friendly acts—be suspicious. Maybe she's no friend at all. Maybe she works for the other side. Alasdair and his crew must have needed some inside people. Maybe MacLeods, like MacGregors, were a hereditary St. Matthews family. Maybe the Neo-Skulls had a women's auxiliary—the Neo-Skullettes? Or maybe I'd been Thea Kozak, girl detective, too long.

I shrugged. "I have no idea. Just thought I'd stop by and see."

"Oh. Too bad. I was just wondering if she was okay." The wide-eyed enthusiasm faded to a dejection equally dramatic and equally implausible.

"So you haven't seen her, Cassie?"

She blinked a little, surprised that I'd remembered her name, then shook her head. "Not for days," she said. "Not since...not since her brother...since that awful thing happened."

That wasn't what she'd told me last time I'd come looking for Shondra. Girl ought to get her story straight. "So you have no idea if she's in there?"

Her shrug was airily delicate. "Not a clue." She looked ruefully over her shoulder at her room. "Guess I'd better get back to work." She retreated, closing the door behind her, but I didn't hear the click of the latch.

I knocked on Shondra's door again. "Shondra, if you're there, let me in. It's Thea Kozak. I need to talk with you."

I expected her to be there. Where else was she going to go, if she wasn't with Coach Adams? Frank Woodson, maybe? But while her brother had taken Woodson's concern at face value, Shondra seemed to dislike him. I'd try her teammates next, starting with Jen and Lindsay. I had their numbers from this morning. I took paper from my briefcase, wrote my message and my cell phone number on it, and pushed it under the door. I waited a little longer, hoping she'd respond. When she didn't, I left.

I consulted the list and my campus map. I'd grabbed a handful of those after giving my copy to Bushnell, figuring I'd probably keep losing them and keep needing them. Jen and Lindsay were in Henderson Hall.

This time, I got in the door all right, but ran into a wary adult before I was five feet into the building. She was handsome and imposing, with the well-put-together style I admired and could never achieve. She had a great haircut and knew how to use make-up. Women like her always make me feel frumpy. Her smile was pleasant, but there was a firmness and certainty about her that made one thing clear: there was no way she was letting me pass.

"I'm Molly Weston, the head resident. And you are?"

"Thea Kozak, from EDGE Consulting, we're working with the school on issues around Alasdair's death." She knew this. I'd been at the faculty meeting. But it didn't hurt to remind her and I wanted to appear cooperative. "I'm looking for Lindsay Davis and Jen Reilly."

"I think Lindsay is in. I'm not sure about Jen." She waved a hand toward the open door behind her. "Why don't you come in and tell me what this is about?"

"I'm trying to find Shondra Jones. I wanted to see if either of them had any suggestions about where she might go."

"You tried Jenna Adams?"

"Yes. And Shondra's dorm."

"I see. If you don't mind my asking, why are *you* looking for Shondra? Why not someone from the school?"

It was a fair question. I decided it deserved the truth. "Technically speaking, I *am* someone from the school, as long as I'm working for them." I let her absorb that, and gave her the rest. "I'm doing it because no one else is bothering, and I'm concerned about her. I was the one who picked her up at the hospital this morning. When we stopped for lunch, someone in the parking lot tried to run us down."

I stopped. This had to sound like too much answer.

But Molly Weston didn't look surprised or suspicious. "Go on," she said.

"Then the police came, and one of them, Lt. Bushnell, the state police detective who's investigating Alasdair's death, questioned her." Her eyebrows went up and I nodded. "He was rough...said some pretty harsh things about her brother. We were going to ride back with Frank Woodson because my car was damaged but before Bushnell finished, Shondra ran away. As far as I know, no one has seen her since."

She listened attentively, as though she cared about what I was saying, but her face remained skeptical. "Why aren't you taking those concerns to Craig Dunham? Her advisor? Or

Security? Aren't they in a better position to help?" She wrapped her hands around her knee and leaned forward. "It's not a good idea to traipse through the dorms, asking for Shondra. I think our students are upset enough already."

I debated whether or not to tell some more truth. It seemed in short supply on this campus, and I had no idea where this woman stood or what she knew. On the other hand, she was the only person, other than the coaches, who'd voiced concern about the impact of all this on the students.

"Shondra doesn't trust her advisor. She feels betrayed by the way her complaints about Alasdair were handled. I don't think she has any kind of relationship with Dunham. I already tried Jenna Adams and she put me off."

Mrs. Weston studied her hands. "Why do you think Jen and Lindsay might be able to help?"

"I'm not sure they can," I said. "But she sometimes confided in them. She may be physically big and act tough, but she's still just a sixteen-year-old girl. The only person here she's close to has been arrested. Her room was trashed and all her things destroyed. Yesterday, she either took, or was given, an overdose of drugs. She's out there all alone and she may still be at risk from certain elements on this campus."

I watched her closely as I said this last, to see if she'd react, but if she knew what I was referring to, she didn't let it show.

She slowly smoothed her skirt, evidently considering what I'd said, and looked at me, a serious look. For a second, I thought she was going to help. Then she unknotted her hands, rose, and walked over to the window, staring out with her back to me.

Finally, she turned. "You've been frank, so I will be frank in return. You wouldn't have any reason to know this, but Jen Reilly hasn't had an easy time here at St. Matthews. This year she seems to be back on her feet, regaining some of her confidence. I'm not willing to allow her to get involved in anything that might disturb that recovery. Not even to help out a friend." She picked up a coffee mug from the table and drank.

"All I want to do is talk with them, Mrs. Weston. I'm not asking to take them around the campus with me, scouting out Shondra's secret hide-outs. It's not like I want them exposed to any risk from Alasdair's Neo-Skulls."

The mug slipped from her hands, splashing coffee on her light blue rug.

"What do you know about the Neo-Skulls, Mrs. Weston? I think they're a serious problem for St. Matthews…or perhaps I should say, a serious threat to St. Matthews' girls, but they can't be stopped if everyone pretends to know nothing about them."

"I'm sorry," she said, looking at the mess instead of at me. "I'm afraid I can't help you. And you may not bother Jen Reilly."

"What about Shondra? Don't you care about her? Don't you care that the Administration seems to be condoning the sexual harassment and possibly the assault of young girls?"

"I'm sorry," she repeated. "I'm not in a position to change the culture on this campus. You'll have to take that up with Todd Chambers. But I do everything I can to make the girls in this dorm safe."

"Is everyone a part of this conspiracy?" I said. "Has Chambers got you so cowed you're all willing to sit back and let this happen if it means St. Matthews will get fancy buildings from big bucks donors? I doubt that what happened to Jen is an isolated incident."

She shook her head sadly. "The incident with Jen happened before Chambers got here. Yes, there are problems here. They're isolated incidents, but they happen. We just have to do what we can. This is a beautiful place with a fine faculty. We give our students a good education. You have no idea how difficult it would be to find this somewhere else…two faculty positions and living conditions like this."

She walked purposefully to the door and opened it. "Good evening, Ms. Kozak."

Before I left, I fired one last shot across her bow. "I don't

261

know whether there are mandatory reporting laws here in New Hampshire," I said, "but if there are, and you have knowledge of harm, or the threat of harm, to the girls in your care, and you haven't reported it, when all of this comes out and parents jerk their kids out of St. Matts, your problem won't be finding another good position in a lovely place. It will be trying to find a glimpse of the sky through jail bars." I left her with a shocked look and one hand spread like a starfish over her hardened heart.

I knew I should just go back to The Swan, eat bonbons until my meeting with Suzanne, and leave. Mother Theresa couldn't do anything with these people. I stomped out to the car, got in, and slammed the door. Then, because losing my temper would get me nowhere, I pulled out my phone and dialed Jen Reilly's number. It rang a few times, then asked me to leave a message. I disconnected and tried Lindsay. Never say die Kozak. I must have a perversity gene.

"It's Thea Kozak," I said when she answered. "From this morning. I'm sitting in my car behind your dorm. I need your help, if you're willing. Shondra's missing."

"She's out of the hospital? When she wasn't at practice, I thought maybe they'd kept her another day. Nothing keeps Shondra from practice."

"I picked her up this morning, took her to see her brother, and then...well. It's a long story. The short version is that my car got damaged and we were going to get a ride back here with Frank Woodson, but Shondra ran away."

"Oh, well. You couldn't know this, but she doesn't like Mr. Woodson."

"Look." I was feeling a sense of urgency. Shondra was out on this campus somewhere with those incriminating pictures, and no one could be trusted. "I just tried to come see you and your dorm head, Mrs. Weston, wouldn't let me."

"Yeah, that's how she is. She's okay," Lindsay said. "Just a little too protective. Better than Shondra's housemother. That bitch...I mean...well, you've met her, haven't you? She treats Shondra like some dangerous creature about to go out of control. Shondra said it used to make her want to do mean things, but after a while she figured it wasn't worth it."

"Mrs. Leverett didn't notice?"

"Something like that." Lindsay laughed. "You want me to come down?"

"If you can. I really need to find her. I think Alasdair's friends, whoever they are, pose a real risk to Shondra."

"You bet they do," she interrupted. "We never got a chance to talk about this, but Alasdair and them…I've heard…have done some awful stuff and not just to Jen. We can't stop it, so we kind of work together. You know, protect the new girls and all. But stuff still happens. Look, I'll be right down."

"When is curfew?"

"Ten."

It was 9:20. "What if she tries to stop you?"

"From dashing to the library? How could she? This isn't jail."

I snapped the phone shut, sucked in a breath, and let it slowly out. I was losing my temper. I haven't got ESP, but I've got an acute sense of impending disaster, and right now, the inside of my head was like a railroad crossing—clanging bells, flashing lights and big striped barriers going up and down. I hate situations where I'm not in control. Even more, I hate the ones where I know something's going on and I've only got the faintest clue what it is.

Lindsay came around the corner of the building. I opened the door and got out so she could see me. As she raised an arm and waved, a dark figure came racing toward her from the trees behind the parking lot, heavy feet thudding on the tarmac. As it crossed the pool of light from the solitary security fixture, I recognized Shondra.

Lindsay saw her at the same time, veered away from me, and went to meet her. I saw the two heads come together, bend down, and rise like a pair of startled deer to look at me. Then they both raced off into the trees. I took off after them.

## CHAPTER TWENTY-NINE

I did pretty well for a while, following their thudding feet through the maze of dormitory buildings and up the slope toward the rest of the campus. As they came up the hill toward the main road, they were briefly silhouetted against a street light, two long-legged figures with flying hair. Then they were swallowed up by trees on the other side.

It was dark and I didn't know the campus. I lost them when we got the section of the campus that housed the classroom buildings. There were muffled voices, the scrunching of feet, and then a door clanged. I couldn't tell where. I surrounded by buildings with multiple entry doors. I hung around, watching for the shafts of light that signaled an opened door, and listened, in case they came reemerged. There was nothing but night sounds.

What now? I could go back to the dorm. Catch Lindsay when she returned. She was due pretty soon with curfew at ten. But I was betting she'd blow off curfew if Shondra needed her help. They might see if they could get Jen Reilly to join them. I could go back and watch for her but it was kind of a long shot.

I considered my options. Right now, I had two priorities—finding Shondra and finding that camera, both the same task, really. On my secondary list were all my questions about the Neo-Skulls, who had been driving that little gray car, why someone had attacked me and Shondra, and whether she was safe on this campus. All the questions on my secondary list really lead up to the big questions—why, with a campus murder and all its fall-out to deal with, did Todd Chambers so determinedly resist our help and refuse to keep Shondra safe, and why was he so complacent in the face of a crisis? What did he know, or think he knew, that explained his behavior?

I thought the answers began with identifying the Neo-Skulls. I assumed that they were behind the attack on me and the trashing of Shondra's room. I wasn't risking my head again. If I could identify them, I'd give that information to Bushnell, who was probably a competent cop even if he was a jerk, and beat a hasty and sensible retreat.

Right now, I was standing in a dark parking lot with no idea what to do. If Molly Weston and the coaches were examples of how cooperative people on this campus would be, I might as well just go back to the Swan and pack. Chambers had things buttoned up pretty tight. Was that the source of his arrogant confidence? That it didn't matter what he allowed to happen on the campus because no one would talk?

Shondra Jones had gotten people talking and gotten the parents upset, and she'd been marginalized. If the Chambers had their way, she'd probably be tossed out on her ear as a lesson to others who thought about making waves, if she survived her return to St. Matthews. Andre had called Shondra my latest waif and I guess he was right. While others might see a tall, fierce, aggressive woman, I saw a terrified sixteen-year-old who was in over her head. I was feeling very guilty about suggesting she stay at St. Matts. I should have taken her to the nearest bus station and sent her home.

Standing on this vast campus on a cold October night, I was at a loss about how to find her or how to help her by fixing the dangerous situation on this campus. I also knew I couldn't leave while Shondra's situation was so precarious. Who was my best resource for identifying the Neo-Skulls and finding Shondra?

Todd Chambers knew the campus and the identity of the players, but he wouldn't help. He just wanted me gone. I didn't know how much Dunham knew, but he lacked backbone. That left Woodson. Security people usually knew a lot. He had staff who could help me find Shondra, and if he knew his student population, he might be able to help me identify the Neo-Skulls and assess how dangerous a threat they were. He seemed like my last hope.

I got out my map and clicked on my flashlight. The campus security offices were at the far back of the campus, housed in one end of a long building that also garaged the maintenance vehicles. If he had any sense, Woodson was home sipping a medicinal Scotch, but he'd seemed conscientious, so maybe while things were in a state of high alert, he was still at work. I clicked off my light and headed back to the car.

I'm a great believer in walking, but it was easily half a mile from where I was to where I wanted to be across a dark campus. After last night, I was taking no unnecessary nocturnal strolls. I climbed into the Jeep and fired it up. I was already getting attached to the big engine, the comfortable leather seats, and the sense of power and superiority that came from sitting up high. If I was going to live with Maine winters, maybe I needed a Jeep.

I wound my way through the maze of roads, following the signs to Buildings and Grounds and Security. I parked in front of the dimly lit building and sat a moment in the warm, dark car, planning what I'd say. Unlike Chambers, who had constructed his own reality, and his cowed underlings, Woodson might see the wisdom of the argument that making the campus safer protected his job.

Maybe it was sleuth's intuition or maybe the fact that people on this campus came out of the dark and knocked others on the head, but I decided to be careful. Instead of jumping out, slamming the door, and bounding into the building, I sat and studied the area around the building for movement. All was still. I shut off the Jeep's interior lights and slipped quietly out, not quite closing the door.

The Security office was to my right, but the nearest entrance seemed to be about twenty feet to the left. Set into the wall between huge overhead doors was a regular door, looking like Baby Bear's door next to the others. Through its small window, I could see into the cavernous interior of the garage, lit enough for security if not for good visibility. There were variously-sized green trucks and vans with the St. Matthews seal in gold letters. At the far end of the building were campus security cars with light bars on their roofs and beyond them, a door in the end wall marked SECURITY.

The garage was empty. I tried the knob, expecting it to be locked, but it turned in my hand. Why should I be surprised? Security around here was, depending on your point of view, notoriously—or reliably—lax. I entered, expecting any moment that someone would materialize from behind one of the hulking trucks demanding to know why I was there.

My footsteps sounded unnaturally loud on the cement floor as I headed toward Security. A sudden, resounding clang from the other end of the building sent me darting behind the fender of a large truck. The clang was followed by a mechanical roar as one of the doors rose slowly on its tracks and a van drove in. A man hummed to himself as he spent several minutes opening and slamming the van's doors. Then his humming was drowned out by the descent of the garage door. I heard him leave the building and the big room fell silent again.

My pounding heart was as loud in my ears as the door had been. I straightened up, turned, and ran smack into a small car completely covered with a blue plastic tarp, which had been hidden from my view by the truck. Carefully, I raised the tarp. Even in dim light, I could see the badly damaged right front and smears of tell-tale red paint. It was the same small gray car that had run into me earlier. I dropped the tarp, crept quietly to the back, and copied down the license number. Now what was I supposed to do?

Obviously, it no longer made sense to try and see Frank Woodson. He knew the police were looking for this car. Hiding a car used in a deliberate assault wasn't minor. If the car was here then he was part of what was going on. He and Chambers and the Neo-Skulls.

Finding the car here, and its implications, suddenly let me see the picture in the jigsaw puzzle I'd been working on. Most of the picture, anyway. If I put together what Jen and Lindsay had said, the note on my windshield, Lindsay's comments tonight and her housemother's peculiar behavior, Chambers' 'refusal to get it' finally made sense. He got it just fine.

He was indifferent to Shondra's situation, and to the possibility of a crisis involving female students on his campus, because he'd been letting them be victimized all along. He had managed to keep the lid on thus far, and he was arrogant enough to believe that if he calmed the parents with that letter and silenced Shondra, things could go on that way. Keeping Alasdair and his friends out of trouble was worth millions.

Okay, that answered the way he'd handled the stalking part of it, and another question that had troubled me—why they wanted Suzanne instead of me. Not because she would be more accommodating but because, if they fed her a carefully vetted segment, she was less likely to connect with students, as I had, who would tell her the truth.

Was I being unfair to Suzanne? I didn't think so. She would have kept her temper and stayed polite. She also wouldn't have pushed them as hard toward the truth as I had, or gone forth as forcefully to check their stories, and so she wouldn't have learned what I had. Because she dealt with schools on day-to-day issues and I came in when there was trouble. Which is why she didn't get knocked on the head and charged by small gray cars. Would she have questioned their investigation? Believed Shondra? That I didn't know.

It was a peculiar truth to be facing in the chilly dimness of a cavernous garage, but insight comes when it comes. Now another hard question loomed. Why had Chambers regained his arrogant equilibrium so fast after Alasdair's death? He'd gone off to the hospital in a shaken state and returned remarkably restored. What had happened while he was gone?

One possible explanation was that MacGregor still promised the money if they named the building after Alasdair. But that would have freed him up to concentrate on his crisis, yet he'd still been too distracted to deal. So what was it? Was I giving him too much credit by assuming that undistracted, he would have handled things competently?

Down at the far end of the garage, the van's cooling engine gave a sharp, metallic ping, bringing me back to the trap-covered car. In my heedless youth, I might have tried to sort this out for myself. Now I had no problem interposing the professionals between myself and the bad guys. A car that had been used to attack me was being stored in a campus facility. Under these circumstances, I was not constrained by any duty to my client. The police needed to know it was here, no matter what questions might ensue. And cops meant Bushnell.

Much more carefully now, I walked to the door, eager to skedaddle back to the relative safety of The Swan, dump the whole mess, including Shondra, in Bushnell's lap, gather up Suzanne and get out of town. I had my hand on the knob when I heard voices outside. I ducked down below the window and pressed my ear against the door.

One of the speakers had his back to me, his words an indistinct mumble. The other, facing me, was Woodson. "I don't know whose car it is. It doesn't belong to any of my people. Could be a student with an illegal car, looking for someplace to leave it overnight. They do that all the time."

The other speaker must have turned, because suddenly I heard his voice, quite distinctly, saying, "It was just an incredibly stupid idea to use that car instead of dumping it somewhere immediately. Now we've got to find a way to get rid of it. Permanently. And without anyone noticing." Todd Chambers. "What on earth were you boys thinking?"

"You told us to get Shondra."

"Not you, for God's sakes. Not in a public place, using *that* car."

"Fuck, man. Frank said follow her and keep our eyes open for chances. That big broad hadn't been so fast, we'd have done it, too. One less nigger to foul up the landscape."

"Minority, Alasdair," Woodson corrected. "Minority."

Until that moment, I'd never understood the phrase 'makes my blood run cold,' in a literal sense. Now, the full enormity of what I was overhearing hit and iciness jangled through me. If

269

Chambers and Woodson were talking to Alasdair MacGregor, if, as Jen had said, he was alive, then they knew someone else had been beaten to death and dumped into that fire.

I gritted my teeth against the shakes and listened. "You aren't even supposed to be around anymore, Alasdair," Chambers said. "That was the deal we made. We've really gone out on a limb for you here, and you're screwing everything up. Suppose someone sees you?"

"They'll think they're seeing a ghost. Everyone knows I'm dead. Besides, Toddy, I'm having way too much fun with this."

"Well, we're not," Woodson snapped. "You were supposed to leave this morning. Your grandfather hires a car and driver and you don't show. Someone's going to see you, or hear your voice, and it'll blow this wide open. If that happens, Alasdair, you're not walking away from this anymore than the rest of us. You understand that, don't you?"

"Oh, please, Woody, spare me your tale of drama and sacrifice. It's not like you both aren't getting what you want out of this. You get me, your chief troublemaker, off your hands. Once I'm gone, Todd and Charles 'Mister God' Argenti can go back to realizing their dream of taking this place back to the dark ages. You get rid of Shondra Jones, and you get Grandfather's money for your arts center. With *my* name on it."

Alasdair gave a derisive snort of laughter. "Toddy, here, loses the principle thorn in his side and can go back to humoring his crazy wife. The fact that Shondra has pictures of Woody screwing a student conveniently disappears along with Shondra, and his job is secure. So don't whine to me about the risks you're taking. Life's full of risks."

"Not at this level, it isn't," Chambers said. "To you, everything is a big joke, but we've got a lot at stake. We still haven't found that camera or those pictures or Shondra."

"She's got the pictures of Woody boning that little piglet? His wrinkled old ass pumping? She get that?" Another manic hoot of laughter. Alasdair must be on high something. Shondra had mentioned drugs. "It's almost funny, isn't it, that while I'm

270

targeting her, having my fun, she's targeting you. And you thought what?" His voice rose, "That you could ... how did Toddy put that? Contain her by making everyone think she was crazy?"

"Watch yourself, son." There was a warning in Woodson's voice.

"What have I got to worry about, Woody? I've got immunity. You do anything to me, you both hurt yourselves. I'm only good to you alive. That's what grandfather said, and that's what grandfather meant."

There was a loud crash, like someone had kicked something big into the side of the building, and Alasdair gave his crazy laugh again.

"Stop that, you idiot." Rage boiled in Chambers' voice. "There are security guys in there. You want them to come out to see what's going on and find you?"

I wished I had my tape recorder to capture this conversation. I also wished I possessed the ability to become invisible. Sooner or later, they were going to come in here and do something about that gray car. They couldn't leave it here. Someone would notice. Maybe Woodson could control his own people, but there were so many other people in and out during the day, and people are naturally curious, especially about damaged civilian cars parked in a business facility. About anything under a tarp.

I backed away from the door, looking for a place to hide. Inside a vehicle or under it were obvious places. But if they were obvious to me, they'd also be obvious to anyone looking for me. Woodson was smart. Pretty soon he'd connect me to that Jeep. Too bad I wasn't tiny like Suzanne. There were a hundred places she could have hidden. Finally I found it. A curved snowplow blade pushed up against a back wall. Where it curved away from the wall there was a space just my size. Quick as a wink, I wiggled into it.

It was dusty and airless, with cold metal on one side and cold cinderblock on the other. Still, it felt relatively secure. Who knew how long I might have to be in here? One thing was sure.

271

I hadn't found it a minute too soon. I'd just gotten settled when the door opened and their voices were in the room. I muffled my breath with a sleeve and listened.

Their voices rose and fell, hollow and indistinct through the metal, as they decided what they'd do about the car. The passage of time felt physical, each minute stroking me slowly, teasingly, from head to toe as the chilly metal sucked heat from my body. I became nervously aware of two things. First, that where I'd parked might be blocking them from moving the gray car out of the building. Second, that my phone was unreachable in a lower pocket, and when I wasn't at the Swan, Suzanne would call.

"So where the hell we gonna dump it?" Woodson said. "You got any clever ideas?"

"Just out there in the woods somewhere," Chambers said.

"Out there in the woods somewhere? You think we're what? Up in Alaska or something? You have any idea how many people are through there every day? Not just our kids, out for a run or looking for someplace to screw? Half the damned town uses these woods. You've been here two years and you haven't noticed?"

"Douse it with gasoline and burn it?"

"And get every fire department from six towns?" Woodson sneered. "And that would be if we hadn't already had a serious fire. Another fire on this campus and we'll probably have the governor and the National Guard called out."

"Somewhere else then," Chambers said. "What about those…what are they called? Quarries? Aren't there some of those around? Someplace nice and deep. Dump it off the edge and that little car is never seen again."

"That would be fine," Woodson said, "if you know of any quarries around here. I've been here for years and I don't."

"Justin Palmer's family's got a summer place pretty close by, it's on a lake that's really deep," Alasdair suggested. "They own, like, all the land around the lake, so nobody's going to be around."

"You know how to find it?" Woodson asked.

"Sorta."

"You've got to do better than sorta. We can't go driving this thing all over hell and gone, trying to find the place. The cops are looking for this car. Assuming we can figure out how to get there, you know for sure that no one's gonna be around, no one is living there?"

"He said it was empty. Before the thing with that girl...before all this shit...bunch of us were going up there this weekend...have a party. We do that lots."

The thing with the girl? Bingo. The puzzle was complete. The shudder that ran through me wasn't from the cold metal but from their cold hearts. The abduction and assault on a 12-year old girl had been all over the news. This was what had happened that made Alasdair's departure necessary. Something more serious than harassment of female students and date rape. Chambers had taken that in stride. This was gang rape of a child.

Bored, perhaps, with their tame depredations, or perhaps given the official word they had to cool it on campus for a while, Alasdair and his cronies had gone cruising for adventure and a victim. They had picked up a girl, assaulted her, and dumped her. Far from school, thinking they were home free. So why hadn't they been? Did this have something to do with Shondra's nannycam? With whoever was dumped in that fire?

It was clear that deciding how to dispose of the car would take a while, and I knew Suzanne would call. I shifted so I wasn't lying on my pocket and started inching the fabric up to get at the phone. I was scared stiff and shaking. I had no illusions about what these guys would and wouldn't do. They'd do anything necessary to cover their miserable asses. Look what they'd done to Jamison and Shondra. To the guy in the fire.

Every sound I made seemed enormously loud as I inched toward the phone. Finally, I worked it out of my pocket. Now I just had to flip it open and turn it off. Slowly, slowly. It was like being in a straight-jacket. There wasn't room to bring my other hand around. I'd have to do this one-handed. Despite the cold, my hand was slick with sweat. As I flipped it open, the phone slipped away with a small clang.

I held my breath. Had they heard? No one said 'aha!' or 'what was that?' but the garage had gone completely silent. I heard the clatter of footfalls, the sounds of doors opening and shutting. They were searching the garage. Damn! Why hadn't I just gone home? I'd promised to be careful. Now I was shut up in a garage full of murderers.

Trying to move quietly, I wiggled down, searching desperately for the phone. I touched it, but it skittered away. Another small, damning noise. It gave me another idea for my design business, assuming I got out of here alive. When I finished with Kevlar business clothes and steel-toed pumps, I'd work on a line of rubber phones. I was clearly unsuited for my present career.

Somewhere in the building, a huge blower shuddered and came on with a whoosh, filling the room with its roar. I felt around for the phone As I flipped it open, it rang. One small, three-note ring before I silenced it. Footsteps converged on this end of the garage. Breathless, I hit off, listening as they checked the vehicles again. The empty barrels. The tool cupboards. I squinched into the smallest ball I could, ducking my head so only dark hair, and not white skin, would show if someone glanced in.

"The fuck!" Woodson yelled, kicking at something that flew against the wall beside me, rebounding with a horrific clang. I gagged my startled noise with a sleeve. "There is someone in here. I know there is."

"Maybe they're outside," Chambers suggested.

"Maybe. All right." Clearly, Woodson was in charge of operations. "You two…go out that end door, split up, and each of you take one side of the building."

"I'm not supposed to be seen, remember?" Alasdair said in a mocking voice. "Maybe you should go."

"It's you that keeps forgetting. All right. You stay here. We'll check outside."

Their footsteps moved away. Alasdair stayed nearby, singing a wordless tune to himself as he poked noisily around. I could hear him shuffling through the tools, then his footsteps coming closer. Suddenly, something crashed into the metal near my head with an enormous, reverberating clang. I didn't scream, but I did jump. Then it clanged again and again, flailing against the metal of the plow blade like a clapper against a church bell. All the time, Alasdair was practically shrieking with glee.

By the time he finally stopped, I was wishing Andre *had* made me wear a helmet. My head was ringing and I felt like I'd been pummeled. Just when I had started breathing again, he reached in, grabbed me by the hair and jerked so hard I thought I was being scalped. This time, I did scream.

The hand relaxed. "Come on out of there," he ordered. He sounded way too pleased with himself.

# CHAPTER THIRTY

I crawled out, dirty and shivering, my head still ringing. A few feet away, Alasdair was swinging a shovel back and forth like a pendulum, wearing a maniac grin. "Gotcha!" he said, so blasted proud of himself I wanted to snatch that shovel and whack him upside the head with it. People had told me he was bad, that he was evil, that he was a spoiled rotten bastard who got away with everything. What they hadn't said was that he was a monster. Right now, that big grin told me the monster was sure his luck would hold and he'd get away with murder.

"Excuse me, but what the hell's going on here?"

It should have been Woodson and Chambers returning, but it was the slightly dim security guard who'd rescued me on the path last night. What was his name? Donnie.

"Hey, Donnie," I said. "Thea Kozak. You rescued me last night when I got knocked on the head? This is one of the students. He keeps menacing me with that shovel. I think … " I slowed enough to suggest a pause, "he's gone a little crazy."

Most security services were familiar with students gone temporarily wacko. Donnie turned to Alasdair. "Put down the shovel," he said in a calming voice. "We don't want anyone hurt."

Alasdair grinned a loose, loopy, anything-but-normal grin. His pupils were big and his eyes were red. "No way, Jose. I drop this and that bitch is out the door faster than a weasel in heat."

"I hope you can deal with him," I said. "I was looking for Mr. Woodson and found this nutcase instead."

Alasdair lunged at the guard, swinging the shovel wildly. Donnie picked up a bigger shovel with a longer handle, and the two of them began a duel which would have been absurd if I hadn't know what Alasdair was, and who was waiting outside.

As I headed for the door, I grabbed the phone, punching Bushnell's number to call for help.

He answered on the first ring. "It's Thea Kozak," I said. "Listen …"

"How ya doin', Mrs. Lemieux?" he said.

"Not good. Don't talk. Listen." I was talking as fast as a car salesman reads the small print. "I'm in the grounds and building facility at the back of the campus. Where Security is. Alasdair MacGregor is here with me, not the least bit dead. Chambers and Woodson are here, too. I need help. Now. They're going to Justin Palmer's …"

"You been drinking or something?" he said. "You want to try that again?"

I never got to try anything. A sudden peripheral motion made me pull back as Alasdair turned from his duel with Donnie and swung at me, knocking the phone right out of my hand. If I hadn't pulled back, I would have taken the blow full in the face. As it was, he tore the skin off my knuckles, almost tore my ear off, and dislodged a patch of scalp. I screamed as a gush of blood cascaded down my neck.

Lithe as a dancer, he skipped across the floor and brought his foot down on the phone. I clapped a hand to my wounded head, pressing hard, as Alasdair turned on Donnie again, flailing madly. He knocked the shovel out of the guard's hand, then lunged forward and drove his own shovel hard into the guard's stomach.

Woodson and Chambers came flying through the door as Alasdair pulled his shovel back and Donnie collapsed on the floor, screaming, both hands clutching his stomach. Alasdair raised the shovel to strike again. Woodson jumped forward and twisted it out of his hands, throwing it far from both of them with a decisive clang.

"What the hell are you doing?" he demanded.

At the same time, Chambers spotted me, one hand braced against the wall, the other pressed against the flowing blood. "Oh, shit," he said.

While he was looking to Woodson for direction, I planted a bunch of bloody prints on the wall beyond me, in a spot that was dark and shadowed. Maybe they wouldn't notice, and since it didn't look good for me right now—Bushnell was probably sitting on his sofa laughing his ass off instead of flying to my rescue and Woodson and Chambers could hardly let me go, knowing what I knew—I wanted to leave as much evidence of my presence as I could.

"That your Jeep out there?" Woodson said.

"Yes."

He held out his hand. "Give me the keys."

I fumbled, trying to get them out of my pocket without dropping the pepper spray. Hard to do one-handed, but my other hand was busy. The extended hand flicked angrily. "Come on. Hurry it up."

I got them out of my pocket, but then I dropped them. As Woodson bent to scoop them up, he noticed the phone. "What the hell's this? Alasdair…what's with the phone?"

"She was making a call," Alasdair said, "so I hit her, then smashed the phone."

Woodson picked up the phone, pushed a few buttons, then shoved it in his pocket with a look of disgust. "You smashed it, Alasdair? Not a smart move." Woodson looked at me. "You call somebody?"

"I would have if that looney tune hadn't hit me with a shovel."

I felt sick. The sight of blood always makes me queasy. It's worse when it's my own. The hot feel of it running down my neck, the slightly metallic smell, the sticky warmth saturating my clothes. My knees felt like jelly. God. If I got out of here alive, I really was going to reform. But that was a big if. I had to focus on right now, on their moves and interactions. On ways to maximize my chances of survival.

To lower my profile as an adversary, I tried to appear weak and shaken. Woodson might not buy it, he'd seen me under duress before, but he was pretty distracted, trying to manage things, and assumptions about women's vulnerability are the usual default mode. Unless he was an incredible actor, Chambers became a dolt under pressure. Alasdair was the unknown quantity. No one can predict a jittery, hopped up lunatic druggie. All that was certain was that he was entirely at ease with a frightening level of violence and apparently without a conscience.

We were all standing between a pick-up truck and one of those long vans the school used to transport sports teams. I took a couple uncertain steps toward the truck and perched on the inadequate running board. I closed my eyes, gritted my teeth against the pain, and tried to regroup.

At my first move, Woodson had tensed and taken a step toward me, but once I was sitting with my head between my hands, he relaxed and turned to Chambers. "Guess we'll have to take her with us."

"What about her car?"

"Take that, too."

"Leave it there?" Chambers said. "That means we'd have to take three cars." From under my hair, I watched him slide a glance at Alasdair. "I'm not sure he's in any shape to drive."

Alasdair watched the guard writhing on the floor with a look of pleasure that was revolting. No wonder he'd been so persistent in tormenting Shondra. Making people suffer evidently fed some sick need. "I'm fine to drive," he said.

Woodson shook his head. "You and Todd will go in the gray car, Todd driving. Ms. Kozak and I will take her Jeep. We'll have to figure out what to do with it later. For now, I don't want it sitting here…someone might notice. And wonder."

Chambers pointed at the man on the floor. "What do we do about him?"

Woodson looked down at the groaning man on the floor—his own man—and shrugged. "I'll have to think about that," he said. He walked over to the man, bent down, and pressed his fingers against the man's neck. Almost instantly, the body went limp.

"Hey," Alasdair sidled up and poked the guard with his toe, "that was cool. How'd you do that?"

"Shut up," Woodson said. "I'm trying to think."

I didn't know if he'd killed the poor man or merely rendered him unconscious. What I did know was that he'd done it with chilling efficiency. And I'd actually thought he was nice. I was glad I wasn't making the noises my body wanted to make. My torn scalp hurt like crazy and my knuckles were skinned almost down to bone. My ear felt hot and swollen and was so painful I'd checked twice to be sure it hadn't been torn loose.

I assessed my chances of escape. There were no doors near me and I already knew there were no places to hide. I'd have to wait until we got outside. Maybe then I could make a run for it. The woods were close, the lighting was poor. It was only three against one.

I lowered my bloody hand and left a few nice handprints on the truck. Then I got up and shuffled toward Chambers. "Todd, is there a towel around here I could use 'til I can get to the infirmary? Even some paper towels would help."

I waved my hand at him, scattering blood around. Then I grabbed his arm, closed my eyes, and swayed right up against him, getting blood on his sleeve and on his chest. "Sorry...I...God...what is going on here? That crazy student who hit me looks just like Alasdair MacGregor. And what did Mr. Woodson just do to that poor man?" I clung to him fiercely as the floor undulated a few times and then settled down.

"I think I ought to lie down somewhere, Todd. I'm not feeling quite right." Banking on my belief that Chambers wasn't a very brave man and most likely a squeamish one, I ran my bloody hand over my face, smearing it until I had to look like I was painted for war. He tried to shake me off and slide away. I clung to his arm.

"Jesus, will you leave me alone," he yelped, jerking his arm out of my grasp. "You're getting blood all over me."

"Sorry." I manufactured a smile as least as loopy as Alasdair's. "I wasn't thinking. Can you excuse me, please. I've got to get to the infirmary." I took a few tentative steps toward the door.

"Forget that. You're not going anywhere. Now sit down and shut up." Woodson grabbed my shoulder and steered me back to my seat on the truck. As soon as he released me, I slid off the seat onto the floor, putting two bloody hands down to brace myself. "Oh, Sweet Jesus, you're going to get blood everywhere. Todd. In the Security Office there's a box of tee-shirts I got for the guys. Go grab a couple, will ya."

"Alasdair." I heard a bunch of keys being tossed. My keys, probably. "Go move that Jeep, will you, so we can get the other car out."

"Sure thing, Boss."

They had to be pretty pathetic, both of them, to let bottom-dwelling scum like Alasdair push them around and smart-mouth them like this. It made Woodson and Chambers, corrupt and soulless as they were, seem a little less frightening. But I had to remember—they had both colluded to help with, or at least cover up—the death of whoever had been pulled out of that fire. Probably the boy I'd read about in the paper who'd gone missing. It was his car they were conspiring to hide.

Like everything else about this ugly business—Shondra's pain and Jen Reilly's, Jamison's situation—the fact that some parents were huddled together, worried sick about their missing child didn't matter to this crew.

"Todd, when you're done with that, could you look in that storage cupboard there in the back, find me a roll of duct tape?"

Oh no. No way. I was not submitting to another duct taping without a fight. The list of physical invasions I am keen to avoid is long. Broken noses held the number one spot, until they were edged out by getting shot, but getting wrapped with duct tape gives me serious creeps. I could do such a riff on the uses of duct tape, from a personal grooming perspective—replacing the chemical peel and the bikini wax, for example—that I could audition to be a stand-up comic. But all I wanted was to be a stand-up gal. Stand up to these assholes and go home.

I heard the roar of the Jeep's engine, the squeal of tires, and a thud as Alasdair ran into something with my rental car. The little jerk. How could he be so successfully evil if he was so incompetent? Because no matter what he did, he got bailed out? Because the things he attempted didn't need skill, they only needed lust and self-centeredness and a total lack of values?

But he had been sufficiently devious to mess with Shondra for a long time without getting caught. And if he'd only left town like he was supposed to, he was close to getting away with murder. Maybe his mental condition was deteriorating or his drug use accelerating? Maybe somewhere deep in the tattered remnants of his soul, corruption was taking its toll.

"Oh, shit," Woodson said. "What's that dumb bastard done now?"

"He's not dumb," Chambers said, dropping a couple tee-shirts on the floor beside me. "He's just indifferent. Why should he care whether he gets it right? You know …" There was a thoughtful pause. "Even if we do get rid of the car, and Shondra, and he leaves like he's supposed to, I don't see how we can trust him to keep his mouth shut and not, in some moment of drugged out honesty or bar braggadocio, claim credit for the things he's done here."

"Yeah," Woodson said. "If you only had the money from Grandpa MacGregor, we could solve several problems at once, couldn't we?"

"That's just it, Woody." Chambers voice sounded suddenly lighter and more cheerful. "I *do* have the money."

They bustled about, getting ready for our trip to the country, while I wrestled with one of the tee-shirts, trying to tear it into strips with my wounded hand. Eventually I managed to fashion a reasonable bandage around my head. They were packing a big green duffle bag with shovels, flashlights and rope. I winced as I saw that Woodson was wearing a gun, but my insides really shriveled when he selected a nice, shiny axe—what a boy scout would call a hatchet—and stuffed that into the bag.

Trust me. I'm no axe murderer.

Alasdair came back from jockeying the cars.

"You run into something?" Woodson said.

"Fuck, man. Some asshole parked this big black Lincoln right behind me. I didn't even see it." He shot a nasty grin at Chambers.

"Goddammit, Alasdair," Chambers exploded. "Can't you do anything right?"

Alasdair gave a 'who cares?' shrug. "What you gonna do, Toddy? Sue me? Fuckin' hard to do when I'm dead."

Woodson grabbed the tape from Chambers and looked at me. "Stand up and turn around," he said. "We've got to get moving."

I was in no hurry. Wherever we were going was worse for me than here. I perched on the running board and thought about all my efforts to try and make Chambers 'get it.' To open his eyes to the issues concerning the safety and well-being of his students. The reputation of his school. The job that had to be done. No wonder he'd blown me off. He didn't care about anything but himself and his "legacy." Whether he knew it or not, his "legacy" was going to crash and burn, even if I didn't survive this. Eventually, Bushnell would come looking for me and I was leaving a trail a blindman could follow.

"Goddamit, I said stand up and turn around." Woodson grabbed my arm, hauled me roughly to me feet, spun me around and slammed me up against the side of the truck. Macho asshole cop stuff. I half-expected him to finish the job by ordering me to put my hands on the roof and spread my legs. Instead, he barked, "Put your hands behind your back."

I didn't. Instead, banking on his unwillingness to shoot me here, I just turned and stared at him. "Why do you want me to do that?"

He wanted to say, "Because I said so." The words trembled on his lips. What he said was, "So you won't try and get away."

I held up my mangled fingers. "If you're going to tie my hands, could you do it in front? Otherwise, I'm going to be leaning on these." He could see what I meant. I bit my lip and waited.

283

Alasdair had that eager, ugly, hungry look again, like he was hoping I would have to beg, and Chambers looked bored with the whole proceeding. If he hadn't been the brains necessary to stage-manage all this, I could almost have felt sorry for Woodson. It's hard to be the only smart kid in the group. Any group. Even a group of killers.

"All right. In front." Woodson sighed. "But no funny stuff."

As if there were anything funny about this. With my hands in front, I had a shot at undoing a seatbelt, opening a car door or window, or grabbing the steering wheel. Possibly even getting the spray out of my pocket. It was infinitely better than the cramped, shoulder-wrenching position I'd be in with them behind me and I wouldn't be rubbing the remaining skin off my knuckles. "Thank you," I murmured.

"Hold out your hands." He wrapped them in enough duct tape to fasten an elephant to the ceiling, then grabbed my elbow and started steering me toward the door. "Todd, you drive the gray car with Alasdair. I'll follow you in the Jeep." He held out a hand to Alasdair. "The keys?"

Alasdair danced away. "I want to drive the Jeep."

"But you don't want to get caught, remember?" Woodson reminded him. "And if you drive either car, your driving will be erratic enough to attract attention. On second thought, maybe you'd better come with me, just in case Todd gets stopped. Now give me the goddamned keys." Alasdair gave him the keys.

"Gets stopped?" Chambers said. "Why?"

"You've seen the front end. You've got a headlight out, a crumpled fender, a missing bumper. That's why we're taking back roads and driving below the limit."

"Well, I don't know, Woody, maybe you should drive the gray car and I'll take the Jeep."

"Jesus Fucking Christ, Todd, what are you thinking? You want to drive an unfamiliar car on unfamiliar roads with the consultant broad all covered with blood AND Alasdair because what? You think it's safer? Trust me. It is a lot easier to explain a crumpled front end than to explain Ms. Kozak."

"Couldn't we just put her in the trunk? I can handle Alasdair."

He could handle Alasdair. It was that kind of thinking that had caused this whole mess. He couldn't handle his own dick in a dark room. At that moment, I was so sorry I'd never taken Chambers into the back room and knocked him around. It might not have improved the current situation, but it would have made me feel better. Woodson seemed to like Chambers' idea. Man had probably never spent any time in a car's trunk. It isn't pleasant. Chambers was such a bleeping inconsistent asshole he was bound to be one of those brake-riding stop and go drivers who'd knock me around like crazy.

"Good idea. You drive the gray car. We'll put Kozak in the trunk, and I'll lead the way with Alasdair." He held out a hand. "Take the keys, Todd."

"But I meant …"

"I know what you fuckin' meant, Todd. I'm saying what we're gonna do, okay? And can we just goddamned do it before someone comes sniffing around or poor old Donnie there wakes up? Can we please or do you need to have some goddamned meeting first? We've got our asses in a sling here and you wanna talk?"

I'd gotten cold while I was hiding, and I was colder now that the adrenaline shock of getting injured was fading. Sometimes, if I get mad enough, the anger can generate some heat, but not this time. I assumed I'd have plenty of time enroute to think about a plan, but in the end I'd have to play it by ear. And I only had one good one. Right now I was using it to listen for the arrival of the cavalry, but without a lot of hope. It was Andre, after all, who had the high opinion of Lt. Bushnell.

Woodson took my arm in a grip that conveyed all of his anger and frustration, and pulled me toward the door. "If you'll just step this way, Ms. Kozak, your chariot awaits."

## CHAPTER THIRTY-ONE

It was not a sweet chariot, though it did swing low. It was an icy, miserable, bumpy chariot that smelled of stale beer and cigarettes, of cold pizza and automotive products. A truly stomach churning combination, so that when I wasn't silently cursing—Woodson's spate of profanity seemed to be contagious—or considering my options once the trunk was opened, I was working hard on trying not to be sick. It would have been even more unpleasant to be rolling around with that.

I was supposed to be thinking about survival. But there wasn't much I could do until we arrived and I saw the lay of the land. I contented myself with gnawing on the duct tape. Slow going since I frequently needed to use my hands to brace myself, but I made some progress. When we finally rolled to a stop, I gathered myself to react quickly but the trunk didn't open. Instead, I heard Chambers asking querulously, "This is stupid. Why are we stopping here? Someone might notice the cars."

"Because Alasdair needed to use the facilities."

Woodson had a way of sounding almost bored with the whole business, as though he wasn't really a part of it. Was that how he thought of it—some business for St. Matthews he had to take care of, or was being blackmailed into taking care of? Just one more thing that needed to be done to cover his own ass? From what had been said, the only thing he needed to worry about personally was Shondra's tape. Except that he'd hidden the car, and knew about the dead boy. No. Whatever tone he affected, he, like Chambers, was in this up to his bony ass.

"What's wrong with the side of the road?" Chambers demanded. Still the petty and peevish bureaucrat. Did he still not get it? He was an accessory to one murder and planning another.

Didn't that call for some level of gravity?

What was wrong with me? I was wrapped in duct tape in the trunk of a car and I was still thinking like the guy was my client and I was worried about his public presentation. I wasn't so naïve as to think that all murderers were serious people who went about their task in a serious way. Most murders, and murderers, are pretty stupid.

"I don't think he's answering the call of nature, Todd. He's answering the call of chemicals."

"Answering the call of …oh …yeah. I got it." Chambers sighed. "That boy is monstrous." He was just figuring this out? I wanted to pound on the trunk and taunt him, but there would have been little satisfaction in it. Maybe a good Christian rejoices when the blind finally have their eyes opened, but the spirit of charity had left me a while back. I was just curious what Chambers would say about dealing with their monstrous charge.

"You know this is never going to work, Woody. Getting rid of the car is only a small piece of it. That boy's less reliable and trustworthy than a 2-year old. It's only a matter of time before he's drunk or drugged out and starts bragging to his buddies about how he killed someone once and got away with it."

"Or he'll forget about his new name and say, oh, man, you know who I really am? I'm Alasdair MacGregor and I'm supposed to be dead," Woodson agreed. "Any idea what arrangements MacGregor has made, anticipating this kind of thing?"

"As far as Gregor MacGregor is concerned, Alasdair is a high spirited boy who got into some trouble at school."

"You mean he doesn't know …" Woodson trailed off. "Come on, Todd. He has to know. The call that brought him running was about a body, for Chrissake."

"Some people have an amazing ability to only see what they want to see, Woody."

I thought Chambers ought to be held down, screaming, while someone tattooed that on his ass, so it would be right there, ready to read, whenever he was about to stick his head up there.

They were both silent, then Chambers said, "We both know MacGregor didn't hand over that check because of some boyish hi-jinks. So, you got any ideas?"

"Same as you. That maybe we can kill two birds with one stone. Get rid of our too-curious consultant, kidnapped and killed by Alasdair, and ..."

"Why would Alasdair bother to kidnap her? Or kill her?"

"Because she asks too many questions. Because she found Alasdair—so he killed her and took her body up to the camp to dump it, but when he was driving away, he was so crazy and high that he drove into the lake. Which still leaves Shondra so distraught at all the trouble she's caused, she takes an overdose."

"That's already been done, Woody."

"Yes, well, her last attempt was thwarted by the quick action of the St. Matthews staff, but this time, alas, she succeeds."

"But we can't find her."

"Don't worry. We'll find her. Eventually she'll turn up and we'll get that camera. You've got Sidaris and Adams buttoned up, worrying about their contracts, and who else is there?"

"Not just their contracts," Chambers said smugly.

"You mean their tawdry little affair?" Woodson said. "Who'd care about that?"

"Al's wife, for one. So you don't think Shondra will head for home?"

"She hasn't got any money. Her family hasn't got a pot to piss in. Besides, big brother's in jail up here, so she'll stick around for him. She might even show up to play basketball. She does love it, you know."

"Ah, yes," Chambers said. "I'm seeing the press release even now. St. Matthews community mourns the tragic loss of star basketball player. Until personal problems derailed her, Shondra Jones appeared headed for star billing in women's college basketball. School struggles to rise about series of tragedies. Et cetera. I'm going to have fun writing that one. I wonder ..."

I could see some holes in their plan, like what to do about Jamison Jones and how to explain the body in the fire. Like wouldn't Grandpa MacGregor know how to get his money back? More were popping into my head all the time. Once again, Chambers was being arrogant and overconfident without thinking things through. This time, though, I didn't have the slightest desire to set him straight.

I thought they'd forgotten about me, there in the trunk, but someone patted the metal with a firm hand, and Chambers said, "Do you think I can get EDGE Consulting to help me write those press releases?" He laughed. "I'm sure, if she's listening, that our holier-than-thou consultant is having a fit in there. She thinks I'm shockingly inattentive to the needs of my students. Most of my students." He patted the metal again and their voices moved away. Perhaps to discuss the details of *my* death.

He couldn't have known he was doing me a favor. Nothing cures a wallow of pain and self-pity like getting good and mad. And when I get mad, I don't get fuzzy-minded or impulsive, I get focused. His bit of nastiness was just what I needed. I formulated the first part of my plan—to be as limp and uncooperative as possible when they opened the trunk. If they had to drag me out, their hands would be busy. I was no small woman, it would take both of them to do it, and that would give me a chance to get on my feet.

After that, I'd see what my options were. But one thing I knew for sure—Alasdair was going to know that both of us were marked for death. That they weren't just disposing of me—they were double-crossing him. He was such a wild card who knew how he'd react? Maybe he'd hit *them* with shovels.

Plan or no plan, I was scared. My teeth were chattering and periodically, the ball of fear in the pit of my stomach sent out flashes that zinged through me like electric shocks. The odds— three against one—weren't good. Especially when one of them had a gun. But hope is what keeps people going. I was hoping that Alasdair could be persuaded to turn on them, and that Chambers, despite his fundamental corruption and flashes of bravado, would prove as weak as he seemed. That would leave Woodson.

Eventually, the car door slammed and we were off again. I could only hope this part of the ride would be shorter. So far, it had been miserable and would only get worse as the night grew colder and the road rougher.

By the time we finally bumped to a stop, I felt like a kernel of corn in a popper. I'd never thought of popcorn as bruised before, but I was bruised. When the trunk lid lifted, the rush of cold air was almost intoxicating after stifling in the fug of my own blood and fear. The air smelled woodsy and earthy with nuances of the rustling lake water I could hear in the distance. There was no moon, no stars, no flashlights. Only the trunk bulb. But after an hour in the rocking darkness, even that dim light was jarring.

"All right," Woodson commanded, "sit up now so we can get you out of there."

I didn't move.

"I said, sit up!"

I moaned weakly and curled into a tighter ball.

"Do as I say, or I'll hurt you."

Like what they'd done already was a tender caress? I waited, trying not to tense up, to see what nasty thing he'd do. He reached in, grabbed my hands, and squeezed the wounded one. Tears filled my eyes. I screamed. A good, loud, long scream, just in case there was someone within hearing distance, and because it feels better if you yell. I was going to make this as hard for him as possible. He wasn't a sadist, like Alasdair. His was a more practical cruelty. He had a goal to achieve. So did I. He released my hand and I flopped protectively onto my stomach.

"Jesus. I've got blood all over my...Todd, come help me get her out of the trunk."

"You've got a gun, haven't you?" Alasdair said. "A real freakin' gun. Haven't you? Why don't you just shoot her? Wouldn't that be the easiest thing?" He giggled and his busy feet shuffled on the gravel. "Come on, Woody...let's see you shoot her."

"Alasdair, you know anything about cars?"

"Sure."

"Okay. Then tell me this. What's underneath the car's trunk?"

"Rear tires?"

"And?" Alasdair didn't answer. "I'll give you a clue," Woodson said. "What makes a car go?"

"You mean you shoot the bitch and the whole car blows up? Man. That would be so cool. Body parts everywhere and a big fuckin' explosion? Do it, man. Do it."

I could picture him jumping around, that look of sick excitement on his face. Go on, Mr. Woodson, entertain me with flying body parts. Do it, man. Do it. A ripple of fear and disgust ran up my back, tightening the skin like an invisible tailor was at work.

More feet crunching on the gravel. Chambers coming closer. I felt his breath as he leaned in and looked at me. Stale old coffee breath with a mint overlay. In the distance, a car engine sounded briefly and then died away. Not close enough to be the cavalry coming to my rescue, but then, I hadn't expected them.

"Hold on," Woodson said. "Did you hear that?"

"Yeah, there's a road on the other side of the lake," Alasdair said. "You can hear the cars sometimes."

"I thought you said these people owned all the way around the lake."

"Did I? I meant they owned a lot of land up here. You know...like they seriously own this whole side. But there's no one around. You can see that. No houses. No lights. No nothing. I've been up here lots and never seen anyone."

"Can we get on with this? I don't like to leave Miriam alone so long...she's very nervous." Chambers sounded peevish, like these menial tasks of killing people and disposing of bodies and stolen cars interfered with more important things.

"Thea." Woodson's voice was low and close to my ear. "If

you cooperate, this will all go much easier." His logic escaped me. Why would I want to make it easier for him to kill me? He squeezed my shoulder, as if he meant to be reassuring. The same hand that had just deliberately hurt me.

"You going to tell Alasdair that, too, Frank? That if he'll just be a nice boy and cooperate, killing him will be much easier for you and Todd?"

"You shut up." His hand touched the back of my neck, the fingers tightening. I'd seen what he'd done to that guard. Didn't want to become unconscious, helpless as a sack of potatoes. I squirmed away from him, burying my head and shoulders deeper in the trunk where he'd have a harder time reaching me.

"You're crazy if you think Alasdair and I are going to cooperate in our own deaths. We're not idiots, you know. I mean, look…he didn't get away with everything he's gotten away with and then fake his own death just so you two bozos could bring him up here and really kill him…leaving you with clean hands, your Alasdair problem solved and Grandpa MacGregor's check in the bank. Right, Alasdair?" With my head buried in the trunk, I had to shout to be heard.

"The fuck she talking about?" Alasdair said.

"Trying to postpone the inevitable by distracting us," Woodson said. He grabbed my arm. "Come on, Todd. You get her legs."

Chambers grabbed my legs, which they hadn't bothered to tape. I jerked free and kicked. He swore and grabbed again. I kicked harder. "Help me, dammit!" he said. "Where's that tape? Alasdair? It's there in the bag." He let go.

If they tied my feet, I wouldn't be able to run. Tie my feet and hands, cover my mouth and then kill me. Was it time for a new survival strategy? Cooperate and maybe they wouldn't bother with my feet? Maybe the only person I was fooling was myself. "Sure, Alasdair, help them out," I said. "Just remember. You've run out of hall passes, too. You're next."

"You shut up."

With a shoulder-wrenching jerk, Woodson pulled me toward him and landed a hard, open-handed slap on the side of my head. He might as well have grabbed the loose flap of skin and jerked. The pain level went to code red and my head started gushing blood again. I curled up inside myself, trying not to cry, losing heart suddenly at this enormous task of trying to survive. It would be so much easier and less painful just to give in.

Out in the woods, there was a loud rustling, then a crash and a snap. "Just a branch falling," Woodson said.

Scuffling feet and Chambers' mumbled 'thanks' told me Alasdair had handed over the tape.

I rolled over on my back and opened my eyes. Was this it? My last vision of life on earth was to be the underside of a dingy trunk lid, the determined faces of two men meaning to kill me and a manic little sadist against the backdrop of a bit of night sky?

I pushed the fear that threatened to overwhelm me out of my head and pulled up a vision of Andre, earlier tonight, sitting on the couch before the fire, fingering his wedding band. Heard his voice saying, "Look how far hope has brought us."

I must not lose hope now. I owed it to my husband, to myself, to Shondra and Jamison Jones and all the students at St. Matthews. I was leaving here alive. I was going to watch the sun come up. I was not letting Frank Woodson and Todd Chambers win.

# CHAPTER THIRTY-TWO

"*Morituri te salutamus.*" In my romantic, novel-reading childhood, it was something I'd always thought I wanted to say. It had never been something I'd wanted to mean. I didn't mean it now, either.

"Do I detect a note of resignation?" The shadow of a smile touched Woodson's mouth. Then his thin lips drew back into a hard line. "Put your feet together and don't try kicking again or you'll be sorry." There was a ripping sound as he tore off a long silver strip of tape.

"Oh, I'm already sorry, very sorry. Maybe you can tell me this. Please. I know that Alasdair's going to drown…going into the lake with the car…but what do you have planned for me? I missed that part of the discussion."

Alasdair was standing a little apart, his back to us, looking out toward the invisible lake, bobbing and swaying like he was dancing to music inside his head. He didn't appear to have heard what I'd said.

"I think you'd rather not know."

"That bad, huh?" He nodded. "When we…it…gets to that point, could you…uh…do that thing you did with Donnie, so that I won't…so that I'm not …" My stomach rolled and I stopped talking. I didn't want to be sick.

"Awake?" he supplied helpfully.

"Awake," I agreed, choking down the hot acid that stung the back of my throat. To sleep. Perchance to die.

Chambers hovered nearby, ready to assist with Operation Thea Removal, his expression an unattractive combination of prissy and squeamish. The sacrifices the poor man had to make for the sake of his career. His legacy. It was terrible.

It felt like we'd been here for hours as I skipped from one

emotion to another like crossing a river on rocks—each step uncertain and unpredictable, unable to find steady footing. I'd counted thousands of breaths, each bringing me closer to what they intended to be my last. It had probably been less than ten minutes.

But ten minutes was too long for Alasdair. Suddenly he turned away from his self-involved dance and came back to peer into the trunk. "She's still in there? Come on. Let's get her out. Let's get this thing done. I've got a ride to catch." In the hand swinging loosely by his side, he held the axe.

Fear exploded in me like dynamite. Far away a siren moaned. Chambers and Woodson turned to look. I jerked at my hands, tearing through the last of the tape, pulled them apart, and pushed myself out of the trunk, springing past them and taking off down the road. I ran like the devil himself was chasing me. Or a crazy maniac with an axe. I ran for my life, straight down that dark and bumpy dirt road with three men chasing me, one of whom had a gun.

The words "broken field running" were muttering in my head. A strategy to avoid giving Woodson a straight shot. But it was damned hard to zig and zag when I couldn't see the ground. It seemed a better strategy to get off the road and into the woods. Sure, the sounds of my feet clomping over branches and rocks would be louder, but there would be lots of cover, too. As soon as I got around that curve I could dimly see up ahead.

I came around the curve and almost slammed into a car standing in the roadway with its lights off. I didn't wait to see if it was friend, foe or merely some local who'd come out to go parking or jack some deer. I thought I heard a voice yell, "Hey," but I wasn't stopping for anyone or anything. Not until I'd put a good safe distance between myself and the guys with the guns and axes.

I veered off the road into the woods, my arms raised before my face for protection. Branches slapped at my arms and snagged my hair. Sharp sticks scratched my cheeks and fore- arms and stabbed at my legs. Fallen branches and tangles of brush rose to trip me.

I moved through it all with the inexorable momentum of a juggernaut. Scraping, banging, and crashing my way deeper and deeper into the forest, tripping and falling and pushing myself up and going on, unable to hear whether I was still being followed because of all the noise I was making, and too afraid to stop and listen. Once, I heard what sounded like a gun shot. A commotion of voices shouting and then more shots.

When at last I paused to catch my breath, hands on my thighs, my chest on fire, I heard someone behind me and saw the broken beams of a flashlight filtered through the trees. Grimly, I used my sleeve to wipe the blood away from my eyes and started off again. I ran until my chest was exploding and pain stabbed my side, the thud of my feet reverberating through my skull.

I ran for my life, and because training with Andre had made me strong, it was a hell of a run. All those hours in the gym were finally paying off. I ran through the trembling muscles and the cramps and the gasping, pushing on, looking for that second wind until I stumbled up a slope, tripped over a slippery rock at the top, and tumbled down the other side, landing hard on my hand and jarring my head.

I lay there on spongy moss, groundwater seeping through my clothes, waiting for dizziness to subside so I could scramble up and go on. I could still hear my pursuer crashing through the woods. See those yellow beams getting closer, slicing through the forest like rays emanating from the hand of an evil wizard. I wobbled unsteadily to my feet, trying to pick out an escape route. He was so close now I could hear him panting. I crawled out of the open toward the darker shadows that meant brush, and shelter.

Suddenly, he was there at the top of the slope, the flashlight beaming down as he searched for me. I lay very still, glad I had dressed in black, hoping I just looked like more darkness, as the beam moved slowly over me and then moved away. My heart stopped when it found me. When the beating resumed, I thought he must be able to hear the thudding that filled my ears.

Then the beam stopped and moved slowly back toward me and I heard Alasdair's maniac chuckle. "Gotcha! They promised me I'd get to do this and I'm going to." For effect, he used the beam to illuminate the axe. All this way through the woods, he'd brought his favorite toy because Chambers and Woodson had told the little boy that if he was good and cooperated, he'd get to chop me up.

That must have been the conversation I hadn't heard because they'd moved away. It would have defied belief if I hadn't known all the events leading up to this. I scrambled to my feet, slightly blinded by the light, and staggered around, looking around for something to use as a weapon. There were some good-sized rocks, but I wanted a sturdy stick. No much of a weapon against an axe, but it would keep him at a distance.

I hurried away from him, back into the woods, searching the dark forest floor until I found the darker shape of a branch. Alasdair followed at a leisurely pace, keeping me fixed in the beam of his light, chanting "Run, run, as fast as you can...you can't beat me, I'm the Gingerbread Man." A vicious little monster with all the time in the world. Toying with me the way a cat plays a mouse.

Farther away, I heard someone call my name. Good guy? Bad guy? I didn't dare answer.

I also didn't dare turn my back on him, no one turns her back on a man with an axe, so I was backing away from him, my going ever more unsteady and uncertain. Reflected light gave his face an eerie yellow cast, his features hidden in shadow, as he came steadily on, determined and horrible. Maybe I should just drop the stick and run. I'd stayed ahead of him before. But my skin crawled at the thought of that axe.

I scooped up a rock and hurled it at him, my aim awkward with my bandaged hand. My 'good' hand. He gave a hoot of laughter. "Leave me alone, you bastard!" I heaved another. It struck his forehead and wiped the smile off his face. He yelled and charged at me, waving the axe. I yelled back and in my own form of crazy bravado, I lowered my stick and charged, holding my sturdy long branch before me like a lance.

I struck him in the chest. He missed me. We galloped a little way past, turned, and charged again. This time my blow glanced off his thigh and his just missed my knee. Way too close for comfort. I valued my limbs, so this time, when I got past him, I kept right on going, scrambling up the slope and back the way I'd come. Bad guys or no bad guys, I wasn't lingering to duel with this monster.

Once again, fear made my feet fast. I come over the top, careful of the slippery rocks this time, and started down the other side. But when I raised my head, I saw another flashlight coming toward me. I veered left, away from both of them and farther away from the road, not knowing how much longer I could do this. My clothes were wet. I was chilled and my stamina was running low. Increasingly, my feet landed badly.

Behind me, Alasdair imitated a madman's laugh. A high, lunatic chuckle. "Run, run," he chanted. "Run, run, run." Why wasn't he getting tired? Was it the drugs?

My lungs burned. All the air I was sucking in didn't seem to be enough. Ahead, low, dense, darker shadows suggested thicker brush. I slowed so my steps were quieter, then dropped to all fours and crept toward it. I reached some fluffy, low-spreading branches, lowered myself onto my belly, and burrowed deep into the pungent, prickly evergreens. I felt around until I found a good-sized rock. Then I curled up into a shivering ball and waited.

Through the thick branches, I got glimpses of his flashlight beam as Alasdair searched and listened, searched and listened. Once his footsteps retreated and I thought he'd gone, but then that bobbing beam was back, moving slowly over the ground, searching for my tracks. I'd probably left an obvious trail, crawling in here. But the brush was too thick for a quick escape and if I moved, he was going to hear me. I lay with my face on the prickly ground, taking shallow breaths, tensed in anticipation of a sudden blow.

I had seen the aftermath of a person attacked with an axe.

Now, unbidden and unwanted, that scene floated into my head. The deep gashes in counters and floors, everything smashed, dried pools of black blood on the floor, streaks and splatters of flung blood on the ceilings and walls. A good forensics expert could recreate the whole scene quite accurately. A good lay imagination did just fine, too. A shudder rippled through me, my skin puckering in waves. Fear pooled like acid in my stomach.

Not more than five feet away, feet shuffled and a branch snapped with a gun-fire crack. "Come out, come out, wherever you are," Alasdair whispered.

I could hear the swish of branches as he searched. Coming closer. Moving away. Moving back. All the time, reciting bits from children's games. "Simon says put your hand on your nose. Take three giant steps. Tag. You're it. Am I warm or am I cold? I'm getting warmer, aren't I? Aren't I? Aren't I?"

A snap. A crack. A swish. An explosive "Gotcha!" The branches above me parted and his light blazed down onto my face.

I grabbed two big handfuls of crumbled leaves and sticks and needles and hurled them into the dark blur behind the light. "Fuck!" he exploded, the flashlight beam waving wildly in the air as he pawed at his eyes. I hurled my rock at him, twisted sideways, and stood up, pushing my way through the springy, resistant branches.

Swearing and grunting, he plunged after me, swinging the axe. It sliced through a branch inches from my hand.

Another light burst out of the trees behind us. A loud voice shouted, "New Hampshire state police. Drop your weapon and put your hands on your head."

I reached down inside myself and called up the reserves, a spurt of energy that sent me flying from the entrapping branches into more open forest. I ran toward the light. Toward the finish line. Toward the end of this race for my life, Alasdair right behind me.

The voice spoke again. "Drop your weapon, son. This is your

last warning."

Alasdair came on. A gun exploded and suddenly, I felt emptiness behind me. A rush of cool air in place of the heat and noise of his insane pursuit. More explosions. I flung myself toward the light, my knees buckling, and I was caught by strong arms and pulled up tight against a metal nametag, the wiring of a shoulder mike, and a Kevlar-clad, iron-hard chest.

## CHAPTER THIRTY-THREE

I wore a jaunty bandage over the stitches in my head and an unflattering set of borrowed green scrubs. I was trying to hold the cup of tea Bushnell had offered between gauze-swathed hands. I looked like a prize-fighter about to don her gloves. But my hands shook and the tea kept spilling. I gave up and set it down. I felt small and exhausted and chilled to the core. I didn't believe this shaking would ever stop.

"Pretty dramatic rescue," I said. "How on earth did you find me?"

"Hold on." Bushnell shoved back his chair and left the room.

I didn't have the wits to wonder what he was up to. Wondering took effort and I was using the little bit of starch I had left to stay upright. What I longed to do was curl up on the room's ugly vinyl sofa and sleep for a thousand years. Sleep until the aches left my body and my head healed and my mind healed and the sun finished coming up and a dozen rainbows filled the skies. Sleep until I figured out how I had come to be traveling down this particular road. Why my life was so different from other people's and what I could do to change mine.

I'd take up knitting. Read novels. Bask in the sun. Maybe I'd learn to use a digital camera and tap dance. I'd always wanted to tap dance. But I was big and clumsy and so I'd left dancing to the smaller, more agile girls. But now I thought—who cared? I didn't have to be good at it; I only had to have fun. Seemed like I was entitled to have some fun. Climb up out of the sewers of other people's problems and start living a normal, regular life. Let someone else be "Ms. Fixit" for a change.

He came back with a blanket and wrapped it around me. "You should have let them admit you," he said. "You're a mess."

"I just need to rest," I said. "Hospitals never let you do that. They're too busy taking care of you to leave you alone. Trust me. I'm kind of an expert on this subject." The blanket felt nice. I pulled it tighter around me and leaned back, resting my head against the wall. My eyelids slammed down like lead shutters. "How did you …"

"Those two girls," he said. "Shondra and Lindsay called me right after you did. You must have said something to them about going to see Woodson. Or maybe Shondra guessed. At any rate, they went over to Security looking for you. I guess they felt guilty about running away. They looked through the window and overheard enough to know what was going on. One of them had my card, so they called me."

Bushnell handed me the tea. "The last thing you said to me was Justin Palmer's camp, so I asked them about that. They told me who Justin was. About Alasdair and his friends taking girls to the camp. Jen Reilly knew a lot more than she was saying. Can't blame the girl, though. She was terrified of them. We found Justin Palmer and made him give us directions." It didn't sound like they'd asked politely.

"Look, I know that right now you're probably feeling anything but heroic, but you have no idea how much good you've done here. What you've helped put a stop to."

"I don't know what you're talking about."

"I'll explain. But first…you're probably going to resent this…I called your husband. I told him he had the bravest, smartest and fastest wife this department has ever seen. You know what he said?"

Bushnell shook his head in wonder, as if he couldn't imagine a marriage like ours. "He said 'and the most beautiful. Or she was. How many stitches this time?' I told him twelve, they wouldn't show, and that you were going to be fine. He says to tell you that he's got the rest of the body parts."

"That's good news," I said. "He's really not upset?"

"Oh. He's upset all right. What did you expect? He made me promise to see that you got a huge breakfast, a hot bath and went right to bed." I could swear Bushnell actually blushed. "I don't think he meant I was supposed to personally supervise those last two."

Caretaking at a distance. That was my Andre. I couldn't quite imagine telling some sister cop to give him breakfast and a bath and tuck him into bed. I considered those my prerogatives. But if I couldn't be there? Maybe the breakfast part. He was a man who loved to eat. But that was all. Andre was a shower guy, not a bath taker, and given the way we liked to shower, I wasn't delegating that job to anyone. Nor the going to bed part. Maybe I wasn't as easy going as my spouse.

"You're smiling," he said.

"I told you I was a newlywed."

"Yeah?" His eyebrows rose. "I don't know how he can let you …"

We were getting along okay right now and I wanted to keep it that way. I didn't have the emotional capacity to handle anything negative. There was plenty of that coming down the road as we debriefed this thing. "I don't, either," I agreed. "It's just one of the great things about Andre. He respects who I am."

I changed the subject. "Shondra and Lindsay and Jen," I almost said, 'my girls,' "are they okay?"

"Better than okay, I think. They're pretty proud of themselves for having the initiative to act when all the adults were sitting on their hands. Shondra's happy about her brother, and …" His serious face brightened. "They all want to know how they can be you when they grow up."

"That's hogwash. No one, in or out of their right mind, would want to go through this." I held up my bandaged hands. "Or feel like this."

"I meant being courageous enough to stick to your guns and in the process uncovering a festering mess of abuse and corruption, getting an innocent man out of jail, rehabilitating the reputation of an outstanding female athlete. Instead of folding your tent and going home to write some dull report."

"Right now, going home to write some dull reports looks

very attractive."

"I'll bet it does." He scooped his jacket off the back of a chair. "You want to get that breakfast now?"

"What time is it?"

"Coming up on 0600."

"Can I keep the blanket?"

"I'd like to see someone try and take it from you while I'm around."

He held the door for me and I trudged through. Everything, including my feet, was sore and tender. I felt about eighty. And not a spry eighty, either. I was heading toward the lobby when he put an arm lightly around my shoulders and steered me in a different direction. "This way, unless you're in the mood to play Meet the Press."

"Can't say that I am."

His car was parked outside the door, engine running, Gabriel Lavigne behind the wheel. It had actually been Lavigne's chest I'd run into, his hands that had gripped me tight. His name was probably indelibly imprinted on my cheek. I didn't know. I wasn't about to go looking in any mirrors. I was teetering on the verge of a plunge into deep self-pity. I didn't need anything to accelerate my fall.

Lavigne observed my cheery face and the way my chic beige blanket complimented my verge-of-nausea green scrubs and turned up the heat. Bushnell leaned in and carefully fastened my seatbelt around me. TLC, cop-style. Then he got in the back.

"We're going out for breakfast, Gabe," he said. "Ida's, I think?"

"Yes, sir," Lavigne said, and we were rolling.

We ate in a booth way at the back, the kind that had high walls for privacy, and following Andre's instructions, Bushnell ordered me the biggest goldarned Lumber Jill breakfast on the menu. Their own selections weren't exactly modest. There's nothing like a good dust-up with the bad guys to whet the appetite. With two bandaged hands, it was like eating with mittens on, but I managed. When food is available and I've got the time, I'm pretty good at finding ways to get food into my mouth.

After a lengthy session of unbroken eating, I unmittened my fork and looked at Bushnell. "Alasdair … is he … did he?" I knew it had taken four or five bullets to stop him, but he'd still been alive when they put him in the ambulance.

"He'll never wipe his ass with his right hand again," Bushnell said bluntly, "which may not matter since he'll probably have to shit in a bag, but he'll be around to stand trial."

I looked down at my decimated pancakes, the oozing remnants of my eggs, the few lonely potatoes scattering the vast expanse of plate, glad I'd finished eating. I wished I hadn't asked. I wasn't ready to process this information. Still way too close to all the sensations of Alasdair chasing me through the night. To the awful toll that level of fear took. It was wrong to want another person dead. I knew that. I also knew that that was the only way I, and a lot of other people whose lives he'd messed with, would ever feel completely safe.

"Hey." Gabriel Lavigne, who to my dazed and weary eyes really did look more like an angel than a cop, set his warm hand very gently on my arm. His smile was tender, his expression slightly worried. "You don't want to talk about this right now, you don't have to. You went through a real bad time last night. It's okay to wait until you're ready. Don't go pushing yourself just because you're so responsible."

Okay. So I couldn't talk about Alasdair. Stalker. Rapist, I now realized. And cold-blooded murderer. But I wanted the rest of the story. "That boy…the kid who went missing. He was the body in the fire?" Bushnell nodded. "How did Alasdair find him?"

Bushnell set down his fork and leaned forward to answer, but I held up a hand. "There's another whole piece of this that I'm missing. About the girl. They kept talking about a girl, and something Alasdair had done, as a reason he needed to disappear? That's the 12-year-old over in Keene?"

Bushnell nodded again. "MacGregor is a monster," he said.

While I was being poked and prodded and x-rayed and cleaned up and stitched, they'd been out interviewing. Putting the pieces together. Never mind that it had been the middle of the night. The wheels of justice never stop. Now they took turns explaining it to me. "The body in the fire was a local kid…a townie…used to deliver pizzas and subs to the dorms. Also sell some dope. Alasdair and his buddies were customers. Sometimes the kid hung out with them. He was a nice kid, malleable, kind of a loser. They were boarding students and couldn't have a car. He had a car."

"They wouldn't have killed him just so they could use his car. It doesn't even make sense that they…or even Alasdair, would kill someone just so he could quietly disappear. There's so much money in that family, Alasdair could just have left." I tried to puzzle it out. Kill some poor schmuck of a kid just to get Jamison Jones in trouble? It was consistent with Alasdair's level of malice, but it seemed too risky. "Sorry. I interrupted you. Go on."

"You need to go back to The Swan and get some rest," Bushnell said. He reached for his coat. "You aren't ready for this."

"Finish the story."

Lavigne assessed me with his worried eyes, taking in the whole bruised, bandaged, trembling mess. "You sure? We can always do this later."

After last night's callous indifference, it was comforting to have someone act concerned. "If I need you to stop, I'll tell you, but I think I have to have the pieces … to understand." I pushed some potatoes around, remembering things.

"Woodson and Chambers. They knew. They both knew…and they didn't care at all. Last night they … their plan was to let Alasdair kill me with the … uh … well, you know about that. Then they were going to kill him. Incapacitate him somehow, put him in that car, and send it into the lake so it would look like he'd killed me and then accidentally driven into …"

Bushnell handed me his handkerchief. Surprised, I touched my face and found tears. They were right. I couldn't talk about this yet. The fear from last night was crawling like worms under my skin. I closed my eyes. "Guess you're right," I said. "Maybe all this should wait. Just promise me they're both locked up."

"We promise," Bushnell said, grimly. "And with your help, we should be able to convince the judge they're both flight risks and keep them there." He slid out of the booth.

"Just one question," I said. "Why kill the boy?"

"He was with them when they snatched that little girl and assaulted her. He didn't participate in the attack, but he was there. He was driving. Then his conscience got to him. He was going to tell us what they'd done."

"So they killed him, made it look like he was Alasdair, and Alasdair was supposed to take off."

"Might have gotten away with it, too, except that he insisted on hanging around to see what would happen next," Lavigne said. "And your friend Shondra Jones got Jamison to tape the whole plan on the nannycam."

"She what?" I popped to my feet, staring at both of them. Some detective I was. St. Matthews had been a veritable pit of snakes, and I'd only seen one or two. How had I missed so much?

"We all missed it," Bushnell said, reading my mind. "Might have gone on missing it if you hadn't poked around until you made them so upset they got careless. Oh. She didn't know she'd taped it. It was just an idea of hers. Her brother put the camera in Alasdair's room and just happened to tape their whole plan. Thing is, the nannycam only gets pictures, not sounds, but a lipreader can make out a lot of what they were saying. They were just using Jamison to cover Alasdair's get away…and to get back at Shondra for taking pictures."

"But the other guys. They're rapists, too. And accessories to murder," I said. "How many are involved? Are they arrested?"

Bushnell shook his head. "We're still sorting it out. But there will be more arrests." He hesitated, then decided to tell me

307

something confidential. "There was only sperm from one guy in the Keene case, although she said there were four guys. So one of them was either too stupid...or too arrogant...to use a condom."

I thought we all knew it was arrogance. "Take a look at which parents have pledged big bucks for the arts center," I suggested. "I think Chambers extorted those pledges in return for condoning their son's activities."

I didn't see how St. Matthews was going to recover from this disaster, but I didn't care. With my stomach stuffed with warm food, exhaustion had socked in like a sudden, dense fog. I could barely stand.

Luckily, I was with two guys who serve and protect for a living. They closed in on either side like an honor guard, marched me out the restaurant, and whisked me off to The Swan, where Lavigne started my bath, Bushnell laid out my jammies, and then they both beat a hasty and discreet retreat.

# CHAPTER THIRTY-FOUR

I woke around three, jolted into consciousness by something dropping into place. My brain must have already been up and working, because the realization fit neatly into a web of questions I'd had about Todd Chambers' behavior. On the morning after the murder, Todd Chambers had been unavailable. When he had finally appeared in response to Bushnell's summons, he'd appeared dazed and ineffectual. At the end of the day, he'd gone off to the hospital to check on Gregor MacGregor. By the time he'd returned that night, his demeanor had changed. He'd become arrogant, indifferent to my advice and to the needs of his community.

His absence in the morning was better explained by the necessity to keep Alasdair out of sight at his home than by his wife's supposed breakdown; his confusion by the difficulties of working out a plan while being forced to deal with the cops and a real crisis, including the fact that someone was indeed dead, and by his inability to convey private information to Gregor MacGregor. At some point while he was away from the school, two things must have happened. He had conveyed the information about Alasdair's faked death to Grandfather MacGregor; and he had been reassured that if Aladair was gotten safely away from the reach of the law, the hoped-for arts center donation would still be made.

It was a comfort, if only a small one, to understand that it wasn't that I'd managed the situation so badly, or that I'd failed to communicate effectively with my client because I was a poor communicator. I'd correctly sensed the resistance and the fact that something was intimidating his staff. I'd even recognized that major changes needed to be made on the campus to make his students safe. What I hadn't recognized—and few people would have—was the depth of personal corruption, and consequent indifference to his community, that I was dealing with.

I thought of how hard I'd struggled to avoid judging my client; to keep an open mind and stay on St. Matthews' side. To put a good face and a positive spin on the situation for the St. Matthews community and the outside press. Feeling like a weasel and a fraud the whole time. Could I have done it differently? Should I have trusted my instincts when even my own partner was urging me to lighten up and try to go along to get along?

Some might say the instincts I should have trusted were Bobby's. He said we should pack our bags and leave. But if I'd packed my bags and left, Shondra would have been disgraced and expelled, if not outright killed, Jamison would have stood trial, and Alasdair would have gone away and assumed a new identity, having gotten away with murder. And all the students at St. Matthews would have gone on living with the same level of unsafe indifference. Especially the girls.

Had Chambers even recognized he was condoning rape and murder? Had he cared? Or had he simply fixed his eyes on the drawings of his arts center, listened to Miriam's insidious voice at his side, and locked that knowledge out of his brain? I could tangle with a hundred bad guys, and never understand how someone could be that corrupt.

They must have left an armed guard or the world's scariest "Do Not Disturb" sign, because no one bothered me until almost four. Then there was a tattoo of insistent knocking. I was ready to emerge from my cocoon and start dealing with life again, so I yelled, "Just a minute," minced on sore feet to the closet, and wrapped up in a cozy white robe. My visitors were Shondra and Jamison Jones. I'd never seen them together before, and it was a sight. They more than filled the doorway.

I didn't even see Mrs. Mitchell standing behind them until they'd moved into the room. "I'm sorry," she said, "but they've been waiting downstairs for hours. I guess they got impatient and slipped past me."

"It's all right," I said. "I wanted to see them anyway. I don't suppose ..."

"Coffee?" she said. "Tea? Some sandwiches? I could fix you all a tray." She glanced at my bandages, then quickly lowered her eyes. "I heard about last night. It must have been terrible."

"I wouldn't want to do it again."

"No," she agreed. "I don't guess you would." Impulsively, she reached out and patted my shoulder. "You look like you could use some soup. I've got a lovely one if you're up to it—creamy pumpkin with ginger and smoked mussels. And some scones?"

Who would pass up an offer like that? I was at The Swan, after all, and Mrs. Mitchell was a wonderful cook. I nodded eagerly.

She plucked an envelope out of her pocket. "Your partner asked me to give you this."

I took it reluctantly. It wasn't like Suzanne to communicate by notes, and the way things had been going, I wasn't sure reading it was going to be a pleasant experience. She probably wanted to dissolve our partnership because she couldn't stand the scrapes I kept getting into. Today, I almost didn't blame her. I wasn't enthused about my scrapes, bangs, cuts or bruises, either. Anymore than I was pleased to be adding the memory of being chased with an axe to the gallery of horrors in my head. The word 'hatchet' would never again summon images of diligent boy scouts.

I stuck the envelope in my own pocket and invited Shondra and Jamison to sit. The room might not feel so crowded if they weren't towering over me. He thanked me politely in his wonderful voice and took a seat. Shondra remained standing, shuffling her feet and staring down at her shoes.

"Sit down. Please," I said. "You're making me uncomfortable."

She looked at her brother. He nodded and she sat down beside him on the couch. I sat in the chair and waited. I'd expected her to speak. She was the one who seemed to have an

311

agenda, but it was Jamison who finally did, splaying his fingers on his knees and leaning forward earnestly. "We're sorry to be barging in like this...so soon and all. I don't expect you're feeling up to company. You don't look so...like...uh." He wisely let that drop. "But me and Shonny...we wanted to ..."

His huge hands were doing pushups on his knees. He looked at his sister, but she was still studying her shoes. "You were the only one around here who believed in us, and here we almost got you killed."

"How do you figure that?"

"Well, Shonny knew Woodson was dirty...but she run...ran away and left you with him, when she could have told you what she knew."

"Yeah. And I could have told you about those tapes...showed you what I had...and then we both would have known, only, you know...you worked for *them*." Shondra said. "And by then, I didn't trust nobody. When Woodson showed up, I figured you were in on it."

"I don't blame you," I said. "You had good reasons. Both of you. There are a couple things I still don't understand that you might be able to explain?" Jamison nodded, Shondra reluctantly seconding him. Still extremely cautious, despite her choice to come here. Had it been her choice? She might just be doing what her brother told her to do.

"Okay. Last night they said you had a tape of Woodson having sex with a student. How did you get that?"

Shondra grinned. "I stole it."

"From him?"

"Of course not. From Cassie. That's where I got the camera, too. That's what they were looking for when they trashed my room."

"Cassie had a tape of Woodson having sex with a student?"

"Cassie had a tape of Woodson having sex with her," Jamison corrected. "It was part of their insurance policy— Alasdair and them. A way to keep Woodson and his security force off their backs."

312

The U.S. government wasn't this thorough. What a tragedy that such clever young minds were wasted on such sordid works. Stalking. Blackmail. Rape. Murder. "The things they did," I said, "why would she want to be a part of that?"

"Not the sharpest tool in the shed," Jamison said.

"And she thought Alasdair was a hunk," Shondra added. "She did stuff to make him happy. He like told her that she was a part of their special club, you know?"

So I'd gotten that right. While all this was happening, where were the adults? "So, Shondra, you took their camera and used it to spy on them?" She nodded. "And where's that camera now?"

"Gave it to that cop."

"Bushnell?"

"Yeah." She followed this with a string of expletives. And why not? Until he'd rescued me from a would-be axe murderer, I'd felt the same way about him. He'd showed us both his hard side.

"I learned something, though. That I've got friends I didn't even know I had," she said.

"That's something, isn't it?"

She went back to studying her shoes. I wanted to leave her to it, she was only sixteen and she'd been through a hell of a hard time, but I had one more question. "The drug overdose. What was that about?"

"I was dumb."

"Meaning?"

"I already told that cop," she said, sullenly.

"Shonny," Jamison said. "The woman maybe saved your life."

"Cassie," she said, giving the words up like they were her last treasures. "When I saw what they done…did…to my room, I felt sick. She's standing there, drinking this Coke and she shoves it at me, says am I gonna throw up, I'd better drink it 'cuz it would help. I was that mad I wasn't thinking about what she was and all, so I did. Then I took off down to the gym. It's where

313

I go when … you know … I get upset. The door to Coach Adams' office was open. I went in. I was feeling pretty strange by that time, so I lay down on the couch."

She shook her braids, as though the sequence still puzzled her. "Next thing I know, I'm at the hospital."

A knock signaled Mrs. Mitchell's return with a big tray holding tea and soup and scones and a plate of homebaked goodies that made Jamison smile. We settled into eating in an almost companionable way, both kids falling on the food like it had been days since their last meal. It might have been, for all I knew. It's hard to eat when you're upset, and their past few days had been terrible.

My big questions had been answered, but I had another. "Are you two planning to stay at St. Matthews?"

"I think I will," Jamison said. "Have to hope that with Mr. Chambers gone, things'll get better. Shonny?"

She picked up the last brownie, shot us a defiant look, and popped it into her mouth. "I was gonna leave," she said. "But last night, after we called that cop and everything, me and Lindsay and Jen sat around, waiting to hear what was happening. Mrs. Weston, she let me stay in the dorm with them and she made us cocoa and popcorn. She started a fire in her fireplace and made us sit there. And we. And they …"

Her voice trailed off and she shot looks at me and her brother, like she was daring us to challenge her. Whatever came of this, the chip on her shoulder had become so huge it was going to take a long time to wear it away. Then she dropped her eyes. "They told me how much they wanted to be my friends and how hard I always made it. How much I mattered to them and that they didn't want to give up. They told me how much I meant to the team. Lindsay said how just by being there I made everyone else a better player."

She looked up again, straight at me. "No one ever said a thing like that to me. They said I probably didn't know it. That people hadn't told me 'cuz they figured I already knew. They said I *was* the team. That I was the heart and soul of it." Her beautiful eyes were filled with wonder at how, in the midst of all this ugliness, she'd been given a gift. "Jen said that when I play ball, it's like watching magic happen."

"Shit, girl, and you believed that?" Jamison's teasing voice was warm with pride.

She tossed her head. "I'm tryin'."

And I was crying. Too damned grateful that something good had come out of all this to act grown-up and distant. I wiped my eyes on my sleeve. Tried to say something, but I didn't have any words.

Jamison went into the bathroom and returned with a box of tissues. "You'll be tired," he said. "We'd better go."

"Yeah." Shondra got up, too.

"Jen and Lindsay," I said. "They'll be good friends to you, if you'll let them."

"I know that." She swept out of the room.

Jamison lingered. "My sister ..."

"I understand about your sister," I said.

"Yeah." He smiled. "I guess maybe you do."

I was alone again, my brain beginning to generate lists. Things to do. People to call. Details. Details. Details. As I crossed to the desk to grab a sheet of paper, the envelope in my pocket rustled. Suzanne's note. Might as well get this over with. I pulled it out and tore it open.

Inside were a folded sheet of paper, and something wrapped in tissue. I unwrapped the tissue and a small, exquisite angel on a golden chain spilled into my palm. It wasn't one of those cute little cupid-like angels. It was an elegant, rather fierce-looking angel, with powerful wings and a big sword. I slipped it over my head and the angel settled, firm and hard, against my skin.

Suzanne had written:

*Mea culpa. I should know by now that you're not impulsive and abrasive, you are compulsive and incisive. That's why I made you my partner and why I should do everything in my power to hold you rather than driving you away. I'm sorry I've been so distracted. It's not you. It's me. We can only hope that this, too, shall pass. Here is your guardian angel. When I saw it, I knew it embodied the attributes of the Thea Kozak I know and love. Wear it in GOOD HEALTH.*

She had underlined 'Good Health' three times.

I set down the note and reached for another tissue, my sturdy little angel shifting gently against my chest. I'd only worn it for two minutes, but I felt better already.

I wiped my eyes, blew my nose, and picked up the phone to call Andre.